BREAKDOWN

SARAH MUSSI

HOT
KEY
BOOKS

First published in Great Britain in 2014 by Hot Key Books
Northburgh House, 10 Northburgh Street, London EC1V 0AT

A CIP catalogue record for this book is available from the British Library.

ISBN: 978-1-4714-0191-6

1

This book is typeset in 10.5 Berling LT Std using Atomik ePublisher

Printed and bound by Clays Ltd, St Ives Plc

www.hotkeybooks.com

Hot Key Books is part of the Bonnier Publishing Group
www.bonnierpublishing.com

To B.

*May you escape from the underworld
and find your road.*

LONDON 2084

PART ONE

The force behind being is the bee. Without this little creature, all life on our planet would cease to exist.

Unknown

1

The light fades. I crouch and peer into the blackness. I can't see anything. Can't hear anything. But it won't be long. They're out there. They'll catch our scent soon.

'Nana?' I whisper.

My arms ache, my eyes itch with tiredness and I'm so hungry. So cold. I can't carry her any further.

'If you lean on me, could you hop?' I ask. I don't know why I say that. It just makes things worse. She can't hop. She's doing the best she can.

'I know, I know,' I say, 'but it's only one more street, if we could just get down to the water's edge.'

'I'm sorry,' she whispers.

I know she is. I know she didn't mean this to happen. I know she thought she'd be OK. She wore a blanket over her coat, took a stick. I know.

'I just wanted to get you something.'

'I know,' I say.

'For your birthday,' she whispers. 'You have so little.'

Through the paling dusk I see her lips drawn tight against her teeth. See her eyes: dark hollows.

A yowling echoes from afar. Still streets away, but they know we're here.

'Nan,' I say. 'You gotta stand up. On your good leg. You've got to.' I snap at her 'cos she's got to.

She tries, staggers, clutches at me. We both nearly go over.

'Let me lift you.'

She whimpers. I don't listen; I lift anyway. We're nearly there. If I could get her to a row boat.

'Melissa,' she whispers. 'You go.'

I don't answer. I try heaving her up onto her feet.

I check the street. Still nothing. Quickly glance at the steps down to the water. We can make it.

Nan struggles to keep her balance. Groans. Her face, ghastly grey. I keep watching the street. Only the burnt-out city. Broken buildings. Sour smell of river. Please, God, don't let them find us.

I know what they'll be doing: sniffing the air, trying to locate us, howling out to their numbers. Gathering themselves together. Waiting till they are enough.

I turn my head back to Nan. She looks at me. She knows.

I look away. Look at her ankle.

The fracture is so bad I can see the bone glistening in the dusk.

'Melissa . . .' Her hand reaches out, her fingers clasp onto mine. I swallow and try to unclasp them. *We must move.*

She pushes the package at me.

'Here. Go. While you can still outrun them.'

I heave and somehow get her balanced against me.

'Melissa.'

I take as big a step as I can. Nan lurches, unsteady.

'Please,' she says.

'No,' I say. 'We can make it. They won't come yet. We still have time.' Please, God, let us make it.

'Even if we make it,' she says, 'this break won't heal.' She draws her breath in. 'We've no reserves left.'

'We'll see,' I mutter.

I try to think if I could get help. The patrols, maybe? I scan the street again. Nothing but derelict houses. Graffiti. Piles of rubble. Candlelight showing in a window.

The army won't help. They'll either leave us or take us to the camps.

'Take the shoes.' She pushes the package at me again. 'Harvest the rest of the crop. Stay away from the soldiers.'

They'll probably just leave us. What use would we be?

'Here's the rest of the coupons. You know what to do.'

I see she's slipped her arms from her coat and is struggling to give that to me as well.

'Why the hell did you go out?' I say. 'Why the hell didn't you wait for me?'

'I'm sorry.'

And I am too. I don't need the shoes. I don't need her coat. I need *her*.

And why didn't she wait? That's the rule. Never go out – not when it's getting dark. Just wait. But I knew why, as soon as I got in. I knew as I checked the flat, saw her coat gone, saw the food on the table.

'They're good shoes,' she whispers.

The yowling is closer now.

If we can make it to the river. We can jump. The tide will carry us. They won't follow.

I take the shoes. I try to smile. I can't swim.

'And you need them.'

A great gap opens up in my heart. I catch my breath.

'If you put them on, I'll try,' she says.

I know she can't make it. I know what'll happen. I want her to know that I know.

So I squat down beside her on the kerb, pull off the rags tied round my feet, quickly slip on the shoes. They're warm. They're soft. They're beautiful. 'Thank you,' I whisper.

'And the coat,' she says.

My chin is trembling. I adjust my headscarf. Hesitate, then thrust my arms through the coat sleeves. Button it up. I dig my hands deep into its warm pockets. Her door key is still in one. The coat smells of her. I know what it means. I accept. I know what it means to accept her coat.

She nods her head. 'Good.'

And then I see them, at the end of the street. They're there, sizing us up.

'Now you try,' I say. 'Please try.'

She tries. Her teeth clenched, her face knuckle-white. I gather her to me in the failing light. Support her with one arm. Hold her hand in mine with the other. Try not to crush her brittle bones. She takes a first little hop. She makes a half-swallowed noise. I hold her hand so tight.

They'll delay a little longer. It's dangerous even for them. They know that. They'll be inching forward on their bellies, waiting for one to be bolder than the rest, waiting for one to lead the charge.

'Keep trying,' I say.

She whimpers again.

We reach the quay. Reach the steps. I hear the river slapping against brickwork. Smell its sour tang. *We're nearly there.*

'Keep going,' I say. I glance behind us. Shapes edging closer. There's a lot of them.

'I'm sorry,' she says.

'Shush.' I hold her very tight to me. 'Just keep trying.'

How to manage the steps? No handrail. If they don't attack straight away, if a row boat comes, if I can get us both down to the water . . .

I didn't eat the food, even though I'm starving. I didn't need to check her coat twice. I saw she'd taken all of the coupons. I knew the shoe boat was coming. I knew they'd rip her off. They're crooks. I heard they had blades. I'd tried to hide their arrival from her. Like I try to hide my thinness, like I try to hide the fact the potato crop was stolen. And that I'm burning Dad's books to keep us warm. Nan won't burn books, not Dad's. They're all she's got left. Except me, Melissa, her little honey. Her sole survivor. Left orphaned with her. 'Your parents starved themselves to feed you,' she said. 'My child of Greek myth. My little honeybee. Why should I not give you everything I can too?' Yes, I hide things. I have to. And I hid the news of the shoe boat because I knew she'd try to get me a present. And I knew she'd trade what we couldn't afford. And I knew she'd fall.

Again.

'Please try.'

And I try. I try to lift her. *We're so close.* But months with only shrivelled potatoes have left me weak. My arms slip. She jolts to the pavement. She cries out.

And then they come.

9

2

There are ten or so of them. Big thickset pit bulls, cross-bred Staffs. All of them feral, survivors of the streets, eating whatever they can. They creep towards us.

The lead dog is squat and dirty white. An old warrior. His muzzle scarred, jaw drooling. He snarls. Huge yellow teeth. Flecks of spittle pepper his chest.

'Stay back.' I step in front of Nan, heart racing, suddenly dizzy. But I know how to fight dogs. Everyone learns that, sooner or later.

I crouch and wait. Nan tries to give me her stick, but I prefer my bare hands. I wedge my foot against a crevice in the pavement. I stare at the dog. And I wait.

This one doesn't care. He's so hungry. He doesn't care about my crouch. He doesn't care about the staring. The smell of blood has made him bold. He doesn't even try to turn his head to meet my gaze, doesn't waver. He just lets out a short series of snaps, cranks his tail round, emits a low, long growl, hackles raised.

I crouch lower and shake my head in that strange sideways warning motion, like a bull before a charge. The dog hesitates, stops. He flicks his eyes away, notes my stance. He barks, edges back. My shaking head worries him. Good. Dear God, let him back off. Behind him the pack jerks to a halt. If he goes down, they'll back off. Maybe.

He draws back his maw. Fangs shine in the gloom: short, stubby upper jaw; long canine incisors.

I grind my teeth, bare them at him, growl softly. I have to get this just right.

He springs towards me, paws reaching, muzzle open.

Then I grab his front legs and rip them apart.

With a cracking sound, he goes down.

Despite his wide-shouldered stance, his ribs are just as narrow as a greyhound's. I hear them break. But he's heavy and I'm weak. I can't hurl him away, back towards the pack, where they might stop to gorge on him instead.

He drops like stone. I slide down. I'm not crouching any more and the pack can't reach him without reaching me. And I can't fight them all. Even before I hit the pavement, I know I've failed. I've survived so many dog fights. But I've failed.

The next dog lunges.

I raise my arm to guard my throat. It's well wrapped. I've taken precautions, but he sinks his teeth in. And I feel them. *Don't pull away. Don't lower your arm. He won't let go. Thrust forward into the jaw. Grab the back of his neck. Push down on his spine. Body slam into the bite.*

Jab at his eyes.

Break his neck.

But a third is at my side and as I slam down onto the second, he strikes.

11

Get up again. Hold your ground. Don't let them wear you down.
But I can't get up. I can't hold my ground.

And then I see Nan.

She's raised herself up. For a second she's poised against the wharf, like the great Goddess Hera: arm raised, lotus-tipped staff in hand, the dark water behind her. Then she brings her stick down. The dog at my side howls.

The stick breaks. Nan falls. The dog jumps back.

I roll free.

I struggle to my feet. Two dogs have hold of Nan. One has sunk his muzzle deep in her ankle. Another is dragging her along the dock. I hear her cry stop suddenly. Two dogs are at her throat.

Like lightning I'm up, screaming, jumping towards her, kicking, punching.

I stamp on the dog at her ankle. I kick and kick at the dogs at her neck. But pit bulls never let go.

And I catch the terror in Nan's eyes. I'm trapped. Smaller dogs are dragging the big, dirty male away; the rest are closing in.

No time to crouch. No time to wait for one to spring and use that trick again. Instead I pick up a rock, a piece of loose concrete. I turn back to the dog at Nan's neck. I raise my arm to strike him dead. Nan lashes out.

I don't know if she meant to.

Her blow catches me by surprise. I spin back. I'm toppling on the edge of the wharf and everything is caught in slow motion. I can't hold my balance. I can't get back to her. I'm falling. I'm falling off the edge, off the quay, into the river. I kick out. I paddle the air. I scream: '*NANA*.'

My call hangs on the air. The river beneath.

No answer. No scream. No growl. No crunch of teeth on bone. No sound of dragging.

The impact of water.

A distant howl cut short.

Icy waters closing over me.

3

I'm going down.

I can't stop.

I don't feel the water, or the air cut off.

I thrash my arms.

I kick.

I flail, force my legs. I'm held under by the drag of water. *I must breathe.* I drive myself back up through the pressure pushing me down.

I kick and kick and hold my chest in tight. I reach up with my arms. *There's only water.* I open my eyes. *Only water.* I breathe.

Only water.

So cold. I can't kick. Can't thrash. Can't swim. I'm going down.

This river has no bottom. So very cold. But I stop. I don't hit anything.

The coat's heavy. It tangles around my waist. Where's the surface? I open my mouth. I can't breathe.

I can't breathe.

And I think of my life and how much I loved it even through the fear and the poverty and it flows before me playing out my

*days and hours and minutes . . . Nan's embrace I can smell her
I feel her arms around me holding me I see the empty streets and
the ragged people and the gangs and the dogs and the coupons in
the ration book all blue and faded and no food in the stores and
the rats and the army trucks and hiding and there's no time to
wonder how I can remember such things and days spent with Nan
trying to pollinate the tomatoes that she'd grown from an old seed
packet that she'd traded for a bowl of potatoes and using a feather
that I'd found at the bottom of the garden and trying to tickle the
pollen dust from stamen to stigma . . . her little honeybee . . .*

There was no tomato crop.

Kick again.

*. . . and Nan and her stories of before the bombings of holidays
in Scotland in the mountains of the big sky and the heather all
purple and the bees, and how I am her little Melissa, whose name
means honeybee, called after the nymph of the mountains, who
cared for the boy Zeus, who fed him on milk and honey and hid
him from his murderous father, Cronus, and for her deeds was
turned into an earthworm to dwell forever in the underworld . . .*

The underworld . . .

Kick.

Under the waterworld . . .

And Nan reaches out her arms towards me . . .

*And holds me and she's smiling and it's warm and green and
it's home . . .*

A wave of light and noise. Something says, '*Mon dieu.*'

Searing pain. Something is punching me. It hurts. I open my
mouth. I spew out. Choking. Spitting. Something yanks me
from that dim green hollow where I'm settling. My stomach

hurts. I'm being punched. My stomach. My chest. Something is punching my chest.

Hot lips are pressed on mine.

Hard lips.

They hurt me.

They punch me.

A hand drags me upright.

'*Is she going to be OK?*'

A blow lands on my back.

Hot hard lips pump into me.

'*Quinny? Is she?*'

A child's voice. I try to see, but the pale green bower has turned black.

I splutter. Jerk forward. Gasp. My whole front heaves. I'm choking. I'm gasping and it hurts. It hurts so much. I can't breathe. I swallow air. I swallow water. I can't breathe. I start to slip back down again towards that green haven. *Nan is there, waiting* . . .

'I don't know.'

I hear another voice.

'Please let her be OK,' says the child.

I don't know who he's asking. He's asking me. There's such an ache in his voice. It holds me. I see Nan's face fading.

I feel a small hand in mine. '*Be OK, girl, please be OK.*'

He won't let me go. Against everything, I open my mouth and cough and retch and let the darkness in.

'Please.'

He's calling me.

It's so painful, I cry out.

16

'She's alive.'

I hear the ring in his voice. It holds me there.

'Don't let Careem get her, Quinny.'

I cough and gasp.

'Breathe,' says the voice. Another thump lands on my back.

And I breathe. I open my chest and despite the cold and the pain I breathe and cough and breathe.

'Good. Now, listen.' A hand drags me into a sitting position. 'You don't have long.'

I sit there coughing water and spitting it out. My throat raw. I open my eyes and try to focus.

It's a boy – tall, broad shouldered, kind eyes, handsome. I stare at him. He's from the east. I can tell by his matted look and the weapons. I can tell by the tattoo across his forearm. Hastily he rolls his sleeves back down. But I've seen it. Bone Cross Bone. I must have been swept sheer past the Tower. I've fallen into the hands of a ganger.

'Do as he says,' urges the kid.

In between sucking in air and retching, I turn my head and look at him. The kid's thin, scraggy; about six. He's squatting right beside me. He peers into my face.

'You gonna be OK, girl?' he says.

He's got pinched cheeks and huge eyes. His hair might once have been blonde but it's uncombed and unwashed and falls in locks.

'They bit you, didn't they?' he says. He touches my arm. I start to shiver. My teeth chatter. I can't control the rattling.

'Lenny, we gotta go now,' says the ganger.

'We can't leave her, Quinny.'

'Yes, we can.'

'But if we leave her, she'll die.'

'She'll know how to take care of herself.'

'Do you?' says Lenny, peering into my face.

'We can't take her.'

'But the dogs will find her. Careem will find her. She's bleeding.'

'I told you it'd be better if we left her in the river.'

'But you didn't.'

'I know.'

'So now she's ours,' says Lenny. His bottom lip creases up.

Quinny sighs. I lean forward to stop myself from falling back. 'Come on, Lenny, we can't.'

'Why d'you save her then?' His face screws up, hands in fists.

Quinny sighs again.

'Then you go. I won't.' The kid folds his arms across his skinny chest.

'Then she'll be your responsibility,' warns Quinny.

'OK.'

'And we gotta get Careem to agree.'

'You get him to agree.'

The older boy squats down in front of me. He peers into my face too. His eyes large and dark. 'Girl,' he says.

'Melissa,' I splutter.

'Well, Melissa, if you can stand up and walk, you best get the hell out. My little bro wants to keep you. I can't promise nothing. If your legs work, get up and get going.'

'We live in Games City,' pipes up the kid, as if that explains everything.

18

Games City. I've heard of it. The old Olympic stadium from the glorious years when Nan was a girl, when kids had phones and homes were warm and there was food. That golden time when everything grew and the sun shone. And people filled up their leisure hours with eating and shopping and sporting in stadiums like Greek Gods.

Games City, the games ghetto, home to the gangers, the outcasts, the people even the army don't deal with.

Oh yes, I've heard of Games City.

I look up at Quinny. Don't say anything. Just shiver. He offers me his arm. I don't take it. How am I going to get west, back home again?

I push back my shoulders, try to inhale without coughing. *Don't think about Nan.* Think what to do. Can I get away? Can I fight off dogs? How will I get back? I think of home, the potatoes still in their dish on the kitchen table, the empty cupboards. The bed where Nan and me used to sleep.

I catch my breath.

Think.

I try to get up. My legs are too weak.

'I'll help you,' says Lenny.

He grabs hold of my arm and pulls. I stagger to my feet.

'Steady,' says Quinny, and I can't stop him from catching me and holding me upright against him.

'You heard what I said.' His lips are close. His voice urgent. His breath hot and strange against my face. 'Get going, Melissa. Don't mind Lenny. I can't keep you unless Careem says.' Reluctantly he lets me go. 'Just get the hell out.'

So I try to. But I don't know where. I'm miles away from

the west side. I stagger away from the dock. It's dark. I could find a bin, a container, a broken building? I could barricade myself in?

I did that once with Nan when we were caught out after dark. She showed me how. I look up the wharf, looking for a container of any kind, an outhouse, an old lock-up garage, an arch – a doorway, even. I squint into the night.

And I see them.

Carrying firebrands and chanting. Banging steel. Faces glittering in the torchlight, savage and dark. More than twenty strong.

And they're coming this way.

4

Maybe it's the danger, maybe it's the fight in me, but I won't die. If a pack of dogs can't take me out, they won't.

I cough, but I straighten up and drag Nan's sopping coat around me. They make straight for us, surround us, firebrands burning.

'Nice one, Tarquin,' says their leader.

Tarquin, not Quinny.

That leader's got to be Careem. Long black coat, full grown – not like Tarquin – about thirty and mean, like a back-street dog, and just as scarred. One side of his face like a meteorite blasted it.

'Boss,' says Tarquin.

Lenny hangs back, goes quiet. He hides behind his brother, clings on to him like he's tomorrow.

'Details?' says Careem.

'We . . .' starts Tarquin, then corrects himself, shoves Lenny's fingers away from his arm. 'I found her crawling out the river.'

You liar, I think. *You hauled me out. You didn't find me crawling anywhere. I was gone. I was in the green hollow.*

Careem motions with a finger. Two of his gang stroll forward and push me. I kick them.

'Sparky, too,' says Careem.

'Good shoes,' says one of them. He pulls at Nan's coat. 'Coat's OK, bit wet.'

They laugh.

'Take off the shoes,' says Careem.

I think of Nan down by the wharf, clutching our last book of coupons, waiting for the boaters. I think of her hurrying home, the light fading, her not seeing so well. I think of her falling all alone on the street.

Her brittle bones.

I think of that.

'I'm not giving anybody these shoes.'

'Please give him your shoes,' whispers Lenny.

'No,' I say. I don't care. I don't care if they throw me back in the river. I don't care if they break my legs and leave me for the dogs. I don't care. Nan wanted me to have these shoes. And now she's dead.

I look Careem straight in the eye. And my will is stronger. Stronger than any stick or blade or heat these gangers carry.

And Lenny sees it, and Tarquin sees it.

And Careem sees it.

'No.' I shake my head.

There's a hush. A dry, stuffy laugh. They look at Careem.

And he's puzzled. He's looking at me, like he's thinking up just the right thing to say, something to show everyone that no soaked girl, pulled out of no stinking river, can out-spark him. He's thinking and he's timing it, so that whatever comes out keeps him on top.

They're all waiting.

'I know where you can get better ones,' I say at last. I let that sink in. I bite my tongue, so I don't rush on. Nan told me: 'I survived this long, because of one rule. Grow tough – tougher than everything – and talk less.'

'And not too far.' I point at a sign. *WESTMINSTER 3 miles.* I let that sink in.

'And enough for you all,' I finish.

Careem doesn't jump. He knows the rule too. He lets someone else do that.

'Yeah?' says one of them. 'Where?'

'Like I'll tell *you*,' I say.

That annoys him. 'You will,' he says, all menace.

'Not.' I mean it. They know I do.

'What d'we do?' says the ganger. He looks at Careem.

I've got to play this my way, or I really will end up as dog bait or back in that stinking river.

'I'll tell him.' I point at Tarquin.

Tarquin frowns.

'Yes,' says Lenny, then shuts up.

'And I'll only tell him if you leave me an' my stuff alone.'

They don't know what to do. I look up at Tarquin and say, 'Dog's Law. I'm your spoil, aren't I? That's right, you know it.'

Everyone knows it. Dog's Law: finders keepers. Since the bombings everyone's been finding and keeping.

But I'm not sure it applies to Careem.

Tarquin pulls a face. I see Lenny slip his hand under Tarquin's arm again.

Tarquin steps back and nods a bit. He shrugs. 'Yep, I found her, I guess.'

23

Careem watches. This way he doesn't have to do anything about me. So he nods as well, all too big-shot to be challenged by any street find. He crosses over to me, grabs my hair, hauls my face up to his.

For a moment I look into his eyes. For a moment I think he is going to snap my neck. For a moment all my swagger is gone.

Then he laughs. 'Some looker, ain't she!'

He sweeps my damp hair back from my face, lets out a low whistle. 'Woo, even dripping like a skunk, she's got the boom,' he says.

The rest of the pack snigger.

'It's your call,' announces Careem. 'Dog's Law applies. You found her. If you wanna go for the shoes that's OK by me.' Careem nods, somehow pleased. 'I get the haul of shoes. I get to trade them. You get to take her back and have her for the rest of tonight.' He laughs. 'After that I've got something else in mind.'

I can see Lenny really tugging on Tarquin's arm now. I can see his small upturned eyes.

'And no bruises, and make sure I'm happy when I see the shoes.' An unspoken 'or else' lingers in the air.

Tarquin jerks his head. It could mean anything. I guess it means he'll go for the shoes.

I don't feel anything screwing over the boat people.

'I'll keep her,' says Tarquin. 'Lenny needs shoes.'

'You got till tomorrow then,' says Careem with a wave of his hand. 'Kaylem and Nailey – stay with them and make sure that girl don't go nowhere.' And with that he turns. Two of the gang remain. The rest of the pack starts banging tin pans again. Then they're gone.

I sink back down onto the pavement.

Tarquin starts on Lenny. 'Don't do that.' He shakes Lenny's hand off his jacket.

'OK.'

'Nothing's OK,' says Tarquin.

'You said we could keep her and we did,' says Lenny, smiling.

Tarquin shakes his head.

Kaylem and Nailey laugh.

I look around. *What are my chances?*

'We can't keep her, Len. Even if we get the shoes, even if everyone's happy. It's only for tonight. That's all.'

'No,' says Lenny. 'You said.'

'Well, it was a promise I can't keep.'

And I can see from the slump of his shoulders that he isn't just saying that because Kaylem and Nailey are there.

5

I can stand up.

'So walk,' says Tarquin.

I take a few steps. The coughing starts again. The coat's too heavy. I try to wring water out of it. I should take it off and leave it. But I'm not going to. I catch at a corner of the cloth and twist. I feel Nan's key on its plastic-photo key ring, still in the pocket. The key ring she got so long ago.

I can almost hear her telling me about it.

'I was nine years old when I went to Scotland. We stayed in a tiny cottage in the mountains. There was a pond, a loch and hills all round. I bought this key ring in the local shop. It's not the same cottage, but just like it. I was so happy there. I promised myself I'd keep the key ring till the day I died.'

A lump forms in my throat. My nose stuffs up. It's so cold. *Till the day I died*. My hands shake.

Don't think about Nan. Not yet. Not now. Focus on staying upright. Focus on moving forward. Focus on getting away.

Lenny comes nearer. He slips his thin hand in mine. 'It'll be OK, Miss. I won't let them hurt you,' he says, like he's the All Powerful.

'That's good, then,' I whisper back.

That little hand in mine helps. We trail along behind Nailey and Kaylem. They turn to check on us. Kaylem is huge. He looks like he's been fighting dogs all his life and every bone in him is meaner than them. He takes in my trembling. 'She's not going to give us no bother,' he says to Nailey and then he ignores me.

And I'm not. If I tried to make a run for it I wouldn't get far. But he's stupid to underestimate me. Just because I can't give him any bother right now, doesn't mean I'm never going to. Stay stupid, I think.

I take in everything – the cracked asphalt, the broken kerbs. When I get away, I'm going to need to know the route back. *Just focus on staying upright. Focus on getting strong. And notice everything. Get through these streets, cross these roads. Mark their names.* I look at the rows of houses. Some with little lights flickering through barred windows. One with a stone lion by the door. I look up at the sky. The dull iron-grey night. *I'm going to stay strong, Nan. You don't have to worry.*

Soon we get more dogs. They're ready to attack. But Tarquin bangs his metal pan behind us. Kaylem and Nailey bang theirs up front. The dogs circle us for a while. Then they slink to the back, and follow.

Tarquin doesn't stay at the rear all the time. He catches up and falls behind and catches up again in a little pattern that he seems to know well. When the dogs try to close in, he bangs the pan really hard with a length of metal, right in their faces.

As more dogs appear, Kaylem picks up rocks, pieces of

27

broken pavement. He throws them at the dogs. He's a pretty good shot. Nailey bangs the pan. The dogs whine and race off and regroup.

But there is a lot of dogs. And I'd have thought that when they get to critical mass they won't care about the rocks or the banging. They'll just come anyway. But I'm not sure. I'm not a ganger. And I'm not a dog. And those lengths of metal look scary.

Lenny squeezes my hand. He tugs at me. 'I know you're tired, Miss, but you got to keep up. They won't try and get us if they know we ain't tired.'

'OK,' I say.

I stumble on, down streets, round corners. It's so cold the coat starts to stiffen.

'Knock it, Miss.'

Lenny thumps at the coat. It crackles slightly.

'Keep knocking it. That'll stop it freezing.'

I'm shivering so much I can't even knock the coat. Lenny knocks at it for me. Tarquin bangs his pan. Kaylem and Nailey bang theirs.

When we're some way from the river, Tarquin falls into step with us. 'Where're the shoes then?' he says.

'On a boat.'

I don't care. Those traders always rip people off. They took all our coupons. They let Nan go off alone into the dusk. They knew the danger. They don't play by the rules, do they?

'Where and when?' says Tarquin.

'Docks under Tower Bridge.' Dog's Law works both ways.

'Clever.'

28

I can't see what's clever about it. I think it's stupid. Running a shoe boat into London. Course someone's going to find you. Most black marketeers wouldn't dare. They knew the danger. Nobody's got any shoes these days. So they were set to make a killing, weren't they?

Their risk then.

'How many on board?'

'Don't know.'

'They got knives?'

I look at him. He looks pretty handy, like he could deal with any number of stupid traders. I notice the shock of dark, matted hair flopping over one eye. If you combed that hair out or cut it back, he'd be OK. I don't know why I think that.

'No matter,' he says.

An icy wind blows against me. I shiver. Nan's coat is so heavy. If he thought getting the shoes was going to be easy that's not my fault. An empty window rattles. A piece of broken, yellowing plastic blows down the street.

'Len, you go with her.'

Lenny looks up and tries to hold on to him.

'I won't be long.' Tarquin shakes him off.

'Can't I go with you?'

'Then who'll take care of her?'

Lenny doesn't answer.

'Don't make me remind you of what I said down by the river.'

Tarquin calls out to the two others. 'One of you wanna come help with the shoes?'

Nailey and Kaylem don't bother to reply.

'I won't be long.'

'The boaters always got knives,' I say.

Tarquin hands the stick and the tin pan to Lenny. 'Drum me up some help,' he says.

At the next street he slips into the shadows and sprints off. At first the dogs don't notice he's gone. Then they do. One of them howls. A bunch of them look like they're going to follow. Lenny starts banging the tin pan. The banging seems to refocus their attention. They move back towards us, settle into the old rhythm, and we trudge on.

'Soon be there,' says Lenny.

I'm so cold I hardly care.

'An' I'll look after you till Quinny gets back.'

'If he gets back,' I say.

'It'll be OK,' says Lenny. 'An' he'll bring the shoes.'

Shoes, I think – all this for shoes.

'There you see, I'm always right,' says Lenny suddenly, pointing at something.

I look up.

And ahead of us, bang in the centre of an open wasteland, are the white walls of Games City.

6

We'd heard about the place, of course, Nan and me.

People had warned us how the Light of the Lord had gone out there. People got quite biblical on the topic, cautioned everyone that a new breed of humans was evolving. A breed as cruel as Herod, that could survive radiation, could multiply like cockroaches; could infect things.

And they were spawning in multitudes in Games City.

But as I trudge up towards its ramshackle barricades and its towering walls, this new evil breed of mankind is not the first thing I notice. The first thing is the smell.

It belches out at me. Sour like a bad dream. Even before we get there.

And the closer we get, the worse it is.

Across the barricades and into the old VIP lounges, and it's so thick I can't breathe. Saliva rises in my mouth. And however empty I thought my belly was, I'm sure I'm going to spill it right there. I nearly do, though my stomach's so shrunk it can't be much bigger than a pod.

I try to cover my nose with my coat sleeve, try to stop myself retching. How can people stand it? And I think of all the stories. It must be true then. Radiation must've changed them. They must be like cockroaches, happy to live on filth.

And I know I can't stay here. That's for sure.

Kaylem and Nailey march me down to the arena.

The once-gleaming, white-spoked Olympic Stadium with its glorious racetrack, which Nan told me all about, is now riddled with ramshackle alleyways. Lean-to sheds. Tin shacks. Hovels of buckled boards. Everything huddled together. Pools of filthy water. Mud. Sewage. Slime-covered concrete. Cracked paving. Litter. Rubble.

And stench.

A brindle dog slinks towards us, its tail between its legs. Oh hell. They've got dogs here too.

'She's a tracker dog, Miss,' says Lenny. 'And she's my friend, ain't ya?' He fondles the dog's head. She tries to wag her tail.

Kaylem sees and steps over. 'Get,' he snarls, and whacks the dog around its muzzle with the iron bar.

The dogs squeals and runs off.

'You didn't ought to do that,' says Lenny. 'She's still got a bad mouth from before.'

'Shut up,' says Kaylem.

Oh Nan, where are you? Don't abandon me here. Not with these gangers and these dogs.

Please take me with you.

Take me to a place where we won't have to scrabble around in dirt trying to grow a few scabby potatoes, hoping this year some apples will fruit on the old tree.

Take me to a place where the bees are back.

We heard that once – didn't we? That the bees were coming back. That somewhere, up-country, in the far north, in the mountains, somehow, they were there. Buzzing on lavender-coloured heather. Not biome bees – real bees, honey bees, collecting nectar, dusting pollen from blossom to blossom.

How long will they take to come south? How many years must we wait?

But we'd have waited, Nan, just the two of us. We'd have sat by dying fires, thrown books on to keep us warm.

How you cried, Nan, when we did that, and said: Not the books – not a life without stories, not a world without the Gods. How you held me close and called me your hope, your little Melissa, and reminded me of my name – Melissa, the nymph of the mountains, who was cursed to dwell in the underworld until Zeus, grown from the child she rescued, took possession of paradise and took pity on Melissa, transforming her into a beautiful bee and sending her back to earth to regenerate the souls of men.

'To regenerate the souls of men.' That's what you said, Nan. 'That's the task, Melissa.' How often did you tell me that?

But, Nan, we got by, didn't we? We used the embers to cook those potatoes, dried our sodden feet, told our own stories.

And you said, 'The sacrifice has been made. The earth has been punished. The bees will return.'

We'd have waited together.

While those bees were coming.

Lenny's upset. He tries to call the dog. But she's too scared to come. We're marched into the centre of the racetrack. I stare at the piles of refuse around me.

I can't stay here.

Kaylem shoves me, says, 'Get close to the fire, then. Dry yourself out. You ain't going to fetch nothing if you look nasty.'

I don't move.

Oh Nan. Are you there? Can I follow you? Please? To that other place?

Is it different there – over the doorstep of death? Is there a hearth with real logs burning brightly and a pot of stew bubbling and clean clothes in the closet and shoes for every day of the week . . .?

Kaylem slaps me hard across the back of my head. 'I don't ask twice.'

It's only when Lenny pulls my hand and leads me to the fire that I move. My ears ring. 'Miss, you got to do like they say or we can't help you.'

'That's it, you watch her,' snaps Kaylem. He rolls his iron bar to Lenny. 'Whack her with this if she's trouble.'

'Please, Miss?'

I get up and go close to the fire. I take off Nan's coat and hook it over an upturned grocery trolley so it can dry out. Then I sit where I can dry out too. The smoke curls itself all around me. I'm glad. I cough, but the smell of smoke shuts out the stench.

Kaylem and Nailey walk off. They head towards some

34

benches at the far side of the arena. Noise. Something like music. Oil lamps flicker. A lot of shouting.

'They're doing drinking, Miss,' says Lenny. 'Old Ma Taylor's brew. And playing checkers.'

Nan's coat drips and steams. The brindle dog slinks back, her belly close to the ground. Lenny croons over her, feeding her scraps of things from his pocket.

'I gotta feed her,' he says. 'And she's one of our best trackers. But Careem hit her bad last week an' broke some teeth. She's still recovering an' she can't eat easily no more. Can you, doggy?' He tickles her shoulders.

I scrunch myself up as tight as possible and stay next to the flames. They die away. Nobody tends them. I start to get cold again. If there was wood nearby I'd risk another slap to get it. Lenny watches me.

'Got to watch you,' he says. 'Tarquin says.'

'I know.'

'I'm not going to hit you, though.' He toes away the iron bar Kaylem rolled at him. 'Even if you tries to escape. I won't hit you, Miss.'

'OK.'

'But please don't try. You might get away and then they'll beat me.' He sits scrunched up as well, his too-big head on his scrawny knees. The dog nuzzles him. Lenny watches me with his oversized eyes and I think: *I can't escape right now. I'm too weak. It's too cold, and it's night, and there's dogs, and Nan's dead. But I will. And I don't care who they beat.*

But I don't say anything. I just watch him back with my eyes all squinty.

Not that I want *him* beaten.

'I really ain't going to hit you,' says Lenny and he rolls the bar even further away to show me he ain't.

'I wish you *could* get away, though,' he says, quite unexpectedly. 'If you could, I'd go wiv ya.'

I look at him then, my eyes open despite the smoke. 'What'd I want to take a kid like you for?' I say.

He shrugs. 'Don't know,' he says. 'You mightn't.'

'You're damn right.'

There're some ideas you have to kill dead.

Lenny sighs. He scratches the dog's head, lifts up one of its ears and whispers into it, 'You'd like to go wiv me, wouldn't ya?'

Then he just carries on watching me with those eyes in that face on that scraggy neck, like he really thinks there's some kind of paradise that I can escape to and am refusing to take him there on purpose.

I sigh and look out over the stadium. It's very dark. They're still shouting and drinking at the far edge. I wish I could sleep. I wish I could curl up in an even tighter ball and never wake up.

But the kid's got me thinking. I could escape. Maybe not right now, but tomorrow, when it's light, when the dogs have gone to ground. Maybe at dawn. What I need to do is find out how. I remember what Careem said to Tarquin: '*You get to take her back and have her for the rest of tonight. After that I've got something else in mind.*'

Maybe Tarquin won't come back and I can give this kid the slip.

But if Tarquin does come back and thinks I'm gonna be so grateful he pulled me out of the river that I'm gonna be his

36

for the night, he's got another think coming. And if he tries it on by force, I'll kill him.

I really will.

But then again, maybe he might help me. He did pull me out of the river and he did say: '*If your legs work, get up and get going.*'

It's Careem who's gonna be the biggest problem.

'What time do the gangs get back?' I ask.

'At dawn, Miss.'

'What does Careem do with girls like me?'

Lenny shrugs.

What would Nan tell me to do?

I think of Nan and her life: and how as a girl she had everything and how she lost everything, including everyone she loved, except me.

She survived though. And her favourite advice was always, 'Think first.'

Oh Nan.

I try to think. How big is this place and how much do I know about it? I try to remember.

Nan told me how the Queen Elizabeth Olympic Park was the new jewel in the Crown of England. How it cost the country hundreds of millions of pounds. How it featured myriad colours and all the colours whirled to form wheels in pinks and blues and greens and oranges that changed throughout the stadium as they were picked out in paintwork, glass, fabric and lights.

Doesn't look anything like that now.

Raw sewage running down between the seating aisles, sheds and shelters of rusty tin, plastic sheeting for roofs, people curled up on rubbish heaps, men drinking, children sifting through trash looking for God knows what.

Holes full of shit.

Vicious tracker dogs.

Thin, starved faces.

'Why don't you wanna take me, Miss?' asks Lenny.

'There isn't any place to take you to,' I say.

'I could help carry things,' says Lenny.

'What things?'

'Any things you want me to carry.'

'You're not coming.'

'But there is somewhere, ain't there, even if you can't take me?'

'And I haven't got "things to carry" if that's what you're thinking.'

He tilts his head to one side as if he knows better. 'There's the farm.'

I roll my eyes. 'The covered farms are not nice,' I say. 'They're prison camps.'

'No, not them,' he says. 'The little farm.'

'Look,' I say, 'you don't want to end up in a covered farm.'

'I mean the little farm in the north.'

I haven't got a clue what he's on about so I just say, 'Everywhere outside London's got radiation.'

'I know.'

'No you don't,' I say.

He goes quiet.

'It can strike you down, just like that, and all your hair'll fall out and you'll shrivel up and die and that's it.'

He sucks in his cheeks.

'There's no cure for it and nobody's working on one, neither.'

'I know.'

'No you don't. Nobody survives radiation once they've got it.'

'I know. My mum didn't.'

That stops me dead. I should have known. His mum.

I look at him. His bottom lip's trembling. He keeps glancing across the racetrack and then back at me.

'He'll be all right,' I say. 'They didn't really have big knives.'

He nods.

'We'll *all* be all right. Me too. I'm always all right. I'm stubborn like that.'

Immediately he looks more cheerful. 'I knew you was going to be OK, Miss,' he says.

Well, that's nice of him I suppose. And it's true. I *am* going to be OK. I'm going to get out of here and go home. Whatever stupid plan these gangers have 'in mind' for me.

And that makes me smile. The first smile since Nan died. I out-sparked them, didn't I? So I know I can get away, plus I don't care. I don't care if I live or die right now. And that gives me power.

So I crouch there thinking, slowly drying out by those embers, listening to the slight crackle of charcoal burning down and the noises of the ghetto.

I'm not going to do anything to suit them.

Not me.

Not while I got a tongue in my head and a brain to think with.

7

A wailing starts up outside the arena. Right by the stadium gate. The howl of dogs. The sound of tin pans suddenly banging.

'It's Quinny, Miss,' says Lenny, his face suddenly alight. 'He's back and the pack are on him.'

I straighten up. Rub my eyes. The fire's only embers. I'm dry. Nan's coat's dry. I pull it back on. 'The pack are on him?'

'The dogs, Miss. Trying to stop him getting through.' Lenny's already on his feet and doing a little dance on the spot. 'Me and her is going to go and help.' The brindle bitch jumps up as well.

'OK.'

Just as Lenny is about to leave, Kaylem reappears.

'Leaving?' he snaps.

Lenny's face falls. 'Quinny's back,' he says. The dog bolts away. Lenny remembers. He's supposed to guard me. His dance changes. No more hopping. Now he shuffles slowly on the spot.

Kayem shrugs. 'Well, lucky for you, I can take over.'

Lenny's eyes widen. A look of relief. Quickly followed by a look of alarm. Kaylem isn't trying to be helpful.

'Go on.' Almost a smile from Kaylem.

Lenny looks at me, looks at Kaylem, starts running anyway for the stadium gates.

Kaylem chuckles. It's not a nice noise. I wish Lenny hadn't gone. Small as he is, he'd have been there.

'All on your own now, are you?' says Kaylem, as if he can read my mind.

And without any further ceremony he lays a hand on my arm and drags me upright. Our eyes meet, just for a second. His lips part. I can read what's in his eyes.

I scream.

Lenny stops, turns, catches the picture of us there, Kaylem's hand on my arm, dragging me.

'Get,' yells Kaylem.

Lenny turns away, runs fast towards the gate.

'Now you,' says Kaylem. 'Let's see how much boom you got.'

I look at him, balance, twist my arm free. I start to back away, clutch my coat around me. I take two steps back. Behind me two gangers suddenly appear from nowhere. They close in. I stop. No way back. I look from them to Kaylem. No way forward.

I'm trapped.

The two behind drive me on. Kaylem smiles, his arm ready with an iron bar. I stop. I let out one shrill cry. A hand from behind descends over my mouth. I bite down, but it's clamped too tight. Someone kicks my knees out. I half-fall, stagger. I try to drag Nan's coat even closer.

'Not here, you clods,' snaps Kaylem. 'Drag her to the south end. Then beat it. Cover my back.'

Two of them grab my shoulders, hold my elbows in, pin me against them. They drag me, kicking, away from the fire, towards the darkened edge of the racetrack.

Where the light stops, they stop. They leave me. I struggle to my feet. Kaylem comes in close, grabs my hair, drags my face up.

'I wanna see the look in your eyes when I do you, boom-ting,' he says.

The other two snigger.

'Get lost, you lot,' snaps Kaylem.

They move off. Like a flash I try to step away. But Kaylem holds me. Pulls my hair. It's so painful I cry out. My scream is swallowed in the darkness. Cries drowned out by the clamour. My heart stops. His hand goes over my mouth. I kick. There's no time to think. I try to hit out.

With one savage motion Kaylem kicks my feet out from under me. I'm falling, thrashing. I'm flat on the grass. My head hits the racetrack with a crunch. I hear my skull thwack. He tries to kick my legs wide. But I fight. I kick back. I rip at him.

'Come on,' Kaylem says in an excited tone. He leans his weight on my chest. 'Tell me how you like it.'

He grabs my hair tighter and twists my face to meet his. Then he slaps me hard, flat-handed around the curve of my head.

'Don't you like our little game?' he says.

I spit in his face.

'Little ho.' He laughs. 'Let's see how much I can make you hate it, then.'

He pulls my hair taut.

I can't twist.

'You know what I want.' He grabs at my coat, starts yanking it open. I struggle. He leaves the coat and slaps me harder. The violence catches me by surprise. My eyes water. I try to kick.

He forces me flat and kneels astride me, pins me down. He's heavy, too heavy. He stinks of alcohol.

'I'll kill you if you touch me,' I hiss. 'I swear to God.'

He just laughs. Then he reaches for the coat hem. Roughly tugs it up. I can't fight. I'm no match for him. If I could hurt him, scratch out his eyes, find some weapon . . . I flail my arm around, search for a stick or piece of stone.

'Sparky.' He laughs. He tugs at my jeans and pulls hard on the fistful of hair, so I arch back. He fumbles at his own jeans.

I can smell his breath. I can smell his stinking boozy breath.

'Let's take a look.'

I jerk my head. My hair tears out. His hand loosens. His grip slips. I wrench my head round. I scream loud. It rips out of my throat. Then I bite his wrist.

He leaves the jeans, finds my throat. With one squeeze, I'm choking. I can't breathe. My head spins.

There's a blur in the darkness.

I'm gasping and choking.

But someone is there.

And Kaylem is wrenched aside.

His weight crushes me. His hand lets go of my throat. I gasp for breath.

'Let her go. She's not your spoil.'

It's Tarquin.

Kaylem grunts. 'What's your problem? Don't want me to get in there first?'

I feel a force seize him off me, feel the impact of foot on flesh, hear the crack of something hard on soft tissue. A belch of air escapes from Kaylem's lips. I smell it, foul, stinking. Then

43

he shrieks, high-pitched.

The weight of him suddenly gone. The night air, cold, welcome.

'You broke Dog's Law,' says Tarquin.

Kaylem can't answer. He seems winded. I sit up, drag Nan's coat back around me.

My fingers trembling.

'You broke Dog's Law. If Careem don't deal with you, I will.' Tarquin's voice is deep and dangerous.

'You – deal with me?' Kaylem's voice, breathy, acid.

'Get moving.'

'You can keep your Dog's Law and your bitch.' Kaylem staggers to his feet, sucks in air, then stays there, doubled up. 'Watch it, Tarquin,' he breathes. 'You shouldn'ta done that.'

'Move.'

'You've started something now.'

'*Va te faire foutre, trouduc,*' hisses Tarquin.

'I'm warning you.'

Tarquin doesn't answer again. Instead he's at my side. Kaylem moves off, threats under his breath.

'You OK?' Tarquin says.

I stay quiet. I don't trust myself to speak.

I roll slowly to one side, try to lever myself up. Tarquin crouches beside me, staring at me. He reaches out his hand to steady me. I clutch it.

'You got back,' I whisper. My voice shaky.

'I got back.'

The night seems to swirl around me.

'Did he hurt you?'

44

I don't answer. Suddenly I remember – 'Lenny?'

'He's OK.'

'Don't go.' I keep hold of his hand.

'OK.' He moves in close, puts his arm around me.

I sit there, trembling, trying to get control of myself. My throat tight, hoarse from screaming. I cough. I swallow. It hurts.

Tarquin raises his hand to my face. Gently wipes my lip. Flicks his eyes to mine, holds them for a second, looks away.

'Lip's bleeding,' he mumbles.

I nod. My heart hammers. 'I bit it.'

'He hit you.'

I nod.

Tarquin's jaw tightens. He mutters something beneath his breath. I think he says '*Batard, branleur.*' He's swearing in some ganger tongue. Then I hear him say, '. . . and you so beautiful.'

I let myself lean against him.

'I'll get you somewhere safe.' He pulls a rag from his pocket. 'I'm sorry,' he says. Then gently, ever so gently, before I can flinch away, he wipes my lip and cleans the blood and dirt off.

8

I'm off the racetrack, in a changing room. Smoky oil lamp, dry floor. I huddle down into a corner. *Can I trust him?* He drove Kaylem off, but . . .

Tarquin sees my shrinking now we're alone. 'You're safe with me. I'm not Kaylem.'

And I'm not stupid. Nan taught me: *Never trust a man and you'll never go wrong.*

I keep my distance from him.

'I want to help you.'

I press myself further into the corner and wait.

'Is there anyone I can tell outside?'

'Anyone who'll pay, you mean?' I say.

'I can't help you if you won't trust me.'

'Trust you? I trust you, all right. As soon as I tell you about anyone, I trust you to go and rob them.'

'I won't rob them.'

'You went to rob the shoe boat.'

'I won't rob them.'

'There isn't anyone.'

Tarquin squats and looks at me. He seems to be searching

for something. 'There really isn't, is there?'

I shake my head.

'We don't have anyone either, me an' Len.'

Does he think I'm like him, then? That we're the same? Am I supposed to spill my heart out and cosy up to him and share our aloneness?

I narrow my eyes. 'You've got Careem and Kaylem, and all of Games City.'

He sits down next to me. 'No I ain't.'

There's something in the way he says it that makes me sorry. I try to imagine life in this place – the squalor, the violence.

'I understand,' he says. 'You've been half drowned and nearly raped and you don't trust nothing. I don't blame you. But you can trust me. An' I'll show ya you can.'

His eyes are dark and liquid. His face is kind. He did rescue me. But I'm not ready to let go of Nan's advice. *Men only want one thing. That's the way they are. Don't ever trust them.*

And he can't seem to take his eyes off me. Instinctively I pull Nan's coat tighter.

'I'll be outside,' he says. 'You're still frightened. You ain't gotta be frightened of me too. I'll be around though. I'll make sure you're OK. I'll send Len in to keep you company. He don't frighten you, do he?'

I just watch him. His voice soft, caring, with a slight trace of something foreign. He lifts his hand as if to touch me. Then lets it fall.

'You got reason to be afraid, though,' he says. 'You really have. I ain't never seen nothing as beautiful as you.'

Lenny is here. He strokes my hand. 'I'm sorry, Miss, 'bout Kaylem.'

I press my lips together.

'I'm really sorry. I shouldn'ta left you.'

I squeeze his hand.

'But I ran and fetched Quinny.'

'Thanks,' I whisper.

'You ain't gonna die, are ya?'

'If I don't eat something, I might.' I try to make light of it.

'I ain't got much food, Miss,' he says, 'but you can share mine.'

Lenny pulls a bit of meat off a bone he's been picking at. Hands it to me. It's only the tiniest bit and it'd scarcely feed a cat. I'm grateful though. I take it. I haven't tasted meat in a long time. Nan and I lived off our back yard. And that was all vegetables – it's only one snap with my molars and a little bit of pushing up and around with my tongue and it's swallowed. My throat's sore now. The meaty greasiness remains in my mouth.

'What kind of meat is it?' I say, a sudden horror rising up in me.

'Dog,' says Lenny.

OK. I don't know whether to laugh or cry. Dog. Maybe I just ate the dog that ate Nan.

'More?'

Lenny holds out another tiny piece. I'm so hungry and my belly's growling and the smell of grease on my fingers is torture, and it's like the morsel I've tasted has woken months

48

of starvation in me.

But I look at Lenny – so skinny, like he hasn't eaten well for weeks either. I shake my head. I haven't got the heart to take it off him.

'No, I'm OK.'

Lenny looks at me; a little worried crease starts up around his eyes. 'You gonna be OK, Miss?' he asks.

I shrug.

'It's being here, ain't it?'

It's so many things.

'It's the big picture, ain't it?'

'The what?' I say.

'When it gets really bad here, I go there,' says Lenny.

'Where?'

'To the big picture.'

I look at him, puzzled.

He nods. 'I do.'

I wait for the next extraordinary thing he's going to say. But instead he runs off, right out of the locker room, his short little legs and ragged shirt flying.

And I sit there and wonder about him, such a funny, skinny little kid. But before I'm through wondering he's back, all panting and flush-faced in the lamplight.

'Look,' he says. He holds something out at me. A book. An ancient, tatty kid's book with a hardback cover that's half hanging off. I don't even want to touch it.

'It's the other place,' he says. 'The little farm in the north, the one with the big picture you can go to.'

'No you can't,' I say.

But he isn't listening.

'When I grow up I'm going there,' he says. And he sits down beside me and snuggles up to me.

I don't know what to do.

For a start, he smells. He smells of pee and of this place, and secondly I'm not used to kids. And I'm not sure I trust them, either, so I push him away.

Nan told me.

Children are tricky. They can spy through stuff. They can reach right inside you. They can see the real thing even when you can't. They can catch you out and suddenly blurt out something you've no idea was there. They can ask you a question that you have no answer for.

'Look,' says Lenny, moving right back up next to me. He flips open the book's front cover and points. It's hard to see because it's so dark. Some kind of picture.

'What is it?'

'The other place,' he says.

I peer down, but I can't see anything. 'It's just a book,' I say.

'But books tell the truth, don't they?' says Lenny.

That's one of those questions I don't have an answer for. I don't know if books tell the truth or not. So I just puff out some air and say, 'It's a book. There's no "other place" *you're* ever going to get to.'

I didn't mean to say it so harsh.

Lenny goes quiet. He doesn't cry.

'I guess not,' he says.

He sits there blankly, biting his bottom lip.

I didn't even give him a chance. I want to say something to make it better.

50

'Well,' he mutters, all ancient before his time, 'maybe I ain't going yet. But you're wrong about the other place. It is there.'

And I see that if I don't back off, as like as not he'll get upset. So I don't say anything. I just sit there for a bit and Lenny looks at me, like I'm going to say something important.

But I just carry on sitting there trying to think of something to make it better.

And I remember how Nan and I used to sit together and how she'd stroke my hand and tell me of Mount Olympus and the story of the boy, Zeus, and how the nymph, Melissa, fed him milk from the goat, Amalthea, and how one day a horn broke off the goat and became the great horn of plenty, the cornucopia of the Gods, from which all good things flowed in abundance.

And Lenny and I sit there. Like Nan and me. Like Melissa and the boy Zeus.

The cornucopia from which all good things flowed in abundance.

And I look around. And it's obvious there's not much abundance flowing here. And I think maybe I could make some up, tell him a story full of good things – like Nan did for me? I wonder what kind of abundance he'd like. Maybe I could make up a story about this secret place he's so keen on.

So at last I say, 'Maybe it's true. Maybe there is a secret place. But you haven't got any right to go around talking about it like that, or it won't be a secret any more.'

'O–K,' says Lenny very gravely. 'I'm not gonna do that again.'

'Because it doesn't like being talked about,' I say lamely. I don't really know what kind of story he'd like. Somehow I don't think a Greek myth about the boy Zeus will do, even with the cornucopia in a secret setting.

Lenny nods his head solemnly.

I rack my brains for something else to say. 'Because it's a secret place.'

'I know.'

'So why did you?' I hiss.

'Because,' whispers Lenny, 'I knew you'd know.'

That stumps me. He looks up into my eyes like he's really sure I know all about his secret place.

'Because you was in the pictures.'

'I'm what?' I say.

And Lenny slowly counts through the pages. With only the light from the smoky oil lamp I can't see a thing. But he knows what he's doing.

So I wait.

And finally he turns up a page. 'There,' he says. He points at something, all shadowy. 'That's you.'

'I see.' I know better than to upset him again, so I pick up the oil lamp, hold it close, squint at the picture until it comes into focus. There's a spring sky, all fluffy clouds. There's a girl standing in a valley outside a little cottage. Roses trail round the door. The girl is willowy and has my smile. She's wearing a coat like mine and above her in the sky, blue birds are singing. And it is kind of weird because she does look a lot like me, but then again she doesn't, because I never smile these days.

And it's just a book.

'But it doesn't make any difference,' I say. 'It's still a secret and you mustn't tell.'

'OK,' says Lenny.

'Not unless I say,' I add.

'OK.' He nods very seriously and snuggles back down beside me.

'Because it's our secret?' he says. 'Just you and me. Ain't it?'

'All right,' I say.

'And if you could get away and if I carry the things, you might take me there?'

9

Lenny falls asleep. I don't. I'm too restless. With a smile I remember – today's my birthday. I tread the floor, heart beating. I keep going over Careem's words: *After that I've got something else in mind.*

Happy birthday, Melissa.

I need air. Clean air, not oil lamp or wood smoke or the foul stench of this place. But I'm too scared to go outside. What if Kaylem's still around? I should go out though, and see if there's any hope of escape. Nan would tell me to.

'You must always get up and fight back, Melissa. If you give up on yourself, few will help you.

'You must strive to be like Melissa, your namesake, the mountain nymph. The myths tell that when her neighbours tried to make her reveal the secrets of the boy Zeus, Melissa remained silent. In anger, the women tore her to pieces, but Demeter, the sister of Zeus, sent a plague upon them, causing bees to be born from Melissa's dead body and the bees swarmed on Melissa's enemies and stung them to death.

'You must always fight back, my honeybee. Sting your oppressors, swarm on your enemies.'

I force myself to go out and look. *Even if only to find something to protect myself with . . . an iron bar, a sharp piece of rusty metal, the right words.*

I leave the locker room and climb up the ramp to the racetrack.

I see him at the exit, dark against the early dawn. His locks falling to his broad shoulders. He's standing guard. I could go back without him noticing. He doesn't know I'm here. I don't know why I feel so nervous. I hear Nan's voice, what she would say: *Get to know him. He's saved you twice. You don't have to trust him. Just use him.*

I walk softly up the concrete slope. I'll speak to him. Suddenly I don't mind speaking to him.

'Thank you for earlier,' I say.

He doesn't turn. I just see him stiffen, just a bit. 'Thank you too, for being nice to Lenny,' he says.

I draw level and rest on the edge of the barricade beside him.

'He told me you was nice,' he continues.

The racetrack lies like a dark lake encircled by a ring of hills. The trash is transformed by the moonlight into ripples of silver.

'There's no way out,' he says.

'OK.'

'In case you was looking.'

'I needed air.'

'And I'm sorry.'

'Sorry?'

'Sorry I brought you here.'

In the light from the stars I can see his face, the square angle of his chin.

55

'I'm sorry too, if the thing with Kaylem brings you trouble,' I say.

'It doesn't matter.'

'I'm always trouble,' I add.

'Lenny likes you.'

I remember Nan saying, 'Beauty is a gift. Use it wisely.' I start thinking about just how to use it here.

'Lenny ain't got no one to care for him.'

'He's got you.'

'Ain't the same.'

'You took care of me,' I point out.

'You can pay me back.'

'Pay you back?'

'Take care of Lenny for me, give him love, and I'll try and save you from Careem.'

For some strange reason my heart drops. He saved me for Lenny.

'You got the shoes all right then?' I remember his words. 'Even if we get the shoes, even if everyone's happy, it's only for tonight. That's all.' And I remember how he left the rest unspoken: *because Careem's got something else in mind.*

He nods. 'I'll try an' save you anyways. Like I said, you can trust me.'

'OK,' I say. 'But you need to know, I'll be trying to save myself too.'

He turns and looks at me.

'Just letting you know. I'm not "spoil". I don't *belong* to anyone. I'm getting out of here one way or another, whatever it takes. Whether I owe you for Kaylem or not. I told you I'm trouble, and I'm not joking. Kaylem is a dead man. I'll get my own back on him. You just watch. And from the moment you hauled me out of the river you got yourself into it too. So expect more.'

I turn on my heel.

I don't know why I'm so angry.

I stomp back inside. It's not just because I've landed here.

It's Tarquin.

It's entirely irrational. Which just makes it worse. But I don't think I've ever felt so angry with anyone ever before.

10

I do eventually get to sleep. That is, I slip in and out of consciousness a bit. Not really sleep. Just a shutting down of everything.

I'm grateful. I can't think any more. Don't want to think any more. I want to turn it all off. Maybe dream of being in that other place with Nan.

Lenny doesn't let me rest for long, though. That's the thing about little kids, they don't let you do anything. I swear they must know better, but they just pull on your sleeve and yank at your hand and just when you're dropping off and you're so very nearly there, where you know it's going to be so lovely, and birds are singing by a waterfall and you're holding a huge chunk of bread and about to sink your teeth right into it, they wake you up.

Lenny shakes me. He's got hold of a few bits of glowing wood and a broken old bottle with more oil in it and a fresh rag wick. He lights it.

'You can read it to me now,' he says and shoves his tattered book under my nose.

'No, I can't,' I say. 'I can't read.'

'Yes, you can. I know you can. I saw you read that street sign down by the dock.'

Trust kids. 'Even if I can read, I'm not reading to you.'

His face falls. All the sparkle goes out of his eyes. Back comes the guilt.

'OK,' I say, 'but only once and that's it – and when I've had enough I'm stopping.'

He smiles immediately and pushes the book onto my lap. I open it up. He cuddles up close. This time I don't push him away.

'OK,' I clear my throat. 'Once upon a time –'

'Where does it say that?' he asks.

I point at the picture. 'Once upon a very annoying time,' I say.

'Read what's there,' he says.

'I'm not going to read anything if you keep on interrupting me.'

'OK.'

'Once upon a time there was a farm.' I stop. There really is a little farm in the book. I stop and peer at the picture. There's a mountain in the background and the same little cosy cottage with a farmyard in front of it. Well, a kind of farmyard – looks more like a garden and a pond with wild ducks swimming on it. And there're the roses around the door.

'Look.'

Lenny puts a grubby finger on one window. There's a girl looking out of it. The girl who looks like me.

'Go on,' says Lenny, turning the page for me.

There is a picture across both pages. It's a close-up of the farmyard and all the things are labelled. One little farm cottage.

Two stone outhouses for storing logs. Three cottagers – an older girl, an older boy and a little kid. The boy and the girl are my age and they're smiling. The little boy is jumping up in the air with his arms flung skywards.

'That's me,' says Lenny and this time he plonks his finger down right on top of the little kid. I can see this isn't the first time he's done that. The kid in the picture has dirty marks all round him, like Lenny's been sitting here and pointing himself out to himself in that faraway place for a long time. He's pretty nearly rubbed the kid's face clean off the page. He's pointed out the girl too. She's none too clean either.

'That's me and that's you.' He points down on the girl.

I don't ask, 'So who the hell is that?' about the last cottager. Instead I quickly move on to the four berry bushes and the five wild rabbits and the six apple trees and the seven fishes in the brook and the eight ducks in the pond and the nine birds on the roof and then I look around for ten. But there isn't any ten.

Lenny gets this shiny look in his eyes. 'Turn over the page,' he whispers. 'This is the best bit.'

I flip the page and the whole double spread is full of tens. There are ten bees buzzing away and all over it is written stuff like: ten bees visiting ten cherry trees, and ten bees calling at ten bramble bushes and ten bees pollinating ten vegetable plots and ten bees collecting honey from ten wild meadows filled with foxgloves and buttercups and harebells and moon daisies, where ten woolly sheep graze while ten lambs frolic and ten hens lay ten eggs each in ten henhouses . . . And in the middle of the page are ten big old beehives.

I've never seen a bee before. I can't tell if they look like the

60

pictures or not. I saw a couple of wasps once, but we don't get many of them either. There must be bees somewhere though because we still sometimes get apples in London. Not many and mostly they're shrivelled, but Nan said: 'Where there's apples there's bees. And it shows they're coming.'

There isn't much else in Lenny's picture book, so I start telling him a tale of my own. There's only so long you can go on saying three birds and two bunnies and counting them up and imagining those bees really existing before you get bored. I turn back to the first page to where the girl who looks like me is.

'Once upon a time this girl fell in a river –' I start.

Lenny gasps.

'You don't like that story?' I ask.

'What happened?' he whispers.

'Are you sure you want to hear it?'

'It's about you?'

'Yes.'

'And me?'

'OK.'

'And the secret place?'

'I suppose so.'

So I carry on. And the tales of abundance start to flow. I tell him all about how he and I go to this place, our secret place, our hidden valley . . . a place where a stream forever trickles its pure waters through a glade ripe with hazelnuts and blackberries; where a tiny crofter's cottage stands empty, its woodshed full of hewn logs, its gardens brimming over with wild spinach; where grouse and pheasant are plenty and the mountain pools hold huge perch . . . and how we sit on little chairs every night in front of a little fireside and eat from bone-china plates and tell stories . . . and only I know the way there, and only I can show him . . .

And just when his eyes are as round as saucers, I make him close them, and I pull Nan's key out of my coat pocket and I put it in his hand. I close his fingers around the key.

'And that's the key to the front door – the one that is covered in roses.'

He opens his eyes. He stares at the key in his hand. He turns it over, peers at its plastic-photo key ring and gasps.

'*It is*,' he whispers. His eyes are full of magic. His finger traces the mountain frozen in the plastic, the croft and the pond with the duck on it. The word SCOTLAND in tiny silver letters.

And a dreamy look mists up his whole face – as if he's already there in that other place. He lifts his head and looks at me.

'Will there be real food there?' he says.

'What d'you mean?'

'I mean *real* food, not book food?'

'There'll be bread and soup and roast duck,' I say, 'and blackberry crumble.' Nan told me that. She told me how she stayed at a bed and breakfast in the Scottish Borders and they had bread and soup and blackberry crumble.

'No,' he says, 'like dog meat.'

I frown. 'Is that real food?'

'Yes,' he says. 'That's what we get here, dog meat and potatoes and a few things the gangs bring in.'

'Well,' I say. 'There'll be real food in Scotland, but you are going to love the book food better.'

'I know,' he says. His little face is all grave. He nods wisely to himself like he knows all about the book food.

'And I get to feed the ducks, don't I?'

'If you want,' I say. 'As long as you don't make pets of them.'

'Because we're going to eat them?'

'Yes we are,' I say.

I close the book up. The wick on the lamp is blowing sootily. I feel tired. Every bone in my body has had it.

'Could we just keep one of them? If it had ducklings?'

I look at him. 'I'm not doing any deal on the ducks,' I say.

'I could go without my roast duck to make up?'

I sigh. 'OK,' I say and I close my eyes. 'But only if it has ducklings.'

11

I wake to the sound of tin lids banging and the smell. The sound sends a shiver into me. What's gonna happen now? I've got this really bad feeling I'm about to find out what Careem's 'something else' is.

Whatever it is, I tell myself, I'll get away. And if I don't, he'll pay for it.

I'm all curled up inside Nan's coat and I want to stay there. Desperately I push my nose deep into its folds, try to smell her, try not to think of last night. The coat smells of old rags and wood smoke. The river has washed Nan right away.

'Oh Nan,' I whisper.

A hand shakes me. A voice wakes me. Someone pulls back the edge of my coat.

'Hey, Miss, they're back,' whispers Lenny.

And I can tell from his voice it's not good.

'We need to get down to the racetrack,' he says.

I roll over and stand up. I brush my hair back. I wipe my face with the sleeve of the coat. So hungry, so dirty.

'Water?' I ask Lenny. I'm thirsty. I don't trust the water but I need to drink. And I'm going to wash. I don't want to look like them.

It's morning, though there's no sun yet. *Think about escaping. Remember?* Lenny fetches me a glass bottle full of water. I let it stand for as long as I can so the sediment settles. I stretch the hem of my T-shirt over the bottle mouth and drink. I only drink the first third of the bottle. Even that tastes stale. I use some to wash my hands. I pour the rest into my cupped palms and wash my face. Lenny watches wide-eyed.

'You're so pretty, Miss.'

I comb my hair with my fingers.

'You're prettier than all those things in the book world.'

'C'mon,' I say.

In the pale light we set out for the stadium. We don't get any further than the first aisle before Tarquin appears.

'I'll take over now.' He ruffles Lenny's hair. His smile is wide, his lips full.

When he draws level with me I hiss, '*I need to get out.*'

He laughs and shakes his head.

'*You need to get Lenny out too,*' I add. '*Get him to some other place.*'

'Once you're here, there ain't no other place.'

'Says who?'

He shakes his head. 'We all belong to Careem.'

I'm the one who laughs then.

'I wouldn't laugh,' says Tarquin.

By the time we get to the stadium track, the fire has been rekindled. Through the pale light, people drag fuel over and pile it by the flames. Boards and planks and sawn timber and old window frames and furniture and seating. They stack them in ragged piles. They break the boards up. They fold them, stamp on them, twist the sheets back on themselves until the ply splinters and gives.

Alongside the fire, on the ground, is a row of metal bowls. And women. They're hardly more than girls, though they look old. One of them has a tiny sickly baby tied to her front. They're setting up little stalls, like something's going to get traded. They fill the bowls with water from a few huge jerry cans. They light fires between three stones and heat up the bowls. There's a silence about them, a heaviness that scares the hell out of me.

The gangers come in banging the pan lids again. And Tarquin darts over to join them. A deafening stream, they march into the centre of the arena like some returning army. They kick up turf and beat the pan lids like drums. Everyone falls quiet.

And then comes Careem. He's still got that long black coat on. He walks in at his own pace, looking about him, noticing everything. All swagger. A little girl scuttles into his path – a woman grabs her up, smiles a scared 'Sorry'.

I remember his words again. His unspoken threat.

'And make sure I'm happy when I see the shoes.'

A trembling starts up under my ribcage. Let him be happy about the shoes. I can't make out if he's happy or not.

'It's not about keeping others happy,' Nan would say. 'It's about showing them you're dangerous. Trust in fear. Not smiles, Melissa. It'll keep you safer.'

She's right. And I *am* dangerous. And in ways he won't expect. I breathe in and try to relax.

Everyone stops what they're doing and clears a path for him. As he strides past they bow their heads. He gives nothing away. Just puts on his own little show.

Fleetingly I wonder how Tarquin did get the shoes. Did he do it alone? What did he do to the traders? I don't care about them, anyway. I learned a long time ago – you got to put yourself first.

Careem makes his way casually down to the centre of the arena. He's got the strut down to perfection. He winks at a few girls, favourites maybe, wags a finger at someone, who goes bone-white. He holds his hand up to stop encroachers. They immediately back off. He accepts a gift from a gang member without a nod or thanks.

He makes out like he isn't looking at anything. But he is. You can see he's as sharp as they come. Sizing everything up. And nobody seems to notice he's doing it. Nobody except the two guys closest to him. Nailey and Kaylem, maybe.

And Tarquin.

I see Tarquin following just behind. I watch him too. His eyes are everywhere but his face doesn't give anything away. In the rear a group of ten or fifteen gangers are lugging loot into the arena.

Careem sits down on a huge armchair under an awning. The gangers wait with their load, near the fire. People crowd forward. I stagger as they shove me aside. Must be about a hundred of them, maybe more, all pushing forward. Must take a lot to feed them.

Careem raises a forefinger, brings it down. The gangers tip everything at his feet: three dead dogs land with a thump. A full shopping trolley tips over. Potatoes, mushrooms, jars of homemade goods, something like a sack of flour spills into the mud. A cart covered with a plastic sheet, an old suitcase with a broken zip – clothes maybe. The girls press forward. One woman steps up, takes charge.

Above the clamour I hear her shrill voice as she points to people. 'You count the potatoes. You get that sack up. You clean this one.' She toes one of the dead dogs.

I've never seen anyone skin a creature so quick. They pounce on it and get its head and paws off before you can look away. They dice it up and share it out and quarrel about the tail.

'Now that one.' She points at the second dog. 'Then dress the last one for the chiefs.'

While some of them start on the second dog, others go through the contents of the shopping trolley. Dividing it up with razor-sharp precision. Careem still makes like he isn't watching, but he is. He's watching all right. So are Kaylem and Nailey.

Everyone knows Kaylem and Nailey are watching. Nobody likes them. You can tell. Specially Kaylem. Everybody gives him a wide berth. I hold my breath. I haven't seen the shoes. I don't know what to think. But I know Tarquin got some. Where are they?

'Listen up,' says Careem. He doesn't shout. He doesn't have to. Everyone is suddenly listening.

'There's only three dogs today because of her.' He points at me in a bored way.

There are murmurs of disappointment. A shuffling noise, angry muttering. Some of them shout: 'Chuck her to the dogs . . . that's what Careem should do. Throw her to the dogs . . . How's three going to feed anyone? . . . After the crew have had their fill?'

68

Careem laughs. 'You're a bloodthirsty lot,' he says. 'But don't worry, she'll pay. She's for the Governor General.'

The mob falls silent. My blood freezes.

The Governor General.

Nan warned me about the General. Kept me hidden. Showed me how to wind a scarf around my head, hide my face. 'Those poor girls,' she said. 'The General is evil. He ravages the beautiful. Like Aristaeus in the Greek myths, he desires what is not his. Aristaeus was the keeper of the bees, but he deserted his hives to chase another man's wife. The Gods punished him and the bees died. The General also desires what is not his – young girls – and because of him the bees won't come back.'

There's a murmur of approval and shouts of: 'Too good for her', 'Get a good price' and '*Careem!*'

Careem waves a lazy hand. Some of them are still grumbling. Two youngers stagger forward hauling in a swag of something. I eye it anxiously, hoping it's the shoes. They drag it right up near the fire. Careem motions them to stop, then ignores them and their burden.

Instead he waves Kaylem forward. He points at the bloody carcass of the third dog.

There it lies skinned, yet still intact. Its eyes glassy and staring. Kaylem picks it up, slits it from gizzard to pap and scoops its entrails and organs out. He cuts something off from between the dog's back legs, holds it up with a lewd gesture, thrusts it up and down. Then laughs. He spits the dead animal right from anus to jaw and slings it between two iron poles over the fire.

Kaylem doesn't look at Careem, but when he's done with

the dog, he jerks his head. A smile lingers in his eyes and then he sniffs his fingers.

'You turn it,' Kaylem orders a younger ganger.

The boy wraps his scarf around his hand, drags the end of his jacket over it, grabs hold of the iron pole and starts turning the dog over the fire.

'The girl,' Careem says.

'That's you,' whispers Lenny, giving me a little shove. 'Don't argue with him. Please don't, Miss. Do what he says then he won't hurt you.'

I stumble forward. Kaylem and Nailey punch me to the ground near the swag. I slip, land on slime, kneel near the offal. I can't take my eyes off it. The smell. The ground is slick with it.

'Wanna see what she's paid already?' says Careem.

The crowd draw in tighter. Shouts of approval run through them. 'Yeah,' says one voice above the other, 'and it better be good.'

'Oh, it's good all right,' says Careem.

And with another nod he indicates that Kaylem and Nailey can show the people what they swapped their dinner for.

Nailey steps forward, rips the end of the swag open. Out tumble the shoes.

I can't quite believe it. I can't quite believe there's that many. Those boat people must've been rolling in it. How on earth did Tarquin carry all that? But he must have – there they are just lying in front of me.

The grumbling takes on a less threatening tone. Someone even whoops. I try to get my heart to subside a little, but it doesn't listen to me. Hands reach forward.

70

'Don't touch,' says Careem very silkily.

One of them makes a mistake. Either it's that or he didn't hear Careem or he doesn't care and thinks it worth it. He jumps right forward, straight at a pair of lace-up trainers, and grabs them.

Kaylem flicks up a hand. The blade arcs and sweeps down through the soft skin of the boy's throat. The kid drops. Blood sprays out across the shoes.

12

There's a huge intake of breath. Nobody moves.

I crouch there, my heart crashing against my ribs.

'Now look what you done,' says Careem mildly. 'You messed my haul.' He stands up, steps forwards and prods the dying kid with his foot. The kid's eyes roll up. He claws at his throat, jerks. A low gurgle.

Careem shakes his head, sits back down. 'What a waste,' he says, nodding at his two guys. They step forward and pull the kid off the pile of shoes and away to one side. 'Put him out for the dogs,' says Careem. And as an afterthought, 'Set some of Shukri's boys to trap any that come. Put him to some use.'

Kaylem hauls the dying boy off like he's already dog bait. I kneel there. In shock. One of their own. It's just like Nan said. 'Kill or be killed. Think. Stay alive. Do whatever you must. Or you won't stand a chance.'

'Make a line,' shouts Nailey.

People are scared. They're scared to disobey. And they're scared to come near the shoes. 'Hurry up,' yells Nailey. A few straggly lines start to form on the far side of the fire.

Careem turns to the guys quietly waiting round him. 'Each

of you take a pair,' he says. They don't stop to match them up much, or check sizes. They just bend down and take whatever's nearest.

'They'll swap later,' whispers Lenny. I glance over my shoulder. He's crept up right behind me, all big eyes and scrawny neck. And suddenly I'm afraid for him. I want him to go back, stay away from those shoes. But he creeps up alongside me, puts his hand in mine. And I can see he's looking at something in the pile.

Near the centre is a little cache of kids' shoes. They're tied together by their laces. Nobody's taken them yet. I look at them and think of the kids that once wore those shoes.

The gangers are just taking the nearest ones. My heart's still hammering. I look at Lenny's feet, so raw and scarred. I look at the blood splattered over everything.

After most of the gang's chosen, Careem calls Tarquin forwards.

'OK,' he says, 'you got them, though they cost us in dogs. Now you choose.'

And as I'm kneeling there I see the way Careem does it. How he keeps his power over this stinking ghetto. Tarquin didn't cost them anything. What was one more ganger going to do that twenty of them couldn't? If they only got three dogs that was all they were going to get. Saving me didn't cost anyone anything. But Careem doesn't want Tarquin to get any kind of thanks for getting the shoes. So he makes out he's a dead weight, keeps him waiting till last.

And he kills the boy who tried first.

Tarquin heads straight into the pile – right towards the kids' shoes. Swiftly he reaches for them, unlaces a pair, stout boys'

73

boots. He holds them up for Careem to approve. Lenny draws in his breath. Nobody draws a knife. Careem flickers one eye. Tarquin steps out of the pile and backs away.

'Don't want none for yourself?' says Careem.

Tarquin shrugs. 'Don't mind.'

'But?' says Careem.

'If you think I did good then let me keep the girl,' says Tarquin.

Everything suddenly goes quiet. The silence is terrible. I can even hear the slight patter of rain on the shoes.

Immediately Tarquin knows he's said the wrong thing.

'Please,' he adds.

Nobody moves.

'Since Ma died,' Tarquin quickly defends, 'Lenny ain't got no one to stay with when we're out. I take him along on account of this. I need someone to leave him with. Someone who'll treat him right. So I can stay out longer. Get more swag. And he likes the girl.'

Lenny's face lights up.

But Careem's doesn't. Nailey leaps forwards.

'No,' I scream. I can't help myself.

There's a terrific whack and a baseball bat cracks clean across Tarquin's ribs. The blow sends him toppling backwards.

'I don't think you was listening,' says Careem. 'I said you can have a pair of shoes.'

Lenny's hand slips out of mine. He's trembling. He's gone whiter than a ghost.

'You put your foot out of line once more and I'll sort Lenny out for you. Forever,' says Careem very softly.

13

Lenny starts crying. Kaylem moves closer. Lenny shuts his mouth. But it's me that Kaylem comes for. His hand descends on my coat and I'm hauled up in front of Careem.

'Girly,' Careem drawls. 'Looks like you've been making friends already.'

'And enemies,' adds Kaylem.

'Well?' Careem's eyes hold a question.

I don't answer. I've got a feeling it's best not to be too sparky.

'You were right about the shoe boat – I don't want no one saying I ain't a reasonable man, so you can keep your shoes and your coat. Fair enough?'

From the corner of my eye I can see Lenny. Keep Careem's attention. Maybe he'll forget about Lenny for now. So I focus back on Careem. He seems to be waiting for an answer. And I think I've got just the right one for him.

I've figured it out. My card.

He won't kill me. He won't even touch me. He wants to trade me to the General, doesn't he?

It's an ace.

'Well.' I raise an eyebrow. 'Seems you're pretty handy at

flouncing around in a long coat and dealing with dead dogs.'

There's a collective intake of breath. I take full advantage. I step up closer to him and daintily wipe my hands on the side of his armchair. I tilt my face to its best angle and look at him. Then I drop my voice. 'As for me, I like my men a lot more –' I flick my eyes up, gaze deep into his – 'potent.'

He knows what I mean. *You're no match for me. I'm for the General.*

Kaylem steps up, ready to execute me on the spot. But Careem's floored. He can't execute me without what I said getting back to the people. If he executes me he'll lose a lucrative deal with the General. Both things will undermine him. He motions Kaylem away. Struggles to reassert control.

'Don't think you can weave your magic on anyone else round here.' He waves his hand at the crowd. 'You got to save it up. You get me?'

'No, I don't get you,' I say.

'You got to save it up for someone special.' He says the 'someone special' all low and sexy.

Kaylem lets out a long guffaw. 'And you thought I was rough.'

Tarquin makes to stand up. I don't know if he was going to do something, but before he's even on his knees Nailey's got hold of him.

Careem calls one of his women over. You can tell he wants to be rid of me as quickly as possible. 'You and Dena get her cleaned up. Check in the haul. We got a few clothes that'll do. Choose something revealing. She's going to the Governor General as soon as she's ready.'

The Governor General. Aristaeus.

76

Nan told me the whole story.

'Nobody reads the Greek myths any more. If they did they'd know that the death of the bees was a punishment because Aristaeus desired Eurydice – and she belonged to another. She belonged to Orpheus.

'To understand the story you must understand the symbols.

'Aristaeus is mankind – greedy, ready to take what is not his own – and Eurydice is nature, bounteous, beautiful beyond compare.

'The bees died because of mankind's greed. It was a penalty for our misuse of the natural world. Man's excesses upset the balance of nature, brought death, brought starvation.

'Wasted populations.'

I am transported back to my childhood, Nan and me and Dad's books and the mythical beauty of Greek islands, where vines clung to sunny walls and turquoise seas lapped on golden beaches . . .

Not wasted wilderness outside the door.

And I remember her warnings.

'Eurydice was beautiful beyond the dreams of mortal men. None could see her and not desire her.

'She was beautiful, Melissa. But not more beautiful than you.

'And Aristaeus caused her death. Caused her to dwell forever in the underworld.

'Do not let the General see you, Melissa. He is an abomination.

He is an Aristaeus. He uses all his power to scour the country for young girls. And he will drag you down into the dark.

'Old tales tell old truths.

'Only Orpheus can lead you back from the underworld, only he can save you once the General has seen you. You must find your Orpheus, Melissa, before the General finds you.

'To be so beautiful is a blessing and a curse.'

14

I grit my teeth as Dena, a woman with pock marks and greasy hair, douses me in icy water. Two others take rags and gritty soap. They scrub me raw.

I cower, shiver. 'I can do it myself.'

Kaylem is standing there, watching, laughing. 'Careem's orders.'

'*Let me do it,*' I hiss at Dena.

'Or-ders,' reminds Kaylem. He leers at me, enjoys my nakedness.

There's no way I can cover myself. *You'll pay for this*, I think.

'*Please,*' I say to Dena. I think even she finds Kaylem revolting. She motions for the others to stop. 'Dry yourself,' she says.

She throws me a cloth. I shiver. I cover up, rub myself quickly. My skin tingles as I try to get some warmth into me.

'Could I drink some water?' I ask, my teeth chattering.

I stand there, shivering, the towel barely stretching round me.

Dena steps back and looks at me. 'Get the clothes.' She scoops water from one of the buckets and passes it to me.

As I sip the water, they sort through the clothes. It seems

they have a supply of dresses reserved for those to be sent to the General.

Dena's not satisfied. 'The dark green dress.'

One of them goes out and returns with a dress. It's very flimsy, with crossed straps at the back and cut low at the front. The skirt clings to my legs. It's beautiful in a way, but I hate it. It makes me feel young and vulnerable and powerless.

Kaylem leans up against the wall, laughing, twitching his crotch, making rude gestures.

'You're too thin,' remarks Dena and pulls the dress tighter around my waist to show my shape. She fastens it with a safety pin. 'Eat this,' she says and thrusts a cold cooked potato into my hand.

I glance up at her. She doesn't look back. There's something sorry in the angle of her shoulders. That's all.

I eat the potato.

Careem arrives. He strolls in, his long black coat swishing as he walks.

'Think she'll do?' he says to Kaylem.

The two of them exchange a knowing look.

Careem examines me. He looks for skin damage. I realise Kaylem was very clever in the way he slapped me. Bruises don't show up around the back of the head and, except for a thinning of hair on my left side, a cut on my inside lip and a few blue shadows on my neck, there's nothing to show.

Careem sees the bruises on my neck, though. 'Not happy about that,' he says.

Dena finds a scarf – wispy, pale. She drapes it round my neck.

'Speak to Tarquin,' Careem orders Kaylem.

'It wasn't Tarquin,' I say.

The blow lands on the side of my head just behind my ear. I reel, nearly fall. Dena steadies me.

'I said, speak to Tarquin. She was in his care and he knows better.'

'Delighted to,' says Kaylem.

'Get Nailey and get her out.'

I'm marched out, dizzy, my eyes watering. Through the arena, across one of the footbridges. A chill wind blows. In this skimpy dress I have nothing to shield me.

'Keep moving,' orders Careem. 'We don't want her looking like a dried dog when we get there.'

I think: *Get where? How far? Can I break free? Run?* I can scarcely walk in these stupid shoes they've squeezed on me. I see a car, an army jeep. It comes gliding out, stops right by us.

'Get in,' orders Careem.

He yanks open a door and gets in the front. Nailey and Kaylem bundle me into the back. One on either side. The car moves off. It slowly negotiates the bumps in the road and heads through the ruined streets of the east. We pass a few straggling gangers carrying heavy loads of broken furnishings. Firewood. One woman with a tin basin full of bits and pieces.

'Grow tough and stay tough.' That's what Nan would say. 'And when the going gets tough – get tougher.'

Maybe I can't run, but I can stay and fight. And that gives me an idea.

I let my shoulders fall slack and a blank mask settle across my face. Even the tiniest pinprick can pop a bubble.

Make your pinprick count, I tell myself.

Make sure you burst Careem's little bubble.

At the barracks, through the swing barrier, at a manned outpost, the jeep stops. We're outside a large stately building. A squad of soldiers, six, come at the double to the jeep. Careem casually steps down from the front seat. He nods at me. 'Brought a little treat for the General.'

The soldiers hold their guns at the ready.

'You and you, step out. Stand by the car,' they order Kaylem and Nailey. 'You and the girl this way.'

Careem laughs, flicks his wrist at the two gangers. 'Amuse yourselves, boys,' he says.

And then we walk. Careem takes my arm. He twists it. 'Walk nicely,' he says. 'If you fail to fetch me a good price, I'll let Kaylem have you – with no conditions about spoiling the goods.'

So he knows.

When the going gets tough, I think, *I'll put my plan into action.*

We're ushered into a wide hall. Instantly I can see where all the country's wealth has gone. It has the grandest interior. The furnishings are all in red. The ceiling is divided into panelled compartments, each showing ancient emblems. Light filters in through stained-glass windows. Coats of arms, paintings, frescoes, statues. Solid brass gates bar an entrance to some kind of chamber. At the far end on a dais is a throne, ornate, gilded.

I think of Nan and her tales of the Gods. I stare. *Was Olympia like this? Did Zeus sit on such a throne?*

Careem sits down on a carved seat near the dais. 'Walk,'

he says, 'there.' He points into the centre of the room. I obey, totter over, stand there, faint, hungry. 'Where's all the sass now?' jeers Careem. 'Cat got your tongue?'

Get tougher.

I try not to teeter in the impossible shoes. Instead I feel for the safety pin Dena used on the dress. I loosen it. I twist the sharp end out. *Look for his weak points. Just one careless moment. I'll take his eye out. That's all I need. Bastard. A few minutes of chaos. I'm outside the ghetto. I could kick these heels off and get clean away.*

I hear the click of boots on stone. I hear the ornate brass gates squeal open. Something creeps out, staggers to a nearby table.

A silky voice says, 'Take it away. Give it to the troops. It's got no use left.'

I look up, focus my attention.

It's a girl. A long-legged, striking girl. Once a beautiful girl. Her face is bruised. One eye black and swollen. She staggers, holds on to a picture. Her thick golden hair falls in waves onto her thin shoulders. Everywhere, she's covered in black bruising. Around her delicate ankles and wrists, raw wheals, like she's been tied down by wires too tight.

Two soldiers march up, take her by the arms, lift her almost bodily. She seems to have no energy left. They support her and half carry, half drag her out.

Careem laughs.

The gates creak open again. The same click of leather on stone.

They open. Through them marches the General. He's much shorter than I imagined. Short and old. And there's something about his eyes. They slide over the floor and over me. He smiles. His teeth – broken, stubby – slope backwards into his mouth.

I tighten my grip on the safety pin.

He seems to be drying his hands. As if he's just washed something off them. He marches straight up to me. Grabs my chin, forces it up. Then he looks.

He likes what he sees. I can see his pupils widen. I can see his lower lip fall slack. He lets out a long, low whistle. He rips my dress down. *This is it.* I respond. My arm comes round fast. My knee comes up. I smack the side of his head. I drive the pin in until it hits bone. I find a use for the stupid shoes. Stiletto heel right on his foot. He jumps back. I knee up again, but miss.

'And spirited too,' he says, slamming his hand to his head. It comes away tinged in blood.

Shit. I missed his eye.

'Haven't had one like that for a long time, have you?' says Careem.

The General lets go of my chin, turns and faces him. 'Don't waste my time. How much?'

Careem chuckles. 'I want twice the usual for this one.'

'Twice?' remarks the General, but I can hear the excitement in his voice.

So can Careem. 'Plus guns.'

'So you *are* going to waste my time,' remarks the General. 'I'm not going to arm gangers, however many girls they find me.'

'Can't blame me for asking,' smiles Careem.

'I can just take this one and give you nothing. You're in my garrison,' threatens the General.

'But you won't,' says Careem, 'because there's nobody else

84

who can get you stuff like this, not as good, not as sparky. C'mon, she'll be a lotta fun, and you know it.'

The General considers this.

'And you know I'm your man. You can call me up any time. If you get a little problem down on your farm, or you need to shift a bitta cargo, or want to hunt a runner down, I'm your dog.' Careem leans insolently on the arm of the carved chair.

The General seems to mull over Careem's usefulness. He strokes his chin, runs his thumb along his upper lip.

'You need a good dog in them wilder places,' Careem adds.

'All right, twice the usual. Take half now. But I want her delivered here on Friday after those bruises have faded.' He points at my neck. 'I don't want spoiled goods. I don't like to touch anything marked. I like to see my own handiwork. I thought you knew that.'

'Mistake,' says Careem. 'One of my boys got too keen – her being a looker and all that.'

The General nods. 'Bring her back spotless and intact,' he says. 'I think you understand.'

'Yes, sir,' smiles Careem. 'On Friday, she's all yours.'

15

I'm back in Games City. I can't sleep. I sit and hug my knees. I should have escaped while I was out. No way. No chance. *Think. Come on. You've got to be able to outthink them. What can you do? Who can you work on? You must get out. If you can get out, you can go home. You can hide. The General doesn't know where you live. Careem doesn't know where you live. They don't know where you live. London's big.*

I hang on to that.

London's very big. I've heard gangers at night. But I've never seen them during the day. They've never seen me before. *Get out then. Hide. Get away. They won't find you. They'll never see you again.* I look at the walls of the room and sigh. I notice that the stench isn't so overpowering any more. Has it gone away or do I stink like them now?

Think. Come on. They want stuff: food, fuel, weapons. They're trading you for stuff. Can you tell them of some other boat that's coming in from the north? A boat loaded with guns? It'd be a lie. *Lie through your teeth.* Would it work? When they find out it's a lie – I don't want to think about that.

But I think anyway.

You'd be long gone. You can lie as much as you like as long as you're long gone by the time the truth settles.

Remember what Nan said about lying. 'If you're gonna lie, make it a good one. Do it upfront and bold. Don't be shy. Lie your heart out. Make it work for you. But make sure there's only one thing in the story that's a falsehood. Sandwiched by the truth a lie will work. Then get as far away as possible.'

Who can I lie to? I try to think of all the faces I've seen. Not Careem. He's too smart. He's a born liar. He'd know. And he doesn't care about anything except his hold on Games City.

Tarquin.

He tried to help even before they brought me here. He told me to run. I should have run. I would have. If I could wind back time, I'd run. I'd rather the dogs got me than the General.

I could hardly sit up, let alone run.

Tarquin's got a heart, though. He's on my side. He's been on my side all along. I've seen it. I've seen the way he looks after Lenny.

Of course. So obvious. Lenny.

That's the way forward. Work on Lenny. He's Tarquin's weak point. That's what'll force Tarquin to help me.

What is it Lenny wants?

I lie back and stare at the ceiling of the locker room. Not much of a ceiling to look at. It's all falling in and covered in black mould.

And as I'm lying there the door unlocks. And Tarquin stands there. He's holding his side. He looks tired.

'I'm sorry,' he says.

'You're sorry.'

'Yep.'

'I suppose I should thank you.'

'You don't need to.'

'For trying to save me from Careem.'

'I didn't do it for you.'

'I know.'

I go quiet.

Lenny slips in past him. He's carrying his book. He tries to settle himself down in my lap.

'Let's look at my book,' he says. Like it's the cure for every evil.

I sigh. I'm tired.

Tarquin stands there, half leaning on the door.

'You look nice,' says Lenny. 'You smell nice.' He pushes his little face against my arm.

'I'm tired,' I say.

'Why?' he says. 'You slept already.'

'I didn't.'

'You did. Quinny said I wasn't to disturb you.'

So that's what he told him. I sigh again. 'I haven't eaten much,' I say. 'Nearly nothing since you gave me those scraps yesterday.'

'Oh.' A worried look passes across his face. He gets up and disappears.

'So you told him I was sleeping.'

'He's too young to know about the General.'

'And you didn't want to upset him.'

'No.'

'What will you tell him after Friday?'

Tarquin turns his head away.

It isn't long before Lenny's back. He dumps himself just like before, straight into my lap. He holds himself awkwardly, concealing something behind his back.

Then he says, 'Guess what I got.'

'Your book.' I sigh.

'Oh,' he says. He pauses. 'Yes, I got my book, but guess what else.'

I can't guess. I don't want to guess. I'm tired and I want him to go away. The deal with Tarquin is over. I need to think up some way of getting out of here.

'I got you this,' he says, and he whips his hand round like it's a big surprise.

And it is a big surprise. In his hand he's got a little bowl of food. Some kind of root vegetable stew with a few pieces of meat.

I look at it and I can't stop my mouth watering.

'Thank you.' My voice breaks.

He's so happy. It must be his meal for the day.

'I'm not sure I can eat it all. You help?'

He wriggles in delight.

'If you sit with me we can read your book and eat.'

'But, it's all for you, Miss,' he says. 'Because you're nice, Miss, and nobody ever read my book to me before.' He looks thoughtfully at the food. He pushes his finger into the mix, licks it, then shakes his head. 'I don't need to eat every day.'

'Are you sure?'

'OK, I'll just eat this part.' He draws a line through the food.

'OK. You got a deal.'

I don't ask for anything to wipe my hands on, I just use

my fingers, and before I know it I'm shovelling in all the food on my side of the line. It tastes so good. My stomach cramps slightly. I can't really swallow, but I keep on shovelling.

And when it's gone I run my finger round my side of the bowl. I let the taste linger. I tell my stomach to stop twisting and trying to chuck it all back up.

Lenny gets himself comfy. He curls up beside me. He props the book open on my knees. I don't mind. He looks up at me. I nod my head. He nods his. It's our secret. He looks out for me and I give him what he wants most.

I know what Lenny wants most.

A future.

So I ignore Tarquin who's still leaning up against the door.

And I start.

'Once upon a time this girl fell in a river . . .'

And as usual I make it up.

'. . . So when all of the others are down by the racetrack, the three of them set out to find the cottage beyond the hills and there was –'

'Me,' chimes in Lenny.

'And –'

'You.'

I point at the third figure in the picture.

'And Quinny!' says Lenny.

I glance up at Tarquin. Will he bite? Can I find the words to weave the spell, to make him fall in love with a future for Lenny? A tiny cottage by a clear brook, safe between green hills, under a blue sky. Will he believe in it? I try to remember all Nan's advice.

'You are beautiful.

'You are so beautiful everyone who sees you will be enchanted. Use it. Some will only think of how they can exploit your beauty to further themselves. Others will worship it.'

So I look at Tarquin steadily. And I speak through my eyes: *Lenny is already in my thrall. I can take him from you. If you do not want to share our future, we will leave you out.*

'And that's Tarquin,' I repeat. And I hold his eye.

I want to smile. I know so well how to do this. But I don't let even a shadow pass over my lips. Nan taught me better.

'Watch the eyes, Melissa. Whether man or child, watch the eyes. When the pupils dilate, seize the chance. Don't hesitate. Don't smile. Don't let them know they are falling. Don't give your power away. And when they are ripe, pluck them.'

'Wait,' says Lenny. He skips the book forward to the very last page.

'Read this page.' He taps it with his finger.

The time is ripe.

I leave Tarquin to puzzle out why he can't tear himself away, why he can't come any closer. Why he feels like he's already on the brink of something so wonderful he must have it. I leave him transfixed, leaning on the door frame, and I find the words.

'And there, spread before them, was the secret valley. There was the little cottage with the tiled roof, and there was the brook that trickled past it, down to the pool where the big fishes swam in lazy circles, and the ducks preened their dappled feathers.

'And all around the cottage grew the hazelnut forest where

the wild deer ran and the squirrels leaped, and the pheasants squawked and the rabbits nibbled the soft turf on the verges by the trees. And there on the little plot in front of the cottage was a tiny garden full of wild flowers: speedwell, eyebright, buttercup, daisy and wild white clover, and they perfumed the air so that the garden was filled with a multitude of buzzing bees.'

I let the honeyed words slip off my tongue. I look back up at Tarquin. I don't smile. I don't offer anything. I know how the mind works.

Nan taught me. 'Be contrary. Show them something they can't have and let them suffer.'

'Read it again,' says Lenny.

I shake my head. My throat is all caught up. I remember now how Nan used to tell me a story, how I used to hang on her words when I was as small as Lenny.

'Can't,' I say. My voice chokes. I bite my lip. 'I'm not going to tell any more.' I look at Tarquin.

Lenny immediately understands. 'Go away, Quinny,' he says. 'Go away or she won't tell about the cottage.'

And my triumph is complete.

Tarquin stands there, stubborn, silent. He wants to hear all right. I press my lips up tight. I let him struggle.

'Please tell,' says Lenny.

I keep my eyes fixed on Tarquin and shake my head. 'I made it up.'

'No, you didn't,' said Lenny. He shoots an angry look at Tarquin. 'Look – it's in the book.' He points to the picture across the double spread. 'You couldn't have made it up, 'cos there it is.'

'It's just a story.'

'But you've got the key. Show Tarquin the key, Miss.'

'No.' I shoot a look at Lenny. My eyes say, *This is our secret, have you forgotten?*

'A key?' says Tarquin. He crosses the floor, picks the book off my lap. A puzzled look clouds his face. 'There's no words on this page. Where did you read from?'

'I told you I made it up.'

He shakes his head. 'No,' he says, 'that was real. Nobody could have made that up.'

'Go away,' says Lenny, suddenly sulky.

'If I made it up or if I didn't, it doesn't matter,' I say. I look up at the walls, at the twisted lockers. 'On Friday you know I'm going.'

'Going?' says Lenny in alarm. 'Without me?'

'Yes, without you,' I say.

There's a small, strangled squeal. Lenny shoots a look at Tarquin.

'Is it true, Quinny?'

Tarquin nods.

Lenny just sits there, wooden, all curled up against me, biting his lip, glaring at the picture, refusing to look up.

And I think, *I've got to make this work. I've got to get Tarquin to believe in me. I've got to make him believe there's somewhere to go to. I've got to use whatever I can. Use Lenny. I've no choice. If he wants to hold on to Lenny, he'll have to bust us both out. Because I've got to get out of here.*

Before they send me to the General.

16

Suddenly there's this great clanging. Tarquin straightens up. Something like alarm seems to spike through him. 'They're summoning us to the arena,' he says.

Lenny sits up.

I wait for Tarquin to do something, say something. My brain's really working now. If he falls for it, let him fall for it, then maybe I can get away, maybe –

Nailey busts in. 'You're needed up in the arena. You.'

I don't say anything. I stand up. Nailey nudges Lenny. 'Not her, you.'

'What's wrong?' asks Lenny.

'Extraordinary meeting.'

'I'm scared,' says Lenny. Tarquin reaches out a hand to help him up but Lenny doesn't take it.

'It's nothing. Nothing bad,' says Tarquin. 'We'll be OK.'

'You don't have to come,' Nailey says pointedly at Tarquin.

'Why just me?' Lenny looks up at us all.

'Just move,' says Nailey. 'I'll take charge of *you*.' He grabs my arm, drags on it like I'm some kind of dog. Like I can't be left alone with Tarquin in case he bruises me again. So I follow.

Lenny holds on to me. Tarquin follows too.

We all stumble through the dark corridors and up onto the stadium walkway. Others are heading to the arena too. They're grumbling.

I grope with my hand along the rail, miss my footing. Tarquin catches my elbow. I lean on him.

Lenny grips my hand tight.

'What's it about?' he whispers.

'Don't know,' whispers Tarquin. He's not happy. After a few moments he adds, 'I think it's the other gang. They arrived earlier.'

'Which other gang?' asks Lenny.

'Not from inside the stadium,' says Tarquin. 'From down Limehouse way.'

'Them?' asks Lenny.

'Yep,' says Tarquin. And I'm none the wiser except that from the way Lenny says 'them' I know they're not nice.

But even 'not nice' might open up a door for me. I glance up at the old exit sign, swinging broken on its backing.

I slow down. I let Nailey get a good ten paces ahead. 'Tarquin,' I whisper. 'If you can get me out – that place with the cottage does exist . . .'

Tarquin shakes his head. I try to read what that shake means. Did I move too early? Then he shoots a look at Nailey. I understand.

'If you could –'

'Shush,' says Tarquin.

But the seed is planted.

'You shouldn't tell her to shush,' says Lenny.

95

'And you,' snaps Tarquin.

'If you'd left us alone, she wouldn't have decided to go without me on Friday,' says Lenny sulkily.

'You're right, you're trouble,' says Tarquin, throwing a look at me. It's the first time I've seen him so edgy.

My heart sinks. Maybe I played my hand too early.

'I want to go with her to the secret place,' says Lenny.

Nailey's waiting for us. He catches what Lenny says.

'You'll be going someplace all right,' laughs Nailey. 'And it ain't gonna be no secret.'

We turn through the entrance and enter the stadium.

We're not the first there. Figures trickle in through the athletes' entrance and some have already gathered in the centre. Lenny's friend the brindle tracker dog trots over. Nailey kicks out at it.

In the middle of the arena, squatting around the fire, are new faces. They're scruffy and bearded. They look a lot older than Careem's crew. They're bone thin with rags tied round them. They smell like this place, but they look worse. Instantly my blood freezes. Lenny lets out a small whine and clutches tight to my hand. He pulls on me and hangs back.

Nailey lets go of my arm, moves off, goes up to Careem, points us out. Careem nods.

'Be OK,' I say to Lenny. 'Think of the cottage and those ducks. We'll go there after all this and lie out in the garden, check the hens are safe in their hen runs, and munch on blackberries.'

'You promise?' he whispers. 'You won't go without me again?'

'I promise.' I squeeze his hand.

96

'What?' says Tarquin.

'Our secret,' says Lenny.

Careem stands up. His gangers start banging their tin pans. Everyone gathers behind Careem.

The two groups face each other across the fire. I can feel the tension in Tarquin. 'Just watch out,' he says.

'OK.'

Suddenly he turns to me, grabs hold of my hand. His palms are slick with sweat. 'If anything kicks off, get Lenny back to the changing rooms. I'll get you out.'

I nod. I want to smile. The seed is growing. 'Careful, Melissa,' I hear Nan warn. 'Let the roots grow first. Water it gently. Roots can grow in darkness – don't let in the light too quickly.'

'And if nothing kicks off,' I say, 'is that still a deal?' I make my point. I only help if the deal works both ways.

He looks at me. Reluctantly nods.

The pan banging reaches a crescendo. Careem raises his hands. In each one is a long bone. He waits till the noise subsides. 'Careem of Bone Cross Bone Crew salutes you peeps,' he says. He knocks the bones together.

On the far side of the fire, the leader of the Limehouse Gang stands up. The rest remain squatting like tribesmen. They're armed with every kind of weapon going. There's a real hush. Everyone strains to hear their business.

'Buffalo Badman of Limehouse Boys greets your peeps too.'

Careem knocks the bones again. 'Times is hard and it's Dog's Law, but we're better off working as allies. The Blah-Blah says south gangs getting up a bevy and Brixton Boys joining up with Peckham Shooters and Catford Peel Dem Crew.'

'That's what we heard too,' says the big guy, Buffalo.

'Yeah,' says Careem. 'So Limehouse and Games City Bone Cross Bone gonna get up a horde too.'

A gasp goes through the people. They swallow it quickly, try not to let their dismay show.

'I don't like them,' says Lenny. 'They're mean.' The brindle tracker creeps forwards. She licks Lenny's hand.

I want to laugh. It's not exactly like Careem is kind and the Bone Cross Bone Boys are saints is it?

'I'm scared,' says Lenny.

'What of?' snaps Tarquin, but I notice he stands in front of Lenny, putting himself in between the Limehouse crew and his little brother.

'Guster says they eat people,' says Lenny.

'Shush,' says Tarquin.

'Nobody eats people,' I say, smoothing Lenny's hair back.

'I'm still scared.'

Careem waves the bones again. A hush falls. 'Give my Limehouse brothers a cheer,' he says. There's a half-hearted cheer – no pan banging, and a bit of mumbling.

Careem whips round. The mumbling stops. A hush replaces it. 'Give my friends a better greeting,' he says, his voice low and dangerous.

There's a strained cheering. A few claps. And then silence.

'We've entered into a deal with them,' he says. There's no clapping.

'If anyone don't wanna do the deal I can take yous down to the coast, over to the continent and trade your arse.'

Deadly silence. Everybody knows the continent is a

wasteland. Everybody knows France had the most nuclear hits. Nobody wants to be sent down the tunnel there.

'All right,' says Careem. 'You give them respect. They're allies now and we're going to make the usual fealty ties.'

'What's that?' I ask.

Tarquin doesn't answer. He's gone pale. He's pushing Lenny behind him.

'Yeah, so you bring one of your youngers to us and we'll raise him as a Games Ganger and we'll give you one of our youngers to be raised as a Limehouse Boy. Cement the good will,' continues Careem.

I feel Lenny's grip on my hand tighten.

'We brought you one already,' grunts Buffalo. He shoves forward a little girl. She's been stripped to the waist. Buffalo spins her round like she's a top. Her back is a lattice of lash marks. She's so thin every rib shows.

'She's had a fair bit of use, but she's well trained and'll do anything.' A filthy laugh goes through the Limehouse Boys.

'But it sounds like you prefer boys?' yells one of them. There's another dirty laugh.

'Some of us do an' all,' another adds.

'Yeah, we prefer boys,' says Careem, unabashed. 'And I've got just the one for you.' He looks around. Tarquin pushes Lenny out of sight.

'You,' calls Careem, pointing a bone right at Tarquin. 'Bring him out.'

A chant goes up. 'Len-ny. Len-ny.'

Lenny's hand grips mine till it hurts. But there are other hands working against ours. They tear him from me, push

Tarquin sideways, drag Lenny out into the centre of the arena. The brindle dog suddenly growls.

'There he is,' says Careem. 'He's been a bit spoiled, so it'll do him good to toughen up. You do what you like with him.'

Lenny's shaking, trying not to cry. Tarquin is whiter than a ghost. 'No!' he yells. He tries to struggle forward. Kaylem approaches him, wielding an iron bar. 'I'll go instead,' yells Tarquin. 'I'm grown. I'll be more use.'

Careem doesn't even bother turning his head. Kaylem lowers the bar. Tarquin ducks, kicks out. The bar spins out of reach. Tarquin goes to shout again. Kaylem's fist crumples into his face. His cry is cut short.

'We'll make the exchange tomorrow,' says Careem. 'Bring your younger over and we'll kill a dog and roast it.'

Lenny shoots me a terrible look.

I didn't know I cared about him. I didn't know his little-hand holding and his snuggling up had found a door in my heart. My chest freezes. I can't speak. I can't take in that look.

They let him go. He runs, stumbles, finds me.

I cling on to him like he's my own flesh. Tarquin struggles up, blood dripping from his nose. He stands in front of us. Broken.

And Careem is laughing and doing high fives with the other gang leader. He waves his hand, as if that's all there is to us – no more favours, no more future, no more nothing, and his two henchmen come and roughly pull us over.

'Lock Tarquin and Lenny up with the girl,' orders Careem. 'Let them have their little fond farewells. Ain't nobody gonna say I'm a hard-hearted man. Use the secure room, down by the lockers. We don't want any of 'em trying a runner, do we?' He guffaws, vulgar, loud-mouthed, raises a bone and shakes it at Tarquin. The message is clear: *You had this coming. I told you I'd deal with you. You ain't nothing. I'm the boss. You're gonna get it now.*

Nailey and another ganger shove us out of the arena.

Tarquin turns on me. 'You witch,' he shouts, his voice cracked, venomous. 'You wait. See what I'll do to you.'

My eyes fly wide. My throat closes up. *Tarquin?* I can't take it in.

I thought he was on my side.

I thought I'd won him over.

As I pass near, he lunges out. My heart stops. The ganger hauling us stops short, knocks him back.

Nailey comes forward, grabs Lenny and cruelly twists his arm. 'You don't do nothing to her,' he snaps at Tarquin. 'I'll break Len's arm right now if you try – if she gets one mark on her, you're dead.'

Lenny stares like a sleepwalker. His face shocked, drained of colour.

'She bewitched us,' screams Tarquin. 'We was all right till she came.'

Lenny seems jolted into action. 'It ain't her!' he screams, twisting his head up. 'It ain't her, neither.'

'Lock 'em up and report back to Boss,' yells Nailey. The second ganger pushes Tarquin and me into the cell. Once we're well away from the door he steps back, leaves. Nailey lets go of Lenny and shoves him in too.

'You wasn't never all right.' Nailey sneers. 'You always thought you was better'n us. See where it's got ya now.' He slams the door shut, slides the bolt into place.

And there we are, Lenny and me and Tarquin, locked in, looking at Nailey through holes busted in the door. And Lenny's crying and I'm just sitting there and Tarquin's seething and cursing. And Nailey's saying: 'I'm gonna be watching, and if you touch her, if you switch on her, even one little finger, Careem's gonna slit your gizzard and watch the dogs guzzle it.'

And I don't know what hurts me most: going to the General, or Lenny being handed to thugs.

Or Tarquin's sudden hatred.

17

After a while we hear pans. Through the holes in the door we see Nailey get up. 'I'll be back,' he warns. He shakes a finger at Tarquin. 'And you've been told.'

We hear his tread receding down the corridor.

Instantly Tarquin's on his feet. He bounds across at me. I shrink back. Lenny jumps up too.

'*It's OK,*' hisses Tarquin. '*I didn't mean any of those things.* Listen. We've not got long.'

I look up, confused.

'There's only one way out and that's through that door.' He gestures at the door. Welded metal. Rusty. Locked.

'And there's no way they're going to open it and give me the chance to take them out for any cheap trick.'

I position myself as far away from him as possible. Isn't this the same person who was trying to take *me* out a minute ago?

'I'm a ganger. I know how they work. The only way I can get them to open that door is if they think I'm gonna hurt you.'

I blink.

'And even then it won't be easy. They'll need to believe I will and still believe they can stop me.'

Had he thought this through, right from the stadium?

'Lenny, I didn't mean it, OK?'

'And *are* you going to hurt me?' I ask. I don't know what to think.

I look at his face through the darkness of the room. Try to read his mind. Lenny looks at both of us. Eyes wide. Tiny face streaked with tears. He doesn't know what to think either.

'Quick,' says Tarquin. 'Nailey ain't gonna be away long. As soon as he's grabbed his share of the food, he'll be back. He'll stand outside that door an' keep watch. Only chance to get it open is to make him believe that if he don't, Careem'll do him too.'

'But how do we do that?' I say. I see he's right. If I get hurt, Careem may kill Tarquin, but he'll also lose the deal with the General, and he put Nailey on duty. So Nailey'll get it too.

'Hit me then,' I say. 'If that's what it takes, hit as hard as you like. You know how this works. Just make sure we get out.'

Lenny runs to me, pulls on my hand. 'No, Miss,' he sobs.

I squeeze his little hand. 'Lenny,' I say. 'Sometimes we have to do things. You just stand over there and don't look.' I brace myself for the punch. 'Come on,' I say, 'I get it. We don't have long. Let him see me bruised and bleeding.'

'Not like that,' hisses Tarquin. 'We gotta time him, so he'll think he can get in and stop me and save his own neck. Len, you stand there where he'll think he can grab you. Twist your arm like before.'

Tremblingly Lenny obeys.

'And I'll hit you first, where he'll think it won't show.' Gently Tarquin touches the crown of my head. 'Then your

104

nose. Not too hard – enough to make it bleed. Sight of blood will fetch him.'

Tarquin steps up close, balls his fist, draws his arm back, screws his face up, concentrates as if punching me will hurt him too.

And we wait, poised in some strange tableau, hearts racing, until we hear footsteps.

'Now,' says Tarquin. 'Start screaming.'

Immediately we hear Nailey coming, Tarquin bursts into insults again. Vindictive. Vicious.

I scream. The footsteps quicken. My heart pounds. Lenny sobs.

'*HELP!*' I scream. '*HELP ME!*'

The footsteps come running. And Nailey's shouting, rattling the door, pressing his face to a hole.

And this is it.

I brace myself.

But no punch comes. No flat-handed slap. No tight fist. No gush of nosebleed.

Tarquin moves close, bends over me, screams insults and between his teeth sobs: '*I can't do it.*' And instead of hitting me, he staggers back as if I've pushed him and bangs his own head against the wall.

Sodding hell! What's wrong with him?

Nailey yells. Threatens. Lenny sobs. I look at Tarquin. He really can't do it.

Holy shit. Think of something, Melissa.

I look around. *A fistful of gravel, scraped down my face? Fall to the floor, grab some?*

It won't do anything. When I brush it away nothing will bleed. No rush of red.

Think. Think. You're losing the advantage.

But there's nothing.

Time's running out. Nailey's withdrawing his face from the hole. Now! Or our chance'll be gone.

I spring forward. Tarquin's shown me the way. I throw myself at him. Scream savagely as if all the witch in me has burst loose. I scratch him viciously across his face. He raises his arm to defend. I spin away from it, as if he's punched me. I crack my head against the wall. Bone on concrete. '*BASTARD*,' I scream.

I reel back. My mind spins. I taste blood, hope to hell I've done enough damage. I let out a volley of screeching. Nailey's back, cursing. I'm about to throw myself against the wall again. Strong hands hold me.

'Melissa.' Tarquin's voice, pleading, guttural. But I struggle against his hands. Like a wild cat, I am all teeth and nails and spite.

Tarquin holds me steady.

'*Do something!*' I hiss. I start screaming again. Ear-splitting. At the top of my voice. Struggling in his grip. '*I'll kill you! I'll kill you!*'

I shake him off me. I throw myself around the cell. I bang into the door. I kick it. Throw myself at the floor, at the walls. Tarquin can't stop me. Twice I break his hold, scratch at him, tear at his hair. And scream at the top of my voice, 'I'LL KILL YOU!'

At first Tarquin's too confused to do anything – except hold on to me. Then at the top of his voice, 'WITCH!' he yells. His voice breaking.

Lenny starts too, high-pitched, hysterical. I can't tell whether his screams are real or not. I think they're real. They make me afraid. Lend power to mine. I scream and scream until my lungs burn.

There's no doubt something terrible is going on inside the cell. Maybe it's the tone of my voice. The shrill shrieking. Lenny's cries, ear-piercing, heart-breaking. Nailey slings back the bolt, kicks the door open. He draws his iron bar up, is about to bring it down on Tarquin's head when, faster than lightning, Tarquin strikes.

One punch to the side of Nailey's face. It looks nothing. But Nailey staggers, slips sideways. It seems as if he suddenly ages. His knees crumple. His head snaps back. He sags, goes down, banging on the wall as he falls.

Tarquin steps in close. Lifts Nailey's head, jabs another punch into his temple. What he couldn't do to me he does tenfold to Nailey. 'C'mon,' he says. 'Out.'

I rush to Lenny, hold his shoulders, take his hand. 'C'mon.'

Lenny tries to wind his little fingers about mine. Then lets go, confused.

'It's OK; *I'm OK.*'

We leave.

Tarquin drags the metal door shut behind us, slides the bolt into place. 'He won't wake up for hours,' he says. 'Let's get out, hide, think.'

We run down a long corridor, take some steps up, some steps down, round a corner until there's nowhere else for us to go, except out onto the terraces. Out into the open arena where the racetrack loops below.

'Under the bleachers,' whispers Tarquin. 'Crouch low. Get to the store hollows, where they keep swag. This way.'

He leads. We slink behind a row of seating. We find one of the cavities where they used to pack the chairs away, in those old days, that long ago, when seating mechanisms worked, when fans cheered athletes to glorious triumphs.

We creep into a hollow and squat. Blood drips from my nose. Blood congeals on Tarquin's scratches. Lenny shakes and shakes, in silence. And Tarquin, his eyes too dark to fathom, stares at me through the shadows.

'Melissa,' he whispers. 'Melissa.' He takes my face in his hands, turns it and inspects the damage. Then very gently he cleans the dirt from my cheek. With shaking fingers, wipes the blood.

And after it's all done, he holds my scratched and bleeding hands tight in his own.

We crouch together under the bleachers. Lenny's trembling so much I can feel his heart beating through his thin shirt. Tarquin doesn't speak. He wipes the blood away from his own mouth. It smears across his lip. I feel so sorry for him, but I must strike now. *Watch the eyes, Melissa, wait until they fall, wait until the load is too heavy, then attack while you have the chance.*

In the shadows of the plastic seating, I watch. I pull the key out of my pocket.

Now.

'I know you're getting out. Take me with you. The cottage is there. Careem will never catch us. I'll show you the way.' I press the key into his hand.

Tarquin twists uncomfortably, takes the key, holds it up to the light, looks at the picture set in plastic, looks at me.

If you're gonna lie, make it count. Do it up front and bold. Don't hesitate. Lie your heart out. Make it work.

'The cottage belonged to my nan. It's mine now.' I press up close to him, put my lips to his ear. 'The pond is there,' I whisper. 'The ducks are there. The hazelnut forest is there. The bees are back. The valley's hidden. The hills blocked out the radiation.' *Please God don't let him know too much about radiation.* 'It's OK there. We were going, me and Nan, but she got ill. I know the way. *Just get us out.*'

A shiver runs through him. I hold my breath.

Lenny draws in close, wipes his sleeve across his nose, sniffs, chin puckered tight. Tear tracks stain his cheeks.

'*Shush,*' Tarquin warns.

'Please don't let them take me.'

Tarquin puts his arm out, pulls Lenny close. 'I ain't gonna.' His face's tight. His voice crushed. 'Careem can choose some other kid. There's some that'd like it, even.'

Lenny buries his face in Tarquin's shoulder. 'He ain't having you,' promises Tarquin.

From the racetrack below comes laughter. A dog barks. More laughter. They don't know we're out.

Yet.

Lenny's small frame convulses. The air grows tight around us. The seating above shakes a little.

'Shush.'

'Careem ain't thinking,' mutters Tarquin. 'I'm his best scout. I got the shoes. I got him loads of stuff.' He shakes his head and looks at me, perplexed, betrayed. And I know I'm one of those things he got Careem.

I look back.

His eyes are saying sorry.

'Please let's go with Missa?' Lenny's voice is all broken.

'Where is this place?' says Tarquin, holding up the key.

I point to the letters at the bottom of the key ring. He frowns. Maybe he can't read. 'Scotland,' I whisper. 'It's in Scotland.'

'But Scotland's dirty,' says Tarquin. 'Everyone knows they nuked the place. It ain't safe. Nobody goes there.'

'It was polluted once,' I say, 'but it isn't any more.'

It'll be fine. I remember Nan saying once, 'If you leave nature alone, she'll heal herself. Time. That's all it takes. Time. And everything will grow back.'

Lenny raises his head from Tarquin's chest, sucks in his bottom lip. 'Please, Quinny? Missa says . . .' His voice comes in gulps. 'It's got rabbits – and them rabbits can't live in no dirty places.'

I stay quiet. Lenny will say it better than me.

And anyway this debate on whether it's polluted or not is nonsense.

Because we're not going to go there.

Because even though I've started to believe in it myself, that cottage in Scotland doesn't exist.

18

Seconds seem like hours, minutes like years. We hear people come and go. A sudden burst of shouting. Yells. Barks. I crouch, terrified our escape's been discovered. Then silence. Laughter. Hooting. Hollering.

And in the calm that follows I remember something.

Tunnels.

And Nan saying, 'When I was nine years old, and they'd finished building the Olympic Stadium and were ready to play the games, they created a spectacle. A grand opening. They called it "Isles of Wonder". All the world watched. They sat at home and watched on their tellies.'

I've seen plenty of tellies. Never one working though.

Nan said it was magical. And it wasn't just jumping around and singing and banging pan lids, either.

There were towers that rose out of the ground, and people that came out of nowhere in cars and on bikes and in taxis, then disappeared like smoke. Thousands of people and whole hospitals and power stations and giants. And I believed her.

I still do.

'Tunnels,' I whisper.

Tarquin turns his face towards me. 'What?' he mouths.

'There were tunnels under this stadium. Some of them must lead out.'

He crouches low. 'Why d'you think that?'

'My nan told me about them.'

'There are,' whispers Lenny.

'You been in one?' Tarquin twists to look at him.

'They sent me down one, once.'

'Who sent you? Where?' Tarquin presses his face closer.

'Them bigger boys. One of 'em said he reckoned dogs could get in. It were big and he sent me down there.'

'Where exactly?'

'They blocked it up wiv rubbish,' says Lenny. 'It's under them trash hills.' He stops. His face drops.

Tarquin's shoulders sink too. 'That trash is baggy. Ain't nobody going to shift that pile a garbage without getting noticed.'

'But there must be other tunnels,' I whisper. 'There must be. Nan says they brought in beds and loads of them and doctors and nurses were all jumping on them. There's got to be tunnels big enough to bring in thousands of beds, all at the same time.'

'Lenny means the old entrance to the arena. It wasn't a tunnel that ever went anywhere.'

I reach into my memory. What had Nan said? 'There was one big main tunnel the athletes ran down.'

But that wasn't it. She showed me an old guide to the place. I try to remember what it said. *An entertainment park . . . Over a hundred miles of electrical cables installed in massive tunnels built under the park . . . pylons and vast amounts of wires to be removed from the surface – all so the park could rise like a beacon of hope, so when the flame arrived, relayed there by thousands of torchbearers, it could burn triumphant . . .*

'There weren't no beds,' whispers Lenny, tugging my sleeve.

'Wires?' I say. 'Can you remember wires? Loads of them, all big and round, and cables?'

Tarquin screws up his eyes, seems to be thinking. 'Shafts of cables?'

I nod.

His expression changes. He wrinkles his lip. Down in the arena, somebody throws a bottle onto something hard. The glass shatters.

'I know 'bout them.' Tarquin creases his forehead. 'An' it ain't good.'

A finger of sunshine slips through the seating, lights up Lenny's face.

'Too risky.'

'But are there?' I hiss.

'We ain't taking Lenny down them.'

'I can go,' says Lenny. 'I'll be OK.'

'They're death traps. Even Careem don't know his way through them.'

I look at him, puzzled.

'Nobody knows the way, or if they do they ain't telling.'

I screw my face up into a question.

'You're talking 'bout the roguing shafts, the ones the smugglers use for dealing behind Careem's back.'

Now is the time to push him. I can hear Nan say, 'When your seed starts growing, it's time to hack back the weeds.'

113

'Tarquin,' I hiss. 'You saw that little girl from Limehouse. Look what they did to her! You want that for Lenny?'

He flinches.

Good. Sting him into action.

'They used those shafts for other things too,' he says and shudders.

'So if we don't use the roguing shafts, what then?'

'Please let's use them shafts,' whimpers Lenny.

'If you haven't got a better idea . . .' I force him to meet my gaze, because if his 'better idea' is to trade me in to one of his pals for a safe passage out, he better look me in the eye and tell me.

'Well?' I challenge.

Lenny starts shaking, his eyes fill with tears. 'Please, Quinny,' he sobs. 'Don't let 'em get me.'

One word from Lenny stirs Tarquin more than all my scheming. 'Wait, then,' he hisses. 'Wait, and be ready. I'll check.' He hugs Lenny close, whispers something into his matted hair, and like a flash he's gone.

'Ready for what?' I wonder.

And I hope I know the answer.

19

I can't think. Can't stay still. Can't move. I'm all jammed up under the terraces. And Lenny's trembling. The muscles in my legs have gone weak. My chest is full up with something that crushes it. I can't hardly breathe.

If Tarquin can get us out. *Oh please God let him get us out.* If Tarquin knows where the shafts are. If they're big enough for us. If we can get into them. Squeeze past the wires. Find our way. *Please let us find our way.*

Nan says there are different kinds of courage. 'Some of it is getting out there and fighting back, some is not letting anyone take you for an idiot. But there's another kind of courage too. A much harder one.

'Staying strong on the inside, holding your fear to yourself. Not burdening others with it – especially when they depend on you.'

I look at Lenny scrunched beside me in the gloom. That's the kind of courage I need right now. My heart pounds. My hands sweat. Will Tarquin find them? What if he can't? What if the old electricity shafts are collapsed, or flooded? What if he doesn't realise? What if we get down there and never get out?

Dying down there in the dark.

I hold Lenny tight. He sniffs, chews his lip, brushes the back of his hand across his eyes.

And we wait. And Tarquin doesn't come. Lenny's shivering. I put my arm round him. Poor little kid. I place my lips next to his cheek, kiss and whisper, 'There's a loft in the cottage, and it's got this little bed with a soft mattress and it's got a warm patchwork quilt on it and underneath the bed in bright-coloured boxes are toys.'

I never had many toys, just one doll and some old bricks made from bits of timber.

'It's got dolls with pink faces and an old stuffed-up teddy bear and a train set.'

I've never seen a train, but they are there; I know the army use them to take food north. And there're coal trains too. I heard they come in at Paddington Station.

'There are engines and tracks and coaches and . . .'

'You'll be wiv me?' whispers Lenny, clutching my fingers.

I cuddle him closer. 'Yeah, I'm gonna be with you, and I'm gonna clean up potatoes and carrots and I'm going to make you a stew with those veggies, and I'll put a big fish in that stew.'

'That Tarquin caught in the pond?' whispers Lenny.

I nod. 'That Tarquin caught in the pond, and we're gonna sit round a little wooden table in the kitchen and eat.'

Lenny sighs and shivers and holds on to me.

Overhead someone clumps up and down on the terrace. The seats shake. I stop whispering, hold my breath.

Lenny goes pale. The footsteps move off.

'We're going to get outta here, ain't we, Miss?' He whispers

116

so quietly I can hardly hear him.

'Melissa,' I mouth at him, hoping to dodge the question.

'Ain't we, Missa?' He's almost desperate.

I nod, clasp his thin body.

'We're gonna be like that relay team,' I say, 'that brought the fire to Games City. We're gonna be the torchbearers. That's what. Nobody ever stopped them.'

'Torchbearers?'

'Yeah, the Olympic flame. They brought it in through the tunnels. And we're going to carry it out the same way.'

''Cos it was dark in them tunnels?' he says, confused.

I nod. 'Because it was dark and when it's dark everyone needs a light to follow.'

Nan told me all about the original Olympic Torch. I tell Lenny just like I'm reading it from one of her old books.

'Prometheus snuck into the heavens and stole fire from the Gods. He was a terrific thief and nobody caught him. He snuck out again and gave the fire to mankind.'

'So they could roast dogs,' adds Lenny, nodding his head.

I hug him tight. 'And after that, the ancient Greeks knew fire was sacred. They kept eternal flames burning in front of their temples. They had rituals of torch relays to symbolise the taking of the fire from the Gods, and the Olympic flame was the most sacred of them all.'

'Was that in a stadium like ours?' whispers Lenny.

'No, it was lit in front of the ruins of the Temple of Hera in Olympia. A high priestess lit the flame and passed it to the torchbearers, who carried it, kept it going – to hold back the underworld.'

117

Lenny is all ears. 'The underworld?' he whispers.

I whisper, 'The Olympic Games in London were part of the golden age. Athletes were nobler, stronger, ran more swiftly in those days and the light from the Torch never went out . . .'

'Never?'

'Maybe it went out just a little bit. Later on.'

'When Careem came?'

'Yeah, but we're gonna light it back up.'

He nods, snuggles closer.

'We're gonna hold back the underworld,' I say. 'We'll carry the Torch that'll never go out – just like them.'

One leg has gone to sleep. I ease it sideways.

'But we ain't got a torch, Missa.'

'We've got a symbolic torch, though.'

Lenny nods his head, but I can tell he doesn't get it.

'The book is our Torch,' I say, with a sudden flash of genius.

Lenny puts the book very carefully on my lap. 'You ain't gonna burn it, though, are ya?'

'No, it's gonna be like a torch to guide us, not a real flame.'

'OK.' Lenny looks relieved.

'And you can carry it,' I say, pressing it back into his hands.

He's much happier about that. He holds on to it tight.

Why isn't Tarquin back yet?

Lenny begins to tremble. I try to keep talking. I force myself to tell more stories. In all of them Lenny and I are heroes, like Prometheus. We sneak our flame out of Olympia, through dark tunnels, for the good of mankind. We fulfil the task set us by the Gods.

The task set us by the Gods. 'To regenerate the souls of men.

118

That is the undertaking, my child. That was the task laid upon Melissa, the nymph of the mountains. Until she could fulfil it, the land of milk and honey could never be hers.'

I start to tremble too. *Oh Nan, I need your courage now.* I bite my cheek, force myself to continue: 'And the Torch lights the way to our secret valley, filled with sunlight. And when we get there, we put it on a sacred plinth, open at the page of tens.'

Lenny grips the book. His eyes huge. 'It really is our Torch, ain't it, Missa?' he whispers at last.

I nod, scarcely trusting myself to speak.

'Miss,' he whispers.

'Melissa.'

'Gonna hide the Torch down me vest, so it's really safe.' Lenny nods solemnly at me, his head all wobbly on its scrawny neck.

He thrusts the little book down his top. And suddenly I want to laugh. The regeneration of mankind in a valley in Scotland that doesn't exist. The fire of the Gods stuffed down a ragged vest, next to the beating heart of a scraggy kid.

It's so bizarre, it gives me a kind of courage that the old stories can't. I smile and squeeze his cheeks and tell him how we're gonna do it, and how when we get there we find those hazelnut trees are full of pesky squirrels stealing our nuts, and how we're gonna set traps for them and skin them and make squirrel pie and fix him a coat . . .

And then we hear a soft noise.

20

A tread on the boards. The seating mechanism shifts. I look up. I squint into the dim light. A dark figure. *Kaylem?* My heart cuts. *Oh God.* My breath backs up, right down my chest.

'Quinny.' Lenny lets go of my hand.

Tarquin's back. A tremble shivers down to my toes. The ground seems to shift under me. *Tarquin's safe.*

'Come on, Lenny,' he says.

Lenny doesn't move.

'Come on.'

For a moment I think he's traded me in. *He's leaving me here.* He's made that deal to get his brother out.

The General appears before me: *his watery eyes. His stubby, sloping teeth. The click of his shoes on a marble floor.*

Lenny crawls forwards. *Lenny's going to leave me too.*

They both pause.

'*Come on,*' hisses Tarquin.

Thank God. My legs go weak.

'Thought for a minute you were going to leave me,' I whisper.

Lenny screws up his face, looks puzzled. 'We ain't never gonna leave you, Missa.'

'Keep well down,' instructs Tarquin.

I wriggle out, follow them both silently up the terraces, ducking low behind the rows of seating. I wouldn't have blamed them if they had. Not really. Everybody's got to look out for themselves.

When it comes to my turn, I'm going to.

'We're getting out,' hisses Tarquin. 'We're gonna box up London, get to your cottage.'

I close my eyes for a second. *God forgive me.*

I send a silent prayer up to Prometheus, to Hera, to Orpheus, to Zeus. *Forgive me. I'll help take the Torch from here. I'll carry it as far as I can. I'll do my best to hold back the underworld. I'll try to be there for them.*

But as soon as I'm out, I'm gone.

I'm going home to all that's left of Nan. To a life where I know how to survive. Not one mixed up with gangers. They'll be OK. I try to convince myself. Lenny'll be free of the Limehouse Boys. Tarquin'll be OK. He's strong. He's resourceful.

Forgive me.

Nan said once, 'Survivors survive and that's the deal. They do what it takes, whatever it takes. Don't ever forget that, Melissa.'

But I warn myself. *Don't say anything. Don't give yourself away. We aren't out yet.*

We get up the terraces, away from the racetrack, into an access route, down a curving corridor. My heart pounds. My throat sticks.

'They ain't raised the alarm yet,' hisses Tarquin. 'If we meet anyone, don't say nothing. They don't know Careem's business an' they don't know mine. Peeps in here knows better than to mix business with Careem.'

'OK.'

'But don't let's be seen, neither. It'll land them in it. When Careem wakes up and we've gone, he's gonna ask if they seen us. And they gonna get it, unless they smart and stay shut.'

'OK,' I say. I don't want to land anyone in it.

'Shush now.'

At the bottom of the corridor a small foyer opens out. It's more like a conjunction of corridors. There's some stairs going up, some going down, about five different swing doors to other exits. Only the doors aren't swinging any more. Two are hanging off their hinges. The rest lie crashed on the floor.

We stop, pause. Hear footsteps.

Tarquin lays a finger across his lips, grabs Lenny, beckons us with his hand. We step over one of the doors, press ourselves out of sight into a door alcove.

The footsteps get louder. I keep my eyes on the foyer, glance down the exits. Sound of a heel striking cement. Coming this way. Shoes. Must be a ganger. Voice of a man. Broken, deep.

I hold my breath. *Don't let them find us.*

They pause at the foyer. Two gangers. Then move off. Going the way we just came. They don't look. *Thank you.* We wait till the footsteps fade, ease ourselves out of the doorway. Lenny's trembling. Won't let go of Tarquin's hand.

We take the stairs going down. They're narrow. We turn the first corner. Suddenly there's a terrible banging.

Pans.

They drum out a beat. '*Merde*,' says Tarquin. 'Hurry.'

We race down the stairs. The pans bang on. They cover the sound of our running. The stairs twist round and down. At each corner I'm terrified we'll meet someone. My knees shake. My chest feels like a hole's gone straight through it. At the bottom we pause, sprint down a corridor, take another, dive into shadows, flatten ourselves against the wall. Look at each other. Eyes wide. Terrified.

'They know we're out,' mouths Tarquin.

The pans close in. We signal, mutely shake heads, lay fingers over lips.

The march of feet.

Oh God.

Tarquin presses Lenny behind him, motions me to keep back. The steps halt somewhere near, out of sight. *Please don't let them decide to check down the stairwell.* Someone says, 'He was hanging around here.'

'When?' says the other.

'Before. 'Bout a half-hour ago. Killa seen him.'

'Why?'

The first one snorts. 'You don't know?'

'I don't get it.'

'You for real? Roguing shafts. Moron.' That's the first voice.

'Here?'

'Yeah. Right here.'

'You a roguer, then?'

There's quiet.

'I ain't no roguer. Moron. Nobody survives them tunnels. If

123

I was a bootlegger, I'd be doing it some other way.'

'Yeah,' says the other. Someone laughs like that's the funniest thing they ever heard.

'If he went down there, he's a moron. Careem ain't got no worries.'

I feel Lenny's hand slip into mine. My heart thuds. I hear another set of steps. Someone running. They're out of breath. The footsteps echo down the corridor we just came by. Panting. Some coughing. Someone starts clanging tin pans. Soon pans clang everywhere again.

'Get to the main exits.' Shouting. Excited. Pans drown everything.

Footsteps set off fast.

We stay there, pressed against the wall – damp concrete, flaking plaster. My blood thumps in my neck right below my jaw. Footsteps still echoing. Pans still beating. My knees tingle at the back. I don't trust them to hold me.

We step out of the shadows, turn back onto the corridor.

And there he is.

A huge ganger.

Pan in one hand, steel bar in the other.

Blocking our way.

21

'Thinking of going somewhere, was ya, moron?' The ganger twirls the iron bar with a sudden dangerous speed.

Tarquin steps forward. 'Aw, c'mon, man,' he says.

The big guy laughs, flicks his eyebrows up, licks his lips.

'You know me,' says Tarquin. 'You know what my li'l bro means to me.'

'So?'

'So you know, if you let us past, let us into them tunnels, I'm gonna owe you big time.'

'And?'

'If you don't, I'm gonna kill you.'

The big guy thinks about that. Shakes his head. 'Nah, moron, I don't think so.'

Tarquin shrugs. 'Well, OK, you're a big guy, I might not kill you, but I'll go for your eyes. Blind men ain't no use to Careem.'

The ganger thinks about that too. He shakes his head again. 'Nah, you ain't.'

Tarquin bends, scoops something up. 'Here.' He passes me a lump of loose concrete. 'I'll get him to the floor. You smack him with this, low on the back of the head 'bout there.' He

125

pats the top of his neck.

'Hang on a minute,' says the big guy.

'D'ya want to lose one or both eyes?' asks Tarquin. 'Permanent? Or jus' a few months? She ain't no expert, so you better say. I'll try an' tell her where.'

The big ganger is slow to respond. Tarquin isn't. Like a flash he dives low, tackles the guy at his knees. There's a thump as they hit the floor. Lenny squeals.

'Kick the pan out of his hand,' hisses Tarquin.

I jump forward, kick the pan away. It rattles across the corridor. The ganger twists and lashes out. They roll. I can't get close enough. Fists and feet flying. I jump towards them, bring the rock down anyway.

By sheer luck it hits the ganger on the head. The rock rolls aside. I pick it back up.

Tarquin has him in an arm lock, pressed to the floor. 'Choose,' says Tarquin. 'One or both?'

'OK,' the big guy says. He lets his body go slack, lifts his head up. 'You can go through.'

In one movement, Tarquin leaps up, crouches beside the ganger, then punches him in the side of the head right on his temple.

The ganger slumps to the floor. Out cold.

'Who's the moron now?' says Tarquin.

'Wow,' I say.

'Works every time,' says Tarquin. 'Snap his head to the side, bounce his brain off his skull.'

'Is he gonna die?' asks Lenny.

'Nah,' says Tarquin. 'He'll live, but he'll have one helluva headache.' He gets his arms under the guy. 'No need to blind him. Give me a hand.'

I grab the guy's feet and together we drag him back down the corridor into the shadows.

'Do you really know how to blind someone?' I ask.

'Yup.'

We leave the ganger sprawled against the wall, race back down the corridor. Tarquin picks up the pan and steel bar, hides them. 'C'mon. We're going into the old roguing shafts.'

The rusty iron door near the bottom of the stairwell squeals as we open it. We step through and down a short flight of stairs. We head off into the darkness. The noise of pans dies away.

'We're going to be OK, ain't we?' says Lenny. I can tell by the quaver in his voice he's trying not to let the fear out.

'C'mon,' says Tarquin. 'We ain't got long – we need to get clear before night catch and we can't see nothing. Stay as quiet as you can.'

I don't know how Tarquin can see where he's going. It's pitch black. I grope around. Crumbling walls. Smell of damp everywhere.

'Hang on.' Tarquin strikes something and there's a light, a rag soaked in what smells like animal fat. It's smoky. I choke. Lenny starts coughing. I feel like coughing too. I hold it tight inside.

'Shush.' I pat Lenny gently on the back.

The rag sputters, crackles. At least we can see where we are.

127

We're in an opening. Concrete floor. Concrete walls. Ridges where the old decking has left patterns of sawn wood in cement. Everywhere's covered in dirt. Water dripping from a high place. In front of us another metal door with a round handle, long broken and not shut tight. It makes a terrible squeaking as Tarquin yanks it open. Beyond it is a tunnel.

'Ain't gonna be as "massive" as you thought,' says Tarquin.

I don't answer. Maybe when Nan read that they were 'massive', it meant massively long. This one's barely a metre high. 'But there *is* a tunnel,' I say.

'More'n one,' says Tarquin.

'But we're gonna be OK, ain't we?' says Lenny.

'They spread out in every direction.'

'But you know the way?' Lenny's voice quavers.

'Not exactly.' Tarquin holds up the light, examines the cables. 'I ain't no roguer. I don't like underground places.'

'So how're we going to find our way out?' I say.

'I been down here before, though.' Tarquin runs his hand along a cable, seems to be scraping at its sides, feeling it. 'You start here an' you got to chose a cable, follow it and don't lose it. It'll eventually take you out. That's what they say.'

'But it might go miles,' I say, 'and come out anywhere.'

'It might,' says Tarquin, 'but as long as it takes us out and we don't meet up with any roguers, and we avoid the chambers, you got a problem?'

'We're gonna make it out, ain't we, Quinny?'

'Yep. No dumb old roguer trying to smuggle stuff past Careem is going to stop us.'

There's something in Tarquin's voice that soothes. I want to believe him. Though I know he's only saying it to cheer Lenny up. Roguers are mean. They're lawless bandits, only interested in their own haul. They'll cut our throats if they catch us.

'We'll be OK. You'll see.'

I shake my head.

None of this is ever going to be OK.

Three metal cables lie inside the tunnel. Huge. Twisted. Like long dark snakes slithering in a hole. They run together, half sheathed in bits of piping. Old plastic. Where the plastic is broken, the metal cables twist out, warped, tangled. In places even the cable itself is broken, and a vast forest of wires poke through. I touch up against one. Cut myself. *Oh hell.*

Cuts are dangerous. Nan told me, 'If you get a cut from anything in the garden, anything that's been buried for a long time out of sunlight, let it bleed, wash it clean.'

I squeeze my finger, suck at the blood and squeeze it again.

'Stay away from the wires,' I tell Lenny.

'We gonna have to crawl through the next bit.' Tarquin waves the lighted rag at the tunnel up ahead. Thick smoke swirls. It's very low. We can't walk. He's right – we're going to have to crawl.

'I'm going to put out the light,' he says. 'So I can crawl.'

'I'm scared,' says Lenny.

'You'll be OK,' says Tarquin. 'Wrap this around you.' He passes Lenny his jacket. 'I'll go first, you follow – in the middle.

129

She can go last.'

'Melissa,' I say.

'OK. Melissa.'

The light goes out. Only the aftersmell, the stink of oily rag. The darkness swallows everything. Instantly I bump my head. Bang into cables. I think it's cables. I daren't stretch out my hand to make sure. A drip of water lands on my face.

Lenny cries out. 'There's rats, Quinny. I felt one.'

'Keep the jacket tight round you.'

'I'm scared.'

'Gotta be brave,' I whisper. 'This is the underworld. But we got the Torch, remember?' I duck my head, feel for Lenny's feet. I give one a little friendly tug.

From time to time I keep checking for his feet. I feel how they slowly shift up ahead. The roof gets lower. I get down on all fours. I go like that for a while. I wave my hand above me, out in front. I feel for the ceiling. I feel for Lenny's feet. A cable underneath me suddenly branches off. A new cable branches in from another tunnel. Waft of stale air.

I feel around underneath. Four cables now. That's weird. Maybe two cables came in. The roof squeezes down. I get onto my belly. Where the cable is smooth, I slide along. Where it's broken, and the wires poke through, Nan's coat catches and rips. I try to pull the cloth out from under me. It tears. The walls are slippery. I reach up and touch the ceiling. Something unpleasant oozes between my fingers.

I lose hold of Lenny's feet. I start to panic. A darkness worse even than the tunnel gets into my head. I twist, waving my hand from side to side, like a maggot writhing in its casing. *I'm*

130

gonna be stuck down here, shrivelled up like a mummy in a tomb.

'Missa?' I hear Lenny's voice. Echoey. Shrill. Panicky.

Up ahead? Have I taken a wrong turn? 'Lenny?' I start to haul myself towards him.

'Missa,' Lenny calls again.

'I'm here,' I call.

'Shush,' Tarquin hisses. 'Quiet.' His voice a long way off.

How far've we come? Feels like miles. How far have we got to go?

Without warning we suddenly all end up together, kaleidoscoped into each other. Smell of damp concrete. Acid. Earthy. I can't figure out anything except that we can't go any further. We haven't come out anywhere. We lie there scrunched up in the dark.

'I need to check the cable,' says Tarquin.

Somebody fumbles around. An elbow bumps my face. I can smell Tarquin. He must be right there and what I thought was Lenny pressing up against me is him.

'Lenny?' I say.

A hand closes over mine. It misses my palm and grips onto my fingers. A face presses up against mine. The hand is too big, too strong to be Lenny's. I feel lips on my cheek and warm breath. 'We've hit a dead end,' Tarquin whispers. 'Don't say anything.' His lips move against my skin. 'Don't scare Lenny.'

I half turn towards him, whisper back. 'What is it?' My lips brush against his.

I draw my breath in. His lips are soft and warm.

He strikes the flint, lights the rag.

He reaches over and examines the cabling.

He looks at me. Light of smoky flame. Eyes, glinting.
Shakes his head.
We've lost the cable.
We've come the wrong way.

22

'We're going to have to go to the chambers.'

'What's the chambers, Quinny?'

'Not going to talk about it down here.'

'I don't believe it. How could you lose the cable?'

He lowers the smoking rag, points. A cable's been capped off. He didn't lose it. It never led anywhere.

'Sorry,' I say.

'We go back,' says Tarquin.

'All the way?' I ask.

'Nah, we'll take junctions that lead to a chamber.'

'How will you know?'

'I'll know.'

We set out again. The light's put out. The crawling and the darkness begin again.

'But how will you know?' I hiss from the back.

'Trust me.'

We crawl on, winding back down the tunnel. We branch sometimes into other tunnels. At each junction we take there's a blast of stale, unGodly air. A musty smell that gets mustier. And there're rats.

At one point we stop. Tarquin lights the rag. We see them lined up against the walls – huge, eyes flashing in the light, quivering noses. They don't seem afraid. They snuffle on up the cable shaft, then turn and snuffle back.

'Some of the boys eat them things,' says Lenny.

Tarquin puts the rag out again. 'Let's try and get out of here,' he says.

We keep forking into fresh tunnels. I'm hopelessly lost. The stench gets stronger. 'What's that smell?' I say at last.

'Chambers.'

Suddenly ahead of me Lenny stops, whispers, 'Quinny says to shush.'

We stay there, quiet. Then I hear them. People.

There's no pan banging, no shouting, just quiet voices. 'Who are they?' I hiss.

'Shush.'

Lenny slides back a little, until he's up against my face. He grabs my hand.

'It's roguers in one of the chambers,' says Tarquin very, very quietly. 'We're going to have to wait.'

'What're they doing there?' I whisper.

'Them chambers is under shafts that lead up to the streets.'

'So we can get out?'

'Yeah. But the roguers drop things into them too.'

'Things?'

'When we go out ganging, some of the crew don't bring back all the spoil. They drop it down into them chambers and roguers collect it through the shafts.'

I get it.

'But there's other things that got dropped down into them chambers too.'

'What?' Something drips on my hand.

'In them long ago times.'

'What sort of things?'

'Shush. Later.'

We lie with the rats and the cables, and our hearts pound. We lie there a very long time. I want to cough. I want to put my hand over my mouth, but Lenny's holding on to it. I struggle to suppress the cough. At the same time I'm trying to pay attention. I can hear them in the chamber talking. Voices – two, maybe three. Silence for minutes. Then a voice again.

We lie there listening, waiting. Hours, cold and dark. I think Lenny's fallen asleep all curled up in my arms. I stroke his head, sadly. When we're out, I'm going to leave him. For a second my heart cuts. I imagine it different. If there really were a place. Somewhere far away. If we could be together. Me, Tarquin, Lenny. If we could carry on journeying – just the three of us – towards that somewhere.

'Help others as much as you can,' said Nan. 'But don't take them on. Only the strong survive. And the weak ones know it. They'll drag you down. Don't show them your secrets. Starvation makes monsters of us all.'

After a long time with nothing except the shuffle of rats and the drip of something, Tarquin whispers very quietly, 'I'm sorry.'

'Sorry?' I hardly dare breathe it out.

He leans in close. 'For everything.'

'It wasn't your fault.' I try to shush him, terrified we'll be heard.

135

'Sorry for taking you back to Games City.'

'You didn't have a choice,' I reassure him, hoping he'll stay quiet.

'Sorry for switching on you.'

'Sshh, it got us out.'

'Sorry I didn't believe.' His breath tickles my ear.

I flinch.

'About the cottage.'

I feel a sudden impulse to tell him I lied. Tell him I didn't trust him either, that I was just trying to save myself. Just like him. And was that so wrong?

'Can we be friends?' he murmurs.

My heart skips suddenly.

'Properly. Like on the same side?'

So he knows I'm on my own side?

'We'll need to be – once we're out.' He's leaning in so close.

If we get out.

'OK,' I mouth, staring into the darkness.

'You know, Careem and that.'

I know.

Pause. Solid blackness. He shuffles slightly, seems to draw his jacket up over his head. I feel his arm go round me. He pulls me in close until the jacket covers us and muffles all sound.

'I'll watch your back, try and take care of you if they come,' he whispers into my hair.

'OK.'

'Me and Len ain't got many friends in Games City. It won't make no difference to us.'

'Why?' Suddenly I want to know about him and Lenny and Games City.

'My mum come over from France, down the tunnel from Sangatte. We was trying to get far away like everyone.'

Those strange words. A sudden guess. 'Your mum was French?'

'Yeah. We was stuck in that tunnel and people was dying. I was so scared. I hate being underground.'

I unlace Lenny's fingers from mine and pull the jacket tighter around us.

'The smell.'

'How old were you?' I whisper.

'Maybe eleven. My mum was ill. She was carrying Len.'

'My parents died too,' I say in a really low voice. 'When I was little.'

I find his hand in the dark. We sit there holding onto each other.

'Sorry,' he says.

'What happened then?'

'We got to London an' she give birth, but she didn't last. Len wasn't nearly a year when she died.'

'And you took care of him?'

'Since then. I carried him down me front.'

I smile and remember how Lenny, too, is carrying something precious down his front.

'I tied him on with cloth and fed him and joined Careem's gang. I was 'bout thirteen then.'

I don't ask why he joined. I don't need to.

'I was useful 'cos I spoke French and could run messages and deal with his business down the tunnel.'

I want to ask about France and if it's as wasted as we hear

and if anyone still lives there, but I don't interrupt.

'And Careem sent me down that tunnel time after time and I went 'cos of Len. But I hate being underground. Can't breathe sometimes.'

His grip on my hand tightens.

'And I wouldn't never have turned on Careem, till he turned on Len.' He presses his lips right on my ear. 'He knows that. We had a deal. I work for him and tell him straight what the French do, *la jeunesse Française, les gangs qui contrôlent les frontières* –'

I don't speak French, but I like the sound of the words. I like to hear him whisper them.

'An' he'd make sure Len was OK.'

I try to imagine what life must've been like for him, with a kid to raise and having to go back down into the tunnel where you got stuck and people died and remembering your mum.

'Nobody in Games City helped me. They don't like foreigners. They didn't like me and Len.'

'We can be friends,' I promise and I mean it, although I don't know how we can, when I'm going to leave him.

'So I don't owe nobody nothing – no loyalty, no nothing.'

'I had my nan,' I whisper. 'But she's gone now, and I don't know what's going to happen.'

'We'll get there to that cottage you got,' says Tarquin. 'Be OK then.'

And I don't know what to say.

'We'll have to risk moving soon. Them roguers might have dropped off. They might stay there all night waiting for spoil to come in. But we need to get out and away before Careem sets up barricades.'

'OK.'

'So be very quiet.'

I wake Lenny. Cuddle him. Shush him. Think of Tarquin and being underground and his fear of dark places.

And Nan. 'Find Orpheus. He can lead you out of the darkness. Follow him.'

We crawl slowly towards the chamber. After a few metres Tarquin stops. We lie listening. Only some distant dripping. We crawl forward again.

At last we get into the chamber. Must be the chamber. The stench is unbearable, stuffy, choking.

Tarquin starts to work his way round the walls. Damp concrete. Soft slimy coating.

'Gonna have to light the rag,' whispers Tarquin. 'Or we won't find the rungs.'

Lenny whimpers.

'Shush.' I hold Lenny close.

'Don't look, Lenny. Promise?' whispers Tarquin.

He strikes the flint. There's a spark. I can't see anything. He sparks it again. The oil rag catches. I look around. A cocoon of light in the darkness. Tarquin waves away the smoke. We're in a circular chamber. I can't tell how big. We're huddled up under some shaft. It goes up and up above us.

And all around are human bodies. Limbs flung out at every angle. Bones. Old corpses, shrivelled, dried and thin, in rotted clothes.

I clutch Lenny to me, press his face against my side. The oil rag smoulders. It doesn't flame up the way it should. I look at the walls. I want to retch.

'C'mon,' whispers Tarquin. 'Got to get up there.' His voice doesn't shake. Just a slight hesitation. I remember Nan's words: 'Strong on the inside, holding your fear to yourself.'

I'm glad he can. It helps me hold mine back.

I look up. Rungs in concrete. Black as black. My heart thumps against my ribs. I shiver like I'm about to break sweat.

'We gotta climb,' says Tarquin. The oil rag goes out. 'Shit,' he says. The blackened shapes on the walls wink into nothingness. How're we going to climb up there? Blind like moles.

'Hang on.'

Something rasps and the oil rag lights up again. A flickering halo. 'Grab on these,' says Tarquin. Rusted ladder treads. Dank shaft. Curling shadows. Something slick and dark on the walls. *Shrunken eye sockets, peeling scalps.* I won't look. I've got to step over them. I hold Lenny's face against me. Underfoot something shifts, creaks. I focus on the ladder. Guide Lenny there.

Tarquin hauls himself up on the metal and then the oil rag goes out completely.

'You got to use the metal hoops, Lenny.'

'OK.' Lenny's voice is so faint. I think he saw the bodies. *Sprawled one on top of the other, lengths of bone, shreds of clothing.*

I pull Nan's coat tight around me. In the darkness Tarquin lifts and helps Lenny up from above. 'I'm going first,' he says, 'and you're following and she's coming last.'

'OK,' says Lenny, still very faint.

I'm right behind Lenny. I hang on tight to the metal rungs. Cold steel. My hands start to ache. Keep moving. Next rung. I can't flex fingers. I'm gripping too tight. *Those pale skulls, lips pulled back, teeth in bony jaws.* The rungs are caked with thick layers of something slimy, flaking. I hold on to them. I hold on tight.

We climb. Tarquin goes slowly. He hangs on each bar, testing it, testing the ones above, knocking them clean with his hands, rasping his feet on the ones below.

I get used to hanging on to the rungs and pushing my head flat against Lenny's feet. My shoulders aching.

And then from below there's a shout.

It echoes up the shaft, distorted words, unrecognisable.

But I know what it means.

Somebody's discovered us.

23

Oh God. Dear God. Somebody is down there.

Desiccated corpses, bones of a hand, fingers intact.

'Hurry,' hisses Tarquin.

Quickly we climb in darkness. We put hands around ankles in the pitch black and guide feet to rungs. We slip on the metal. Tarquin swears in the pit of his throat. He's cursing, cursing God, cursing himself.

Great lumps of debris fall on me. They touch an elbow, brush my hair. There's a silence till they hit something beneath. *Empty eye sockets, ribs sticking out, carcasses all rotted away.* I imagine the fall below. I'm hanging over a precipice.

Sometimes the rungs shake where the concrete's been loosened. Lenny doesn't speak. 'Just hurry,' hisses Tarquin.

Once when I put my hand up too far, I felt Lenny hanging on to Tarquin's leg. I want to say something to make him feel safe. I can't say anything.

Caved-in faces, taut grins, white bony skulls, plates separating.

The shout comes again. It's louder.

I hear Tarquin banging against something. Fist on metal. Are we at the top? *Dear God, please let us be at the top.* I hear him swearing again and again, searching around. I touch Lenny's leg. I whisper, 'Going to be OK.'

'OK.'

'Just hold tight.'

'OK.'

'It'll be OK.'

Below, the shouts are louder.

Suddenly there's a dreadful clang and rush of air. So cold. Dust whirls in at speed. My eyes sting. I can't look up. My eyes. I look away. Beneath me, that chasm. Vertical. Dark. I squint back towards the light. The hunched shadows of Tarquin and Lenny loom huge. I narrow my eyes even more. Tarquin is already half out. He drags Lenny after him.

Blindly I push up on Lenny's legs. I try to keep my eyes open. His dark shape wriggles. He slides into a ball of pale light.

And hands are reaching down for me. Holding me tight. But I can feel the rungs shaking below. Don't let the void beneath touch me. *Don't let those leathered faces, those sightless eyes near me.* I'm up the next few rungs. I'm coming out of some kind of manhole into a deserted street.

I'm almost out.

There's a shout.

'C'mon,' says Tarquin. He brushes debris from my hair.

'Please hurry, Missa,' says Lenny.

I am hurrying. My legs tremble. I don't want to miss my step and somehow slip back into the shaft.

I want to be careful. They heave and tug at me, as if they are midwives birthing some reluctant newborn. *Something touches my leg.* They anchor their arms around me. *Something touches*

143

my leg. I scream. I kick.

They roll me and pull.

I kick again. The thing lets go. *'There's something there,'* I shriek.

I'm out.

It's night. There's a very faint moon, as thin as a nail clipping. It hangs in the sky. Grey clouds chase at it.

'Run,' I scream.

'Get up. Move,' yells Tarquin. I can see him clearly against the sky. He's scanning the street.

I raise my head. I'm on my feet. I kick the manhole cover shut.

'Can't we lock it?' I call.

Movement a long way off. Something wailing. Pans. Dogs howling.

'Just run,' yells Tarquin. He grabs Lenny.

Dogs. Pans. The manhole cover.

'Melissa, run. They're coming.'

PART TWO

To make a prairie it takes a clover and one bee,
One clover, and a bee,
And reverie.
The reverie alone will do,
If bees are few.

Emily Dickinson

24

Tarquin doesn't wait. He sets off at a run. Lenny follows. He can't run that good. No kid can run gracefully. He's all knees and feet and angles. But he goes fast. I can hardly keep up. I'm weak. The thought of those raw skulls, peeling skin. Faster. I jump gutters. Swerve round trash piled on the pavement.

We sprint down one street. It forks. There's someone out sifting rubbish. We're still in the east? They hurry off when they see us. Must still be the east. We dash left. I glance down one street, across an open space. Glimpse a shape, ghostly white. The Olympic Stadium.

Run.

I focus on the uneven paving slabs. My stomach feels glued to my back. I'm gasping for breath. Dragging it into my chest in great heaving gulps. *We're half a mile away.*

My knees turn suddenly shaky, my heart crashes around in my chest. We're only just inside the cover of the streets.

But we're outside the stadium.

Overhead the thin moon races, icy bright. And I realise we made it. *We're free.* I get this feeling, like a horse must've felt in that before time, running wild, mane flying, clods of turf springing from its hooves. *I'm not locked up in Games City. I'm not going to the General.*

We speed across an old car park. Tarquin and Lenny are much faster than me. At the far side Tarquin slows and stops. Lenny waits. I reach them, grab hold of Lenny's hand and squeeze it. I squeeze it too hard. He doesn't say anything. He points up at the moon.

'New beginnings,' he says.

'New beginnings?' says Tarquin.

'Yes,' says Lenny.

'Where the heck d'you get that from?'

'Don't know,' says Lenny.

New beginnings? I think about it. No. Not for me. I'm going home. This is no new beginning. This is the end of a terrible nightmare. I'm going home to our flat. Nan and me. Where I know how to take care of myself. Where I'm safe alone. No gangs. No gangers. I set my jaw. Nan would tell me to. And not to think twice.

We set off again. Quickly, we put a good distance between us and the stadium. Through the night comes the sound of pans. We zip through a wasteland of tall flats and into a maze of narrow old streets. Boarded-up windows. Light shining through cracks. Smell of fires burning who knows what. People safe indoors. I want to be safe indoors too.

We make it down to the bottom of a street, round a corner, and that's when we see them. Oh God. We've come the wrong way.

A gang of ghetto boys with tracker dogs. The dogs whine and sniff and get our scent. One of them raises its muzzle and

150

howls. The boys bang pan lids. We take one quick look. We don't say anything. We just grab hold of Lenny, one arm each. We take off down the next cutting. God knows where we're going. I don't ask. I don't care as long as it's not Games City.

The sound of the pans so close puts fresh life in me. We run. Like cockroaches from a match flare, we make for the darkest reaches of the street. It's drizzling. Trying to sleet. The banging covers the crunch of shoes, the rattle of breath. City air. The taste of it. Cold and smoky. God, the sour taste of it. A roofline of houses overshadows us. In the darkness we hide from the tiny moon.

I never knew I could run so fast when I felt so weak. Soon we're down that street and turned into another. It's a cul-de-sac. We back up. Look for a way out. They're all dead ends. We take another street. I'm sucking in great lungfuls of air. Tarquin's panting. Lenny's making little choking noises. We don't stop. Down past mildewed market stalls, dark with damp. Crumbling Victorian houses, more trash, old cardboard, sodden, blackened. Old traffic lights, no lights, no traffic. Dodging twisted car frames, scrap metal all rusted onto the pavement. Rats in the gutter. Past the broken glass of old shop fronts, smashed into tiny shards, glittering like raindrops in the moonlight.

We're not lucky.

We go flying around the next corner and it's blocked off. I can't tell whether it's been blocked off on purpose – whether Careem sent gangers out to block off the whole neighbourhood just for us – or if the blockade's been there for ages. Dumpster tanks right across the road, sheet metal and old furniture. Piled high. There's no way round.

We slide to a stop. Broken glass everywhere. Lenny goes down, cuts his hands. He doesn't shriek or anything. He just raises his palm to his face and watches the blood oozing.

'Hide,' says Tarquin. 'Get down – out of sight.' He scans the street. He seems to spy something. 'There.'

We're across the street, down a few houses, up a set of old stone steps and Tarquin shoulders a door. The rotting timber gives. The door creaks open. And we're inside the hall of a terraced building.

Tarquin jams the door shut. We stand there catching our breath. It's dark. Slowly my eyes adjust. Must have once been a family home. Sodden carpets with brownish patterns. A mailbox with its metal flap prised open. Everything's been ransacked.

'I'm scared,' says Lenny.

'It'll be OK,' says Tarquin.

'I'm scared there's someone in here.'

Tarquin stops in midstride. He stands very still. He listens. He kneels down in front of Lenny.

'Can you hear anything?'

Lenny shakes his head.

We pick our way across the stained carpet, weaving round fallen ceiling tiles. They litter the entrance hall in twisted squares. Some of them are broken and lie in a soggy mess of plaster. We step across them.

'Wait,' says Tarquin. He dodges back to the entrance and roughs up the pale tracks behind us. Lenny waits. I put my hand on his arm. Tarquin scuffs the carpet with his hand. Removes his shoes and tiptoes back to us. Then he leads the way into a long corridor.

'We're just gonna hide out for a bit,' he says.

'OK,' I say.

'Maybe we can spend the rest of the night,' Tarquin says. He's got his head half turned, listening.

'But what if they know we're here?' says Lenny.

'They don't know,' says Tarquin.

'But they've got dogs,' I say.

'Maybe they didn't set up that road block for us – they might've done that some other time.'

'But what if they did?' says Lenny.

'Then they set it there for us,' says Tarquin, 'but they don't know we made it this far. They don't know we're out of Games City. They won't come – they ain't going to waste time – they got to meet the Limehouse Crew and swap over their youngers. You're forgetting about that.'

'I'm not,' says Lenny.

'The tracker dogs?' I say.

'The tracker dogs ain't tame dogs. They're just street dogs. Those boys just taking them along to keep the other dogs off mostly.'

'So they won't follow?'

'They still can track. If they're put on our scent, they'll find us.'

'Then we must keep going,' I say.

'Let's just wait a bit,' says Tarquin.

We sit down underneath the staircase. And wait. He's the ganger, I tell myself. He knows how they operate. The sound of pan banging continues. The drip of water through broken panes. A door creaking upstairs.

'There ain't nothing,' says Tarquin.

'It's safe?' I ask. I don't want to leave.

'We'll hide out here,' says Tarquin.

'OK.'

'Lenny got to eat.' Tarquin stands up. 'I'm going to check the street – see if there's anything. You check in here.' He opens a door. 'C'mon.'

I take Lenny's hand. We crawl out from under the stairs. We step into a room. High ceilings. Huge sash windows. Wrought-iron fireplace.

'No one ain't really lived here for years.'

'But what if they saw us?' says Lenny.

'They didn't.'

'Then why did ya brush out the footprints?'

'They didn't see us. You stay here with her.'

'Melissa,' I say.

'Yeah, whatever,' says Tarquin. He shoots a look at me. 'You stay with him.' The look says: I got you out, we got a deal.

I nod. Not because I care about his deal. I'm sorry about that. If there were a place in Scotland, it'd be different. But there isn't.

And anyway if there were, Nan and me would've gone there long since, and none of this would've happened. But I'm hungry. I'm starved. Maybe he'll get some food. And Lenny's got tight hold of my hand.

I stand in front of the fireplace. Some kind of leaf motif. Blue tiles. Tarquin squats down in front of Lenny. He hugs him and looks him square in the eyes. 'It'll be OK.'

Lenny nods.

Tarquin looks up at me. Locks falling over one side of his face. Steel-dark eyes. Arched brows. Faint blush on his lips. 'Here's the flint. Light a fire. Keep Lenny warm. Make a small one in a back room. There's lotsa fires this time of evening. Nobody's gonna notice one more.'

He passes me the flint and steel and the oil cloth. 'I'll check upstairs, then I'm gone.'

I nod.

He leaves.

'C'mon, Lenny,' I say. 'Let's check the place, see what's here.'

25

I tiptoe back into the hall. Lenny trails behind me. In that before time, rich people lived here. Down the hall, a kitchen – everything gone, except the cooking range, some shelving, old pans thrown on the floor. In the sink, a warped plastic bowl. A toolbox – rifled, rusted nails, a hammer with the shaft broken.

Upstairs, four bedrooms. A double bed in one room, the mattress all sodden and falling out at the bottom. A hole up in the roof. One of the ceilings completely fallen in. Huge damp shadows on the plaster. In another, wallpaper printed with bunnies peels off at the corners. A computer and game box still plugged into the walls, a built-in wardrobe and chest of drawers. They've been emptied. A blue fleece stuffed into a basket.

I pull it out.

'Might fit you,' I say to Lenny. 'If you like it?'

I show him the top: there's a big logo on it.

'OK,' he says. He looks at me. I dust off the hoody and shake it out. I roll up the sleeves. He looks at me.

'Like it?'

He doesn't answer.

'I'm talking to you,' I say.

'You're very pretty, Missa.'

'Let's try it on?'

He holds out his arms. I slip the hoody over them, over his head.

'Looks good. Keep you warm.'

'Till we get to the cottage.'

'Yeah,' I say, 'till we get to the cottage.'

With the hoody on, Lenny looks different. He looks like he isn't a Games City younger so much. He trails around the house after me. I find a blanket stuffed under a bed. OK, but it has holes in. A curtain that has been folded and kept for best. I find it downstairs, in the dining room, hidden carefully in the base of a big table. The table's been half broken up and only the base remains. But the curtain's still there in the cross section of the base. I lever it out with a scorched bracket from the fireplace.

The curtain's dry and thick and heavy and made of some kind of raised, slightly shiny weave. It's nice. If I were back at home Nan and I would make something of it, a dress with enough over for a little jacket maybe – something nice we could trade.

There aren't going to be any more long evenings sewing dresses. *Get that into your head.* Look for anything we can make a fire with. It'll be OK in the back room. Nobody'll see the smoke. Too dark and wet out. *They might smell it.* I check the chimney. Still smells of soot. It's been used quite recently. Squatters, looters maybe. We need to eat. We need to keep warm. Maybe Tarquin won't find anything. That little plate of stew Lenny gave me last night can't keep me going much longer.

I search the house. Whoever was here burned nearly everything up. Scorched screws, twisted hinges, lie amongst the embers in the fireplace. I collect what fuel I can. I peel off strips of bunny wallpaper and build a fire. I lay half-burnt chair legs on top of scrunched wallpaper. I prise off lengths of skirting board. Most of it's gone. The only reason that curtain was still there was because the table base was too heavy to move.

I keep looking. I found that curtain. I got a top for Lenny. Not that the top was hidden. There aren't so many kids around these days. They don't make it. Lots of them get born, but lots don't make it.

Radiation is weird. It's there and it's not. You can't see it, but you can see the effects of it. Like with the children. If there were schools, like in Nan's day, I'd understand. If we hadn't had to burn all those books maybe they would have told me about it, if I'd been able to read them properly.

Lenny catches my hand. I stop puzzling. I carry on searching. If those people were so crafty and careful as to hide that curtain in the base of the table, maybe they were careful and crafty about other things. They'd have put stuff somewhere, bound to have.

In that long-before time, people used to think about how they were going to survive.

Nan told me.

'It was the years after the bombings that were so bad. So many refugees. So many dead. There was no food. All the shops were ransacked. All the canned goods gone. The aid ships came from Australia for a while. And then there were the gangs and the looting.

158

'The army took over. Ordered curfews. They'd shoot you on sight if they caught you out. They started building the covered farms, started removing the contaminated topsoil. People hid and hoarded. Stores of food mostly, then things they could trade – weapons, guns, seeds for planting. They built secret places into their houses and hoarded everything.'

I balance on what must once have been a beautiful sofa. Stuffing falling out of the seat. But still strong. If I were a long-ago person living here, where would I hide stuff? If people came looking, where wouldn't they find it?

'Let's play a game,' I say to Lenny.

He looks at me, blank.

'A game?'

'Yeah.'

The blankness doesn't go away. 'What sort of game?'

'A game you can play here.'

'It's not big enough.'

'Not a sport,' I say. 'Not football.'

'What then?'

'Hide and seek.'

I pass him a piece of fallen plaster. 'Where're you gonna hide it so nobody's gonna find it?'

Lenny's eyes dart around, up to the ceiling. They skid over the floor. He bites the edge of his lip. He's thinking hard about the game. He knits his face tight. Then he leaps up and crosses the room and pulls at a piece of hardboard that's warped and sticking out under the dado rail. It shifts and buckles out. He shoves the plaster lump in there. 'That's where I'm gonna hide it,' he says.

159

How smart. Back in the day, that hardboard wouldn't have been all springing up and out of its fittings. It would have been neatly slotted into the wall and painted over. I go round the room tapping on the boards. I don't actually need to tap much. They fall out.

There isn't anything there. I stop after a bit and let it go.

Lenny still plays the game. He makes me go and stand in the next room.

'You don't look,' he says.

I don't. Well, not at him. I creep to the window, carefully look out onto the street. I scan as far as I can see. There's little light, just the faint moon. No sign of gangers. I listen to see if I can hear pans. I can hear them. Out there, beating a rhythm. They're still looking for us.

A flare between two houses. Firebrands? The pan beat is nearer. Maybe one street away. Please don't let them find this house. Where's Tarquin? When's he going to get back? If he's gone out looting, if he's trying to take out a dog, he might be gone hours. I want him back. Not just because of the food. Though my stomach is still stuck fast to my back. Like there's a hole where it used to be.

Lenny appears with a box. Cardboard, stapled at the corners. Dust caked thick, like grey icing. Chinese letters stencilled on the sides. Inside are packets.

I can't make out what they are. It's so dark in here. It could be food. I rip back the old dry cardboard and pick out the packing. Thin strips of shredded paper. I lift one of the packets. I carry it to the back window. Try and examine it in the moonlight. I've never seen anything like it. Square and brittle and kind of crumbly. At first I think it's biscuits, broken crackers. But I've never seen biscuits like this. I slit open one of the packs. Inside are thin wires of white crumbly stuff.

'What is it, Missa?' asks Lenny.

He reaches forwards and snaps off a piece and crunches it between his teeth. A weird look passes over his face. He tries chewing, but it looks like he can't make it out any better than I can. I flick up another pack. I sit there trying to read what's written on it. The light's bad. The print's too small. Some of the writing has flaked off.

'Noo . . .' I read. 'I think it says "noodles".'

'Noodles,' repeats Lenny. We look at each other.

I've heard of noodles. About five years ago China sent aid ships packed with foodstuffs: rice, dried meat, dried vegetables, noodles. The food was supposed to be for the children. There'd been a very harsh winter. 'A proper throwback to the nuclear ones we had after the explosions,' Nan had said.

We were starving. So many children died. But we never got the food. The army took it. These packets must be from then. Someone must have traded for them, hidden them, meant to come back for them.

'What is it, Missa?'

'It's food.'

'It don't taste like food.'

I turn the packet over in my hand. I crack the white stuff between my thumb and forefinger. Is it still good to eat?

'Maybe they're like potatoes,' says Lenny. 'Maybe you gotta cook 'em first.'

That kid is smart. I look at the package again. I try to read the writing. There's a section in Chinese, but at the bottom of the pack, screened onto the cellophane inside a red-lined box is written: BOIL IN WATER UNTIL SOFT.

We go back to the fireplace. I strike a spark onto the oil rag. Lenny fans the embers with a broken piece of hardboard, feeds in dry tinder, splinters of broken panelling, half burnt bits of old wood. Soon we can remove the oil rag and build the flames, feed a length of skirting on.

At the back of the house, outside the broken kitchen door, is a short patio. To one side a downspout. Under it, a collection of plastic flowerpots – silted up, careened over – have trapped rainwater. I scoop off the water, careful not to disturb the sediment, and half fill a cooking pot from the kitchen.

Lenny trails after me, watching.

'If we boil the water well,' I say, 'it's gonna be fine.'

I don't know how much to boil. I fill the pan up and carry it to the hearth. It takes a long time. Some of the water slops out of the pan and douses half the fire. I shove a piece of brick into the hearth. I balance the pan back on it. After a long time the water heats. I put in two noodle packs. I break them into pieces and feed them in. I tip in the little dried sauce packs that go with them. I stir it and fork it down, mashing the pieces and squashing them in with an old table fork. Then we sit there.

'How long we gotta wait?' asks Lenny. His eyes, huge and round. He's staring at the pot of noodles. They bubble. A frothy scud of foam builds up around the edge of the pan. They smell good. Dry and spicy. 'Can we play another game?' he asks.

'What d'you wanna play?' I say. ''Cos we got to watch these noodles.'

'Let's play living in Scotland.'

'OK.'

'I'm gonna be a duckling.'

'I'm gonna be a pesky squirrel,' I say and I throw bits of grit from the floor at him.

'I wanna be a squirrel too,' he says. And throws the grit back.

'Let's pretend we're hens,' I say. 'This room can be our henhouse.'

Lenny sits up and does an imitation of a hen softly clucking.

'What're we going to eat?' I say.

'Them.'

The noodles have swollen up and filled the pot with white squiggly wires.

'They're our worms.' Lenny picks up the fork and reaches forward.

'Wait,' I say. 'We don't eat from the pot when I'm cooking. Run and get that bowl from the kitchen.'

Lenny runs. He comes back with the warped plastic bowl. I slop a bit of the gluey water into it and swill it out.

'Chuck this outside.' I pass the bowl back to Lenny.

In a flash he's dumped the gluey water outside and skipped back, holding the bowl out to me again. He squawks, 'I want worms.'

I lop a load of noodles into it. The grey mess lies there all lumpy, sticking to itself, but it looks like food. And it smells OK.

We sit together, sharing the bowl. Playing at being chickens. The flames suddenly flicker, like a breeze has caught them. The steam off the noodles swirls.

Someone has opened a door, down the hall, by the front.

163

A floorboard creaks.

I pause my spoon before my lips. Lenny jumps up. I lower my spoon, stand up. 'Hide,' I whisper. 'Be quick. I'll stop them.'

I don't know who it is.

I don't know if I can stop them.

26

'Maybe it's Tarquin,' Lenny says.

'Get into the kitchen. If it isn't, get out the back, keep on running and don't come back. You hear?'

Lenny goes ashen grey, shakes his head. 'No,' he whispers. 'I ain't gonna leave you.'

'Yes, you will,' I say. 'Someone's got to keep on going, now we've escaped from the underworld.' I cup his little face in my hands, thrust his book at him. 'Take the Torch, like they did from Olympia.'

Lenny looks at me blankly. I push him towards the kitchen. 'Shush. Just go.'

I stand up. The noise continues, like someone's creeping around outside the door. If it's Tarquin, it's OK. If not I'll give Lenny as good a start as I can.

I choose a pan, heavy cast-iron. I creep back to the dining room, wait behind the door, pan raised. I'll bash their head in. I stand there poised, arm raised. The room fills with the steam of noodles, the thumping of my heart. The door creaks. If it was Tarquin he'd have spoken out by now. Surely? Someone steps into the room.

I don't wait. *He who hesitates is lost.* I bring the pan down.

A hand catches my arm, twists. I drop the pan. It clangs to the floor.

'Hey, it's me.' Tarquin yanks me towards him, doesn't let go.

I didn't know I was holding my breath. We stand there for a split second, almost touching.

Lenny lets out a little whoop, darts back from the kitchen, throws himself at Tarquin, drags him to the fire.

'You nearly brained me.'

'Why didn't you call out?'

'What if the gang had found you an' was waiting for me to get back?'

'We got worms,' says Lenny. He holds out the bowl, slops noodles at Tarquin.

And I don't know what's come over me, but I haven't even picked my spoon up. I'm holding back. And I'm smiling.

Lenny stuffs a broken board and a drawer from an old chest on the fire. He fans the flames with his hand. Then with a sheet of cardboard. The smoke billows out into the room and curls up over the mantelpiece. The flames gutter in the hearth. Shadows flicker on the walls.

'White wiggly worms,' says Lenny.

'You're soaking,' I say.

Tarquin squats down by the fire, hunches his back, holds his palms to the heat.

I put my hand on his. 'And cold.'

'It's snowing out.'

We sit tight together, cross-legged by the fire, eat noodles. Gloopy and slippery and soft. They taste of some distant forgotten flavour. Something I can't quite fix. Something belonging to Nan's world. Hot spice and salt.

They taste good. I'm pretty sure they're OK. They boiled for a long time. Nan says you can eat almost anything if it's been boiled for over five minutes. Except poison. I'm not worried. I'm too hungry to worry.

And I'm happy.

I don't question it. We got out. We found food. We built a fire. Tarquin's back. We're safe. We escaped from the underworld. The noodles fill me up. My stomach must've shrunk to the size of a snail. Suddenly I feel a bit ill. It's not the noodles. It's just that I haven't had anything for a long time.

'They're out everywhere,' says Tarquin. 'I didn't get no chance to get nothing much.' He tips out a few potatoes. They're small and have been pulled too early.

'How bad is it?'

Tarquin glances at Lenny, sees he's not watching. Then he shakes his head. Lenny lifts up his eyes, looks at Tarquin.

'Where'd you find that?' Tarquin pulls the hood of the fleece down over Lenny's head. Lenny swats his hand off. Tarquin laughs.

'Missa found it upstairs,' he says.

'Lenny found the noodles,' I say.

A smile radiates from Tarquin. 'Clever Lenny. Where'd ya find 'em?'

Lenny beams back. 'Behind them panels in the wall.'

'Anything else there? Behind them panels?' Tarquin says.

I look at Lenny. He looks at me.

'We never checked,' I say. 'Once we got the noodles.'

'Look sharp then,' says Tarquin.

Straight away Lenny puts his spoon down, races out of the room. I hear his feet patter down the hall. The door to the front room squeals. So that's where he found the noodles.

I look at Tarquin. He's still smiling. His face softened by the firelight. He looks almost handsome. If only I could freeze time. If only we could stay like this, sitting by the fire, food to eat, the night ahead.

I reach out and touch his hand.

'Tarquin?'

He raises his eyes and looks at me. They are so huge and dark and soft, like Lenny's.

'Yeah?'

I don't know what I want to say.

'They're out there everywhere, Melissa.'

'It's bad?' I know it is.

'They're checking all the streets.'

'This one?'

'Careem means it.'

'How long before they get here?'

'Maybe at dawn.'

'I see.'

'I ain't never seen so many posses out in one night.'

Lenny comes back. 'There's more, but I can't get it.'

Tarquin shovels noodles into his mouth, puts the bowl down. 'Show me where.'

Lenny races off. Tarquin follows. I pick up the bowl, place it near the hearth to keep it warm. I follow them to the living room.

Another high-ceilinged room. Smashed chandelier. Tall sash windows. Radiators twisted off the walls. Parquet tiling all warped and half gone. Polished marble fireplace, carved in intricate swirling designs.

Behind the old panel boards, another space, tucked so far in that even with an outstretched arm you can't explore it.

'OK,' says Tarquin. 'I'm going to smash into the wall. See what's there.' He crosses to the window, checks the street. Listens.

I listen too. Pans banging about a half-mile away.

Tarquin pulls his jacket off, picks up a chair. It's heavy, but he lifts it easily. I watch the muscles across his shoulders bunch and tighten under his T-shirt. He wraps his jacket round the chair leg to muffle the noise. Then whacks the chair at the wall. The panel splinters. A leg falls off the chair. He swings the chair again. His shoulder blade spading out. A line of sinew on his jaw. A glimpse of muscle tight across his cheek.

'You need a hammer,' I say. 'There's one in the kitchen that might do.' I go and get it.

Tarquin taps the wall with the club end. He gets the claw foot up under the panelling, holds the broken haft tight. He yanks a panel out.

The board yields with a soft squeal. It splinters open. Tarquin claws with the hammer at the pieces until he has a hole big enough.

Pieces of plaster fall out. Dust. Cobwebs, thick and old.

And inside, dark, small and tightly wrapped: a package.

I don't know why it's wrapped up so tightly. It's too dark to see much. Tarquin carries it back into the dining room. He squats down by the fire. Unwraps the packet. It's tied up, rigid in old plastic. The plastic has split and is sharp and dry with age.

Lenny picks up the bowl of noodles, pecks at it, peers over Tarquin's shoulder. Inside the plastic is a padded envelope of some kind with faded writing on it. Inside that is more plastic.

Tarquin peels it all off carefully, like each layer is food. There's a box inside, tied with string. Doesn't look like anything you can eat.

'Can't see to undo these knots,' says Tarquin. He shakes the package, then squats close to the light of the fire.

I look away. It's probably old bank notes. They aren't any use, except for lighting fires. I stare at the fireplace, the high marble mantelpiece. The pale oblong space where a mirror once hung. I've got to get out soon. Leave them. Now Tarquin's back I can leave Lenny.

I'd almost decided to try and cross London when they were sleeping. But I can give that idea up. Not with gangs out. I'm not strong enough to fight off a pack of dogs, either. I gnaw at my bottom lip. Try to think my way through. I'm going to have to wait. Tomorrow. I promise myself. Tomorrow. Once we've got clear of this place. Well away from Games City.

I look at Lenny, his matted hair falling over his face. Tarquin still carefully untying the packet. His broad shoulders, his jaw line. I feel a stab of something, like a particle of ice has lodged in my throat. I wish to hell there were a valley in Scotland. I wish to hell we could go there.

Just leave them, I tell myself. The sooner the better. On your own you can survive. Get out. Before you start caring too much. I look at Tarquin. Tall. Tough. He'll manage OK.

He doesn't need me. Once he knows there's no cottage, he'll probably dump me anyway. He'll probably leave London and go someplace else.

I've never been outside London. The traders say that for hundreds of miles in every direction there isn't anything. It's all been taken and ransacked. But then they would say that, wouldn't they? They don't want anyone else muscling in on their territory.

All the towns have city boundaries, they say. They defend themselves. They don't let hungry mouths in to eat up their food. The roads have been reclaimed by wind and weather and stubborn plants. If you try squatting in the country, you'll find it tough. All the outlying farms have been burned to stop highway gangers settling there. Highway gangers are everywhere on the road.

Well, that's what they say.

Maybe Tarquin'll join the highway gangers.

He's been living on dogs. There're plenty of them in the city. He can live on them and thieving, I suppose, in London. If Careem didn't find him.

And what about me? I'm going to have to live without Nan. On coupons that I can't cash in. On blighted potatoes. *You can do it*, I tell myself. *You're safer on your own. Much safer than mixing with gangers.*

A finger of moonlight filters through the clouds, lays a trembling stripe on the floor. It touches Lenny. He sits cross-legged in it, like some strange child God. Lit up in stardust. He raises his head and flashes me such a smile. The ice in my chest hurts. I flick my eyes away.

They'll probably sell you out to the General the minute they know there's no cottage.

The package lies open, the string neatly balled.

Tarquin is holding something up. 'Look what we just found,' he says.

I look.

It's a gun.

That changes everything.

With a gun I could get away from here. If anything tried to stop me, I could shoot it. I could go tonight, maybe? After they're asleep?

'Not much of a gun, though,' Tarquin says. 'Not a proper one, that's why they wrapped it so tight. Stop it rusting.'

My vision of getting home by morning bursts.

'It looks like a real gun,' I say hopefully.

'Yeah,' he says, 'but it just works on pellets. Look.' He holds up a small container of round silvery balls. He rattles them. 'It's one of them BB guns.'

'Can I hold it?' asks Lenny.

'Yeah.' Tarquin passes him the gun. 'It ain't loaded.' Lenny weighs it in his hand. 'Don't like it,' he says. 'It could hurt my ducks.'

'Could protect them too,' says Tarquin.

'Will it shoot?' I say. I've no time for ducks. No use protecting imaginary ducks.

But Lenny's in his magical world. He's standing up and waving the gun around.

'I'm going to hold the gun,' he says, 'an' when we get to our cottage, I'm never going to use it on nothing – unless some of those wild dogs come and try and get my pesky squirrels or chase them ducks.' He smiles like he is going to have such fun, sitting on the porch and watching out for stray dogs all day.

'All right,' says Tarquin, 'but you gotta let me hold it until we get there.'

'OK,' says Lenny. 'OK, you hold it, Tarquin.'

'Can it kill?' I say.

Tarquin gives me a funny look.

'It could hurt,' he says. 'You'd have to shoot at very close range and catch someone right in the neck or eyes, otherwise you'll just fill 'em up with shot.'

'So it's no use,' I say.

'It'd hurt a lot if you got filled up with shot.'

I suppose so.

'Maybe that's all you'd need.'

I think about it. If you hurt an old dog, a wary, seasoned survivor, maybe it'd back off. But young dogs are pushy. They don't stop for much.

'But we ain't gonna shoot no one, are we?' says Lenny.

Tarquin sighs. He puts the gun inside his shirt, tucks it up under his jeans belt at the back, puts the pellets in his pocket.

'We're just going to keep it safe,' he says.

We sit round the fire. Put on more skirting board. The flames light up Tarquin's face, dance on Lenny's new top. Nobody looks like they're going to sleep yet. I'm glad. In a weird way I want tonight to last forever.

'Can I see it?' I say at last.

Tarquin pulls the gun out again and passes it to me. It's warm where it's been pressed against his skin. I have a crazy desire to hold it against my face. I don't.

'We should load it and keep it there tonight.' I place it on the hearth.

'In case anyone tries to come in,' says Lenny.

'Yeah,' I say. 'Keep it handy.'

'OK.' Tarquin sets about opening up the gun, cleaning it and loading it with pellets.

I fetch more water, boil it and cook more noodles. I shouldn't. But it's kind of like a last supper before I go. 'Specially for Lenny.

'Feed you up,' I say. 'Get you ready for the long trek.'

I encourage Lenny to eat twice the amount that's fair. If I can, I'm going to go off with the rest of the noodles and the gun. As soon as I get the chance. So that's only right, isn't it?

'When we get to the cottage,' says Tarquin, 'I'll go hunting. I'll catch you something nice and cook ya a supersonic ganger special.'

Lenny rubs his tummy.

'And we won't have to eat wiggly worms.'

Lenny lets out a clucking noise.

'I like the worms,' I say.

'Here.' Tarquin picks out a noodle and dangles it in the air. 'Open your mouth.'

I open my mouth. He lowers the noodle in. 'There you go,' he says, 'my little chick.'

175

After Lenny sleeps, Tarquin says, 'How're we getting to Scotland, anyway?'

I bring my head up, sharp.

'How was you getting there with your nan?'

Make up something. Anything. You'll be gone tomorrow.

'We were going on a trading boat,' I say. 'Nan had links.'

'Them links still good?'

'We'll have to check,' I say. 'Get to the riverbank where they trade.'

'OK,' says Tarquin. 'Does the river go all the way?'

I blink.

'Don't know,' I say. 'We'll have to find out.'

'OK. We'll find out.'

He smiles as if he'd like to say more, keep on talking. But instead he makes a space for me to lie down by the fire. 'You're tired,' he says. 'Sleep.'

I lie down. I am tired. I close my eyes. As I drift off I hear him murmur, '*Alors, à demain, ma belle amie, quand nous allons voyager vers l'avenir, ensemble, sur le grand fleuve du destin. Jusqu'à demain.*'[1]

I turn my head, sleepily open my eyes.

'What d'you say?'

'Just good night.'

He's got his arms wrapped around Lenny. Firelight dancing across his face.

---

1 'So, until tomorrow, my beautiful friend, when we will journey out into the future together on the wide river of fate. Until tomorrow.'

I wake in the night. The room's dark. I feel good – not cold, as I ought to. Though the fire's out. My face and arms aren't squashed or numb with the pressure from the floor. Instead of the floorboards under my head, there's something soft. I sit up. It's the thick curtain, carefully folded. Around me a coat.

Someone has lifted up my head, gently. Somebody with the softest of touches has tucked the curtain in, pillowed my cheek, covered my shoulders.

I look through the gloom, make out the shape of the gun laid ready on the hearth. The last packet of noodles. I should take them.

Go.

Now.

I look at Tarquin, curled up around Lenny.

Coatless.

And I can't do it.

Not now. Not like this.

Before dawn, we leave through the back. Sleet drives down. I keep my hands in my coat pockets, trying to warm them. We hack a way through a tangle of dried out brambles in the garden. Lenny gets the worst of it. He's not big enough to stamp them down. Tarquin goes ahead and tries to hold them aside. 'Hurry,' he says. They spin out of his hand and whip back. Lenny doesn't say anything.

We climb over the garden wall, into another back garden. The going there is pretty much just as bad. Impassable in some places. The bushes are high and dense. We start crawling through them instead of hacking them down. It's cold and wet. Almost freezing. The sleet is relentless. I hug Nan's coat around me. It's ripped but still warm. I'm glad of it, and the shoes. I love you, Nan.

We make it to the end of the row of houses. Scratched, shivering. Tarquin is edgy. The sleet turns to fine snow.

'Reckon they've guessed we're outside Games City by now.'

Lenny clutches my sleeve.

I glance down the street. No dusting of snow to give us away yet. Nobody's going to know we camped in that house, unless they check.

'Be OK, Lenny,' I say. I bend down, kiss the top of his head.

Tarquin checks the gun's in his belt, crosses into the street. The snow's settling.

'Melissa, you go last,' he whispers. 'Drag a branch or something behind you. If they see the snow's been disturbed, they won't be able to tell by what or how many.'

I haven't got a branch. My hands are too sore from battling with the garden. I don't want to go back there to get one. I take off Nan's coat. I drag that behind me.

We make it down two streets.

Before they find us.

28

No pans clanging. Just Kaylem and one other. And the empty street.

'Knew I'd find you,' says Kaylem. 'You forgot I was the one who taught you all your froggy tricks.' He smiles. In one hand he holds a machete, rusty, half a metre long. In the other, an iron bar. 'So, Tarquin,' says Kaylem. 'You going to come quiet?'

Tarquin stops dead. 'Don't step no closer,' he says.

Kaylem nods at his sidekick. 'You know we can pan up a posse in seconds.'

'You was always a good boy,' says the other ganger. It's not Nailey. 'Till you met that ho. We don't like to cut up good boys.'

Tarquin doesn't miss a beat. 'Guys,' he says. 'What's it to you if I go? What's it to you if I take the girl? I got my kid brother to look out for and you know it.'

'Quite the little family,' says Kaylem.

'Let us go and I'll owe you one. I ain't never crossed neither of you before all this. There was that time down in Bow when we fought 'longside each other. I had your backs.'

'Ain't up to us now,' says the second guy. 'If it was up to us, we'd have considered.'

'I wouldn't,' says Kaylem.

'See, it's not me,' says the other.

'You had it coming,' says Kaylem.

'It's Careem,' says the other. 'We been sent to fetch you and the kid and the ho back. You made him look a fool, bro. When the Limehouse gang come, he couldn't give them the kid he'd promised. He ain't happy 'bout that and we got our orders.'

'You're making a mistake,' says Tarquin. 'I coulda been your mate on the outside. Mighta been of some help. Us not knowing the future an' that.' He moves his hand round to the back of his jeans, slips it up under his shirt. 'I got my uses and my contacts. Careem ain't gonna last forever.'

The sidekick shakes his head. 'We can't go back until he's happy. Next thing we know, someone else gonna catch you and you're gonna blab and tell on us.'

'I won't ask you again,' says Tarquin. 'Just turn around and walk off. Even if you forget we fought 'longside each other, I don't.'

Kaylem lifts the machete up and takes a step forward.

'Come easy and we'll put in a good word for you,' wheedles the other.

'I'll take out Quin. You hold the others,' snaps Kaylem.

'Bet you're hungry ain't you?' The second ganger turns to Lenny. 'Bet you could do with a good haunch of meat and a bowl of spuds? Nice and juicy,' he adds, all leery eyes.

'I ain't kidding,' says Tarquin. 'I'm asking, just this once, for you boys to let us go. We ain't coming back. We're leaving London. No one'll know.'

'Just give up, Quin,' says Kaylem. He raises the blade and steps closer.

'Well, we ain't going to,' says Tarquin.

And he pulls out the gun.

He points it right at Kaylem.

That stops him.

'Get behind me, Lenny,' says Tarquin. 'And you too.'

I get hold of Lenny and we get behind Tarquin.

'Please don't shoot them,' says Lenny.

'Yeah, listen to Lenny,' says the second guy, backing off.

But Kaylem doesn't care. He keeps on coming. He laughs. 'Where'd you get that from, Quin? Sure it works?'

Tarquin holds the pistol steady.

'It don't work, do it?' Kaylem carries on stepping up, machete raised.

'Please,' says Lenny.

'No closer,' says Tarquin.

'You ain't going to pull that trigger anyway,' says Kaylem. 'You're a pussy.' He's up really close. As bold as dogs.

Tarquin doesn't say another word. He aims the pistol and waits.

And suddenly I know why he's waiting.

He's waiting for Kaylem to be right on him. When he shoots, he's going to do maximum damage. I gnaw up on my inside cheek. I try to breathe. I tug Lenny back further. I hold my breath in. My heart thuds. My teeth are tight against my lips.

'Quinny?' says Lenny. 'You don't know if –'

'You shut up, Lenny,' snaps Tarquin.

'We was your old running mates,' says the second ganger. 'If it weren't for Careem we'd a let you go.' He looks at Lenny. 'Tell your bro, he don't have to shoot no one.'

Kaylem inches forward. He thinks he's got Tarquin's measure. *Shoot.*

How close is close enough?

For God's sake, shoot him, Tarquin.

If I had that gun I'd shoot.

Kaylem creeps on, his knees slightly bent. Only an arm's length away. He raises the machete.

Brings it down.

Tarquin holds that gun rock steady and pulls the trigger. The gun fires. Silver balls spray out. The machete clatters to the ground, spins out of reach. *It works. The gun works.* With a squeal, like he's a dog with a broken back, Kaylem falls. One side of his head spouting blood.

The other guy starts shouting. 'It's OK! Tarquin. It's OK! Don't shoot. You jus' carry on, like you said. Jus' go. You know we always been friends.'

Tarquin backs up a pace, scoops up the machete. 'You,' he says to the other ganger. 'You take your belt off. Sit down in the road. Put your arms behind your back.' Kaylem moans and squirms on the pavement and wipes at the gore on his bloodied face. The other ganger whines, 'Don't do that to me. The dogs gonna get me.' But he sits down and does like he's told. 'I woulda let you go.'

'Yeah,' says Tarquin. 'Here.' He passes the gun to me. 'Shoot him in the face if he does anything,' he says.

I hold the gun. It feels good. I step nearer and crouch down. I hold the gun full in the ganger's face. *I'll shoot you*, I think.

182

You don't know me. I'll shoot you as quick as lightning.

Tarquin takes the belt, squats down behind the boy, twists the belt around the boy's wrists, locks the buckle into place. With the machete Tarquin saws through the remainder of the belt. He tests it, moves to the front and ties the boy's feet.

'Aw, please,' whines the boy.

All the time I push that gun right up close. My hand doesn't waver. I almost wish he'd struggle so that I could shoot and be done with him. He isn't going to take me or my Lenny anywhere. I wish to God he wasn't going to live to tell any tales back at Games City either.

Kaylem gurgles, screams. I glance over at him. One side of his face pitted with shot. Blood everywhere. He looks back at me. Evil. Malicious. But it's a vacant stare. One eye not quite right. I think he's lost an eye. He starts coughing, spluttering. I remember his breath on my face, stinking of alcohol. I don't care if he chokes on his own blood. I wouldn't turn round and roll him over if you paid me in hot meals.

Tarquin doesn't say a word. After he's through tightening the belt, he backs up.

'Don't do this, bro,' whimpers the ganger.

Tarquin toes Kaylem. 'You better not die,' he says. 'You need to sit up and loosen the ties on your partner and pray he helps you home before the dogs come.'

As if by design, a low howling breaks out through the morning.

'Oh, man,' moans the ganger.

Tarquin takes the gun back off me. 'I ain't finished here yet,' he says. 'Get Lenny.' He yells at Lenny, 'Take her hand.'

His voice changes. 'Take Lenny's hand. Walk to the end of the street. Turn the corner and keep going. Don't come back whatever you hear.'

'What you gonna do, Tarquin?' says Lenny. He sounds more frightened about what Tarquin's going to do than for his own skin.

'Don't ask,' says Tarquin.

I don't. I just grab Lenny's hand and pull him back up the street. We get to the corner. Lenny lags a bit. I haul him around it. He doesn't need to know what Tarquin's going to do. I don't need to know. I grab Lenny and hug him to me. 'Your brother knows best in this,' I say. 'You gotta trust him. He was one of them once.'

We keep on walking. Lenny keeps looking back. We wait to hear shots, wait for something. It's like the whole of London's waiting. But the shots don't come. Gradually Lenny stops shaking so much. He starts to breathe easier.

We hear something. I'm not sure what it is. It's not a shot. Lenny jumps nearly out of his skin. I keep tight hold of him. I don't know why. Now would be the very best time to let go, let him scoot off. Lenny wouldn't know what to do. Even if he didn't scoot off he'd just stand there not knowing.

Yep, this should be the very best time.

To leave Lenny and Tarquin, once and for all.

29

I imagine Lenny standing there after I've gone and looking all baffled. Looking like he's thinking: *should I wait for Tarquin? Follow Missa? Go back? Shout out?*

And I can't do it.

Maybe I can't do it at all.

And then I'm foxed. I've got to do it. Go. Leave them both. Before we reach anywhere near Nan's flat.

It wasn't my fault. I'm not the one who locked me up in Games City. What the hell do they expect me to do? But I don't move or run off or anything. I still can't. Not while Lenny's got his little hand curled up in mine so trustingly.

Tarquin catches us up. He comes at a run and shoots one look straight at Lenny. I can see Lenny thinking, like he's going to ask a string of questions. Tarquin cuts through all thinking. 'Where to?' he asks me.

I open my mouth and say, 'West.'

Oh God. I don't want them to come west with me.

I hear Nan's voice. 'Rules of survival. He who hesitates is lost. When you kill a dog, take its head off in one sweep. Don't leave a chance for it to get up and bite you. Don't look into its eyes. Pity is a trap for the faint-hearted.'

But they're not dogs. And I'm not ready. That's it. I'm not ready. I don't want to leave them and go back to the flat alone. I want their company.

I'll pretend we are going to Scotland just a little longer.

Before I know it, it's dusk. And I haven't even tried to leave at all. We're down by the waterfront where Nan died. I don't even know why I brought them here. We're supposed to be going to the wharf where the trade boats moor.

We get to the place. I look around. Lost. As if I'm expecting to see Nan. Tarquin puts his arm round me. Lenny slips his hand into mine and says, 'Don't be sad, Missa.'

'Is this where it happened?' says Tarquin. They stand there with me.

And I don't know why, maybe because they're being so nice about everything, maybe because we're beginning to feel like we're a team, but I can't stand it. The time is right now. If I don't do it now, I'm never going to be able to.

I bend and give Lenny a little kiss on the top of his head. I stroke his cheek, tuck his hoody round him. I look at Tarquin. Our eyes meet. I look away. I stop thinking about the way his skin glows, the angle of his cheekbones, how the muscle on the side of his face bunches when he laughs.

He's going to be OK. He's got a gun. He's going to be more than OK.

'I need to be alone,' I say. 'Just for a bit.'

They nod. I slip away very slowly. Like I'm just going to shed some tears round the back of some derelict building.

As soon as I'm out of sight, I quicken up my pace. When I'm

sure they aren't going to hear, I start to run. I run fast.

I head straight down the street. The flat's only a quarter of a mile away. I can do that in five minutes easily. I know I can get there. I ate well last night. It's almost curfew. This is the dog time of day. But I'll get there.

When I get home, I'll get in, I'll ram the door shut, lock out the world behind me. I'll drop down on the bed. I'll let go. Everything can flood out then. I'll lie there. I don't know what the hell I'll do after that. But it won't matter. I'm not going to stop until I get there.

I make it down through the old high street and up the old estate, I round a corner and I meet them.

A gang of five.

They're holding bars. They're holding dogs. The dogs start baying. The gangers smile when they see what they've found.

I scream, one long pitch of despair. They weren't banging any pans. I can see the street leading to my home. The dogs yowl. The noise that only those kind of dogs can make. Everything was so safe, so quiet a few seconds ago. I was free of Tarquin, free of Lenny, free of all the lies. I was racing home to be with everything that is left of Nan.

I was so very nearly there.

The boys laugh. I recognise some of their faces. I can see what's coming. I turn round. I run back the way I came. And I scream. I run and scream and run. No thoughts. Only Tarquin. Run. Faster. Keep going. Fast.

I glance back. They've loosed the dogs.

Don't stop. Don't fight. Not when two packs are on to you.

30

I round a corner and there's Tarquin. He's running towards me. Thank you, God. I don't know what to think. *Help me.* He must help me. He must know I tried to take off without them. I don't care. I'm so glad to see him.

'Get back down the street. Find Lenny. Bring him here.' Tarquin pulls out the gun. He drops to one knee, holds the gun steady in both hands, shoots the lead dog dead in the face. I race on, find Lenny, grab his hand.

The dog goes down squealing. Thrashes about. His eye's a mess. Everything stops. All the running and the whooping and the cries of 'Cut her down.' An ice front descends, freezing everything in its tracks.

One of the boys calls, 'We're going back. We seen what you did to Kaylem. Nobody here wants to lose an eye. But now you're for it. You hear? Careem wants your head, and Lenny's, in a bag. He's got posses out after you, everywhere, every street. And he wants the ho.' The boy throws a finger at me.

'Come an' take her then,' says Tarquin. 'Scared of a BB gun?' The boy doesn't move.

Tarquin stands back up, holds the gun level. Both hands.

'Don't worry, Melissa,' he says. 'Nobody's going to take you from me.'

A flicker of something shivers in my chest. If I could have gotten away, I would have. I'd have wiped Tarquin's steel-dark eyes out of my mind. I'd have forgotten everything about him. However hard. However much it hurt.

But I know then, at that moment, I'm not going to try and get away again. I can't do it any more.

I hold Lenny tight. He's trembling. I hold him very close.

Tarquin stands tall like a statue. The gangers drag their dogs away. One of them presses his hands together and bobs his head. Tarquin nods.

The boy slinks forward, hauls the injured dog off, backs up. They all back up. All the way down the street.

As they turn the corner, jeering starts. Calls of: 'Pussy man,' and 'Not for long.' Hooting, a crescendo of pan banging.

Tarquin turns to me. 'Where?'

'This way.'

'Your place?'

I nod.

'Sounds like a plan,' he says.

I lead them to my street. I open the side gate to the back garden and the flat. We pass alongside the house into the yard. I don't say anything. I know they know. They don't say anything. Tarquin just smiles. Lenny clings tight. We open the yard gate. Tarquin lets his arm rest on my shoulder, just for a minute. 'Expect you was confused, just needed some time,' he says.

Lenny joins in. ''Cos you was upset.'

I daren't speak.

'I do that,' says Lenny. 'I run away when I can't stand it. I sticks my head in a corner.'

'Being where your nan died.'

They don't say anything more. I don't either. I scuff along the tiled path to the flat door. Frowning. I keep my head up. I pull out the pot by the corner and get out the key. I figure they won't notice it's the same as the one on the key ring with the cottage.

The yard is just the same – straggly potato tops, old brick wall. I unlock the door. I push it open. We go down into the basement. Steep stone steps. Concrete floor. One tiny grille letting in a last sliver of light. Old fireplace. Smell of soot.

I can't think of anything else to do. Tarquin doesn't mention it again. Even if Lenny didn't guess, Tarquin did. I grope around for a lamp and the flint. Get it going. Point to a chair. If he's ready to bury it, so am I.

'The gangs?' I ask. 'How did Careem know? So quickly, about Kaylem?'

'The Blah-Blah,' says Tarquin. 'The pans.'

'Oh.'

'We bang out messages on them.'

'I thought they were to scare off dogs.'

'They do that too. But anyone who's a ganger knows how to hear the Blah-Blah.'

I see. All around me a secret language. Instructing thieves on thieving. Looters on looting.

'Gives a running account of where you are, what swagger you got, blades, dog packs you're hunting, what your business is, where the army are, avoid getting curfewed, sent to the labour farms.'

I didn't know. 'I'll get out wood,' I say. 'If it's safe, I'll make a fire.'

'It'll be safe enough for tonight,' says Tarquin.

The lamp flickers. Everything's the same as when I left. The worn rag rug, tall bookshelves, table in the middle of the room, potatoes still on it. They've got mould on them. Lenny looks at them wistfully. I throw them out. I got more potatoes. I get them out of the sack in the cupboard. I scoop out water from the pail. Wash out a pan in the sink. Scrub five potatoes. I set about cleaning out the fireplace, raking out the ashes. Fetch the firewood from under the steps. Get it going.

Tarquin pulls up the chair and sits. He puts the gun on the table. He stretches out his legs. He cups his hands round the back of his head. His jacket falls open. The fire catches. He exhales, soft air. I drag up a stool. I place it near his feet. 'Put up your feet,' I say, just like I used to for Nan.

And this old, dry feeling comes over me. I see her garden stick by the door. I see her old blankets. All her little pots arranged by the windows with the seedlings in them, limp and drooping. I glance into the bedroom. I see her comb, her mirror, her things spread on the side table.

I want to hold them to me. Grip tight the fossil we found in the garden, her book of Greek stories, pray to all her Gods to take care of her in the underworld. I want to look into the mirror and see if any memory of her face lingers there. I want to gather up her old blankets and wrap myself inside them and lie down on the bed and rock myself into that other place.

As soon as I get the fire going, I go into her room. I don't let myself cry. I'm not going to feel anything again. Feeling is too hard. I stand there. I press her clothes against my face just for a second.

I hear the door. I drop the clothes. A hand touches my arm. I think that it must be Lenny. He still feels things. His feelings flow out unchecked. An arm goes round my shoulder. It isn't Lenny.

Tarquin doesn't say anything. He just keeps his arm around me. I just stand there. He presses his lips against the back of my neck. He doesn't kiss. I just feel him and his lips pressing against me.

The edges of me melt. I don't know where I stop and he starts. Like when you climb a steep hill and you're too weak. No one can carry you, but if you say you can do it, you can. It's like that. Drawing strength out of nothing. Some of Tarquin has got into me, and the two of us are stronger than I knew.

The moment passes. It's stupid to stand there with Nan's old clothes. I go back out and cook the potatoes.

Tarquin follows me. He says, 'We can't stay here.'

You can never go back, can you? Things happen and you can't unhappen them.

'They'll find this place. They'll rip it apart.'

I realise I'm trembling.

'They'll get trackers on to us at dawn – nowhere's safe now.'

He's right.

'How long have we got?' I say. I know we don't have long.

'We should leave tomorrow.'

I thought we might have had a bit longer.

'We daren't risk going back to the waterfront either. They'll watch everywhere we've been.'

192

I don't say anything. I just take down more of Dad's books and pile them on the floor beside the fire. Nobody's going to read them now.

The books burn. The room warms up. I boil a little pan of potatoes. I cook the rest of the noodles. I poach our last egg. I serve it all up. We eat. I find some of the dandelion leaf tea. I brew a pot.

Lenny is warm and full. He snuggles by the fire in the armchair and falls into a deep sleep. He doesn't ask me to read his book. He hugs it to him, as if he's scared we're going to put it on the fire.

Tarquin and I sit facing each other across the table.

'We really got to go tomorrow?'

'If I was on my own, I'd have gone tonight.'

'OK.'

'But.'

I nod. He doesn't need to explain. I look at Lenny on the chair. He doesn't need to explain anything.

31

I bite my lip. I should tell. Now. While Lenny's asleep. While there's still a little time to make a plan.

I take a deep breath. 'Tarquin,' I say.

He looks at me.

'I got something to say.'

But what if he walks out on me? Nothing will bind us together any more. What will I do then?

I could have managed alone, fought off a few dogs, if I was left alone. But I can't stand against Careem. He'll find me. They'll find this place. He'll send me to the General.

If Tarquin walks out on me, where can I go? Alone?

'You don't have to explain,' says Tarquin.

I'm better off if we stick together. I'm far better off. We can go north. Why not? Why not pretend a little longer? North is as good as any other direction. I don't have to tell them yet.

I hesitate, bite my lip. 'Thanks.'

We might never get to Scotland. We might get somewhere different. There may never be any need to tell anything. Ever.

I sit there. I fight hard against this swallowing feeling. I'm all wrong inside.

'You're very beautiful.'

I look up in surprise.

'And Lenny loves you.'

His eyes are shining.

'And I won't do nothing to damage that.'

I try to grasp what he means.

'Like I said in them tunnels, you're safe. I'll protect you, like I do Lenny. I'm your friend.'

'Oh,' I say.

'I'm trying to say, you ain't got nothing to fear from me.'

And I understand. The curtain pillowing my head, the lips on the back of my neck. The silence when I tried to run. The arm across my shoulder. He cares about me for Lenny's sake.

'*Un vrai ami, pas comme les autres que vous avez eu jamais.*[2]'

I shake my head. 'Why do you do that?' I say. 'Suddenly start speaking in French?'

He smiles. 'Some things come easier in my own tongue,' he says. 'An' I like to use it. I ain't got no one else to use it with.'

'Not Lenny?'

'Not Lenny.'

'But I don't understand it.'

'I'll teach you one day.'

I sigh. Get up. It's not just French I don't understand. I don't understand why he doesn't speak it to Lenny. I don't understand him. I don't understand anything. I busy myself. Collect clothes. Clear plates off the table.

'Good idea,' says Tarquin. 'Pack everything that's gonna be useful. And then we gotta sleep. Tomorrow when we're shot

2 'A real friend, like none you have ever had before.'

of London, we'll figure out how we're gonna get north.'

'OK.'

'At first light when we know the street dogs are gonna be tired, before they get the trackers out, we leave.'

I poke the fire. Watch the last book burn.

'Can't figure out much more than that now.'

I go round the place. I pile on the table things that might be useful. I heat up an old iron saucepan on the embers of the fire. I wrap it in the cloth hanging by the grate. I put it in the double bed like I used to for Nan and me. When I'm sure the bed is cosy and warm, I tell Tarquin.

'Lift Lenny into the bed. We can't keep the fire going all night.'

Tarquin lifts him in. He drags Nan's old suitcase into the kitchen. We pack it. We put in thick clothes. We find three good-sized shoulder bags. I give him everything that was Dad's. Everything that's left: a hat, gloves. He finds the old pair of binoculars.

'Take these?'

I nod.

There's not much food left. Some potatoes.

There's only one bed. We get into it. Me and him and Lenny in the middle, all warm and cosy. Lenny sighs and snuggles down. A little smile flicks across his face. The fire shadows play on the ceiling through the open door. I look across at Tarquin. It's very dark. He looks across at me. The light catches his eyes. I imagine him smiling. I smile back. He reaches out a hand, finds mine and holds it.

I wake in the night; the fire shadows are gone. Just a dull

glow. Lenny's got his head on my shoulder. Tarquin's got his arm flung over us both. I look at him sleeping. His darkened face, soft, just a shape. His locks tossed aside. Worry lines smoothed out into a blur. I could have liked his face.

I stare up at the ceiling.

This is the fourth time he's saved you. Can't you trust him yet?

But saved me for what? So that I can leave this place forever and go to some other place. A place that doesn't exist. I stroke Lenny's hair back from his face. I look at him instead.

Nan visits me in the night. In dreams she comes to me, out of that green hollow.

Her hand rests on the book of Greek stories. She wears a cloak of white cotton. 'You have taken the Torch from Olympia,' she says. 'You must understand what that means. Prometheus stole fire. But he could not see the future. He brought only tragedy. Prometheus was punished.'

And from that place over the doorstep, another voice seems to speak. Like one of the Gods from Mount Olympus.

It thunders. 'You have stolen from the Gods.

'The time has come.

'The past is gone.

'There's no way back.'

I turn in my sleep, only half awake.

Tarquin tosses in his sleep, murmurs, *'Pour l'amour de Dieu.'*

The past is gone.

Tomorrow we head north.

32

We leave.

The sun isn't up. The sky glows with a cold silvery light. The city hovers in the mist. It's beautiful, sinister, all blurred edges, sharp underneath. The ground, cold and hard. Frozen solid.

Tarquin drags the suitcase.

Lenny wants to have a go. Tarquin says, 'We're going to have to pull this case a long way. Let me do it for you now. Soon you're gonna be sick of it.'

But Lenny isn't having that. He wants it now. Tarquin laughs and lets him. After ten minutes of pulling and pushing, Lenny is all puffed out.

'See,' says Tarquin. 'When it gets a bit lighter it's easier to pull.'

Lenny clamps his teeth and heaves all the more. It is snowing again.

We head north. Tarquin says it's north. 'At night you can get direction from stars,' he says.

'OK.'

'And in the daytime from the sun.'

'There ain't no sun,' says Lenny.

He's right.

'It rises in the east.'

Of course. Already there is a definite glow over the horizon.

'North is that way.'

'What's outside London?' says Lenny.

Outside London is hills and wild country. I've never been there.

'Will they trail us?' I ask.

Tarquin nods. 'Obviously.'

'For how long?'

'As long as it takes.'

'Why? What use are we any more?'

'Ain't about us,' he says. 'It's the stadium. If they don't bring us back and roll our heads out to show that running away ain't worth it, then everybody's gonna try. They're gonna say, "Careem's a pussy. He can't make nobody do nothing no more."'

'So how're we going to get away?'

'They're going to say, "You can get out of Games City and go the hell where you like,"' adds Tarquin.

'And then,' pipes in Lenny, 'they gonna go and Careem won't have no gangs left to boss 'bout, and he's gonna have to feed hisself.'

'Well, everybody gonna have to feed themselves. By the time they remember why they stuck together in the first place, be too late. Careem'll be done for. Them other gangs from the south, them ones getting up a bevy gonna take over Games City.'

Lenny laughs. 'And all because of Missa.'

'He's taken payment too. If he can't deliver you to the General, he's gonna be seriously messed up. Everything'll go nuts.'

I smile. Seems like I brought Games City to a standstill, overthrew Careem and pissed off the General all in one go. Without even trying.

'So we keep running till then?' I say.

'Got a better plan?' says Tarquin.

The sun climbs over the rooftops. Grey light behind grey cloud. Snow falls. Light. Barely covering the street.

'When we gonna get there?' puffs Lenny.

Tarquin takes the suitcase from him without a word.

'Is Scotland big?' asks Lenny.

'Pretty much,' I say. 'Lots of mountains.'

'Where zactly we going?' He gets out his book.

'Hadrian's Wall first.'

'Adrian's wall,' says Lenny. His eyes, big, round, like he's imagining a wall encircling him, twice as high as the one round Games City.

I don't know what Hadrian's Wall's like. The name popped into my head. Nan told me about a different holiday she went on. Long ago. With her aunty, to Hadrian's Wall. It was an 'outing' she said. 'We had fun, made a picnic there with hard-boiled eggs.'

'We're going to have a picnic there,' I say. 'When we reach it. We'll have hard-boiled eggs.'

'Ain't Hadrian's Wall contaminated?' says Tarquin.

'Maybe,' I say. 'Not the bit I'm going to though.'

He looks at me, perplexed.

I shrug. 'I'm not going to any contaminated bits – which bits *you* going to?'

He smiles.

I change the subject. I need time. I need to figure things out. For a start, I'm supposed to know the way there. Maybe I should try and wean them off the idea.

'Scotland's a long way,' I start. 'It'll take months to walk there. Maybe you're gonna like some other place better?' I put it to them.

Lenny shakes his head, holds up the book. 'I'm going to my cottage. My ducklings is waiting.' Then after a bit, 'And I got the Torch.'

We tramp on. The pavement's broken. Weeds have busted through cracks. Soon the pavement ends. We walk in single file down the edge of the highway.

Nobody's out. Who'd be on the road anyway? Everyone's bunkered down, exhausted after trying to grow a few vegetables, saving their coupons, hoping the spring will bring back the bees.

Hoping the army will stop taking everything for itself.

Maybe there's another reason people aren't on the road. I try to remember if I ever heard anything about travelling outside city limits. If it was OK to do that.

I don't think I did. The curfews at dusk are nationwide. That's standard. Though in London you never see patrols. They don't care about protecting us. They got their own deals with gangs anyway. I don't know anything about daylight patrols.

'Where do all these roads go?' asks Lenny.

'Everywhere,' I say.

'How many other places are there?'

'I don't know,' I say. 'Lots, I guess.'

'How many people live there?'

'She don't know,' says Tarquin.

I don't. Since the bombs, the population has wasted. There might be hundreds of ghost towns, thousands of empty homes. A vast prairie of dead fields.

I can almost hear Nan's voice. 'Aristaeus upset the balance of nature, brought death, brought starvation. Wasted populations when he chased Eurydice. He hunted her with dogs. She fled from him, ran along a river, where a snake, which lay hidden by the bank, bit her.

'There is always a snake, Melissa. In every garden there's always a snake. Run swiftly, run fast, my beautiful child – but be careful – be very careful.

'Find your Orpheus.'

'How far is it?' asks Lenny.

I don't answer. I just gaze at the skyline of buildings, pale grey. A thin film of snow. Early morning haze, blurring roads and streets and sky.

After a while Tarquin says, 'That's a thought.'

He's quiet again for another half mile.

I'm glad I've got shoes. *Bless you, Nan. Thank you for the shoes. How did you know I'd need them? Did your Gods tell you I'd go on this journey?*

'The army use some railway to go north, don't they?' says Tarquin finally. 'Heard 'bout it from a guy at Games City. He rode down the country on a coal train. Said he got off at Clapham Junction.' He drags the suitcase round a pothole. 'If not for Careem, we coulda waited for that train.'

I don't say anything. I don't know where Clapham Junction is. I suppose a train might've helped. But what's the point in saying that?

'Never mind. At least this way the army won't see us.'

I'm still trying to remember the rest of the story about the bees, about the journey through the underworld and carrying the Torch and something about never looking back.

There's no guarantee the army won't see us.

And I'm still wondering about the snake and the garden.

By midday we're clear of the city. We navigate empty suburbs, tangled weeds, slabs of broken tarmac. Graffiti on crumbling walls. A rat running across the road. Some people are out. They avoid us.

We climb up on top of a rise. We take a breath and eat cold potatoes. Tarquin can't settle. He takes out Nan's old binoculars, scans the way we've come. He doesn't say anything straight away. He doesn't have to. He just freezes up and doesn't move.

'How far is it to Scotland?' says Lenny.

'Shush.'

Something's up. I swallow my lump of cold potato. It gets stuck in my throat, I can't speak properly. 'What?' I croak.

'Gangers,' Tarquin says.

'Where?'

'Let's go. They got dogs. Trackers.'

We shoulder our packs and grab the suitcase and set off at a run down the hill.

'Tracking us?'

'Hard to say, but yeah, probably. Careem don't give up.'

We slow to a jog, leave the suburbs behind, the endless streets of barred and boarded up dwellings. Half of them burned out, broken gates, dead bushes.

'I've got a stitch,' complains Lenny. 'Can't we rest?'

'Just a bit further,' says Tarquin.

My heart's banging in my throat and not just because of the jogging. People could've seen us. They could be hiding in the houses. Everyone knows you can trade information.

We hit the open highway. No more houses. We slow down a bit. A huge rusted road sign blocks part of the road. It lies buckled, its blue paint flaking. 'M1 THE NORTH Luton' and a picture of a white aeroplane.

Tarquin looks at me.

I nod. 'We're going the right way.'

Pulling the suitcase gets harder. The road isn't a road any more. Just an endless stretch of broken surfacing, lumpy, cracked. Little hillocks of asphalt peak out, followed by huge potholes furrowed in icy mud. My heart is still racing.

'We need to get off this road,' says Tarquin after a few miles. 'I ain't sure we're allowed outside city limits without travel passes.'

'What's them?' asks Lenny.

'Papers.'

'Why?'

'So the army can control where you go.'

'Like Careem?'

'Bit.'

'But if we cut across country, we'll get lost,' I say. I think of the other road signs up ahead, lying rusted and broken, but still pointing out directions.

'We'll keep going north,' says Tarquin. 'Trust me.'

We leave the road, climb a hillside. It's hard going. Months of ice and snow have frozen the old plough lines solid. I nearly twist my ankle. Tarquin has to carry the suitcase. At the top of the hill we're surrounded by woodland. Wind has felled boughs off dead trees. They block our path. Years of decay makes them treacherous. Up here the breeze is sharper, colder.

We trudge downhill through a meadow. Everything frozen. The snap of desiccated bracken. Over a fallen wooden gate. We skirt a pond, long weeds like tentacles. Across a bridge made of old rotten tree trunks. Not a bird. Not a rustle of anything.

Tarquin stops, raises the binoculars. Desolate countryside, once the greenest of pastures. Pale. Inanimate. In the distance, the skeletons of pylons. The seared remains of a tree.

'This is no good,' says Tarquin. 'We ain't gonna get nowhere like this.'

We head back to the M1. Old bramble everywhere. Lenny looks at the hedgerows and pulls at the woody shrubs. He finds a spider. Long dead, but still a spider. It was alive, not seventy years ago when the power stations melted down, not fifty years ago when we got out of the long winter. Maybe only a year ago. That's hopeful.

It means there were two spiders and they found each other. They got eggs and the eggs hatched and the spiders fed the babies and that means there's still more insects around – living insects, getting caught up in spider webs, and that's got to be hopeful.

One day the country's going to recover. One day, when

Lenny's bigger, there's going to be lots of insects.

One day the bees will come back.

Crops are going to grow, not just in the biomes, not just food for the army. Proper crops for everybody. One day we're going to emerge from the underworld and find that garden.

We go a bit slower. Lenny drags at Tarquin's arm, shows him the spider again. Tarquin's not interested. He just grunts, 'Yeah.' He looks through the field glasses, scans around, leads us back to the road. We take turns to drag the suitcase. Lenny pulls out his picture book from where it's hidden down his vest. He opens it up and jams it against his chest to stop the wind flapping the pages. He points to a picture. It's one of the garden scenes. There, at the bottom of the page, all nice and tidy in the grass, is a picture of a spider.

'See,' says Lenny. 'it's one of them.'

'A spider.'

'An' I found one. That's a sign, ain't it? Tarquin, ain't it a sign?'

Tarquin says nothing. Lenny drags at Tarquin's arm.

'It means we're going the right way. We're on the way. We're going to find everything in this book,' says Lenny. He does a little dance.

I don't know what to say. I cross my fingers. Send a silent prayer up to all Nan's Gods.

'Don't get your hopes up too much, Len,' Tarquin says. He tugs Lenny's locks. 'One dead spider ain't much of a sign to me.'

33

We hear them first, deep rumbling engines. The stones on the road shake. Trucks. Covered canopies. Sludge-green. Filth of ages. Rattling down the bumpy road at us.

It's not good. 'Hide. We've got to hide,' I yell.

They come spluttering through the drizzle. Jerking their wheels round the ruts, ploughing through the pitted mud. The canopied frames swaying crazily from side to side.

'Shit,' I mutter. I grab Lenny's hand. 'Quick. C'mon.' Tarquin moves fast. He grabs hold of Lenny's other hand, shoves the suitcase into a ditch. Lenny freezes in terror.

'C'mon!' We haul him.

'Hide.'

Half carrying Lenny, we race for a gap in the hedgerow. Dead shrubs, woody, brittle, tangle along the roadsides. I catch my footing, trip on brambles, go sprawling. Get up. Run.

'C'mon.'

We dive through the hedge. Fall flat. Press ourselves into the undergrowth behind it.

The army convoy reach the ditch with the suitcase. They don't stop. If they see it, they take no notice.

'Just stay very still. Don't move,' says Tarquin.

Truck engines crank and rumble past us, like a distant earthquake.

'Stay down,' hisses Tarquin.

An image flashes through my head. *A long-legged girl. Once beautiful. Her face disfigured. One eye black and swollen.*

We lie there panting, hearts thudding. Through the gaps in the blackened hawthorn hedges we see a long line of vehicles winding down the hill. The first truck is well past us, past the gap in the hedge. Gunners are sitting on the tailboard with rifles. Thick black fumes choke out and gust up into the air.

Lenny looks at me, waiting to see if it's OK. I raise a finger, place it over my lips, press myself flat in the dead undergrowth. Tarquin tries to quietly tease stems and straggle them over Lenny.

'If they see us, I'll get up. I'll head them off. You stay. You carry on. Get Lenny to the cottage,' he hisses.

I look at him, fix my eyebrows into a question.

'I'll find you. Whatever it takes. Leave a sign at Hadrian's Wall or wherever. Lenny knows the Blah-Blah.'

I lift my head slowly. Roar of engines. Three trucks are past. I press myself into the ground, willing it to shield me. I lie there, my head splitting with a sudden terrifying headache. *We're not hidden well enough. They're going to see us.* Lenny reaches out his hand and takes mine in his. He holds it tight with his unspoken question.

'It's going to be all right,' I mouth.

He's still gripping on with asking fingers.

But it's not all right. And if his hand wasn't holding mine, and I were on my own, I'd roll over quick as a flash, and get myself tucked into that hollow next to the hedge and *nobody* would see me.

But I can't. And I won't try to leave him again. So I lie there knowing the axe will fall.

And it does.

A shout goes up from a truck. A klaxon horn. The convoy stops. A deep voice barks out an order. There's a crash. A noise like a ramp dropping. Soldiers shouting. Engine spluttering.

Then shooting.

Tarquin springs up and races away from us down the hedgerow.

'Don't shoot!'

'Stop.'

'HANDS UP.'

'Don't shoot. Don't shoot!' yells Tarquin.

Another round of fire. I clap my hands over my ears.

34

I don't raise my head, don't open my eyes until I feel a heavy hand on my shoulder. It drags me up.

They aren't gentle. They aren't gentle with Lenny.

They snap huge hands right over his thin little wrists and haul him over to a truck.

They drag me up and stand me next to him, by the wheel.

'Look what a pretty thing we got here.'

My heart hammers. My legs shake.

Filthy faces, stained uniforms, teeth missing, stubbled chins. *Where's Tarquin? What's happened to Tarquin?*

It seems my heart stops. I forget to breathe. *What's happened to Tarquin?*

'Get her to the truck.'

'Where's the boyfriend?'

'He's down.'

Dear God. No.

'She's one hell of a catch.'

'A real lulu.'

'She's gotta be one for the General.'

An ornate brass gate squeals open. Something creeps out, staggers to a table. Black bruising. Raw wheals.

'Where is she?'

Dear God don't let him be dead.

'Let me see.'

'There's a kid.'

'Hers?'

'Get her up there by the truck.'

'Get that runner.'

'He's alive.'

'Bring him in.'

He's alive. I let out all the breath in me. *Tarquin's alive.*

They take the BB gun off him. They beat him about the head with rifle butts. They haul him back to the truck. *He's alive.*

'Names?' barks out an officer.

'Tarquin Carver.'

'You.'

'Lenny Carver.'

'You.'

'Melissa Hambrook.'

'Where're you going?'

Lenny starts. 'There's this place –'

I cut him off. 'We're going to find work,' I say. 'We heard there was work on the covered farms.'

The officer laughs.

'You think you're cute,' he says.

'No.'

The man looks at me.

I look right back. If he thinks I'm afraid of him, he can think again.

I hear Nan. 'That's it. Chin up. The hedgehog curls up to protect his belly. Don't curl up. But don't show them your belly. Don't let them know where to hurt you.'

The officer shakes his head. He forces us into the back of the truck. Tarquin's face is swollen, bloodied. Lenny's gnawing his cheek and scrunching his thin little shoulders up and down.

I don't say anything. I stick my chin in the air and press my lips together.

In the truck, under the canopy, people sprawl on the floor. Dirty. Thin. Their hands long-nailed, filthy. Eyes stare at us. I hear the cab door slam. The judder of the engine. It stinks of diesel. We sway, start moving.

'Are you what all the commotion's about?' says someone.

The truck jolts us. I try to protect Tarquin's head, hold on to Lenny.

I stare back at them. I tuck Lenny into the space beside me, help Tarquin to get comfortable. He's bleeding.

The truck swings round a curve in the road. We all lurch sideways. The truck takes a sharp left turn.

'Three more for the death camps,' mutters an old man, grey stubble, bleary eyes.

Through the flapping canvas, I catch a glimpse of hedges, a long line of them winding down a hill. Blackened hawthorn. I don't believe it.

'At least there's food there,' grunts someone.

'Not what I heard.'

We're going back the way we came.

'Must be.'

'If you steal it.'

I looked over at another man, old trousers, holes, tattered, held up by string. 'They watch you,' he says.

We're going back over the land we've just covered.

'They starve you – work you to death. They're bloody concentration camps.'

I find a space on the floor. I wish I had the blankets. I'd roll them out for Lenny. He could rest. I could hide.

Instead Lenny scrunches himself up, tight against me. I cradle Tarquin's head in my lap.

Back towards London.

Gently I touch his face. I won't tell them.

'Let me look.'

Blood is still oozing over his cheek. I wipe it away. There're two gashes across his cheekbone. *He's alive. Thank God he's alive.* One of them needs stitching. I hold the ragged edges together. I don't know what else to do.

Except to press them close as we head back towards Careem and the General and nowhere to hide.

35

We lurch to a halt.

Another arrest. I can hear them by the trucks, shouting. Voice of a woman. Then I hear her screaming. 'My children! Let me go.'

The woman sounds terrified. I put my arm around Lenny and hold him. His body so thin.

'They'll starve,' she screams. 'They're only little.'

'How old are they?' 'Where are they?' Soldiers, not sure what to do.

I move to the back of the truck and lean out. Was she out looking for food? Left her children at home? I see someone. 'Officer,' I shout.

'The girl,' yells one of them.

The officer looks up.

'Will you get her children?'

'Shut up. Get back inside.' The soldier on the tailboard smacks his hand on my chest and shoves me back.

'They'll starve!' the woman screams.

I struggle up, wincing. Find my place by Lenny and Tarquin again.

'We'll send someone.' Voice of the officer.

'Will they bring them to her?' I ask anyone inside the truck. Nobody answers.

The canvas flap is hoisted up. The woman's pushed in. I see her eyes, crazy with fear.

'We'll take them to one of the farms,' says the officer. 'Now shut up. We don't leave children to starve.'

'Not if you can put them into a harness,' says someone from further inside.

'But will they bring them to her?' I ask.

Somebody shrugs.

The woman screams, a high-pitched keening. The officer smacks her hard across the face.

'We don't have fuel to be running stupid kids up and down the country. You've broken the law. You're out on a public highway. You might be a scout for highway robbers. We don't know. You might be relaying them news, so they can ambush the convoy and kill the lot of us. Your kids will be collected as long as you give us directions – when we reach the farm camp. We're not Philistines.'

At least we're not going back to London.

The woman wails.

'If you carry on screeching, I'll make sure we *don't* get them.'

Immediately the woman stops. She's shaking all over.

The officer in charge catches sight of me. His eyes linger on my face.

Philistines? A story Nan told. Something about the bees. I try to remember.

'We going to a farm?' asks Lenny.

Something about Samson.

'Where they grow food?'

It's a good question. Nan and I got the ration books. On the covers – MINISTRY OF FOOD & COVERED FARMS. We never got what was printed on the coupons though. *Cabbage. Onion. Dried Peas. Bacon.* We got a bit of lard every now and then, but that never came from any covered farm.

Tarquin is so quiet. I put my hand on his cheek. Very gently.

'S'OK. Resting.'

I tuck my arm back round Lenny.

'Will they get the little children?' he says.

'They say they will.'

'Are you sure?'

'That's what they say.'

'Why?'

'Because they said they're not Philistines.'

'OK.'

I look at the people in the truck. If they round up this number on every trip and send them to the farms, they should have enough by now, shouldn't they? Enough hands to produce enough food. So why did we never get what was printed on the coupons?

'What's Philistines?'

'People who do bad things.'

'We're not Philistines?'

'No.'

216

We travel all day. We go more west than south. Nowhere near London, thank God. The last shadows of dusk dissolve into night. The truck jolts to a halt. Someone shouts an order. Voices of soldiers. Tyres on gravel. The truck jolts forward again. Then stops. They order us out.

We climb down from the back of the truck. It's cold. I catch Lenny to me. I help Tarquin. I can see the biomes, huge ghostly domes, going on for miles, weird, like moons caught in the hills, circular, weightless, almost ready to lift up and take off. They're linked up right across the valley.

So these are the covered farms.

I see the fence, chain link, four metres high, barbed wire stretched across the top, the thin moon beyond. A prison camp. I see the rows of terraced houses. All inside the wire. I try to prepare Lenny.

'Remember when we played that game about the hens in the henhouse,' I say.

He looks at me, runs his teeth over his bottom lip.

'Behind the wire.'

'There weren't no wire.'

'Well, there should have been.'

'Should there?'

'Yeah, I forgot to mention it – to keep them safe from foxes.'

'Oh.'

'We got to pretend we're the hens for a while, to really get to know what it might be like to be a hen, living behind wire. Then when we get to our place in Scotland, we'll know exactly what it's like and we can give our hens the best life ever.'

He looks at me, nods his little head and says, 'I'd never've

217

thought of that.'

I stroke his head.

'Is it part of carrying the Torch?' he says.

'Yes. Yes it is.'

Tarquin doesn't say anything. He just looks at me. I wish he didn't. His look is so grateful. It makes me feel so terrible. He should be back in Games City. He shouldn't be here, pressing an old rag up to his swollen face. Feeling grateful that we're playing at being hens.

I drop my eyes.

When everyone's down from the truck, they line us up. An officer counts off groups of eight and dispatches two soldiers with each group. 'Take them to the Induction Centre.'

We're marched along a track, gravel underfoot, old engine parts overgrown with weeds. Broken metal gates. Overhead, iron-grey clouds outlined in the last rays of the sun. Blood red. A high ridge of hills. The fence.

The Induction Centre is a disused village school. Brickwork. Old desks. Filthy white boards. Metal filing cabinets. We're taken from room to room. Stripped down to our underclothes. Issued blue boiler suits. They take Nan's coat. They take Dad's old hat and gloves. They take Lenny's hooded top. They leave us our shoes.

As we file out in our boiler suits, Lenny taps me. He nods very secretively. Then taps his tummy. 'The Torch,' he whispers. 'Got it down me pants.'

In the old canteen an officer numbers each of us. He pricks digits into our arms with a sharp pin. Tattoos some kind of stain. It stings. Like a sewing needle scraped hard across skin.

Like someone scratching on sunburn, like a skinned knee. I feel every stick of the pin.

I look at Lenny, waiting his turn, biting his cheek, his fists balled.

'Imagine it's a bee sting,' I say. 'You won't mind the pain so much then.'

Lenny looks at me, lips pressed tight. 'I will,' he mouths. I hold his eyes with mine till his number's done.

When they get to Tarquin, they see the Bone Cross Bone tattoo. The officer calls someone, points it out. They write it down in a book and prick his number onto the back of his hand.

I'm 278. Lenny's 279. Tarquin is 280.

We're marched into the assembly hall and formally addressed by a tall officer with a cap and stripes. He's got a moustache and a very scrubbed face.

'We run the plantation system here.'

His voice is different – like Nan's – like he reads books.

'You'll be given a fair trial and, if convicted, you'll be expected to work your custodial term out. You work from sunrise to sunset. Harvesting certain crops, you work an eighteen-hour day. You must be in line at the first sign of light. You close when it's too dark to see. You work in gangs with one soldier overseeing you. Women and children work the same hours as men.

'At the end of every day you get in a line to have your produce weighed. Your daily food allowance will only be given to you once you have met your minimum target weight.

'You stay in the village. There will be houses with rooms allocated to you. On Saturday nights you are allowed meetings. You get Sundays off.

'We have an incentive system here. If you're hard working and regularly exceed your weigh-in targets, we can allow you extra food, clothing, time free from work and positions of responsibility. You can use the gardens attached to the houses to cultivate foodstuffs or rear animals for your own use. You may not take seeds or fertiliser or bees from the biomes.

'As far as possible we will keep you in family, kinship and work-gang groups, but we retain the right to move you at any point, to any work gang, or any biome.

'Presently you are on remand, awaiting trial, and will be expected to follow this schedule until you receive your sentences.

'Sunrise tomorrow is at 7.10 a.m.'

He salutes, clicks his heels and marches out.

A smaller man in camouflage steps up.

'And I'm the adjutant. I'm in charge of this section. You get up when we say. You work when we say. You stop when we say. We run this place and you lot are just a pile of shite.

'We'll flog ya if you try anything. We'll flog ya for thinking about trying anything. So get that into yer thick heads. Look at ya! What a pile a wasters. You should be grateful we picked you up. You're the lucky ones – the ones that get fed and somewhere to sleep.'

He doesn't salute or click his heel. He just cracks a whip and belches.

They split us back up into our parties of eight and march us out of the old school and up into the village. Old stone. Slate roofs. Brick walls. They break the groups up and send us to different streets. We're given one room in one of the houses. The whole eight of us.

The bed is just a space on the floor to sleep. But a lot of the floorboards have been ripped up. Lenny finds an unbroken patch and drops down on it. He's so small and thin. I wish I had something to cover him. I think of the suitcase lying miles away in the ditch. No blankets. No warm clothes. Not a scrap to eat. I lie down. Tarquin does too. We huddle together. The others find spaces where they can. Someone argues about being too near the door. My number itches like crazy. I try not to scratch it. I see Lenny scratching his. I hold Lenny's hands still till he falls asleep. I'm starving. I don't think I can sleep.

In the darkness Tarquin's hand finds mine.

In the darkness his lips press softly against my shoulder.

36

It's nearly light.

People are moving about. Someone nudges me. My belly hurts. I roll over and shut the nudging out. Just a little longer. Just a few more minutes before I face today. I lie there trying to climb back into sleep. It's no use. I roll over and stare at the ceiling.

Lenny is already up and gone. He calls to me through the broken window. He's standing outside. I get up. I step over the sleeping shapes huddled together. I push open the front door and get outside. I breathe in the morning air. Fresh country air, like fine weather in London, only better.

'Missa, look.' Lenny's waving his arms and jumping up and down. He's got an apple in his hand. A real, red, rosy apple. Smooth skin. I've never seen an apple looking so fresh, so perfect. Lenny is bouncing and bouncing.

'You can eat it,' he says.

He runs at me. Apple in his outstretched hand.

'Eat it,' he says.

I take the apple. Raise it to my nose, crisp, sweet.

'It's juicy,' he says. 'Bite it.'

I look at Lenny and then bite into the apple. It takes my breath away. The juice spills over my lip. Saliva floods into my mouth. I hold the disc of apple on my tongue. It's so good.

'You see?' he says.

I nod.

'Have more.'

I shake my head. I pass the apple back. I bite down on the crisp flesh poised in my mouth. The taste of it smarts the back of my throat.

Lenny takes the apple back. He nibbles it, holds it out to me again.

'Go on, it's good.'

'Your first?'

'Yes.'

I remember Tarquin. I remember his arm around me in the dark night. I raise my eyes and glance back through the open door at him.

Immediately Lenny races inside, bounces over the others to Tarquin. 'Quinny!'

I follow. Tarquin rolls over. He's awake. His face bruised, swollen.

'Try it,' says Lenny.

Tarquin shakes his head. He smiles.

'How you feeling?' I ask.

'Not so bad,' he says.

'It's good. Missa says so.'

'Nah, you go ahead. I had mine already.'

I don't understand. There's only one apple. Tarquin raises himself up. He spreads his arms wide. He winks at me. I think

223

he's winking. His swollen eye twitches anyway and closes.

I frown.

'Apples.'

'Yes, *one* apple,' I say.

He sighs as if I'm stupid. 'Apples. You know. Eden.'

'What about it?'

'I was trying to give you a compliment.'

'A compliment?'

'I've been in Eden all night.'

I shake my head.

'Aw, forget it. It ain't no good if I got to explain.' He sits up, stretches.

I pause, confused.

Lenny jumps up and down. 'Let's eat it, Missa,' he says. He bites and passes it to me. I bite and pass it back, glad to focus on something.

When we're done I say, 'Where'd you get it?'

Lenny laughs and points at one of the other houses. 'They got 'em in there. They got three. There's kids in there, Missa. Me and them kids been playing farms. They gave me it. There's more inside the biomes.'

I try to imagine inside the biomes.

'There's whole trees of 'em,' he says. 'That's what they tell.'

I look out across the street towards the biomes. Once upon a time perhaps I could've liked this place. Maybe in Nan's day. Rows of small terraced houses, winding up the hill. Little front gardens buzzing with bees. I look around. Not much to like now. Roofs fallen in, not a window with any glass. The house they put us in, abandoned, damp, cold, spattered walls, no doors, no furniture. Floorboards and ceilings ripped up. The front garden, overgrown with those thick weeds. The ones that last without light or insects.

Even so, if I had time and energy I could make it something. Mend the windows, find plastic sheeting or something to tack over them, board them up. Put back the floor – at least make it even, so you don't twist an ankle. Right now you can't even walk on most of it – you'd break your neck.

Someone tried here once. I can see they tried to wash the tiles in the hall. There're patches where they look almost clean. And there's a row of bottles they must've used to store water. We're going to need to store water.

I go outside, to ask someone where to get water.

Down the street a woman's out too. She looks as thin as a pole and pale as moonlight.

'Excuse me,' I say. 'Do you know where I can get water?'

'You the new batch?'

'We need to drink something.'

'They put you in the end house, didn't they?'

'I guess so.' I look back at the house we spent the night in.

'You the ones who've got the little lad?'

'Yes.'

She smiles. 'Come in here. He's already been over, playing with our Tommy.' She leads me into another house, cold, just as dirty. Looks like every stick of furniture's been burned. At least there're ceilings. Every room is full of sad people. They don't look up. They crouch on the floor, huddled into bits of bedding. Nobody's done anything to make anywhere better. They look like they've given up. The woman leads me through the house. Out the back is a garden, or it was. It's hill-high with junk. I'm puzzled. How come you have a garden, and you work on a covered farm, and you don't grow anything for yourself? Nothing to trade, nothing to live off? If Nan and I had a garden that big, we'd be doing something with it.

'Water's there.' The woman points to an old well. 'You can haul water here until they move you, if they move you.'

I pick up the bucket and haul it up full.

'You'll have to bring a bottle though.'

I hurry back and fetch two bottles from the line on the window sill.

We manage to drink some water before a squad of soldiers arrive. They pound the horns on their jeeps and shout out. Down the street the workers come out, blue boiler suits, stooping shoulders. We line up, form a queue.

The soldiers do a head count. Tick us off on a sheet. Someone called Crowley is in charge. The soldiers laugh at us. One soldier flicks the end of an apple core at the line. He shouts, 'Scramble.' Nobody dives for it.

Crowley looks around. The dawn is just flooding the sky in the east. 'Where's Tidmarsh?'

Everyone freezes. Nobody speaks.

'Where is Mrs Tidmarsh?' Crowley yells.

Everyone looks away. Crowley pounces. He grabs a scrawny kid about the same age as Lenny and yells in the kid's face. 'Where. The. Devil. Is. Your. Mother?'

The kid's so nervous he can't answer. Crowley goes to the truck, pulls out a long whip. He sets about the boy.

'She's coming, Mister,' whimpers the boy.

'Why's she not here?' He brings the lash down.

'Don't know.' The boy tries to cover his head with his hands, tries to duck the lashes. Crowley has him by the back of his boiler suit and is laying into him.

Lenny stands there as pale as pale, biting his lip. He looks at the boy, looks up at Tarquin. Crowley brings his lash down.

The boy screams. Blood soaks across the back of his boiler suit in a long ragged line.

Tarquin looks at Lenny and steps forward.

He grabs hold of Crowley's arm. Tarquin's no weakling. Despite the pounding he took yesterday, he twists that arm and Crowley drops the whip. Crowley raises a whistle to his mouth, lets out one long blast.

Oh, Tarquin. What have you done?

Soldiers jump off the jeep.

Why do you have to be such a hero?

I clutch my head with my hands and close my eyes.

37

'Missa!' Lenny's voice jolts me back. He's tugging at my arm, his tiny frame shaking. I hold him to me. Look over at Tarquin, meet his eyes.

For a split second Tarquin holds my gaze. Then he crouches down, presses his ribs and hisses at the boy, 'Get back in line.'

The boy darts away. Tarquin barely has time to straighten up. Three soldiers are on him. It takes all three to restrain him. Crowley steps up. He's got the whip again.

'You piece a shite,' he snarls.

I hold Lenny's face against me, cover his ears, grit my teeth.

Then Tarquin twists. Seems to ripple, as if he has extra joints. The soldiers try to hold on to him. Crowley raises the whip. But before Crowley can bring the lash down, Tarquin's foot shoots out. He kicks Crowley up and under the chin. I hear the impact. A thick thud, a sudden crunch of bone. A spray of blood. Half-strangled scream.

Lenny twists, looks. Crowley is writhing on the ground, holding his jaw.

'It's broken,' whispers Lenny. 'I can do that, nearly. It's how we gangers floor the dogs.'

More soldiers join in. They pin Tarquin to the ground, lift Crowley into the front of the jeep. He's frothing blood. Can't speak.

'Move them work gangs along,' orders one of them.

They make us march off up the street.

Tarquin twists his head up, flashes me a last look. *Take care of Lenny.* And then a bag is pulled down over his head, his hands and feet manacled. He's lifted up and flung into the back of an open jeep.

I grab Lenny and move to the back of the line. I ask a soldier, 'Where're they taking him?'

'None a your business.'

I want to shout in his face. *It is my business. Don't you understand? Everything that happens to him is my business.*

'Get back to your work gang.' The soldier raises a fist.

'What they gonna do to Quinny?' Lenny clutches my hand, pulling me back.

I've no answer. My heart's pounding. I'm trembling. Lenny's trembling too, doing a little shuffle of terror. I bite my lip.

'Are they gonna hurt him?'

'Dunno.'

Lenny looks like he's going to start screaming. *Think of something to calm him. If he starts, they'll take him too.* He's nodding his head in tiny little jerks. Like he's about to have a fit. *Get him to focus on something else.*

'It's part of the story,' I say. I steer him up the street.

His chin's trembling, his fists are balled.

'Just listen.'

Think.

'He's the hero of the story.' We fall into step in the line.

'*They put him in the jeep.*' Lenny's voice has a new shrill edge. *Tell him a story.*

'They put him in the jeep, because before the hero can get to the hidden valley, he has to defeat the enemies and things.'

Lenny looks up at me, chin jerking, tears running down his little face.

'And be tested.'

He's got his hands on his head, clutching his hair.

'Quinny had to save the boy and defeat Crowley, and he did, see? He passed the test.' I take his hands in mine. I stroke them. *Keep him walking. Keep him listening. Focus on that.*

'Was Crowley one of them enemies?' he says. *Good, he's trying to understand.*

'Yes, he was,' I say. 'In all stories the hero has to defeat the enemy and pass through the Valley of Shadows.'

'O-K.' His breath comes in great gasping shudders.

'Before there can be a happy ending.'

'Is there a happy ending?'

'Yes, there is.'

'But what happens in the Valley of Shadows?'

He doesn't understand. I don't know if I do. I try again. 'Our secret valley isn't like any ordinary valley. It isn't just a hollow stretching between two hills. It's the Valley of Sunlight, and it's a place you can go to in your heart, when you feel everything's so awful you don't know what to do.'

Lenny nods, wipes his sleeve across his nose. 'I don't know 'bout no valleys,' he says.

I cuddle him to me.

'Look, we're gonna rescue Quinny and get out of here and go to our valley, together, OK?'

Lenny nods his head, quickly. 'OK, Missa.'

'So you have to keep going, because this is the hard part.'

I move back up the line, keep Lenny with me. I single out one of the older men. He looks like he's been here a long time, tired out, thin as a bone. But his face is kind.

'What'll happen to him?' I whisper.

He doesn't turn his back on me like I'm half expecting. He bends his head. 'Speak softly, young lady.'

'Sorry.'

'They'll take your young man to the pen.'

'Pen?'

'Where they'll flog him.'

My throat seems to suddenly close up.

'It doesn't stand for penitentiary.'

I look at him blankly. He shrugs. 'You're too young to remember America?'

'America?'

'It stands for pig pen.'

'Pig pen?'

'They'll take him to the pig pens and he'll work there.'

Bacon. I remember there were coupons for bacon.

'We've not got enough people to leave any of them idle. He'll work in the pig pens by day and be locked up in the old police cells by night. Unless.'

I wait.

'Unless he's too much trouble.'

38

At the old village green, a triangle of overgrown weeds, they break us up into our work gangs. Most of the gangs go to their biomes. Lenny and I are ganged up with the other new arrivals and taken into a holding area.

It's a long, dark hut. Wooden boards. Grille windows. Thick dust. Smell of sweat. Rank bodies. The people we travelled with last night are there. The moaning man, the one with grey stubble. The woman, still without her children. There are others too. No Tarquin.

We join them. We sit on benches. Lenny clings to me. I try to keep my chin up, my lips tight. *Don't let them flog him.* We sit there and wait.

'What we waiting for?' Lenny whispers.

'We're waiting for the General,' says someone.

The General? I go cold all over.

'It's a court.'

'Court?' says Lenny.

I clutch him tighter.

'Missa, you're hurting.'

'Caught after curfew, held on the highway, planning to thieve.'

232

I loosen my grip. *Shit.*

'Thieve?' A whole conversation starts.

'So you can't travel?'

'Not outside town limits. All those caught out of doors without travel passes in public places get sent here.'

'Highway Robbery Act. Two years' hard labour.'

A soldier enters. I hear him informing the officer on duty. 'Just got word, General wants this court to hold off. He wants to come here himself.' The noise of the others drowns out his words.

He wants to come here himself. Dear God, no.

'Aren't we honoured.' It's the officer on duty.

I strain to listen.

'He's still in London now, something's kicked off there. He'll come here briefly, on his way to Andover.' Voice of the messenger.

I can't catch the officer's reply.

'Not now, not today. Commander in Chief of Land Forces wants him . . . something about deployment . . . MoD involvement . . .'

I miss the rest of the exchange.

'Meanwhile they're to go to Biome Thirty-four and do the harvesting.' That's the soldier again.

'He doesn't want Brigadier doing the sentencing?' That's the officer in charge.

'Apparently not.'

'Problem?'

I focus all my attention to catch the next words.

'Nah, nothing big. It's the girl, the good looker – thinks she may be someone they've been after in London. You know him. Wants to check up on her before he goes.'

Check up on me. My hands go clammy. A cold sweat breaks out.

'Missa?' Lenny tugs my arm.

'We'll be fine,' I manage.

The soldiers are already clearing the courthouse. *God help us. First Tarquin. Now this.*

I keep my teeth set tight, steer Lenny into the line. My knees go weak. *Keep walking. Keep thinking.*

We're sent to Biome Thirty-four. *Delicate ankles. Bruised skin.* We go in through sets of sliding plastic. It's big. So big it could house Big Ben. *I don't want spoiled goods.* It covers four fields. *I like to see my own handiwork.* Hexagonal shaped, clear plastic panels, each about nine metres across.

That whip lashing down on Tarquin.

'We're in the beehive now, ain't we, Missa?'

'What?' *Oh, Tarquin.*

'It's a bit like a beehive, ain't it?'

I look up at the biome. He's right. A honeycomb of plastic panels.

'We're getting to learn how them bees feel now, so we know, ain't it?'

Are you there, Nan? Are you still waiting for me? Have you no words to help?

One of the bees buzzes round me, seems to like my smell.

234

A real bee. So tiny. So loud. It settles on my wrist. It crawls onto my hand, tickles my skin. How can the future of us all be borne on such a small, furry back? I blow it gently. It quivers fairy wings. Buzzes up, circles, keeps rising.

I whisper the words of the nursery rhyme, '*Busy Bee, Busy Bee. Here is the beehive. Where are the bees? Hiding, hiding where nobody sees . . .*'

Was that you, Nan? Did you send me the bee?

I look up at the honeycomb biome, at the flitting bees, at the rows of shiny green cabbages.

Is this what it's like, Nan, over the doorstep of death?

'It's gonna be OK, Missa,' says Lenny. ''Cos it's in the book. This is the big old beehive on the end page, ain't it? See all them honeycombs up there? Zactly the same.'

Each field's broken into sections. We start in the cabbage section. *Try and help Tarquin.* The cabbages are ready for cutting. We get a sharp knife and a basket. *Find out what's going to happen.*

'Don't get any funny ideas,' says a soldier. He counts out the knives, marks each one, and puts our numbers in a ledger.

I test the edge of my knife.

'Attacking an officer: flogging and ten years. Fighting: flogging and five years. Stealing: flogging and two years. Eating on the job: flogging,' intones the officer, just to make sure we do understand.

A flogging and ten years.

We slice the cabbages off their stems. *Keep thinking. Don't feel anything.* We put a dozen cabbages into each basket. And each basket into a big open crate. *We're going to fight back.* The cabbages aren't ratty. They're full and green and kind of silvery grey. *Watch for anything that can help.* They look so good, I could eat them raw. *I won't let him rot for ten years.* Lenny tries. I see him nibbling on the bits that fall off. I don't say a word. He needs food. I stand in front of him. Make sure they don't see.

Find somebody who wants something. Find out what, how you can use it.

And there's not just cabbages. There's onions and tomatoes and beans and carrots. *Use your brain.* And down the centre of the biome are rows of apple trees. And canes, fruit canes, heavy with berries.

And bees.

Loads of bees. Huge bumblebees buzzing around the tomatoes. Honeybees hunting out the blossom.

My first bees.

How my heart aches for Nan. How I wish she could see it. How it'd warm her heart. All this food. Miles and miles of blossom and fruit and food and full-to-brimming with bees and buzzing.

The bees seem to like me too. They swarm around and settle on my hair and boiler suit.

Keep thinking. Even the smallest thing can make the difference.

'Look, Missa,' says Lenny. 'So much.' He waves his thin arm at the acres of greenery.

'I know.'

'But, Missa?'

'What?'

'Why's all this food here and in London we don't get none?'

I don't know.

Lenny tugs on my top impatiently.

'Maybe they only just started growing it,' I say vaguely. *Every garden has a snake. Be the snake, Melissa.*

Lenny shakes his head. 'Them trees is really big.'

He folds his arms over his chest, stands there puzzled. 'They're like Careem,' he says at last. 'There was plenty of dogs, but they wanna keep it all to themselves.' He unfolds his arms and bends to cut the next cabbage. 'Because they don't care 'bout us.' He drops the cabbage into the pannier. 'They going to give it to their own little boys and girls.'

'I'll carry your basket,' I say.

'If I had all this food, I'd share it with everyone,' he says.

I pick up his load and move it over to the next row. I place it halfway up the aisle so he can run and drop the cabbages in and not have to carry it so far.

Watch the others as you cut. Watch for an answer.

'And I wouldn't miss out no one – not even them.'

'I'm gonna put you in charge of the universe,' I say. 'After we cut these cabbages.'

Think. What *does* happen to all the food? It doesn't get into the stores. Cabbage, carrots, onions, bacon, eggs, chicken. Never seen any of them. I always thought there wasn't any, or there wasn't enough, or I just got there too late. *Is this something you can use?*

There are fields of cabbages here, and this is just Biome

Thirty-four. There's more than forty biomes on this farm. And there's more covered farms across the country. And the population's so small. Everyone knows the army take what they want, but to take so much, with the rest of us starving?

Find out what happens to the food. Find out who takes it. Find out if they have anything to hide.

That's a start.

Everyone has something to hide.

They keep Lenny on cabbages, but they send me to water-winding. There's a whole line of irrigation winders. They've got a lot of people doing it. A horse too. We have to push huge screw things round and round. The horse is big and shiny with sweat. He smells slightly sour, but fresh, healthy. I like his smell. I like the huge muscles that strain and bunch under his damp coat. A real horse.

The camp is organised. Rows of cabbages. Irrigation systems. Horses. There must be a weak link somewhere.

But for the next few hours I can't think, except to put one foot in front of the next, winding that water up into the sluices. My shoulders strain, my hands become raw. I can't even watch the others, let alone try to figure anything out.

Just when I think my back's about to break, a young guy steps up and pushes on my winder. I look at him. He smiles. 'It's an Archimedes' screw, and it'll break your back if you don't work it properly,' he says.

'Oh,' I say, none the wiser, except that I know Archimedes was Greek.

'Take a break. I'll wind for you.'

I glance over at the soldier on duty.

'Got it covered.' He winks at me. I let him wind. I find Lenny still cutting cabbages. I squat down by his basket and help him. I listen to the sound of the sluice sloshing the water. I look out across the fields. *Were you once open to the sky? Was all England like this? So plentiful? What happened to the world?*

Lenny stops and looks at me. 'Missa, is this a farm?'

'Yes.'

'Are all farms like this?'

I flip my palms up. 'Guess so.'

'Do you think they'd miss just a tiny bit of them veggies?'

It's a farm all right. With nothing to eat in it. You could starve here, surrounded by huge silvery-green cabbages, if you didn't help yourself.

Something inside me snaps. I'm not going to starve. Neither is Lenny.

I shove as many crunchy cabbage leaves as I can inside my boiler suit.

Whether we make our targets or not, we're not going to starve.

39

By the time the sun's setting, I've got a whole load of carrot and cabbage stashed inside my top. Only thing I need to do now is weigh out and make sure they don't find it.

We stand in line by the weighing slabs, hoping our baskets will meet the targets, so we can get our food rations. People are hungry. They push and elbow each other out of the line. Lenny struggles to lift his baskets of cabbages along. One woman shoves in, bang in front of him. I shove her back. I'm not having it. I stand still to block her trying that trick again. But she's knocked Lenny and he slips, knocks over one basket, spills his cabbages. And they roll down the line.

'Dog's Law,' squeals one man. He bends and picks up two of Lenny's cabbages and puts them in his own basket.

I put down my basket. I'm not having that either. I go over to him and snatch the cabbages back.

'So that's how it is,' he says and pushes me so hard I fall over. I land with a bump. The man strides up to my basket and helps himself.

Lenny races around trying to collect the other scattered cabbages. But they're gone. In desperation I kick over one of the man's baskets. 'See how you like it,' I snap.

The young man who helped me at the water sluice suddenly appears. He's got three of Lenny's cabbages in his hands. He dumps them back in Lenny's basket.

'C'mon,' he says to the queue. 'Let's not spoil the little fella's first day.'

As if by magic, everybody gives the fallen cabbages up without a word. I stand there, mouth open, eyes wide.

The young man strolls up, picks up the man's basket I just kicked over, puts it right. The people in the line put all the cabbages back in it. Then the young man returns my cabbages to me.

'No need to make enemies, you know,' he says.

'Thanks,' I mutter. 'You don't seem to have any.'

'Well,' he says, 'that's the way I like it.'

'Now, young fella.' He turns to Lenny, who's standing there fighting tears, his chin trembling, his thin legs shaking. 'I'll give you a hand with that, shall I?' He shoulders two of Lenny's baskets and heads towards the top of the line.

We've lost our place in the queue, but the young man says, 'No problem. Everyone here's my friend,' and proceeds to talk to the others saying, 'If you don't mind,' and, 'Let's give the young 'un a break, shall we?' and 'Here we go, that's right.' Soon we're at the front, right near the weighing benches.

Our cabbages are weighed. We pass the target. We collect our rations. A hunk of flat bread, a few vegetables. The soldiers see our companion and wave us through.

And miraculously I'm out of the biome – clutching our dinner in one hand and with the other holding on to all the extra helpings I've stashed down my front!

Some distance from the doors, the young man bows to me in an oddly formal manner. 'I'm Harold,' he says.

'Melissa and Lenny – and thanks.'

Lenny is already tearing into the bread.

'So you're the little ganger, eh? The one they picked off the streets?'

'I ain't no ganger no more,' says Lenny.

'That's the spirit,' says Harold. 'I've got something to cheer you up. Wanna see it?'

Lenny chews and nods.

'OK. Choose a hand.' Harold balls both his hands into fists and hides them behind his back.

Lenny looks at him, sucks on a finger, takes time to make his choice. 'OK,' he says, 'if I choose the right hand, I'll be right.'

'Oh no you won't,' says Harold. 'You'll be wrong.'

Harold pulls out his right fist, and with a flourish opens it up right under Lenny's nose. There's nothing in it. Lenny laughs. 'Then it's the other.'

'Wrong again,' says Harold. He brings out the left fist, opens it. There's nothing there, either.

Lenny looks peeved.

'Don't you think he's had enough for one day?' I say.

Harold twists his right hand, brings it forward again and, right in front of Lenny's eyes, he snaps his fingers, says, 'Abracadabra.' And between his thumb and forefinger is the hugest ripest strawberry I ever saw.

Lenny's eyes light up.

The smell of it. So sweet, tantalising. Lenny stares at Harold, takes the strawberry.

'How d'ya do that?'

'Everything's simple when you know how,' says Harold. 'Just a snap of the fingers and a flick of the wrist and there you go. Anything you want. I can get it for you.'

That's far too exciting for Lenny. He sucks his finger again and says, 'No you can't.'

'Go on,' says Harold. 'Try me.'

'OK,' says Lenny. 'I'd wanna duckling.'

'No problem,' says Harry. Quickly he balls his fists again, hides them behind his back. 'Choose a hand, any hand.'

Lenny considers. He doesn't want to be caught out this time. He reaches forward and says, 'I think I'll have that one.' He suddenly puts both hands out and grabs both of Harold's arms at exactly the same time.

'Got ya now,' says Lenny. 'Where's my duckling?'

Harold laughs, says, 'OK, you win.'

'Bring it out,' says Lenny. Then his face falls. 'You ain't got no duckling. You got that strawberry outta one of them biomes. You ain't got no duckling nor nothing.'

Harold brings out first his right hand, snaps his fingers. Nothing. Brings out his left hand. Snaps his fingers. Nothing.

'I knew it,' says Lenny.

'Well, sorry about the duckling,' says Harold with a bow, 'but you can have this.' Suddenly he spins around, crouches down and then throws his arms out, hands clasped together. There in his cupped hands is a bird.

Lenny stares. 'It ain't a duckling – is it?' he says at last.

'It's a pigeon,' says Harold. 'Now do ya want it or not?'

243

'I want it, but I ain't got nothing to feed it on,' says Lenny very solemnly.

'Then I'll just have to let it go back where it came from.' In one motion Harold throws the pigeon in the air. It flies high. Lenny watches it, eyes wider than saucers. The pigeon whirls in the air, circles, comes lower, circles again, and then suddenly turns, as if it knows where it's going, and flies straight off.

Harold turns and winks at me. 'One of the army's homing pigeons,' he whispers. 'But it cheered him up.'

Lenny's still watching the bird.

'Thank you,' I whisper back.

'So, young lady.' Harold turns to me. 'What do *you* want?'

I shake my head.

'Have a think about it. When you're ready, let me know.'

'It'll take more than a snap of your fingers to get me what I want.'

'Pity,' says Harold.

'It is,' I say.

'I don't mean it that way.'

'What way do you mean it, then?'

'I mean that it's a pity you don't believe in magic,' he says.

40

Back in the room with the ripped floor I hold Lenny. He can't sleep.

'Why ain't nobody happy here?' he asks.

'Sshh.'

'There's food. And it smells nice.'

'Let's look at your book.'

He tugs it out from under his top. It's damp, crumpled.

I open it at the tens page where all the bees are buzzing.

'On the farm they had ten –' I pause.

'They've got bees,' says Lenny. 'I seen them today, real live bees in that biome and there's loads of 'em.'

'Yes,' I say.

'And they didn't die, did they?'

'No, they adapted.'

'Adapted?'

'They've got used to living in the biomes. They could probably live outside of them too.'

'But what about the radiation?'

'The biomes don't keep out the radiation. They just keep the bees in.'

'Tell me about the radiation.'

'You know about it,' I say.

'But I don't,' he says. 'I never really did.'

'Well,' I start. 'Long ago, they were pretty clever and they discovered lots of things like electricity and –'

'Proper food,' says Lenny.

'They grew lots of it –'

'On farms.'

'Why don't you tell the story then?'

He shakes his head.

'They invented a way of making electricity from nuclear energy.'

I pause. I can see Lenny's eyes drooping. He's tired.

'And just when nuclear energy made everything work fine, somebody blew it up.'

His eyes open up a bit. He wants to ask: Whadda they wanna do that for?

But his eyelids sink lower instead.

'All of it,' I whisper. 'And then we got this.'

Tarquin visits me in the night. In dreams he comes to me, out of the waters of a great river. He wears a tunic of white cotton. 'I have come to take you home,' he says.

He folds me in his arms. He holds me to his breast. He kisses my hair. He chants a sad hymn to the sound of tin pans beating. The whole of the underworld is filled with music.

'I have paid the price for your freedom,' he tells me. 'Now you must follow me up, out of the darkness, out of the Valley of Shadows, into the sunlight.'

He holds my hand one last time, kisses me until my lips are hot with desire. 'I will lead you to the upper world,' he says. 'And you must believe in me. Follow wherever I go, but do not call out to me, do not tempt me to turn and look upon you, for your beauty will bewitch me, and I will not be able to lead the way. The curse will be unleashed, and you will remain forever in the underworld.'

And together we climb up the long hill towards the light, where the sun forever shines in a valley, where a brook forever runs, and the grass is filled with wild white clover.

But just as we reach the doorstep between the worlds, and he crosses the threshold, I forget my promise and call out, 'Tarquin!'

And he turns, being already in the sunshine. His face is lit up for a moment in dazzling light.

Then the door to the underworld slams shut.

And I am left in darkness.

41

The next morning dawns.

We aren't taken back to Biome Thirty-four. We're lined up and marched to the green, our numbers recorded. We're taken into the courthouse. Once again the long hut, the long benches. There're more of us, new arrivals. They sit on the benches too.

At the far end sits the General.

I feel physically ill. I can't avoid him. The balding head, the watery little eyes, the cruel mouth, the sloping teeth. My heart thumps. I break into a cold sweat. My boiler suit sticks to my back.

'I'm scared,' says Lenny.

I wrap my arm around him. He's shivering.

'What're they gonna do?'

'It's part of the journey,' I say. I hold him close.

He rests his chin on my arm.

'The hard part again?'

'Yes. This is the really hard part.'

One by one, each goes and stands in front of the General's table. The short man in camouflage reads out the charge. He's got a gun strapped to his thigh. Oh yes, I remember him. The adjutant who told us we were a pile of shite.

'Out after curfew.' A girl with mousey hair.

'Loitering with intent.' A young man.

'Two years' hard labour.' Judgement for both.

It isn't any different when it comes to us.

'Where were you going?' barks out the adjutant.

'Scotland,' says Lenny, before I have time to shush him.

'Why?' says the man.

'We was going to live there,' says Lenny. His voice trembles. His eyes seek mine. I don't shake my head. He knows it was our secret. They drag him forwards.

'Explain.'

'We was going to make blackberry crumble.'

The adjutant pushes Lenny to the side. Turns on me. 'I'm going to put the question to you again. Where were you going?'

'We were escaping,' I say. 'We were escaping from the Bone Cross Bone gang. We were trying to get out of London.'

The General smiles.

'And how were you going to feed yourselves?' says the adjutant.

'We had some food.'

'How much?'

'A bag of potatoes.'

'And after that?'

'We'd look for work.'

A look shoots from the adjutant to the General.

He nods.

'Two years' hard labour each. The child can stay in the biomes. The girl is for house service.'

The General looks at me. He's smiling. A light sweat glistens on his upper lip. He leans forward and hisses, '*This is going to be fun, isn't it?*' He flicks an eyebrow up. A soldier steps forwards, wrenches Lenny from me. Drags him away.

Lenny's eyes plead. He raises a hand, as if to hold on to me. 'The hard part,' I whisper.

His thin frame is trembling like a leaf. He twists free from the soldier, races to me, clings on. Instantly the adjutant steps in, whacks Lenny across the head and yanks him off me.

Lenny screams, all legs and arms, stamping, punching, then he's pulled off through the door. At the last moment he turns. His face is lit up by a sunbeam from outside.

Then the door slams shut, and he's gone. I'm left in the darkness.

They lead me out through another exit. No sniggering faces. No jokes. *Poor Lenny.* They all know why I'm singled out.

Two years' hard labour. The General with his watery eyes. *Poor Lenny.* Tarquin flogged and locked up.

O ye Gods. Don't desert us.

42

They march me straight out of the hut, out of the village, down a long lane that must've once been a farm track. Packed earth, patched in places with broken-up rocks. Line of weeds growing down the centre. On the hills ahead I can see the fence outlined against the sky.

Think of something.

But I can't. A long, slow ache starts, as if everything that ever meant anything is draining out of me. Nan. Tarquin. Lenny. It's no use planning for tomorrow. Tomorrow isn't going to be any different from today. We are stuck in the underworld. No torch to light the way. The Valley of Shadows has won.

We turn a corner. The flag is flying over an old manor house. Barns turned into garrisons. So this is where the General stays. We march on. The soldiers are suddenly quiet. The girl's face haunts me. *Golden hair. Frightened eyes. Once so beautiful. One eye black and swollen.* Tramp of boots. One of my laces snaps. What to do about it?

Nothing.

They escort me to the back of the manor house. Tradesmen's entrance. They shove me into the kitchen. Worn, uneven flagstones. Low ceilings with thick, darkened beams. A wooden table stretches down the centre, big cooking pots line one wall.

They tell the woman, 'You're to oversee her now. She's not to be touched. Not one bruise. You know the drill. You're to set it up, leave the room and pack for him. He's looking forward to seeing her before he leaves. He's going straight from here to Andover. MoD business, he says, so pack formal.'

The woman makes some kind of noise in her throat as if she's completely put out.

'After that, put her to work. Give her freedom. Don't break her spirit. He likes to do that himself.'

'As if I don't know,' says the woman.

My days! They're all in it together.

They leave. I sit on a stool, stare at the door, like I'm catching my breath, about to make a run for it. *You better think quick, girl. Better come up with a good plan.*

'Don't even try,' she says.

I look at her.

'There's five miles of nothing but radiated scrub before the fence. It's patrolled. You won't get over it, nor under it, nor round it. If they catch you it's going to be even worse for you.'

Can it be? I doubt it. But I don't say a word. I don't know who she is. I don't know whose side she's on. Probably her own. She isn't going to help me, anyway. She's the one it's probably going to be worse for.

'What d'you get anyway?'

'Two years.'

'Two years is going to pass,' she says, 'a lot quicker than ten.' She starts chopping up tomatoes.

Ten years. Tarquin. I wish my brain would work.

I look at the table. On it is a plate piled high with some kind of flat baked biscuit. Something is cooking too in the pot on the range. It smells good. My mouth waters. I try not to let it.

'Think about it.'

'Where do they take children?' I ask.

She snorts. 'They don't make any allowances for kids, except less rations.' She places the knife on the table, piles up the chopped tomatoes.

'But where?'

'Probably on seed picking,' she says. 'Little fingers, nimble hands. They send them there.'

Poor little Lenny.

'It's not that bad,' she says. She must've seen my face. She sluices off the chopping board – thick, solid marble. Lays it beside the knife on the table.

And I think what little Lenny's been through: his mum gone, the ghetto and the Limehouse gang and Careem. And now separated from Tarquin.

It *is* all that bad.

He didn't deserve it. He's tried to be happy and kind and hopeful. I think of his worried little face. His blackberry crumble. A hole opens up inside my heart.

And I think of Scotland, and even if we did two years and

we left a note for Tarquin telling him we're going on ahead, and we'd wait for him up there by Hadrian's Wall, who's to say we wouldn't get caught by the next patrol and do another two years at the next place?

And anyway, there's no cottage in Scotland.

I'd almost forgotten that.

Scotland is made up of bareness and radiation and no hope. It *is* that bad.

I sink into a chair.

'It isn't them you should be worrying about, anywise,' says the woman. 'It's you.' She pulls a skewer out of a drawer, tests the meat that's cooking in the pot, lays the skewer beside it on the range.

So she knows about Tarquin and Lenny? I sigh. She's going to be annoying.

'I'll put you straight. I'm his aunt, Marcy, and I run his house. I'm not fond of you girls.'

She goes to a cupboard and removes a hammer from it. She crosses over to a chair and hammers at its seat. 'Loose nail,' she says. 'Keeps catching when you sit down.'

So she's a relative, called in because he can't trust anyone else?

'He's going to use you up and wring you out like a rag.'

'Can I have one of those biscuits?'

'Last girl was good looking like you. She went to the quarry pit.'

'Quarry pit?'

'Threw herself off the top into the old stone quarry.'

Great. Very cheerful.

'Couldn't stand any more.'

'I see.'

'And I don't blame her. I've no time for that side of things.'

With that she reaches over, passes me a biscuit and goes out, leaving me sitting there in the kitchen.

I nibble at the biscuit, chewing each bite and pushing it around in my mouth. The whole kitchen is brimming with food. Large baskets line the far wall: carrots, onions, tomatoes, parsnips, turnips, cabbages. Jars of pickles and sauces and preserved fruit stacked up on the dresser. And meat too, simmering in that pot. Not dog. I poke it with the stirring spoon. Looks like tender breast of chicken or duck and sliced up side of bacon.

I'm not going to starve.

Quickly I cross to the baskets. I pick out two carrots, a round red tomato and a handful of lettuce. I take three more biscuits. I fold the lettuce and crunch into it. I pierce the side of the tomato and suck out the sweet pips and inner flesh and, as I finish it off, I tuck the carrots into my pocket. Then I cross to the pot, pick up the skewer, hook out a whole leg of chicken. I pass it from hand to hand, blowing on it, until it is cool enough to bite into.

As I chew and swallow tomato, chicken, lettuce, I feel energy return. Then I pick up the knife from the table. Sharp as a razor. I test it with my thumb.

Don't know if that woman was trying to give me a hint.

Maybe the last girl went to the quarry pit.

This one has a different plan.

43

Slowly I put the knife down again. So what exactly *am* I going to do? I look around, trying to make up my mind. Flagstones, cooking range, crockery, cast-iron pans. There's one there, right on the sideboard. I could grab it. I could smack the General over the head with it and bust his skull.

In fact the kitchen's full of things I could use. My first thought is to grab one.

Such a choice. They're all laid out before me: sharp knife, marble block, skewer, iron pan, hammer. My eyes flick from one to the next. But there's something very wrong about it. Like it's somehow staged. Why would you put a girl like me, who you're just about to abuse, and who you *know* can stab you up – I remember the safety pin and smile – in a kitchen with so many weapons? Are you crazy?

That General is definitely not crazy. He may be vile and revolting and a sadist, but he's not stupid. You don't get to be a general if you're stupid. I've looked in his face too and seen his intelligence – all depraved and simmering there at the back of his eyes. Only stupid people arm desperate victims.

So is Marcy stupid? I think about that. She didn't look it.

And if she is, why hasn't she been fired by now? This isn't the first time he's played this little game, is it?

So what *is* going on?

What was it that officer said to Marcy? 'She's not to be touched. Not one bruise. You know the drill. You're to set it up, leave the room and pack for him. He's looking forward to seeing her before he leaves.'

What was that all about?

The General's coming to see me, as soon as he's done at court, before he goes to Andover. He's coming to check out his latest little toy.

That's it. I'm a toy.

So what's his game?

'You know the drill. You're to set it up and leave the room.'

Marcy was laying weapons out. I didn't take much notice while she was doing it. But she put the knife on the table, then the marble slab, then the skewer by the range, then the bloody great big hammer.

'You're to set it up and leave.'

So that's his game. Give pretty little Melissa a fighting chance. Is that how the game works?

But why? He can do what he likes with me. All he's got to do is call a few soldiers and I couldn't do a thing. But maybe that'd be too easy for him. I remember him saying he liked them 'spirited'. I remember his words at the court. 'This is going to be fun, isn't it?'

And what's the fun if there's no fight? He's a general and a general's a soldier and soldiers fight.

He wants a fight.

He gets off on beating the shit out of his enemy.

He's into submission.

So that's the kind of game he's going to play with me. I try to remember the girl who staggered out of his room in London. The one with the beautiful blonde hair. She'd lost the game. Hadn't she. Because she was a beginner and he a veteran. Because he's been playing this game for a long time. What're the rules then? He played it with her. But remembering her face gives me no clue.

Think.

I pick up the blade from the table again. It's very sharp. It's very heavy. One stab with that and I could finish him off forever. But if Marcy has 'set it up', he'll know I've chosen the knife the minute he walks in. He'll have prepared for that. He'll have his own little knife-defence strategy going on. All ready and waiting. He's playing a warped war game, isn't he? One in which he is always the winner.

I get it. Choose your weapon. Let's see if you can win. A duel. A weird, sicko, twisted duel.

He wants to see what I'll choose and that will determine the kind of game he plays. He'll have some kind of defence for each one of them.

Sick bastard.

I'm not going to play his game. He's not going to be in charge of this fight. I don't need his choice of weapons. He's in for a shock. Because if he wants a fight, he's going to get it. And I'm going to be the one calling the shots.

I'll play a game with him, all right.

A game he's never played with any girl before.

I think back to the streets of London. Back to Nan, who said: 'Grow tough, then grow tougher.'

Quickly I cross the room. I get two kitchen towels, the woven kind. I bind them round my forearms. I don't really need to, but it puts me in the right mood. My fighting mood.

When the towels are tight enough, and I feel I'm ready for the streets, I roll my sleeves back down and sit at the table.

I know what I'm good at. I know the fight I can take to him.

I'm good at fighting dogs.

He enters. A smug look on his face. I watch him carefully. I see his eyes flick from knife to block to skewer to pan and hammer. I was right. He's planned it. He looks across at me, confused. As if he expected something different. Expected I would be more spirited, disappointed I'm not.

I sit there, fold my arms across my chest so I can feel my bound forearms. I'm watching. And I'm ready.

I stand up. 'Shall we play then?' I say.

He looks even more confused. His eyes flick from block to carving knife to skewer again.

'Well,' he says. 'I think I'd like to sample the goods – which, by the way, I've already paid for – before I'm off to Andover. Just a taste, so that I can look forward to savouring you, at my pleasure, when I get back.'

'Go for it,' I say. 'Come and take a little taste, Mr Bigshot.'

He advances. I stand up. I turn to face him. He hesitates.

He's used to people running, crying, cringing, begging. Instead I take my stance. I place my feet about a pace apart, and I crouch, watching.

His eyes travel again around the kitchen, as if he's sure I must have armed myself with something. He doesn't know I prefer my bare hands. I wedge my foot against the cooker. I stare at him. And I wait.

He's baffled. All his little manoeuvres are of no use. He's got to think on his feet now. At last he shrugs as if he doesn't care. He's hungry for his 'little taste'. He glances at his watch. He hasn't got that long.

I crouch down a little lower. I stare a little harder. *He's just a dog, like the rest of them. Bigger, cleverer. Still a dog. You can do it, Melissa.*

He moves round the table towards me. He doesn't care about my crouch. He doesn't care about the staring. Maybe the sight of me makes him aroused. *You've survived countless dog fights.* He doesn't even try to meet my gaze. *You can take him out.* He doesn't waver. He just lets out a short little laugh.

I crouch lower and shake my head in a sideways motion, like a bull before a charge. The General hesitates, stops. He flicks his eyes around, suddenly notes my stance. He laughs again. My shaking head worries him though. *Good. You should be worried. Arsehole. I'm going to break your neck.*

He rubs his hands together. He's still worried.

I grind my teeth, bare them at him, growl softly. *Just another dog. Focus on that. Get it absolutely right.*

He springs towards me, fist ready to punch me out.

I grab his outstretched arm. I twist it sideways, rip it at an

260

unhealthy angle to his body. I feel his shoulder joint jolt. With a scream, he goes down on his knees.

But he's heavy and I'm light. I can't hurl him to the flagstones.

He lunges back at me. Grabs my left arm. I shift, wedge my foot more firmly against the range.

I raise my right hand, feel around for that pot of hot stew. Can I do it? My arm's well wrapped. I've taken precautions. I shift the pot towards me, get a hold on the handle, and quick as lightning I smash the pot right at him. Boiling stew, searing, scorching pain. But he feels it most. My arm is wrapped in five layers of towelling. His isn't.

Good. Get up now. You tosser.

Hold your ground, Melissa. Wait for the right moment.

He staggers upright, screaming.

And before Marcy bursts in, I kick him in the nuts. Hard.

Marcy calls for soldiers.

Soon they're crowding in.

I know when I'm outnumbered. I know when the dog pack is too big for me, so I step back. 'OK,' I say. 'You win.'

The General's writhing in pain. 'Don't let the soldiers in, you *idiot*,' the General hisses, furious with Marcy. 'Send them away.'

I want to laugh. Oh my God. He's embarrassed! His latest little toy was too much for him! Don't let the troops know!

Marcy sends the soldiers off, whips around the kitchen

putting the implements away, and stands there not knowing what to do.

The General drags himself to a chair. 'Fetch a bowl of water, you imbecile,' he bellows at Marcy.

She brings him the bowl. The General thrusts his burned arm into it.

He looks at me, as if he's about to fetch a gun and shoot me. I don't push my luck. He's in no shape to attack me again. Not right now. Marcy faffs around until the General can move, but he still can't stand without groaning.

'I'm late,' is all he mutters.

When he can walk, Marcy helps him out of the kitchen. I douse my arm in cold water too, but even though my skin is fiery red it's going to be OK. The towels did their job. Then I set about mopping up the spilt stew. I keep all the bits, the chicken and the vegetables. I swill them off with water, eat as much as I can and hide the rest.

Before long the General's back. He is in charge of himself now, as if nothing has happened. Nothing except a bandaged arm and second degree burns. He's got a clean uniform on. But he moves very gingerly. He smiles politely. Marcy's carrying his dispatch case. One hand's in his uniform pocket. And as he steps across to me, I can see he's in pain. *Good. Serves you right, you sicko.*

He tries to reach out with his good hand, to touch my cheek. I flinch and step back.

'As for you, my dear,' he hisses, 'I'll be back very shortly. Getting to know you is going to be a lot more exciting than I first thought.' He draws back his lips from his teeth in an ugly sneer. 'But make no mistake, I won't underestimate you a second time.'

I don't bother to reply. He's run out of time.

'Oh no. You've had your fun,' he blusters.

He taps his crotch in the most disgusting manner.

'It's my turn next.'

44

Marcy stays away from me for the rest of the day. She's furious as well. *And* in disgrace. As I move about the house doing boring duties, I hear her alternately weeping then cursing.

Apart from Marcy I don't see another soul for the rest of the day.

I'm desperate for news of Lenny and Tarquin. I must leave, find a way to see them. I get down the lane and across one field. The soldiers stop me, roughly get hold of me, escort me back, shove me around, insult me.

'Try that again, you little slag, and watch what we'll do,' one of them threatens.

He twists my neck and forces my face down onto his trousers, rubbing himself against me.

'We ain't all as sporting as the General,' he laughs.

He pushes so hard I can't breathe.

'And you'll get it from all of us,' adds another.

I don't try again.

I check out the area I'm allowed to roam in. The house, big and rambling, but mostly locked up. The grounds, overgrown rolling lawns. A walled garden. The glass greenhouses where the General grows orchids. Some pens with livestock. I watch and wait and go about my duties: mopping floors, cleaning, polishing, dusting, putting out rubbish, taking in deliveries.

At last someone comes. A knock at the kitchen door.

'Deliveries.'

I cross the flagged floor, open it. There stands Harold, the guy who gave Lenny the strawberry.

'Settling in?' he says.

He eyes all the produce. I don't say anything.

'You'll want the news.'

'Thanks for yesterday,' I say.

'You'll want to hear how the little boy's doing.'

Is it so obvious I'm desperate for news? 'Why're you here?' I say.

'And how your young man's making out in the slammer.'

Tarquin? I open my eyes wide. 'He's not my young man,' I say.

'Bet he'd like to be.'

I close my mouth. Let him think what he likes. I remember Nan. 'Them as stay quiet, learn more.'

'Well I don't have long, so what news d'you want first?'

Who exactly is he? This is the third time he's just turned up. He seems to be able to do what he likes, go where he wants, be everyone's friend, be invisible to soldiers, even. That means he's got to be dodgy.

'I'm never any good at remembering names,' he says. He offers me his hand.

I take it. 'I'm Melissa,' I remind him. 'And it was Lenny. You were kind to Lenny.'

'Pleased to meet you, Melissa. I suppose you know your name means *queen bee*?'

I nod. I like the addition of 'queen'.

'Mine, Harold, means *leader of the army*. It's something I'm working on. Obviously.'

I smile. That was funny.

'Now have you thought any more about magic?'

'No,' I say. 'Sleight of hand and fooling six year olds isn't magic.'

'Pity,' he says. 'I was going to offer to solve all your problems.'

'I wish.'

'You could try believing,' he says. 'After all, it can't get much worse, can it?'

He's right. It can't.

'I want something more than news or strawberries,' I say. 'I want to know how to get out of here.'

He shrugs. 'Isn't that what we all want?'

'I don't know about everybody else,' I say. 'That's what *I* want. Right out, and not back to London.'

'It's not impossible,' Harold says. He eyes me warily.

My eyebrows raise a little.

He makes a motion like he's washing his hands. 'You help me. I help you.' He continues gazing at me, unsmiling, thoughtful. 'Takes two,' he says. 'One hand to wash the other.' He pauses. 'With cooperation,' he adds, 'anything is possible.'

He unloads some baskets onto the kitchen table. All the time keeping his attention on me, watchful. 'Perhaps we have some common ground?'

He carries on unloading the deliveries, piles carrots on the table. He goes out, disappears round the side of the house, reappears with a box of cherries and some onions. 'Perhaps we could come to an understanding?'

He steps back into the kitchen, hangs the string of onions on the back of the door. 'We're all human after all,' he says, 'and this camp was only designed by humans.'

I take a handful of cherries and wait.

Nan always said, 'You can tell when a horse wants to go home. Just give it a free rein and it'll carry you with it.'

I never even saw a horse till yesterday, let alone rode one. But I give Harold free rein. I want to see where he'll take this.

'But only a very few humans control it. One, the current internal manager – he controls the black market – and two, the adjutant.' Harold sits down and watches me closely, his eyes cautious, calculating.

'That foul man in camouflage?'

'And three, the General, of course.'

The cherries are sweet beyond belief. I try not to look like I've never eaten any before.

'Power,' he says, 'isn't given. You have to seize it. Every time you don't take power you allow others to take it from you.'

Carefully I spit the stones into the palm of my hand.

'We can change things,' he says. 'We can achieve the impossible, but we must be ready to cooperate, ready to seize power, ready to use it, don't you think?'

I stay quiet. I don't think I'm supposed to say anything.

He looks at me. 'Are you ready to seize power?'

The air seems to suddenly crackle with a dangerous energy. I'm supposed to say something now. But I hesitate. I change the subject.

'I'd like to hear the news first,' I say. 'Lenny and Tarquin?'

He nods, still attentive. 'Lenny's in a house two doors from where you slept last night with a nice young woman, and your young man's in the prison cells.'

My young man? That's the second time he's said it. For a moment I catch a glimpse of Lenny and Tarquin and me from the outside. A little loving unit.

Harold watches me.

A little loving unit split up and scattered. A lump forms in my throat.

'They're alive,' says Harold. 'That is the most important thing, and with life and *cooperation*' – he stresses the word – 'anything is possible – even a reunion.' He pauses as if he's asked a question.

'Reunion isn't enough,' I say. 'We need to get out.'

He nods again as if I've passed some kind of test. 'With *cooperation*,' he repeats, '*everything* is possible.'

'*Theoretically*,' I say bitterly. 'There's a huge fence and the army between us and out there.'

'True,' says Harold. 'But the army are only *human* and entirely controlled by *only* three people. Imagine if there were a change of power. Imagine if Billson, our current internal manager, were replaced by someone who had a mind to help you?'

'There's still the adjutant and the General,' I say.

'But this new internal manager would have access to all kinds of things.'

'Like?' I take more cherries.

'Well, he'd control all the comings and goings, all shipments in and out.' Harold smiles, a sly curl of the lips. 'To be precise –' he taps the table –

'Food out to London,

'Food out to Newcastle,

'Coal in from Newcastle,

'All rations to all camp inmates,

'All work details, paperwork and supply checks.'

'The army don't do any of that?' I ask, surprised.

He shakes his head. 'Prisoners do everything.'

'So what work detail are you on now?' I ask, suddenly aware that he too is a cog inside this huge prisoner-run system.

'General deliveries,' he says. 'I almost forgot.' He disappears outside again, round the side of the doorframe, and reappears after a minute with a stack of boxes on a trolley. 'General's special supplies,' he says. 'Last of the crop. Let's hope he can make them stretch.'

The boxes are full of bottles.

'Wine: six crates. Brandy, three star: one crate. Produce of Biomes Seven and Eight. You must sign here.'

I've never seen wine or brandy before. I take care not to let my jaw go slack.

'Do you think you'd *like* to cooperate?' he says after I've signed. 'Because when everything's said and done, all you need to do is ask yourself: would a change of internal manager be in your interests? Ask yourself what the current manager does for you now. Then consider what another, one who you'd helped up the ladder, could do for you – if he had the means.'

I smile. *The horse has found his way to the stable, Nan, just like you promised.* 'Tell me more,' I say.

'Here's the thing,' he says. 'I've got access to every house in the camp.' He stacks the crates up by the cellar door. 'I've got cooperation in every terrace, barrack and biome going. I control all the news. That much power I have already seized. I've cooperation on every shift, detail, work gang, train arrival and departure, but I haven't got cooperation in the General's quarters, not since Dora jumped.' He hastily crosses himself and adds, 'Poor Dora.'

'So that's where I come in?'

'So while you consider the offer, d'you want the news in full?'

I nod. I do want more news.

'Lenny's fine. He's in that house, as I told you, on the old village high street. The woman's given him a second apple. She's kind and is looking out for him. Lenny doesn't seem to mind. He's made friends with her kids, 'specially Tommy. He's missing you, though.'

'And Tarquin?' I say.

'He's settling down in the slammer,' says Harold. 'His trial is set for sometime next month. The officer he mangled had to be transferred and won't be back for a while.'

I let myself relax, just a little.

'It's going to be a big case. He'll probably get a flogging and, if he survives it, ten years. He's happier, though, since I gave him news of Lenny, and he's my cooperation in the old police cells at the moment.'

A flogging. If he survives.

'We've got to get out of here before that trial,' I say.

270

'So, are you going to cooperate or not?' says Harold. 'He's got a fortnight's solitary, by the way, to start off with.'

Ten years.

'Can you get us out?' I say bluntly.

'Yes or no?' says Harold, his eyes suddenly narrowing.

I nod, my mind racing. 'When does the General get back from Andover?'

'Maybe a few days, a week at most,' says Harold.

I look up at him. 'What've I got to do?' I ask.

'Just keep your eyes and ears open for now, remember who comes, who goes, what they bring, what they take, what they say, who they say it to. Think about seizing power. How the forest can be felled. News is what I want. Insider knowledge. Intelligence is my business.'

'Is that all?' I ask.

'For now.'

'And later?'

'A bit of borrowing and a bit of replacing, maybe.'

'Thieving and lying you mean?'

'Well, all property is theft if you want to get moral,' he says. 'And, before you ask, I also deal in blackmail.' His eyes go snake cold. 'So if you're in, you stay in.' He watches me steadily, so I get the point. 'Are you in? Speak up, because I told Lenny I'd bring him word.'

I look at him. He's got all the cards, hasn't he? He pulls the last one out.

'By the way,' he says, 'this is yours.'

On the table he puts the key ring. My key ring. With its little picture of the cottage.

'How'd you get it?'

'Ways and means.'

'Can you get my coat too?'

'I get what I like,' he says.

I think of Nan, the dogs, the wharf.

'Please?'

'Nothing easier . . .' He leaves the 'if' unspoken in the air of the kitchen.

'I'm in,' I say. 'I don't know your plan, but I'm in.'

'Good,' he says. 'I'll be back tomorrow with detailed news and a few little jobs for you.'

I nod.

'Till then: one, ears; two, eyes. And in particular, Mrs Fellowes of fifty-two Barlow Street wants news of whether Dora ever got the sewing kit. You could just check on that for her. I believe it was in the General's downstairs study.'

'Here,' I say. I grab the package of chicken and vegetables salvaged from the stew. 'Give them to Tarquin. Get the coat, give it to Lenny. Can you?'

'Of course,' he says. 'I can work magic.'

And with that he leaves.

I find a bit of string. I thread it through the key ring. I hang it round my neck. I look at the little cottage in its plastic setting, the roses, the valley and the mountains. Then I close my fist over everything. I hold it tight. 'If only we were there,' I whisper into my closed hand. If only.

I set about putting away the deliveries. I hope to God Harold isn't all talk. For the first time since we were thrown in the back of the lorry, I allow myself to hope. I'll help Tarquin like

he helped me. I'll save Lenny from this horrible place.
And if the General tries to touch me again –
I'll kill him.

45

I keep my eyes and ears open. I need news I can trade with Harold. Something that will shift the balance of power.

I find out everybody hates the General, except maybe Marcy. He oversees all the farm camps north of London. He oversees the main rail link to the coal mines. This house was once part of a country estate. The village was called Compton Powell. Biomes One to Ten produce luxury items entirely for consumption by the army elite. Biomes Eleven onwards are supposed to grow staple food crops for the nation. The rest of the army takes them.

I find out the farm ships trashy foodstuff up north, to the coalfields, for extortionate rates, and pays very little for the coal. I find out the coalfields in the Midlands are coal camps like this one, but their output is low. They can't turn convicts into miners, apparently.

I find out there's a huge black market inside the camp. Corruption is everywhere. The black market's controlled by the internal manager, Mr Billson – and I begin to understand what Harold could achieve if he had the job.

And he's right. The prisoners do everything, including

overseeing. The army conducts checks, but each work-gang officer varies. Some are Philistines. Some are not. Some regularly flog workers. Most workers are half starved and have to steal to eat.

But I'm pretty sure that Harold knows all that, so I try to listen out for the things he might not.

Marcy, the General's aunt, sends me down to the chicken farm in Biome Six to collect the eggs. It's very close. On the old estate. That's why I'm allowed to go. I'm surprised I *am* allowed to go. But I don't fool myself. The minute I put one foot too far, I'll be for it. Marcy tells me exactly where I can go and where I can't. She especially dwells on what will happen if I don't believe her. She tells me (with some relish) that since Dora, the General isn't going to let any bird fly the coop a second time.

I use the freedom. Though I don't trust Marcy one bit. I remember her laying out the weapons in the kitchen. Maybe she has new orders. Perhaps the General is planning some different game. One where he lets me loose on the estate and hunts me down. I wouldn't be surprised. It'd be no fun for him if I didn't know where I was going. So I explore as thoroughly as I can, noting hiding spots, short cuts, watercourses, and timing myself between points.

I make the trip to Biome Six. I enter the pen, throw the house waste to the chickens, and add a helping of chaff that

275

came in from Biome Twenty-five. I collect the eggs. I crack two into the bowl I brought the waste in. I mix them up with my finger and drink them down. I've put myself on a fattening diet. *Grow tough, grow strong. You won't be able to outsmart anyone if you're weak.*

Then I head back to the manor. I jog to build stamina. On the way I notice that certain points in the stone wall around the estate have collapsed. I notice that some of the walkways can be roped off.

I nod my head.

I know your game. I've guessed it. You'll set me up. You'll open the cage. You'll watch me try to escape. Then you'll hunt me down.

The jog tires me out completely. I'm not ready for his new game. I've got to get out before that. And he'll be back soon. Four days have gone already.

I shiver. *Did Dora really jump? Or did you hunt her up to the old quarry? Did you give her a choice: jump or submit? Or did you use her up then force her over?*

I need news to trade with Harold.

Before it's too late.

I take a shortcut through the coppice and head for the General's greenhouses. On the main door is a sign: NO ADMITTANCE. I suppose that means me too. Though I take no notice. The General's away, and the sign looks very old. Like it was put there long ago when people obeyed rules and there was order and safety.

And I need a quiet place to think. To plan. Plus the sign annoys me. If the General did have it put there, then I'm going in. So I push on the double doors. The locks on them are old;

one door should be bolted to the floor but it's not. It only takes a bit of shaking for both to give.

Inside is an old-fashioned greenhouse, high clear spaces, glass panes, green-dappled light. Wooden frames. Bees hum. Beautiful. The sun sparkles through in diamond patterns. And curling upwards everywhere are orchids. The General's collection: rare, exquisite.

I stand there. Racking my brains for some brilliant plan. All the orchids have exotic names and are arranged alphabetically: *Acrolophia*; *Adamantinia*; *Aerides*, Fox Brush Orchid; Dragon's mouth; Cup Orchid; *Galeandra*, Hooded Orchid; *Galearis*, Showy Orchid.

I stand and breathe in thick perfumed air. Bees dart from flower to flower. Was it like this before? Were there multitudes of flowers? Priceless orchids as well as wayside blossoms? Birds and sunshine? Clouds casting shadows on sunny fields?

I try to imagine it.

Then I hear something. Instantly, I duck.

Voices of two men. Coming from inside, by the walled garden exit. So others come here to plan too. I take a big breath. I remove my shoes. No squeaks. I leave them behind a bed of *Hexalectris*. I slink over behind some *Mesadenus*. I crouch and listen.

'So,' says a deep male voice. Not one I recognise. I peer through the vines. He's in farm overalls with a cap, a belt and army boots. He's plump.

'So,' he says again. 'Over here.'

Another guy, I can't see him, answers. 'Order in from the west country.'

'Right.'

'They want honey.'

'How much?'

'We can charge them double. Their bees didn't survive. They've had to replace the lot. We got them over a barrel. Can charge what we like.'

They move a bit closer together. Are they workers or what?

'How many jars we got?'

'To spare? About two dozen.'

'If we can make that four dozen, we've got ourselves a real deal.' He moves. I move too. I want to see him. I step out from behind a Monk Orchid, move across a pathway and squat down inside a huge towering tangle of vanilla. I get a clear glimpse of him then: a short man in camouflage, carrying a baton. A gun strapped to his thigh. The adjutant from the courtroom shed.

I freeze. The heavy perfume of the flowers suddenly makes me dizzy.

'Army truck going out a week tomorrow?'

'One of ours in charge?' asks the adjutant.

'Yep, Eric from Fourth Battalion.'

'Right, if we get them on that.' The adjutant slaps his baton against the palm of his hand.

'We only got two dozen,' says the one in the farm overalls; then he whispers, 'But I got a plan.'

There's a silence. They drop their voices. I can't hear any more. I try to move closer. I tread on a piece of bark. It cracks. I freeze. My heart starts pounding.

Oh God, don't let them find me!

I crouch there in a cold sweat, waiting.

Through the hum of the bees I hear them still whispering.

So I wait, thinking about what plan they're hatching. Praying I'm not discovered. And suddenly, I get the best idea I've *ever* had. *My own plan.* All my watching and waiting and thinking has paid off.

I've discovered what these people want.

And I know just how to use it against them.

46

I'm biting my nails by the time Harold comes.

And even when he does, we can't talk, because Marcy's there. She's there all the time. It's almost like she knows I'm cooperating with him.

'Patience is a virtue,' he whispers in my ear as we go to unload the supplies from his cart. We carry the crates of vegetables into the kitchen, empty them into the baskets. I stack washed-out empty jars and load them into crates. Together we take the crates back to his cart.

I despair of ever getting a chance to tell him. He's about to leave, when a chance opens up. Marcy gets called out by a messenger.

Harold smiles. 'While the cat's away, the mice will – you know,' he says. 'I'm on two-cartload deliveries up here these next few days. The barracks are really making hay. When the General returns we'll all be back to rations.'

'I've got news,' I say. 'And an idea.'

'I have too,' he says.

'Yours first,' I say. 'How's Lenny?'

'Missing you,' he says and he hands me a drawing. It's of a

cottage. The sun is a big yellow circle in the sky with sunbeams like straight lines and a bush with red blobs that are berries and a rabbit. The rabbit is a bit wonky. It might be a squirrel. In the foreground are three people and they are all holding hands. One is a tall young man, and one has wavy hair and is a willowy girl, and one is small and has a big smile. My heart turns over. A lump somehow ends up in my throat. It sends a tingle up to my eyes.

'Wait,' I say. I pick up a piece of delivery packing paper and take the pen Harold carries for signing. I draw the same girl with wavy hair. She's got her arms around the smiling-face, stick child, and in her other hand she's holding the key. I make the key very large. I don't put Tarquin in the picture, because I'm not sure where to put him, but I draw in a straight line at the top and even though Lenny won't know what that is, I do: it's Tarquin's shoulders. I nip back into the kitchen. I take half a cooked chicken from the cold store. I wrap it in more delivery packing.

I give it all to Harold. 'For Lenny.'

He nods.

'Did you get the coat, and how's Tarquin?'

'I got the coat. I gave it to Lenny. Your young man's in a bad mood, but not in bad shape. Would you like me to take him a message?'

Suddenly I feel flustered. His words again – 'your young man' – hum inside me. I blush, turn away. I *do* want to send him a message. I don't know what, though. I stand there tongue-tied.

'When you're ready,' says Harold. 'Now your idea.'

'I got it,' I say.

'Got what?' says Harold.

'I've got an idea of how to outsmart the internal manager, so you can get his job.'

Harold draws up a chair, his face cold, serious.

'OK,' he says. 'Firstly, be clear. Secondly, realise this conversation could get us flogged or worse.'

I take in a deep breath.

Harold sits, waiting.

'We set the internal manager up,' I say.

'It's been tried,' Harold says. 'He's too smart.'

'Look,' I say. 'Tell me exactly how far he'll go?'

Harold lowers his voice. 'Everything from extortion to corruption to theft to bootlegging.'

'What drives him?' I say. 'What does he want?'

Harold thinks. 'Anything that gives him more power, more privilege, more control over others.'

'Right,' I say. 'What about exporting things? Will he sell stuff on to other camps or is all that internal?'

'It's the adjutant who deals with exports,' says Harold. 'Only the army can deal with anything beyond the fence. But there's lots of produce in and out – that's dodgy too,' he says. 'The produce from Biomes One to Ten, if you can get your hands on it, fetches big on the outside.'

'Then listen,' I say.

'It better be good,' says Harold, 'because it's dangerous.'

'Yesterday,' I say, 'you delivered six crates of wine here. The General's away and I signed for them. You said they were the last bottles of that crop. What if an order came in – from outside – saying they needed exactly six crates of wine and were prepared to pay anything for them? What would the adjutant do then?'

Harold considers. 'I see where you're coming from,' he says.

'Would he dare?' I say. 'Plot with the internal manager to come back to this house and steal wine from the General?'

'Oh yes,' says Harold. He pauses. 'But even if I could find someone to get such an order through, there's a huge problem.'

'What?' I say.

'The adjutant won't come here himself, and Billson, our internal manager, won't come without a cast-iron alibi, *and* a person he'll have set up to take the blame.'

'So we need a witness to destroy his alibi,' I say, 'and an idea of who he'll set up to take the rap.'

'They'll pin the blame on us,' says Harold straight away. 'If we don't catch Billson red-handed, he'll say I falsified the order and you colluded with it – that together we flogged the wine to a third party.'

'Then we'll have to be absolutely certain we catch him.'

Harold gets up off the chair, paces around the kitchen. 'What we need is a foolproof witness to denounce him, one who'll be believed – and we need to be able to get the crates back.'

He's right. But who is there to witness a theft from these cellars? I won't be any good. Not if I'm going to be blamed for it.

Suddenly Harold freezes. 'I know who'd be the perfect witness, who'd be ready to hide in the cellars, who'd denounce Billson and be believed. Oh, she'll denounce him all right.'

I look at him. 'Who?' I say.

'Marcy, of course. The maiden aunt, the one who longs to be in the General's good books. The one who'll do anything for him. And the one who's on site. Who better? That's who we'll put in charge of the wine.'

Of course. 'Set her up too!' I say.

'And after the incident here, before her nephew left, she'll do it. Redeem herself. Atone for making him look a fool.'

'You know about that?'

'Who doesn't?' he says.

'But how?'

'Soldiers talk, you know.' Harold's already heading for the door. 'Time's up. Now what was it you wanted to say to Tarquin?'

'Nothing,' I say. 'You concentrate on the plan, my bit too.' I step in front of him. Block his exit. 'If I help you with this, you'll get us out? Deal or no deal?'

'Your stuff is all possible,' says Harold. 'Always was. Blackmail. A little forgery. Release papers, travel permits. It's getting away with it, that's the tough bit. But once I've got rid of Billson, that's the thing! Now, Tarquin?'

'Tarquin can wait.'

But under my breath I add: Tarquin can wait *for me*.

Because suddenly I've decided, soldiers or no soldiers, carefully designed hunting grounds or not, I'm going to visit him myself.

47

During the course of the day, I raid the kitchen. Cooked chicken, slices of bacon, half a loaf of bread, as many apples as I can carry. I stash the food in little hideaways. The bread and meat under an upturned bowl, behind jars in the pantry; the apples tied in a scarf behind the rubbish bins. Then I sit down and draw myself a map of the estate. I write in every detail I've discovered. I mark the most likely sentry points and shade in the most risky areas to cross. I calculate the timings of the patrols. Impatiently I wait for nightfall.

When I'm certain Marcy's in bed, I creep down to the kitchen, collect the food and stow it in a bag. I tiptoe into the General's study. As quietly as I can, I slide up the sash window. It squeaks. The glass rattles. I freeze. *Don't let Marcy come.* A breeze ruffles the curtains, lifts the corners of papers, scatters them across the floor. Let them stay there. I listen for footsteps.

The first patrol passes. *All clear?* I sit on the window sill and swing my legs up and through. I duck my head and slide out. Across the flower border and I'm outside. Down three stone steps to the Great Drive. *Be very careful.* Soldiers might shoot first, ask questions later.

The Great Drive circles the house. It's wide, covered in gravel. I slip off my shoes. Hold them in my hand, tread carefully, so that no stones crunch underfoot. *Very, very quietly now, Melissa. Somebody will be on duty somewhere.* Carefully I cross the gravelled walkway, reach the steps to the formal garden. *Bit easier here. Hide behind those trees.* Rows of clipped trees like kids' drawings. Duck behind the rosebushes and hedges. *Will Tarquin be there? Will I get a chance to see him? Go back. Before it's too late.* In the moonlight I dart from hedge to hedge, the bag of food clutched tight to me. *Listen for the tread of booted feet.*

In the distance, voices. Soldiers? Maybe not, maybe workers still on their way home? *Don't move.* I stay hidden inside the formal garden until the voices fade.

I wait for the moon to go behind a cloud. Iron grey sky. I race across the wide lawn. At the far end I throw myself flat onto the grass. The drive curves up to the front door. I have to cross it. I lie very still by bushes, listening, watching. *Wait. They are there somewhere.* At last I see the guards, two of them in a small shelter by the walled garden, a thing like a playground house. I inch on my stomach to the very edge of the drive. I'm going to have to risk it. Now, before the clouds clear again. I worm my way across the drive. In the very centre the clouds break. I freeze. *Wait.* My heart pounds. Nothing.

I get into the woodland. Once there I keep close between the trees, watch behind me. It's only about half a mile down to the village. *Run now.* Fast. I pull my shoes back on and run.

On the far side of the woodland is a long avenue where people in the old days probably strolled on pleasant afternoons. I avoid it. I stay inside the tree line. Cross little glades where stone statues cavort. Bacchus, half naked, raises a marble hand with a short staff to the skies. Pan, bearded, horned, on cloven hooves, playing pipes. Eros, bow in hand. Urns on plinths.

For some reason, the statues remind me of my dream, when Tarquin came to me chanting hymns, banging pans. *His lips on mine.* I think of Nan and all her Gods.

Trees stretch up, smooth bark, twisting trunks, pulled out like barley twist on old furniture. Leafless. Cold. There's nobody in the woods. Nobody to follow me. *Be careful, Melissa. Make sure.* I crouch down and listen.

Nan told me that.

Never be too sure. Don't trust completely. The calm comes before the storm. Double check.

Out of the woods. Over the wall. Across the old village square to the back of the police station. Soldiers. Some of them are drinking. I hear conversations, coarse comments about girls, what they would do to them if they had their way.

I hide behind a barrel. *Don't let them catch you, Melissa.* They go on towards the village, swilling back their drink. Scatter. Shout. Move off towards the barracks. As quiet as a mouse, I slip round to the old police station.

Carefully I check the building – one storey high, low slate roof. At each window I raise myself up and peer in. Darkness. Silence. Cold stone. I whisper, 'Tarquin? *Tarquin?*'

Window after window. No answer. I'm three quarters of the way round the building, desperate.

At last, a little window. Too high. I pick up a tiny pebble and stand on tiptoe and throw it in. No glass. The pebble rattles against stone. I can just reach the bars. I hold on. '*Tarquin?*' I hiss.

'*Melissa?*'

Thank God.

There is a God.

'Go back,' he says. 'They'll catch you. They'll flog you.'

I doubt it. I don't tell him. I don't think the General will let anyone flog me. He'd prefer to do that himself.

'I'll be OK,' I say. 'I brought you food.'

I push the handle of the bag through the bars. 'Pull it in.'

'Thank heavens, I'm starving,' he says. 'I've been eating pig swill.'

He hauls the bag through the bars. 'Meliss, I can't do this much longer. I'm going to lose it. I don't wanna make things worse.'

'Hang on,' I say. 'Please, hang on. There's a plan.'

'How's Lenny?'

'He's fine.' No time for details.

'Be ready any time from now,' I whisper. 'You remember the moron guy, by the tunnel out of Games City?'

'Yeah?'

'As soon as I get you out, the guard needs the same treatment.' *Please let him understand.*

'What about Lenny?'

'We'll get him out. Just KO the guard as soon as he releases you. I'll sort everything else out.' I hope I will. I hope to God I will.

My mind starts spinning. *Just get Tarquin out.*

'OK,' he says.

'I gotta go.' I reach my hand as far as possible, press it to the bars, cold steel, chill stone. I push my fingers into the space between.

I'm expecting to feel his hand touch mine, but instead something warm and soft brushes my palm.

'Meliss'?' he says.

I can't answer. My heart's racing.

'Meliss'?' he says again. I feel his breath on my skin, hot, ticklish.

I try to speak. My throat closes up.

'Thank you,' he whispers and he presses his lips into the soft centre of my hand and kisses it.

48

It's not long before Harold's back.

'I've set it up,' he says.

'OK,' I say. 'But you haven't forgotten about Lenny, Tarquin and me getting out?' I say. I push the point home. 'I want your plan for that.'

'It's covered.'

'It better be,' I mutter.

'Right, let's get down to details: one, the wine order for Billson, the internal manager, will come soon, could be any moment. The truck those wine crates supposedly need to be shipped out on is leaving tomorrow afternoon, so it's going to be *very* soon.

'Two, the trick with this is not so much catching Billson red-handed – now that I fixed it so that Marcy will denounce him – but getting believable witnesses to denounce the adjutant. *That* is going to be *very* difficult. He's a powerful person around here and he'll back Billson. If any prisoner denounces *him*, they'll be sorry.'

I sigh. I didn't realise we'd have to oust the adjutant as well.

'But I've got one main man in Barrack Five who'd very

much like the adjutant's job and is ready to risk everything to get it. He's put his squad of soldiers on watching this place round the clock from now on. The official excuse is that I've told them you intend to do a runner.'

'*What?*' I rise to my feet, suddenly angry.

'Calmness,' says Harold quickly. 'That's only the official reason. It works in my favour, so when you go missing, they won't think I'm involved. On the contrary they'll know I tried to raise the alarm.'

'So how does it work in *my* favour?' I can't believe it. Harold is just taking care of Harold.

'Just hang on,' says Harold. 'First things first. Marcy Bruttlesworth, on side. I've informed her of the intended theft. She's enraged. She's going to sit guard over every wine bottle as if it were made of gold.

'But I've told her not to interrupt the theft. Because we want to trace the bottles to the soldiers who're behind it. I frightened her a bit, told her it's part of a coup being planned against the General, and the major in Barrack Five wants to expose the conspirators.

'So when Billson takes the bottles, she's to let him get away with it. I will have him followed by the Barrack Five squaddies. When he delivers the bottles to the soldiers at the truck station, I will get my wannabe adjutant to inform the inspection team that the current adjutant is allowing theft and profiting from plunder.

'Marcy will denounce Billson and will point a finger at the current adjutant as planning a coup.

'The inspection team will descend on the truck, find the

bottles and arrest everyone.

'And finally, Marcy will tell the General. Swear blind she heard them plotting against him, and I will be nominated by every main man I've got for promotion to internal manager. Barrack Five will provide a new adjutant. Marcy will be reinstated in the General's good books and –'

'Yeah,' I say, 'and what about me?'

'That is the beauty of this plan. You won't have to wait for my ascent to power. Tomorrow evening the coal train goes to Newcastle. While everything is in uproar you will go to the prison cells and use your charms, a bottle of brandy and a forged release order, "signed" by the soon-to-be disgraced adjutant.' He produces a bottle of brandy, a piece of paper and some clothes. 'And get your young man out.'

I take the bottle and look at the release paper. It looks genuine. I shake out the clothes: a top and a very short skirt. A kid's track suit. A hoody and jeans for Tarquin.

'What about Lenny?' I say.

'I will be being busy and honest and fully alibi-ed, between Biome Thirty-four with a soldier (who owes me a few favours) and Lenny – who, by the way, I've just had identified for a transfer – and Biome Sixteen, which is right beside the train station. I will escort young Lenny between the two biomes during the late afternoon shift.'

'O-K,' I say carefully.

'So I'll meet you all out back as the train's leaving, hand Lenny over, and my man in Biome Sixteen will swear blind I delivered him, but that he ran off on his own. All that's left then is for you to get on the train.'

It all seems very easy. Bit too easy.

'And how are you going to get us on the train?'

'Leave it to me,' says Harold.

I pray to God it'll work.

'Only one snag,' says Harold.

'What?'

'You mustn't let the charge officer at the police cells check that release paper.'

49

They make their move quickly. I'm almost off guard. One minute I'm running up and down in the big house, cleaning, sorting, chopping endless vegetables, washing endless plates till I'm sick of it. The next minute there's the internal manager with two others at the front door.

'Who are you?' says Billson. Like he doesn't know.

The second one goggles at me.

'Answer him,' says the third.

'Look, be quick,' says Billson, tapping his wrist like he's got a watch there. 'We're here on business.'

I don't say anything. I bob a real old-fashioned curtsey like Nan showed me. She'd learned how to do it for a play once, in her school.

They like the curtsey. The second one still can't take his eyes off me. He's staring. I don't like him.

'Who are you?' repeats Billson.

'I'm new here,' I say.

'Where's Marcy?' says Billson.

I think of Marcy sitting guard in the cellars. 'Gone out,' I say.

'Gone where and for how long?'

'I don't know. She didn't tell me. Ages, probably.'

One of the men laughs.

'Well, we'll need her,' he says. 'So you better go and find her.'

'What'll I say?' I ask.

'Just that she's supposed to be here to report, and she knows better than to leave a new girl on her own in charge of the big house.'

I clock what they're up to.

'OK,' I say. 'But who's going to be in charge, if I'm off?' I look at them like I don't know what they're planning.

'You better be quick then,' says one man, 'because nobody will be, and you'll be for the high jump if something goes missing.'

I'm right. I'm almost surprised. They're so bold. As soon as I'm down the drive fetching the elusive Marcy, they're going to be into the house and out with the crates.

But nevertheless, I curtsey again and bob up and down like I'm a bottle fallen into a bloody river, and then I'm off down the long drive.

And I'm smiling.

I'm smiling for real, because they don't know Marcy's watching everything. They don't know the Barrack Five boys are clocking them this very minute.

I remember Harold's words.

'Those barrack boys will be on duty. Any bottle that goes in or out from now till the General returns will be witnessed.'

I step out down the lane. The way's clear then. Get to the first hedge and duck behind it. Wait. Wait until they've loaded up all those crates of wine and left.

Retrieve the bottle of brandy and bag from their hiding place in the ditch. Change into escape outfit.

And set out to rescue Tarquin.

50

I hide the bottle of brandy, wedge it under the waistband of my skirt, pull my top down over it. Step out of my cover, back down through the old streets of the village, past the first three biomes and down the path to the old police station. I knock on the door. Timid. Acting the part. At last the soldier on duty comes. He opens the door, looks at me. It's a good start. I take a deep breath. My heart is hammering.

'Remember, when you're scared,' said Nan, 'it's just a feeling. It has no use unless it helps you. Remember that.'

'The soldiers up top have arrested the manager,' I say. 'Caught him and two workers stealing the General's wine. They sent me to say you need to get three cells ready.'

The soldier lets out a long, low whistle.

'They're holding him at the barracks.' Breathless. Chest heaving. Breasts swelling. 'It's a long story – seems like the adjutant is in on it . . .' Fans self with delicate hand. 'He's nowhere to be found – and I was there . . .'

The soldier sucks in his breath. 'Come in. Tell me,' he says.

'The officer in charge now says he "don't want any of them in the same cell so they can make up thieving, lying stories."'

I step into the police station. My heart still hammering. 'Oh, maybe that's four cells.' My hands fly to my face. 'Oh no, I've forgotten how many cells.'

That's it. Feel the fear. Let it help. Act confused.

The soldier seems winded by the news. He goes to the back behind the counter of the charge office and removes a bunch of keys.

'So they sent me with a release order for the prisoner you've got here.'

A puzzled look creeps across his face.

'So you'll have enough vacant cells . . .' I stammer.

Use your fear.

The soldier takes the release order and looks at it. He's obviously surprised.

'Wait,' he says. 'I need to check this one because the prisoner we're holding has serious charges against him.'

Oh God don't let him check.

'Oh and they sent you this.' I lift up my skirt, a little too high, and pull out the bottle of brandy. 'They say it's a celebration that they've finally rounded up the thieves . . . and they found . . .' *Stay breathless. Heave bosom.* '. . . whole crates of unaccounted-for brandy. It seems there's been a racket going on for ages.' I smile at him. I put the bottle on the ground and bend forward. My top drops open. My cleavage shows. He can see right down. I pull out the loosened cork. The smell of alcohol is overwhelming.

I don't straighten up. I just lift my chin. I let his gaze linger. I stay breathless. 'I'm so sorry I don't know how many cells . . .' I can see his eyes grow round. His pupils dilate. *Time him,*

Melissa. Wait for the right moment.

'Shall I pour it for you? Do you have a glass?'

He gets flustered. I never thought I would be any good at flirting. But it turns out I am. I leave the bottle on the floor and straighten up shyly, pull my top back up. Blush. I don't like flirting. I'd rather fight a dog any day.

I tell myself: *Keep going. Get Tarquin out.* I gasp as if I'm suddenly aware of the extent to which my top fell open. I run my hands over my breasts. Look distraught.

The soldier's still looking at me. Mesmerised. His pupils fully dilated. I hear Nan's voice. *Strike now. Wait. Time him. You may not get a second chance.*

I toss my hair to one side and smile and look into his eyes. Wide. Seductive. Beautiful.

Strike.

I pick up the bottle. Hand it to him.

He takes the bottle and raises it to his lips.

One slug of that brandy and he wants to cough. Anyone would. I can smell it from here. Raw like liquid fire.

But he can't. Because I hold him with my eyes and carry on smiling and looking. He daren't cough or splutter.

He raises the bottle again and gulps back more. I understand. *He's mine now.*

I act agitated. I adjust my skirt just a tiny bit, show a glimpse of my knees, put my shoulders back, my chest out. I act embarrassed, just enough to keep his attention. I let my legs splay a fraction.

Oh Nan, you'd be so proud of me.

He swigs from the bottle again. He's gone. His eyes are wide.

His face a book. Nan would be beaming. *Your beauty has power, Melissa. Harness it. Make it work for you.*

I keep smiling deep into his eyes. Making him drink more. I lean in a little closer. He stinks of alcohol.

'I've got to report back when the cells are empty,' I stammer.

'What?' he says. He slurs his speech a bit.

'Are you all right?'

He looks again at the release order. 'Shit. Can't check on this smelling of grog.'

This is it, Nan. I've nearly done it.

'I'll get him,' he says. He's staggering a little, but he still knows what he's doing. *Very careful now, Melissa.*

I wait in the old charge office. Dirty cream walls. Flaking paint. Rusted filing cabinets. The soldier disappears down to the cells. I hear him clanking through other doors. He's gone for ages. I sit there staring at the wall. *Oh please don't let anything go wrong.*

Tarquin. Tarquin.

I cross and uncross my legs. I hate skirts.

What's happening back at the house? Have they arrested Billson? Is Lenny on his way? My God, he's taking forever. My heart pounds. My legs feel like they're made of mud, all squishy.

Footsteps returning. The soldier. Tarquin. I shoot him a look. Flash my eyes. He nods ever so slightly.

'Need to get these handcuffs off,' mutters the soldier. 'Where's he to go to?'

Where is he supposed to go to? Oh my God. Harold never mentioned that part of it.

'He's to report to Barrack Five,' I say. I make it up as I go along.

'Any transfer docs? Or bail papers?'

Holy shit.

'It was such a rush,' I say. *Just let him unlock the handcuffs. That's all.*

The soldier looks confused. 'And they're bringing the arrested parties here?'

'Yes, really soon.'

The soldier sighs. He finds his keys. He unlocks the cuffs on Tarquin. He crosses to the desk. 'I can't release him yet. I'll ask the others when they bring the culprits in where he's to go to. They can escort him there.'

But you have released him. Without handcuffs on he's as good as free.

'So you' – he turns to Tarquin – 'sit and wait while we get this sorted.'

I nod at Tarquin.

The soldier goes to hang up the keys.

It's the last thing he'll remember doing.

'Where's Lenny?'

'Shush. No questions.' I put my finger up over my lips. I hand sign him to wait.

Outside, the street's empty. I nod at Tarquin. I point to the back of the building. Tarquin doesn't need explanations. I know what he's thinking.

'He's there,' I mouth.

It's like the sun breaks through clouds. With a little shake, his shoulders seem to broaden.

'Find him and wait for me. The train will leave soon. We'll be on board,' I say and point to the field beyond the back of the old police station, to the little thicket of bushes.

'Get going,' I say. I give him a tiny push. 'Behind the thicket is the railway station. I'll meet you there. I've just got one more thing to do.'

51

I turn on my heel.

I wish I could be there when Tarquin finds Lenny. I'd have liked to see the smiles and the hugging. I'd have liked to see Lenny's face. I'd have liked to see Tarquin suddenly happy. I blink back a sudden rush of something. *Stay in charge.*

The General will be back soon. If I'm going to get my own back on him, I don't have much time. He'll be sorry he ever messed with me.

I race from the back of the police station to the edge of the big estate. I climb the old stone wall and I'm in. A part of me is screaming, *Leave. Join Lenny. Join Tarquin. Forget it.*

The other part is saying, *No. Show him. Do something, however small. Fight back.*

So I do. I march up to the greenhouse. I step past NO ADMITTANCE. I push open the doors. I stand inside inhaling the sweet fragrance of the orchids. I wedge the door wide. I walk down the aisle between the plants. As I go I pick up old flower pots, seedling trays, gardening tools, and I hurl them at the old glass windows. They break with a crashing sound. The bees begin to buzz, alarmed. A breeze from outside suddenly belts through the broken glass.

'Fly, little ones,' I whisper.

I turn into the second aisle. I pick up *Eltroplectris*: Long-claw Orchid; *Elythranthera*: Snake-mouth Orchid.

'Out the window with you.' *That was for you, Dora.*

I smash as much glass as I can. I start to run. I hold out my hand and sweep the pots to the floor. *This is for you – girl with the golden hair.* I run and throw and smash. The bees whirl up in a cloud and find the gaps in the glass. They stream out of the greenhouse.

It's the best I can do.

I will do more, I promise all those girls. *If I have the chance I will avenge you all. Absolutely.*

The orchids are smashed, the bees are gone. It's time to go too. 'The bees are free now, Nan,' I whisper.

And I pray some of those bees will make it into the gardens beyond the biomes. I pray some will make it beyond the fence into the wilderness. I believe they will find a new queen, start a wild hive.

If a spider can survive, maybe a bee can now. Maybe all they needed was someone to set them free.

'The bees are coming, Nan,' I whisper.

52

I run.

I race the length of the greenhouse and out of the other exit. I sprint back down to the stone wall, climb over, up the narrow lane, back to the old village high street. At the turn of the street, I can see the thicket by the railway. I jump a half-tumbled fence and dash across a field.

In less than six minutes I'm back. Lenny's holding on to Tarquin. Tarquin's holding on to Lenny. Harold is standing there, impatient.

'We need to move,' he says. 'It's not safe yet.'

'OK,' says Tarquin, his voice deep, hoarse.

'This way,' says Harold. We set out through trees towards the railway station. As we step over dead leaves rotted soft, I feel a gentle tug on my arm. I turn into the shadows and there's Lenny. He's got his book in one hand and my coat in the other. He looks at me. His eyes radiant. His face looks like it isn't big enough to contain all his smiling. I stop. I squat down. I give him such a hug. I could squash all the breath out of him.

'No time for all that,' whispers Harold.

I want to ask about the internal manager, the adjutant, about

Marcy even. How did it go? What was the look on their faces? But I don't. I can tell from Harold's smile it went well. I can tell it's not over yet, though. He's itching to get back, finish up all those details, call in those favours.

We pass behind the thicket, through a street of boarded up houses, onto a wide avenue that might once have been a dual carriageway. It's been a long time since any vehicles used it. Weeds grow thick in the broken patches of tarmac. There are no army trucks. We cross over and down behind a short row of terraced houses. There's nobody there to see us. Everyone's at work in the biomes.

I look over my shoulder. I won't breathe easily until we're on the train, past the perimeter fence and on our way. Then I'm going to breathe. Then I'm going to let out all the breath in the world.

No sooner have we turned into the siding by the rail track than we smell it – steaming, burning and soot.

'No,' warns Harold. 'This way.'

We pause, uncertain. 'You've got to get on without them noticing,' he hisses, 'or there'll be a squad of soldiers on the next one up.'

But how're we going to do that? I scan the station. Up and down the sides of every platform are guards. They're armed, and they don't look like they are going to miss seeing us.

We stop.

'What're we going to do?' says Lenny.

306

We hide at one end of the station, behind large steel tanks that are jumbled at the end of the cutting. Harold examines the platform. 'Where is he?' he mutters. Suddenly my heartbeat rockets.

What does he mean? The steam from the engine's spouting. The wagon beds are clanking. The train's about to bloody leave.

I hold Lenny's hand tight. He is looking at me with his big eyes. I know what he wants to say. I can hear him already.

'Put the book away,' I say. Lenny lets go of me and stuffs the book down his front.

'Let's wait a little longer,' Harold says. 'It'll be fine.'

But it's not fine. And it gets worse. A squad of soldiers arrive on the platform, as if they're expecting us to be on the train.

'Hang on,' Harold says. 'I'm going to find out what's happening.'

We wait forever. The train starts to shunt forward. My legs tremble. The train stops again.

Harold comes back. 'We need to get out of here,' he says. 'Quick. Marcy has reported you missing from the house. There's curfew out everywhere. They're closing all the barricades. They're going to search this train before they'll let it leave.'

'Oh no,' I groan.

'I'm not going back in them cells. I'm not gonna be flogged an' stay there for ten years,' says Tarquin.

Lenny doesn't say anything. His eyes are wide with fright.

'There's only one thing we can do,' says Harold. 'Jump. Can you?'

'Jump?' says Tarquin. 'Are you mad?'

'There's a bridge not far from here, where the train goes

307

into a tunnel. You can jump from the bridge. Drop's not too far – perhaps four metres onto the wagon beds, as they go through.'

I shudder at the thought of dropping four metres onto moving wagon beds. We could break our necks. Lenny could roll completely off.

'It's been done before,' says Harold. 'We've had a couple of people try to escape that way.'

'Did they make it?' I ask.

'One did,' says Harold.

Not very good odds. I look at Tarquin. He looks at me. He looks at Harold. In the distance the train lets out a long hoot. There's some shouting and a round of gunfire.

'OK,' says Tarquin.

'I'll tell the driver. I'll tell him not to pick up speed until he's through the tunnel. Try to jump onto one of the first wagon beds. The tail ones wobble too much.'

My heart's pounding. I'm not good with heights. I don't do jumping.

I think of the rushing, of hitting the cold, hard bed. I don't know which is worse – breaking my legs, or rolling off onto the tracks and having the wheels go over me.

The gunfire's louder.

'You need to decide,' says Harold. 'They're firing warning shots to let anyone know they'll shoot if they find them escaping.'

'Quickly. They'll be sending soldiers up to the bridge as we speak.'

To jump is crazy, but to stay here?

'We'll jump,' I say. Lenny's got tight hold of my hand. I can't smile at him.

'It's gonna be all right, ain't it?' he says.

Tarquin nods. 'Yeah, it's gonna be all right.'

Harold draws Tarquin aside. I take Lenny.

'Make it to the old bridge,' I hear Harold hiss. 'Get going. I'll try to stall them.'

I can't hear Tarquin's reply.

'Hold him and jump. Be OK. Do it quick. Here's a blanket, sheet of plastic and water. All I could carry.' Harold pushes a bundle of things at Tarquin.

I look at Tarquin and nod. 'Lenny,' I say, 'we're going to jump the train.'

'OK,' he says.

And before I know it, we're running for the bridge, the train's blowing and the whole place is full of steam.

And we disappear into the smoke and steam and swirling air.

We stand on the stone parapet. I can just make out the trailers attached to the engine moving beneath us. We balance, poised, looking down. Tarquin scoops Lenny into his arms. I strain my eyes, looking through the steam, trying to focus on the right moment.

'Roll when you hit the bed. Try to roll straight, that's what Harold said.' Tarquin nods at me.

The air suddenly rises. For a second I can see the coal trucks shunting below. The sound of metal on metal. The long squeal of track. The shudder of engine. I wipe my eyes. They're streaming too. I watch the great beds slide by.

'Now.' I grab Tarquin's arm. We step off the parapet, Lenny in Tarquin's arms.

Suddenly there's empty space beneath me. Then I hit the trailer. Jarring pain. My legs crumple. *Roll, you fool. Roll.* I roll. Pain. Everything sharp with agony. My shoulder. My legs. I'm rolling. It's totally dark. I've let go of Tarquin. Suddenly I'm terrified he's rolled off the side. I struggle to sit up. My hands are grazed, they're all gritty. *Where's Tarquin? Where's Lenny?*

I hear Lenny. He's OK.

'Tarquin?'

We shoot out of the tunnel.

I blink. We find each other. I hug them. Hold them tight.

The pain in my hands forgotten.

There they are in the smoke and the steam and the swirling air. *They're OK.*

The air clears. The steam is blown off across open countryside. I look down the line of the train. We're moving slowly, clunking down the track. Each wagon bed is covered with coal dust, coal slag. We're already as black as the beds. For a moment I glimpse up to where we jumped from.

People. Two people. They're pointing. They've got guns. I don't know if they can see us. I can't hear them. Only the engine and the wind and the rattle of wheels and the shrieking of metal. Then there're shots. They whistle through the air, dangerously near. They've seen us, all right. The train curves round the track. The bridge disappears out of sight. But I know

310

what they're saying.

There you are.
We've seen you.
We know where you're going.
If you think we won't follow you and shoot you down –
Think again.

53

I'm going to give myself five minutes before I remember.

I'm going to take a deep breath before I tell them.

I'm going to try to imagine for the last time that running brook, that hazelnut forest.

Those bees in the wild white clover.

Then I'm going to tell them.

Tell them that, after all we've been through.

When at last we're speeding north.

There is no cottage.

No hidden valley.

No pond with ducks.

PART THREE

Until you have smoked out the bees you can't eat the honey.

Russian Proverb

54

The wagon bed lurches from side to side. Best to lie down. Lenny tries to stand, falls, slips dangerously near the edge. Tarquin hauls him back. We huddle together, lodging the blanket beneath us and round as much of us as we can. We link arms, and clutch the plastic over us. The wind struggles to tear it off. It's so cold.

An arctic gale races down the track. Thick white air. Frozen steam. Droplets of ice bruise my face. Every time we brush through undergrowth, frost showers us. Lenny clings to me. I pull him in tighter. Tarquin presses close on the other side. Keep Lenny tucked in the middle.

The train rattles. We lie as still as possible, too scared to move. Even when my hands and feet grow numb. *Don't give yourself away. Don't let anyone see.* The wagon beds slide sideways on the bends. *Oh God, don't let us lose our grip.* The track's so old. Maybe in places it's gone. They repair it, surely? Maybe they don't. Some bits of track throw us violently sideways. Screech of metal. I hang on. My shoulders ache. My poor legs.

We head north.

'We're getting closer, ain't we, Missa?' says Lenny. I press his cold hand. I take a deep breath in.

'Lenny,' I say.

He looks at me. His eyes grey-brown, round.

My heart thuds. I pull at Tarquin's arm. We curve out of a bend. The train flings us sideways.

'What?' he shouts.

The roar of the train rushes in on us, whips words away.

'Got – something to tell you.'

'Wh-at?' he yells again.

'Tell you.' I must tell them, before my courage fails.

'I'm OK,' says Tarquin.

'Not that.'

He smiles. I see the warmth in his eyes.

'Thank you, Melissa –' Tarquin screams into the wind. 'For rescue.'

I try again. 'It's about the cottage.'

The steam sweeps round, shrouds us in freezing fog. His hand catches mine. He holds it. 'I owe you.'

It's no good.

I can't continue against such odds.

Instead, think.

They're going to follow us. Those were soldiers on the bridge. They'll take the next train.

Could we jump? When *is* the next train? What's the schedule?

Trains arrive at Newcastle, are loaded with coal, go back to the covered farms? Freight beds are split off, sent on to London. Empty beds are shackled back on the engine. One food wagon. Return to Newcastle – get loaded up again. Round trip – how long?

Does it stop on the way?

And is there more than one train? Harold should have told me. *Why didn't I ask him?* If there are more, do all trains go to exactly the same places? Harold was too busy feathering his own nest. He got us out. But he could have done more.

Can we jump?

'We'll get off when we stop going north,' Tarquin shouts over the rattle. He looks up at the sky.

'We gonna stop going north?' asks Lenny.

Tarquin looks at me. 'Scotland's always north, right?'

I don't know. I'm supposed to know. 'The coalfields are in the north,' I say. 'Maybe we can get shelter there, before we cross Hadrian's Wall.'

'We mustn't stop,' says Lenny.

'We'll keep going,' says Tarquin. 'No people, no stopping.'

Lenny rests his head against me. He's shivering. His teeth chatter. I unbutton Nan's coat, slip it round him. It flaps in the wind, tugs at my shoulders.

I try to remind myself that Lenny would have been traded to the Limehouse gang. He'd be there, a sad little skivvy, all dreaming gone.

Did I dream when I was little? Was there time? Sweeping out the fire, selecting half-burned cinders to reuse, sifting ash for the garden, mixing the rest with cooking fat to make soap, checking on the plants, being a busy bee – that's what Nan called it – 'being a busy bee', pollinating the flowers by hand. 'Melissa,' she'd say. 'My busy bee. Melissa, my little honey.'

The train slows, takes a long curve.

'We still going north, ain't we?' says Lenny.

'Yep,' replies Tarquin.

'We'll be OK?'

'We will.'

The light's fading. I can just make out Tarquin's profile.

'Try to rest,' he says.

The train slows. Screech of metal brakes. We must have fallen asleep. We're shunting into a siding. There's lights. Dazzling. Bright. I screw my eyes up.

'*Tarquin!*'

Voices. Deep, with strange accents.

We've been asleep for hours!

The next thing I know Tarquin's hollering. Men hold him tight. I can't figure out what's up. Have the soldiers caught us? I feel hands on me. *Oh God.* They're pulling me up. They're pulling Lenny up. '*Lenny!*' Lenny's hand is ripped from mine. He shouts. Two men haul us along the freight bed: one holds Lenny; I struggle against mine.

Where are we?

'Right,' says one of the men. He's huge and thin. I feel his muscly arm around me. He's covered in something. His clothes are rough, gritty.

'Bring 'em down,' someone orders. We're lifted, dragged, shoved to the edge of the wagon beds. We're passed down and along the track. More hands take us.

So many men. They don't say anything, just hold us tight. They smell strange, sweaty, metallic. I can't move. Tarquin moves, even though he's held by three of them.

'Just quit struggling, young fella,' grunts one. 'No one's going to hurt you.'

No one's going to hurt you. They're not soldiers?

'And you're coming with us whether you like it or no.'

Try to think. Who are they? What's going on?

'Bring 'em in,' says a man.

And where are we?

No moon. They walk us along a platform, swinging smoky lamps. A freshly repainted sign says: Blaydon-Newburn. *Where's that?* Out of the station. Down a road. Long, stony and beaten out of something dark. On either side: buildings. More and more buildings. *Is this Newcastle?* It's cold. We're marched through freezing darkness.

'Take them to the football stadium?'

'No. Up to the council.'

We're led down an alley, through an open place, a black shadow up behind, a bitter wind blowing down, icy cold.

More rows of houses. At last through a wide door. Into an open space. A round table. Maybe an old church hall. Lamplight. They tell us to sit.

We sit.

What's gonna happen now?

319

Lenny's rigid, as if in a trance. I try to reach him. They smack me back. The man who gives orders goes out. Four stay. They all have this thin, grimy look. Three hold Tarquin in an arm lock. He twists. They hold firm. He can't move. I bite at the side of my lip, clench and unclench my hands.

Lenny grips the chair. Pale as a ghost. 'Please sir, don't hurt him,' Lenny says. His voice, sweet like birdsong. The men holding Tarquin almost jump. One of them peers forward at Lenny, looks questioningly at the others.

They stare too. They all stare at Lenny, like they're going to eat him. A sudden chill goes down my spine. I heard that in far-off places . . .

Then I remember Nan: '*Stuff and lies . . . and wasn't it bad enough to find food without scaremongery? Nobody ever ate a person even if they did eat dogs. And we aren't sunk that low yet. Lord knows we need everybody we've got in this God-forsaken, desolate country . . . and there's still order, even if it's the army . . .*'

The men continue staring at Lenny. I scan the room. The walls are old stone. They've been repaired in places. They look solid, but dirty. Not dust, or filth. Something black and grainy. It's hard to tell in the lamplight. It coats the furniture as well.

Tarquin suddenly twists, tries to break free. The men clamp down on him, force him to bend forwards.

Lenny screams. I jump up. One man springs out, shoves me back in my seat.

'Stay put.' He snaps the words out so viciously, I'm sprayed with saliva.

Lenny swallows his screaming. I freeze in my seat.

Think. You thought your way out of Games City and the

farm. These people must need something.

Bargain your way free.

But as soon as they come in, I can see what these people need, and I'm absolutely sure I'm not going to be able to give it to them.

55

They come in – men and more men and more and more men.
All coughing. All thin. At last, only three women. I shudder. The
women look worn out. They look ill. One's got a strange shaped
head. Small. Shrunken. As if her skull's failed to grow.

I don't want to stare, but I find myself staring anyway. So
broken, tired. One of the men, a stooping giant, sees me. He
glares at me, presses his lips tight.

They carry chairs to the table. They all sit. I run the tip of
a finger along the side of my seat. I examine the tiny grains of
dark grit imbedded in my skin. I rub them between the pads
of my thumb and forefinger. Dry. Hard. Not dirt. Coal dust?
We must be somewhere near Newcastle then. The borders of
Scotland, even. We've reached the coal mines.

One of the men hawks up phlegm. The sound of it rattling
in his chest makes me want to retch.

I fix my eyes on the women. The youngest one looks at me.
She's actually not that old. There's something so trampled in
the droop of her shoulders though, it makes her look ancient.

'The council can begin,' says someone. His voice rings with
authority. Someone else starts coughing again, hacking, echoey.

'Evening all.' He's a dry man with skin like leather. 'We got visitors and this time we struck lucky.'

I don't like the way he says 'lucky'. Like in the past sometime they struck 'unlucky'. It makes us sound like street find or spoil.

A few people grunt, 'Good evening.' There's more coughing. Someone spits on the floor.

'If we let you go, you'll sit and behave?' says the man to Tarquin. 'Raise your left hand if you agree.'

Tarquin raises his left hand.

They let him go. He sits next to Lenny and me. There's a pause while everyone seems to be staring away from us, in the direction of something they can't name. Then the man says, 'You don't move, you hear? And you answer our questions.' He wags a finger at us.

I don't like the wagging any better than the spitting.

'And you tell the truth and we'll decide what to do with you.'

Immediately I decide to lie.

'Let's have your story.'

I bring up my head and look him in the eye. I can almost hear Lenny's worry. *Please don't let them stop us going to the cottage.*

So I keep my voice clear like a bell, 'We're looking for a better future.'

So far, so true.

Lenny covers his face. He's trembling. One of the miners breaks into a fresh bout of hawking. I keep my voice steady. *Buy time. Tell them something they'd like to hear.*

'We know it's a tough life up here, but we heard there were jobs in the coal mines, and you're fair and would treat us decent.'

'Flattery is part of deception. Praise is your ally.' Nan's voice coaches me.

They look at each other. Somebody clears their throat. Another starts coughing again. Deep chest-wracking coughs.

I don't dare look at Tarquin. He never left Careem's gang to work down a coal mine. He *hates* being underground.

I don't let anything show on my face, though. I keep my chin up and say, 'We were born down south, and we don't complain about life down there, but we're young and we want to help build up this country.'

'Why did you jump our train?' asks the man. He's not a fool. 'Why didn't you go to the office down south?'

'Ain't open,' chips in Tarquin.

'True,' says one. 'They don't open, hardly ever.'

'We didn't have money to pay the fare,' I add.

Always mix a little truth in with a good lie.

'And there's fellas after you,' says another.

I look at him, don't let my gaze waver.

'Yes,' I say. 'We're wanted by soldiers.'

And always tell the truth when you can't get out of it.

'Now we're getting it,' he laughs.

'And the General, I'll wager, if he's seen you.'

Study your subject. Lying is an art.

'Scum,' mutters the oldest woman.

'We set out on foot,' I say, 'but they stopped us and sent us to a prison farm. But we've left there and now we're here.'

'What'll we do?' asks someone in a wheezy voice. 'Ship 'em back on the next load?'

'There'll be trouble if we don't.'

324

'Maybe,' says the leader. He's looking at Lenny. Suddenly they're all looking at Lenny. He's obviously got something in mind.

He clears his throat. 'Right. It'll go to a vote then.' He turns to us, his voice suddenly sugary. 'I'm Alfred Glover, and I'm headman here. We're the Coal Syndicate Owners' Council, of the reopened Newburn and Throckley pits,' he says. 'We run a cooperative mine here. We make our own decisions, independent of the army. We're going to send you to the houses, while we talk this over.' He smiles at us in a thin-lipped way. 'So if you've got anything further to add?' He pauses, waits, his smile still stretched taut.

I shake my head.

'Then you'll wait for our decision. If we let you stay and work, we'll house you and feed you and you'll join the cooperative and sign up to our terms and conditions, according to *our* council rules.'

I don't like the idea of *his* council rules.

'But if we decide against you, we'll send you back, trussed up like geese if need be.' His smile evaporates. He looks at Tarquin like he'd send him back regardless.

Lenny's face drains of colour. The angle of his jaw sticks out. He clenches the edge of his seat. Tarquin half rises. Instantly I drop my hand over his arm.

The oldest woman comes forward.

I squeeze Tarquin's wrist.

'I'm Bridey,' she says. She's wrinkled and her voice is slightly scratchy. 'I'll take you and the little one to mine.'

I can feel his pulse banging.

'We women live separately from the men. It's our choice. Your fella will have to go with Colin or Bert.' She nods at Tarquin.

'*Lenny needs to eat,*' I whisper, scared Tarquin will explode.

Bridey tucks her grey hair behind an ear. 'Don't worry about your family, young man,' she says, seeing his mind. 'You'll be right next door, and you can talk to each other in the backyards.'

I grip Tarquin harder, whisper, 'I'll make sure.'

But before she leads us off, Lenny breaks free. He runs to Alfred Glover, cries out: 'Please don't send us back to the prison farms. We shouldn'ta never gone there. We wasn't doing nothing wrong.'

The woman with the shrunken head leaps up, holds her arms out to Lenny, shrieks out a mangled cry.

Instantly Alfred Glover's on his feet. In one swift movement he crosses to the woman, slaps her arms down, roughly thrusts her back in her chair. As her small misshapen head cracks against the chair back, she cries, 'No life for a child here!'

No one moves.

Lenny stares first at the woman, then from face to face.

'We was only trying to go north,' he whispers.

56

The terrace of cottages stretches up the hillside. All gone to grime. No sign of life. Just a grey line of grey doors. Everything coated with dust.

We climb up the narrow street. Chill wind, thin sleet. Moonlight. We pass an old churchyard. Rows of small graves. Tiny mounds barely grassed over. One fresh. On top, a wet and wasted teddy.

An old set of steps. Through the door of Bridey's house, straight into the front room. Tiny. Perfect. An antique sideboard. A coatstand in the corner. Stuffed furniture. Every chair cover, curtain, darned and mended. Even the skirting boards intact. Nothing half stripped out. And a coal fire. A real coal fire.

Oh Nan, a burning coal fire.

Glowing coals, dancing flames.

And heat!

Lenny stares at the fire, crowds closer, stretches out his thin hands. His eyes wide.

And china, Nan.

Plates lined up on a dresser, cups hanging from hooks. Real blue and white china *and* a nest of little polished tables. *Just like you used to tell me*. I cross the room and pick a plate off its shelf, carefully wipe the dark patina of dust off. *Real china!* Lenny looks and looks, all eyes. Then he says, small voiced, 'What're them black stones for, missus?' He points at the hearth.

Bridey laughs and says, 'Get away, that's coal.' Her voice tender, like she loves him already.

I take off my coat. Warm my freezing hands. Maybe it's not going to be so bad. Maybe it could work out? Can working down a mine be so awful?

If they let us stay.

'You can get scrubbed down in there.' Bridey points up the stairs to a door. 'There's a proper tub.'

Maybe they won't. Maybe they'll truss us all up and send us back down on the next train.

She brushes past, climbs the stairs. I shake my head. That's not going to happen. I won't let it. We follow her into a tiny bathroom, white tiles, a sink and toilet and bathtub. She turns on a tap. Hot water gushes out. It's not only Lenny now that's got big eyes.

I won't. I'll think of something.

Bridey laughs again. 'We've got our own electricity up here,' she says, and puts down her candle and flicks a switch. The room floods with light. 'We fire the generators from rough we don't sell. It works part of the mine and gives us a decent life.'

I gawp. *Real electricity*.

'If you're prepared for the danger and you work hard, you'll get along fine.' Her tone is cheery, as if we've all already got her vote.

It's so bright, I actually blink.

Bridey turns the light off again. 'But light bulbs is hard to get, so we won't leave it on.'

Lenny's already hopping up and down with excitement, trying to strip his clothes off. 'Can I get in now, missus?'

Bridey smiles. 'Bless the child,' she says.

She plugs the bath. She lathers soap in, turns on the tap again, starts filling up the tub. I've never seen hot water coming out of a tap before. I watch, mesmerised, as it plunges and steams. Bridey brings out some old plastic toys. Yellow ducks and ducklings. She sails them out on the bath.

Lenny looks up at her. His face like magic. He scoops out one tiny duckling caught in a swirl of water and cuddles it to his chest.

The woman bends over the bathtub too. She mixes round the suds. Foam flecks combine with the fine dust in the air. She pushes a yellow duck through the grey bubbles with one finger. She smiles at Lenny with this look on her face, like all she ever wanted was a kid at bathtime, with those yellow ducks.

'You can go,' says Bridey, turning abruptly to me. 'Hannah will find you food.'

I think her eyes have filled with tears.

'I can take care of the child,' she says.

Maybe it's just the soap suds and the bending.

I step back onto the small landing, dismissed.

Maybe it's going to work out. Maybe I can have a bath too. In bubbles, all the way up to my neck. Sit in a hot bath under electric lights!

How I wish you could see it, Nan. Everything just like it was when you grew up. If I go downstairs now, maybe there'll be a working television too, a computer and a mobile phone!

I peer back at them through the slightly open door. Steam half obscures Bridey. She lays out towels for Lenny. She passes him a sponge. His shape wavers in the mist. Ghostly, like a spirit child. She sets out slippers on the bath mat. The slippers are way too big. She bows before him like an antique handmaiden. If he said: 'I command you to bring me a plate of food in the bath!' I think she would.

Half scared he will and I'll be caught watching them, I turn away. I catch sight of a little bedroom at the end of a corridor, its door slightly open. I creep down and peer inside. A child's room. A cot. A stuffed toy cat on a quilt. A set of childish clothes folded and laid on a chair. Another child in the house? Lenny will like that. I step inside. The clothes are coated with coal dust. The room's strangely still. Quiet as the grave.

I creep back down the stairs and peer into the kitchen. Looking for more wonders.

It all seems too good to be true.

Inside the kitchen is one of the other women I saw at the meeting. The young one that looks old. She warms herself by a big cooking range. She smiles at me, pulls up a chair and says, 'You're Melissa, aren't you? I'm Hannah.'

I cross over and sit down. 'It's so nice here,' I say.

'You're very pretty.'

I blush. 'And so warm. I'm not used to coal fires.'

Deep shadows around her eyes. And a faraway look.

'Electricity neither,' I say.

She reaches out a hand to touch my face.

'It's only us that's got it,' she says. 'I mean us up here, near

330

the mine – and when they close up, it'll go off.'

I smile. I don't really understand.

'It's the mine, you see,' she explains, stroking my hair.

I still don't understand. I suppose my face shows it.

'They power up the generator,' she says, 'with coal dust and slack and the graded coal that ain't put on the trains. They use it to make steam and that, to power the winding room.'

I look at her blankly.

'So they can lower the men down and the coal up,' she says.

'Oh,' I say.

'It doesn't go nowhere else, just for the mine and us.'

'That's so clever,' I say. 'All warm and full of light and everything working.'

'It wasn't always like that. It wasn't like it when I was born. They done all this in the last ten years.'

A wave of relief settles over me. Lenny won't mind if there's no Scotland, if he can be here, washed, fed. Other children to play with. If it works out here, we won't need to go anywhere else.

And suddenly I know they'll want us to stay. I see it in the sad lines of her face. It showed in the eyes of the men, when they kept staring at me and Lenny.

'If I could live here and have a warm house and light in the evening, I'd smile all day,' I say.

The woman lets go of my hair, drops her hand. Her fingers tremble. I realise something's very wrong.

'What is it?' I say, uncomfortably aware she's near tears.

She doesn't answer. She bites her lower lip, drags a hand across her nose. She stands up, goes to the sink, splashes water on her face.

I don't know what to say, what to do. I twist my fingers. Suddenly everywhere looks less shining than before.

'I'm sorry,' I say. 'Have I upset you?'

She turns, a sad smile forced across her face. 'Oh no, it's nothing,' she says, her voice empty. 'Just a cold.'

A huge fear starts inside me. *There's something I don't know.* Something I'm missing.

Something I *should* know.

'Is the room upstairs your child's?' I ask, trying to change the subject. 'Lenny'd love to have someone to play with.'

Her face goes grey. Her chin quivers. She makes no reply. Instead she puts a bowl of soup on the table, nods at it and leaves the kitchen.

Somehow I've touched a raw nerve.

And all of a sudden, despite the warmth, I feel cold. My heart starts racing all over again. *I knew something was wrong. I knew it was too good to be true.* I look at the fire smouldering inside the old cooking range. The glowing coals. The dancing flames.

They aren't dancing at all.

They're twisting.

Hungry. Insatiable. Devouring.

Turning everything to ashes.

57

I sip on the soup. What to do? Ignore the signs? Pretend? I've got food. I'm by a warm fire. No Careem. No General. I'm not worrying about Lenny. He's got a woman fussing over him and a hot bath and I'm getting one too. I won't be ungrateful. I fix my brain on that.

But my heart is racing. And with every beat it pounds out, *Beware. Beware. Beware.*

Nothing is what it seems.

Even the surface of the soup is coated with that thin film of black.

Tarquin. *I'll talk to Tarquin.* Maybe he'll know what's wrong. I put my spoon down and blow on the hot soup. *Maybe he is what is wrong? That's it. That's part of it. They want me and Lenny. They don't want him.*

Why not?

The soup steams up. I stop blowing. My heart falters, seems to miss a beat.

Why don't they want Tarquin?

I take my bath, I smile and pretend. Then I lie in bed and think. I lie very quietly, because Lenny's lying asleep beside me.

They want Lenny and me. But they don't want Tarquin.

The shrunken-headed woman who cried out, '*No life for a child.*' What did she mean? That headman, Alfred Glover. So sugary. That row of tiny graves in that old churchyard. That wet and wasted grey teddy. Everything covered in dark dust. A sudden shiver goes down my spine.

The electricity and the tasty soup and the hot baths and the little yellow ducks and the loveliness of knowing that soldiers are nowhere near. Nothing is what it seems.

From somewhere inside my head I hear Nan's voice.

'There's always a snake, Melissa. In every garden there's always a snake. Oh beware, my beautiful child. Run swiftly, run fast –'

Her warning stuns me into action.

I've got to do something. Find Tarquin. I glance at Lenny, fast asleep. His tangled locks all combed out, washed, cut. His head a halo of curls glinting in the lamplight.

Find Tarquin. I get up. I go straight to the window. There's a light shining out from one of the houses. I see the pale square of it on the back yard. *Tarquin?* Maybe he can't sleep either. Maybe that's his light.

I creep back to the bedside. I pull on my shoes. I slip on Nan's coat. I get to the door. It's locked.

It's locked.

I try the handle again.

I'm locked in.

I can't believe it.

Hannah and Bridey locked me in?

I'm tempted to rattle the handle, kick the door. Shout. Scream. *How dare they?* But I don't. Instead I swallow my breath, press my lips tight, check the lock and smile.

Without a bolt on the outside, no lock can hold me. Certainly not this flimsy one.

I squat down. I push gently on the base of the door. It gives slightly. I try the top. No bolts. Good. Now the lock.

It's a simple pin and tumble affair and the key's still in it. Quickly I take down one of the posters tacked to the chimney breast, and try the old trick of slipping a sheet of paper under the door and poking the key out. Fingers crossed. *I'll find you, Tarquin.* It nearly works, too; the key falls onto the paper, but as I try to drag it back under the door it sticks. *Shit.* The gap isn't big enough.

I hunt around, remove a loose nail from the wall. It's the right thickness and the shape of the nail head gives me hope. *I'm coming, Tarquin.* I set to work.

I slide the nail into the lower portion of the keyhole to act as a tension wrench. Then I use it to apply a twisting force to the cylinder, first clockwise and then counterclockwise. I experiment until I feel the firmness of the stop. Clockwise. Yep. *Gotcha.* There's that telltale bit of give.

I insert my hair clip as a pick into the upper part of the keyhole and feel for the pins. *This is going to work.* With the pick in the keyhole, I press up and along, feeling out each individual pin. One after the other I push them up. *I'm gonna get out, all right.* I feel the pins spring back down when I release the pressure. I work out which one is the hardest to push. *You know you can do this, Melissa.* I turn the nail to increase the torque. *Gently does it.* Then I press up hard with the hair clip.

The stubborn pin yields, slips completely out of the cylinder. I hear a faint click as it falls back out of its housing.

One down – how many more to go? Can't be more than five. Probably only a couple. I feel for the next stubborn pin. Yep, just one more. It gives without trouble. *You see.* Only a double mortice-lever lock.

And I turn the handle.

As I pass Hannah's, maybe Bridey's bedroom, I poke out my tongue. *Take more than a cheap tumble and pin to stop me.* But before I go downstairs I creep to the end bedroom again. I want to check something out.

Quietly I push open the door. As I expected: empty.

I think I'm beginning to understand.

I pad through the rest of the warm house, out and down to the back door. None of the stairs creak. None of the doors whine. Everything works. They have time to oil hinges, mend floorboards.

The back door is bolted on the inside. They obviously didn't think I'd make it this far.

I slide it back and escape into the night.

58

Outside I hurry towards the square of pale light. Everywhere is order. The vegetables all grow in straight lines. All are neatly covered in plastic. There's some kind of chicken coop and a tiny greenhouse at the end of the garden. In the shadows, I see a beehive beside it. I hope there's bees inside. Can bees survive up here?

I reach the pale square. I look up at the light from next door. My heart's hammering. I don't want those women to discover I'm out. It's not that I'm scared of them. When I think about it, they're probably only following council rules. But Lenny's still there, and being caught might mean being shipped back.

I stand there, pressing my hand against my face, biting the inside of my cheek.

I stare up at the window. *What to do now?*

Suddenly a voice.

'Meliss'?' It comes from somewhere just behind me. I jump. Standing in the shadows by the greenhouse is Tarquin.

Tarquin.

A rush of something sweet and wonderful. My fears evaporate. *He came out to find me. Together we'll find a way.*

Maybe they don't want him, but they won't separate us. We've come so far. We've been through so much. This sad, dust-blackened place can't part us. And suddenly I understand something about myself.

I'm scared of losing him.

And with that understanding the old spectre rises.

The lie.

The fear that when Tarquin learns the truth, he'll leave me. There, I've admitted it to myself.

I don't want to lose him.

No need to tell him yet, though. I look up at him, smile into the darkness, throw my arms out. My voice falters. But I *should* tell him.

We're alone. There may not be another chance.

But I only manage, 'You can't sleep?'

Oh Tarquin why didn't I tell you everything right then?

He smiles. 'Crazy,' he says. 'Here we are with good food and the best bed in ages and neither of us can sleep.'

Why didn't I trust you? Why didn't I open my heart and let you in?

We both stand there.

'Let's get into the greenhouse,' I say. I'm still nervous about being out. We slide open the door, step inside.

We could have faced things together.

He brushes against me. I shiver as if an electric current has short circuited inside me. My voice trembles. 'I –'

'*Moi aussi* –' he says.

We just stand there.

And I know that if I turn now and raise my lips to him, my

338

life will shoot out of control, like a great river over a great cataract and I'll be swirled away in its current.

So I don't.

I stop myself.

'I'm scared,' I whisper.

'*Moi aussi*,' he whispers back.

And I know that if I ever kiss him, I will be his. And I won't be able to ever make it on my own again.

'Of this place,' I add.

My heart stands still. I'm trembling. I think he's trembling too.

He seems to nod, draw away.

I don't trust myself.

It would be a terrible mistake.

The wind rattles at the greenhouse. Drops of rain patter on the glass.

'Yes,' he breathes out. 'All this "have a cuppa", like they're figuring to sell us something. Nobody ever done that sort of thing without them knowing exactly why they done it.'

'They tried to lock me in,' I whisper.

He straightens up. 'What?' he says.

'They seemed so nice, but they locked me in and – Tarquin – there's no children.'

He steps back from me.

I step away too, hold myself together.

'We ain't gonna stay here then. We'll just head out. Carry on going north.'

And I want to go with him, steal back in, bundle Lenny into my arms and leave. *Now.*

But.

And that's the problem. There's nowhere out there.

I take a deep breath. *Be sensible. Lenny needs rest. He needs food. Tarquin needs food too. Neither of them had the General's kitchen to plunder.*

'Let's wait a bit. Tomorrow. See what they say?'

'I don't like being in a different house from Lenny.' No trace of a French accent now. I'm glad. His ganger voice doesn't confuse me.

'Or you,' he says suddenly.

'Me?' My throat dries up. Confused again.

'I don't like being away from you.'

I don't know what to say. My heart hammers. I hold my breath.

'You stick near Lenny, right?' he says.

'Yes,' I whisper.

'You stick right by him all the time?'

'OK.'

'And whatever they decide at the council, we meet out here tomorrow night?'

'OK,' I say.

'And you bring Lenny too.'

'All right.'

'And what d'ya mean they locked you in? How come you're out then?'

'I picked the lock.'

He chuckles. 'Melissa, Melissa, ganger girl.'

'There're no children,' I repeat. 'There's something wrong with the children.'

'How?'

'That churchyard on the way up, and Bridey and Hannah so sad, and there's this bedroom in the house, like some sort of shrine, like a child died in there.'

Tarquin freezes. The pale moonshine fractured by the glass gleams in a ghostly halo around him.

'And everyone coughs so much,' I say.

'Maybe they're sick, like in France,' he says slowly.

I shake my head. I don't know what it is.

'We ain't letting Lenny nowhere near no sickness.'

Suddenly I feel terribly cold.

'Could be TB,' he says. 'Or radiation.'

Maybe it really is worse here than down south.

'Look at how they wash everything. They've got polythene over all them vegetables,' he adds.

I don't have any answer. It could be all of that. Though polythene won't keep radiation out. And there's that thin film of grit everywhere.

'There's sickness round here,' he says, 'and we gonna get out.'

'Could be inbreeding,' I whisper. 'There's so few women and all those men.'

'Well, it ain't OK,' he says, 'an' we're leaving.'

I look at him. *I'm going to have to tell him.*

I stand there. Trying to convince myself there might not be TB or radiation or anything. I try to remember Nan telling me about the picture on the key ring.

'They say hills offer protection – some deep valleys are in a rain shadow. The worst of the fallout misses the valley. I used to dream that valley was safe and you could still live there – or would be able to one day – when the worst was over, and the bees were back.'

Maybe the worst is over. The north should be OK now.

'Let's wait and see?' I say. 'We can't leave tonight. We need to rest.'

'If I had my way, we'd leave, and now.' Tarquin slams his fist down on a bench. Plant pots rattle. Something falls to the floor with a metallic tinkle. 'An' I ain't going back to no ten years' hard labour,' says Tarquin. 'I'd rather deal with Careem.'

'Tomorrow,' I say.

'And I'll kill that General if he touches you.' Tarquin tenses up as if some new thought has struck him.

The bolt of electricity is back. It shoots between the two of us. And I tremble from head to toe. And I look up at him and the wild light in his eye.

'No.' I try to laugh. 'He's my spoil. I'll kill him myself.'

'I won't let him touch you.' In one swift movement Tarquin pulls me to him, his eyes blazing. 'I'll strangle him with my bare hands.'

My heart pounds. I can't breathe. His breath on my cheek. I'm shivering. I'm balancing on the top of that waterfall.

About to plunge over.

And as he tightens his grip around me, I feel the rush of the current. And when he presses himself against me, I try to hold back.

I mustn't. I can't fall.

Over that cataract.

Into that abyss.

342

59

A noise wakens me.

Lenny's side's empty. The sheet thrown back from the mattress. Where is he?

I sit upright in bed.

'Lenny?'

'Here.'

A voice from the window. A grey shape against a grey dawn.

The noise again. That's what woke me. A kind of gong. Not like any gong I've ever heard.

I'm out of bed, into clothes, helping Lenny tug his top on in the dim light. Cold boards underfoot. Scent of burning. I smooth my hair, wash my face in a basin. Running water. Bridey enters, she looks surprised. The door's unlocked. She says nothing. Then we're down those narrow stairs. Hannah holds the door open at the bottom.

'Good, you're up.'

'What is it?'

She smiles. 'Call to the mine.'

I give her a blank look.

'The men go down and when they're all down, we got to

follow them.'

'Us too?

'Surely,' she says. 'You've asked to join us, and council rules say you have to visit a coalface before we sign you. That way we all know what we're all getting into. We can't abide deserters up here.'

A trembling starts in my knees. Suddenly I hear Nan's voice louder than ever. 'Beware, my honeybee. Eurydice was trapped in the underworld. A dark unholy place, land of the lost, land of the buried.'

'And Tarquin?' asks Lenny.

'We'll meet him at the pithead,' joins in Bridey.

I nod at Lenny. 'Be OK.'

'After they've worked their shift, they'll tell us their decision,' says Bridey. 'It's no use fretting. The men are the mine and the mine ain't nothing without the men. We live by the power in their arms. That mine saved us all. If we hadn't got down there, we wouldn't be here now. The men will decide. And they never decide quickly, not until they've slept on it, and not till they've worked a coalface. Then they'll sit us down and tell us their decision.'

She puts a rough-cut hunk of bread into my hands. Then on a sudden impulse takes a carrot from the table and presses it into Lenny's.

'Eat it, child.'

Lenny turns to me. He breaks the carrot in half. 'I'll save some for Quinny,' he says.

'Eat it. This too.' I break off some bread.

He shakes his head. Puts the half carrot in his pocket.

We get to the pithead. Beside the winding gear waits the only person I want to see. My cheeks suddenly seem hot. And I can feel myself smiling. Though his first smiles are for Lenny, I know he's watching me. He picks Lenny up, gives him a bear hug and tosses him in the air.

He throws his arms around me. Squeezes. My heart races.

'You're going down pit,' reminds Bridey. 'Collect your tokens.'

'Why?' asks Lenny.

'Identification in case of fire,' explains Bridey.

'Fire?' says Lenny. 'Is there gonna be a fire?'

I imagine all that coal burning underground like in the pits of hell. I imagine us caught down there. Nowhere to run. Hungry flames. Suffocating heat. *Tarquin. Lenny.* Ashes. My chest tightens. The only thing left: metal tokens.

A sweat breaks out across my brow.

'It happens,' says Bridey, her voice flat. She passes us the tokens. We string them around our necks. We collect a hard hat, safety lamp, overalls. I catch Tarquin looking at me. I think of last night. The pressure of his arms.

'You'll need to see what you're joining,' says Bridey. 'It's a good sign that they've called you down mine. Some as wants to work here, don't get invited to pit.'

His eyes are searching mine. I remember how I pulled away.

'This is Aidan.' She hands us over to a young miner.

I had to. Had to keep a clear head. Survival is all that counts.

We enter the cage at the pithead.

'You're not coming?' says Lenny, suddenly taking Bridey's hand through the bars.

'Bless the child.' She strokes his hair. 'I'll be here when you get back.'

The cage, a steel box, is about as wide as a cupboard. It holds nine of us, packed tight. Tarquin can't stand upright. There are six other miners with us. They crouch as if their chests were already on fire. I press myself close to Lenny. Can't avoid being crushed against Tarquin. My heart hammers. My pulse pounds. The steel door shuts. Somebody works the winding gear. Down into the pit. Down into the underworld.

Suddenly we drop. My stomach squirms. I crouch too. Hold Lenny tight. The void opens. A swallowing feeling, as if a fish has dived through my intestines, and a bursting sensation in my ears. Then complete blackness.

Near the bottom, the cage stops abruptly. Almost like it's jerking back upwards. I hang on to Lenny in the darkness. Somebody lights lamps, hands us one each. We crawl out of the cage deep underground.

My bowels seem to shrivel. *I'm here, Nan. Here in the underworld.*

A smoky smell of old fires and hot nights greets us. We're down under everything. Above us the bones of extinct things, earth, stone, struggling roots of growing plants, threatening to

346

crush down. I look up at the low ceiling of the first gallery. It's only kept up by wooden props, thin as lampposts.

I close my eyes. Hold my breath. Steady my nerve. When I reopen them for a minute I think we're back inside the tunnel under Games City. Escaping from Careem. Tarquin's hand finds mine. He presses my fingers. The abyss opens up inside me. I hold on to him. How brave he is. How much he must hate this place. If he can be brave, so can I.

For what seems like miles we trek along cramped passages. Single file. Only Lenny can stand. The rest of us stoop. No way to hold any hand. Tarquin bangs his head. Every minute I think we'll find the miners working. At the very next gallery, surely?

I stumble at the rear, trying to guide Lenny when I can. Down the dim-lit galleries, three metres wide, only half that high. On again. Tarquin is bent forwards, almost double, like some strange, crouched apeman. If only he could stand to work here. If they want us. We could be together.

On either side, walls of slab shale. More thin, wooden pit props hold up the roof. Above us girders bulge into absurd curves. We duck beneath them. What if they fall? Underfoot, thick dust, angled chunks of shale, coal mud, glittering tracks of anthracite. Down the centre of the gallery runs the tub track. Sleepers to stumble over, not quite a pace apart. Everything soft grey.

Like blind things we stumble on. *This is the underworld, Nan. I know it. It's always been here, deep inside me.* Past strange machines, bunches of tools hooked on wires, mice scuttling from the dim beam of our lamps. Pit ponies. Poor sightless things: working in darkness, born in darkness, dying there.

'Do they live down here always, mister?' asks Lenny.

'Aye,' says the miner, Aidan, his voice still young, though he looks ancient. 'They ain't never seen daylight.'

I shudder.

Lines of coal trucks. We press against the wall for them to pass. Bit by bit they crank and jolt towards the shaft, towed by some infinite steel cable. We shuffle through curtains of sackcloth and thick ventilation doors, held open by the hands of small children. *So there are children.* Ferocious hot air. It smacks out at us, sucked past by shaft fans.

'Have to get the little lads and lasses to flap the doors,' says Aidan.

'Why?' asks Tarquin.

'Keeps the deeper workings ventilated.'

'But why children?' insists Tarquin.

'Some of them shafts too narrow for a grown person.'

Lenny stops by the child opening the door. A small girl with a grimy face. Whites of her eyes staring.

'Here,' says Lenny and presses the half carrot into her hand.

The miner laughs. 'Don't pity her too much. You'll be a trapper too, doing the work yourself afore long.'

Tarquin stumbles, stops. Turns sharply round and looks at the sad figure of the little girl, squatting by the door.

'And you'll get a good beating if you falls asleep.'

Tarquin puts his arm round Lenny. 'I don't think so,' says Tarquin.

'Men's lives depend on fresh air,' says Aidan. 'And we can't work the mine without it.'

'But do the children live down here, like the ponies?' asks Lenny.

348

'A trapper's job never ends,' laughs Aidan.

'But they don't live here,' insists Lenny.

'They dies here, though,' says Aidan. And this time there's no laugh in his voice.

60

Children dying down here in darkness.

That row of grassy mounds. The roof falls to only a metre. We're forced to crouch lower. A pain starts in my knees. *Children squeezed into narrow shafts, flapping heavy wooden doors.* I'm tired of stooping after only such a short time. Even Lenny can't stand up. *'No life for a child.'* I bend double, keep my head twisted round so as to see the beams, so as to duck around them. *Hour after hour.* Forever crouching. A crick starts in my neck. *Day after day.* I think of the empty bedroom. Is this what happened to the child at Bridey's house? *Did he fall into that final sleep? Was there a fire?* My thighs ache.

They need the children to work the ventilation shafts.

They need Lenny.

We come to a long portion, where it's really low. We go slower. Will we never get there? I have to crawl along in a semi-squatting position. Tarquin has gone ominously quiet.

I reach out my hand to touch him. He doesn't respond.

Suddenly, terrifyingly, the roof opens out. An old fall of rock has left a vacuum above us. We can stand at last. I walk upright, trembling.

But if we leave here, where can we go?

Another low stretch. A series of beams. I crawl. I go lower. Down on all fours. At the end of the line of beams, my knees refuse to lift me up again. I try to get up. And I can't.

'Can't,' I whisper.

'Only a short way now,' says Aidan.

I creep towards the coalface, the far-off roar of the conveyor belt steadily drowning out all speech. *I'll have to tell Tarquin.*

'We've only DONE A MILE,' Aidan shouts. 'Some of us working at Greenleigh Gallery TRAVELS THREE AND A HALF MILES BOTH WAYS.'

I don't care. I slump in the coal dust, rub my calves, my thighs. Try to flex my neck. *Only cold mountains. Nothing to eat.*

We crawl under the last pit props and finally see the shiny coalface ahead.

No shelter.

Lenny will die.

It's about a metre high. Overhead the rock ceiling, underfoot rock again. The yellow light of our lamps is quenched in a fog of coal dust. The deafening racket of the conveyor belt drives out all thought. We crouch like living fossils in a metre or so of open space pressed on each side by tonnes of solid planet.

We'll all die.

And there in front of us is the petrified black forest of our prehistoric world. Cast in swirls of leaf and bark, whole trunks, whole trees, whole woodlands.

I squint into the darkness of that distant past. Dust in my eyes. I imagine bowers of shady green, tangled carpets of wild flowers, a world filled with tiny buzzing insects. And birdsong.

A world I've never known.

All turned to stone.

'There – it – is,' yells Aidan.

'What?'

'Black – gold.'

A forest forever frozen by some dark Midas touch.

And on either side, a line of squatting men, stripped to the waist, polished black as the landscape in front of them. They drive their shovels under the fallen coal. Their torsos shining in the half shadows as they fling the slack over their shoulders.

A metre behind them, the sliding conveyor belt. Gleaming coal rippling by. A dark, prehistoric river.

I watch their shoulder blades saw and slack, shovel and sag. I shudder.

It's appalling. Crouched there in this subterranean hole, moving monstrous quantities of ancient jungle. How do they do it? Kneeling, squatting, all the time?

And the heat.

Suffocating.

Coal dust down your throat, coal dust up your nose, coal dust in your eyes, under your eyelids, coating your hair, clogging your clothes, beneath your nails, beneath your skin, inside your mind, inside you.

And the noise.

Deafening.

Everywhere, like the rattle of gunfire.

'Seven or eight hours,' yells a miner – I think it's the tall, stooping giant. 'We'll – come – up and – tell you our decision – whether – you're in or not – seven – or eight hours.'

Seven or eight hours.

Down here.

God help them.

Coming back is worse. I'm tired out and dispirited. Nobody with a soul could bear this work. Tarquin is right. We must leave. The journey back to the shaft is uphill. My knees are trembling. Even the lamp becomes a bother. When I stumble, I drop it. And it goes out. And we must all stop until I light it again.

Ducking the beams is an effort. I forget to duck. I try walking with my head down; then I bang my backbone. Tarquin has already banged his. A dark patch stains across his shoulders.

After three hours underground, two miles travelled, crouching like gorillas, I'm totally exhausted. My thighs so stiff even stepping up into the cage is difficult. I can't step anywhere. I can't even walk again. I try resting my back against a wall and balancing against it in a curious sidelong gait, so as not to bend my knees.

At the pithead Bridey notices. 'So you've seen how 'tis ta work down pit, eh?'

Lenny doesn't reply. His little face is terrified.

Tarquin can't answer. His face is twisted. His jaw set tight.

'It's what we all do,' she says. 'But it's always hard at first. Still, 'tis the reason we can sit by a fire and sup on vegetable potage.'

She looks at Tarquin's shoulders, those once broad, straight shoulders.

'You'll be fine,' she concludes.

Lenny looks up at Tarquin with big eyes.

'You too, Lenny,' she says. 'You'll make a fine trapper.'

I shudder. None of us says a word.

'They'll be calling us soon. Best to get ready and know your minds.'

61

They haven't washed. They haven't eaten. They haven't returned home. Nine men and three women sit on metal chairs around the table.

We stand and wait. Above us the winding gear and arched roof of the pithead.

'We've made up our minds,' says Alfred Glover.

All of them nod.

'You're in.'

They nod again.

'You'll be given a bed and board, and willing hands to help you fix up a home. You'll get paid in kind, same as us. You'll be given shares in the mine.'

He smiles his treacly smile and waits for us to say something. I cast a glance at Tarquin. His face is set in stone. I let go of Lenny's hand. I try to bob a curtsey. My knees are too stiff.

'Thanks,' I say. Someone's got to say something. I flash Tarquin a look. *Just pretend. Till we think of something.*

'You're a pretty lass and God knows we can all do with a pretty face,' says Alfred. He turns the full beam of his attention on me, and leers. Openly fascinated. 'Will be nice to get to know you better. See more of you.' He puts his hands together, palms in.

My heart sinks. There's a pause. For a moment I think that's the end of it. Then an old woman I haven't seen before stands up.

'My mother,' grunts Alfred.

'You've noticed we need women, and we need children here,' she says, straight to the point. 'We've hardly got a dozen young ones left. All of them are needed in the mine and even though we're working them day and night, there's still not enough of them to keep the mine ventilated. Some of 'em won't make it through the winter and we got to keep output up or we'll all starve. You've come along with a young one, and they tell me he's already popular. He's good and small. Make a fine trapper in the deep workings. We'll expect more.' She nods her head at me in a rough manner and sits down again.

Alfred Glover separates his palms.

'We're glad to have you. Not many want this life,' she adds as an afterthought.

The woman with the shrunken head bursts into tears. I notice Hannah slips an arm round her and cries too.

'You may well cry,' snaps Alfred's mother, rising again. 'But you're not the only one who's lost a child to the mine.' She spits the words out at Hannah.

The stress level in the room shoots up. There's a quick nodding of heads.

'And if you wasn't so sickly, you could breed us a few more,' adds the woman unkindly. 'And ease the work on the ones left.' She points a thin finger at Hannah. 'If you'd tried, maybe your boy wouldn't've gone.'

356

Hannah hangs her head. Her shoulders shaking.

Alfred Glover quickly picks up a pen and signs a document laid out in front of him.

Tarquin is about to explode. I can see his tension like a fuse burning. I grip his arm. *Not now. Remember the locked door. Wait.*

But he can't. He's got to speak. And I know what he's going to say. But as he opens his mouth, the door bursts wide. In runs a young man. He's holding a paper. He rushes straight up to Alfred.

'*Communication!*'

Tarquin stands there, mouth still open.

'Communication,' pants the messenger again. 'Carrier pigeon.'

Everyone waits while Alfred unfolds the note. Not a chair squeaks.

Alfred takes an age reading it. At length he raises his hand, reads out. '*Believe fugitives arrived at pithead last night. Girl, young man and boy. Wanted. Deliver back on next cargo. By order Governor General.*'

'No,' sobs Lenny.

Tarquin sees his terror, swallows his words.

'Send 'em back,' shouts someone.

'We won't go,' warns Tarquin.

'You won't go,' says Alfred.

'No.'

'You're part of the mine now.'

'We still won't go.'

'You're part of the mine and you'll do what I say.'

Tarquin stiffens.

'*Just hang on,*' I whisper.

'This mine is independently owned and operated. General Hammond don't run it. And he'll not interfere with my running of it. I sign up who I like. We've got our own charter. I've already signed you. So he's too late. If you've committed a crime we'll see to it here. You won't be going anywhere.'

You won't be going anywhere. A cold shiver runs down my spine.

'I see,' says Tarquin.

Lenny squeezes my hand, terrified.

'He won't take silence for an answer! He'll be on the next train up here!' shouts out one of them.

'Let him come,' murmurs someone. I realise it's Bridey. She's snuck into the room and moved up close. She places her hand on Lenny's shoulder. 'Let him try. He'll not take my boy from me,' she says.

'And he can't take what he can't find,' adds Alfred's mother.

'You want the girl and the little lad that much?' asks Alfred, still staring at me.

She nods. 'We gotta breed some strength and beauty back,' she says, 'or there'll be no younger ones left to run the mine when all of you're old.'

'Scabs' Law then.'

'Scabs' Law?' asks Tarquin.

'Old term for when you crossed a picket line,' explains Bridey. 'Headman just set a picket. Nobody'll tell the General about you, where you are, or if you ever reached here. All of us got a duty to each other. We'll hide you, lie for you, stick with you. Nobody's a scab in this community.

'As long as you stick with us.'

It's night. Tarquin will be waiting. He said to bring Lenny, but I look at Lenny's little face, his damp golden curls stuck against his cheek, so sound asleep. I let him lie. There's no lock on the door tonight. I creep down through the house, through the kitchen, softly open the back door. Let myself out. Cross the garden to the shadows behind.

'We're not staying here.'

'I know.'

'Didn't you see that girl down the mine?'

'I did.'

'I can't live like an alien bent double in darkness.'

'I know.'

'I'm used to outdoors. I'd rather roam the streets, fight dogs.'

'I know.'

'Then why d'you sound so disappointed?'

'It's a roof over our heads. And they need us, I guess.'

'They need Lenny.'

'And food.'

'They need Lenny and you, not me.'

'They'll protect us from the General.'

'They need Lenny, so as they can send him down the mine.'

I bite my lip. I can't bear to think of Lenny down the mine, flapping those heavy doors. Living in darkness.

'And you, to breed more children, so as they can send them down there too. The ones that don't die.'

A cloud runs across the face of the moon. The greenhouse

falls into shadow. I think of the smell of smoky fires, hot nights, of the fossilised forest. We can't stay here. I know it.

But where?

'Don't you care they want to breed you, send your babies into a pit?'

'OK.'

'OK, what?' He sounds so fierce, so disappointed.

'You've made your point.'

'So tomorrow night, when we've got some food and clothes together, we're out of here.'

62

I lie awake. My mind filled again with the horror of that mine. Its deep black jungle like a living thing, filled with bloodsucking parasites, draining me of every happy thought.

In the darkness, I hear Nan's voice.

'The underworld is a terrible place, Melissa. It is the land of the living dead. Do not get trapped there. You are a child of the light. Queen of a thousand blossoms. Beware the darkness.'

And I remember the story.

'When Eurydice disappeared, Orpheus travelled to the underworld to soften the heart of Hades. And Hades allowed Eurydice to return with Orpheus to the sunshine – on one condition: Orpheus should walk in front of her and not look back until they both reached the light. He set off with Eurydice following, but enthralled by her beauty he hesitated, he turned to look at her, and she vanished forever.

'Do not cause others to look back, do not hold them by your beauty, Melissa, lest you remain forever in the underworld.'

And suddenly I remember my dream. When Tarquin came to me clothed in white cotton and took my hand and led me forth . . .

But if we leave here, where can we go?

Oh Nan, there are many kinds of underworlds. Many shades of darkness.

To be back safe with you, by the fireside, with your book of Greek myths. That enchanted world. To open it up at my favourite drawing: Gods sporting, maidens cavorting, over them honeyed skies of gold.

Oh Nan . . .

Where else is there in this God-forsaken land?

I don't sleep well. And the morning brings worse.

'Soldiers have come,' says Bridey as she stirs a cup.

'Already?'

'Arrived on a special, early this morning.'

'The General?'

'Not yet.'

'What's a special?'

'A small engine that can run the lines.'

I sit down, rest my head in my hands.

'He must want you pretty bad to send soldiers the minute he don't get a reply.'

With a chill I remember.

Aristaeus desired Eurydice – and she belonged to another – yet still he did not repent. Still he pursued her.

I shiver.

'We'll stick by you,' says Bridey. 'Me and Hannah already

362

love that boy of yours and your young man's good and strong.'

I don't point out that he isn't 'my young man'.

'None of us is scabs,' joins in Hannah. 'And we don't like the army up here,' she adds in a whisper. 'They don't pay us for the coal on time. They send us rotten vegetables and they stop us from trading fairly.'

She was beautiful, Melissa. But not more beautiful than you. And Aristaeus pursued her to her death. Caused her to dwell forever in the underworld.

She goes out to the standpipe in the back yard, starts pumping water up to the header tank.

'It's you he wants,' says Bridey. She poles flat cakes with a long handled spatula into the little side oven by the range.

'I know.'

'Beauty is a blessing and a curse,' she says.

'A blessing?'

'Look at the way your young man worships you,' she says.

I raise my head. Tarquin worships me?

'Even a blind man could spot it.'

I raise my fingers to my face, touch the curve of my cheek, the tip of my lips.

'Half the men in this community already swooning.'

'Not really?'

'Why d'you think our Albert, the headman, took you in, give you shares without even a condition? Why d'you think he didn't turn you straight over when that communication came?'

I shake my head. 'He'd already signed us?' I say.

'It's on account of the others. Albert's only loyalty is to the mine. But a face like yours gives them something to dream about, when they're down there in the dark at the coalface. He knows that. He's a man too. Seeing you, touching your hand, maybe breeding with you. That's all. Even he dreams of it. Dreams are food for the soul, as keeps you going, through them dark hours. We need dreams up here. We got to keep going. We've got a good thing – that mine has saved our lives, but it'd suck the heart out of you.'

Lenny bounces in. He runs straight up to Bridey and throws his arms around her waist. He buries his face in her apron.

'You,' he says, 'smell nice.'

She puts her arms around him. Raises her hand to her eyes. Brushes them.

'If anybody scabs, by Christ the Lord, I'll kill them.'

63

I stand in the kitchen. *Soldiers.* They'll search for us.

Leave no stone unturned.

'Tarquin?' I ask.

'Don't worry. There was a meeting in the night. Your young man was brought to reason. He wouldn't let us take you both to stay in the pits, but he'll be well hidden down there himself by now,' says Bridey. 'Take more than an army of soldiers to search them mines. And they're lazy buggers them soldiers. So it's you we got to worry about now.'

'They'll do a house to house search,' says Hannah. 'Bound to.'

'Before they check the mines.'

The two women step into the yard, seem to be arguing. Lenny sits at the kitchen table. He's got two fried eggs in front of him. He's looking at them, like he's planning every mouthful.

It starts to rain. Bridey and Hannah take shelter by the privy, carry on arguing. The rain drives against the windows, batters the roof. I pace around.

'If they find us, Missa, how will they know it's us?' asks Lenny.

'They know what I look like.'

'Do they know what I look like?'

I think about it. They probably won't. They won't really know what Tarquin looks like either. His face was all swollen at the farm. And Lenny had dreadlocks then. He's had his hair combed and washed and cut now. I look over at him: curls, sweet little face. They might not even be soldiers from the farm.

They'll know it's him because of me.

They're not gonna forget my face.

Perhaps I should turn myself in?

Bridey comes back in, wipes her hands, tucks a strand of grey behind her ear. 'When the soldiers come, you're to go out back and hide in the geese coop,' she says. 'I said it wasn't the right place to hide you and my boy, but it's the safest.'

Lenny cheers up. 'It's a good place, missus,' he says. 'We was pretending we was hens before. Now we can do ducks.'

'Geese,' I say.

He decides at that point to cut off the white of the eggs and fork the yolk into his mouth in one go.

'You got to make sure them geese don't squawk, that's all,' says Bridey. 'Talk to them. Croon to them. Geese like that. If they honk and squawk, the soldiers are going to look there. If they don't, the soldiers're not going to know anybody's inside. Geese are nasty creatures if you stir them up. Them soldiers won't want to do that.'

'Our geese ain't scabs, though,' calls out Hannah. 'They

love us and they hates soldiers.'

'We can read them geese my book,' says Lenny. 'You can tell them a story about how they're going to lay ten eggs each like them hens do, Missa.'

I smile at him. I try to harness that other kind of courage. 'Better go and practise then,' I say. 'So they get to know us.'

Lenny needs no more encouragement. He finishes his breakfast, gets his book. We go down to the coop.

'Watch out for their beaks,' warns Bridey. 'They can give you a nasty peck.'

At first they make a terrible honking. Bridey comes out twice to check. She says, 'Best you come in and hide under the beds or someplace. This ain't working.'

But I don't think hiding under the beds will work either, so I set about talking properly to the geese. Soon they calm down. They like Lenny's cooing and they like eye contact. Soon Lenny's petting them and tickling their feathers. I'm tolerated too. One actually lays her head on my lap. I'm just about to take a short break, stretch my legs, when there's a banging on the door.

Bridey runs out, skirts flapping. 'They've come,' she hisses. 'They've searched all the houses up to us. Stay quiet.'

My heart hammers. I put my arm round Lenny. 'Keep cooing to the geese,' I whisper.

Lenny lets out little soft, cooing, goosey noises. The geese coo too, adding just the odd satisfied cackle.

I hear the soldiers. Steel-capped boots. Loud voices. 'Stand aside. What's this?' Furniture being dragged. A metal bucket clanks.

Five minutes? Have they gone? I'm trembling all over. They're in the yard. 'What's in there?' Voice of a man.

'That's the privy.' Hannah's voice. 'Toilet.'

'And that?'

'Greenhouse. Tomatoes.'

'Check it. Bring some.'

I hear footsteps. The sliding of the greenhouse door.

'That?'

A shout from far off. 'No tomatoes here.'

'Coop and pond for the geese.'

'Geese in there?'

'Yes.' Bridey.

My heart hammers on my ribs. I nod at Lenny. He lets out a little coo. A goose gives a contented cackle.

'Check it,' says the soldier.

I hear footsteps. Lenny's eyes are wide with fright. I nod at him again.

He coos a second time. I break out in sweat. The geese cackle again, softly. One steps out and waddles halfway down the little ramp. I can just see it. It trembles its neck, ruffles its feathers, cocks its head to one side, flumps down, tucks its head in, scratches.

The soldier tramps nearer, big boots, heavy tread. 'Catch it. Do for later.' The goose doesn't like that. Boots. A scuffle. It stands up, sticks its neck out, lets out a nasty nasal honk, flaps its wings, goes straight for the soldier with an angry hiss.

Boots crashing. The soldier jumping back?

'Blimey!' he screams. 'Those things are lethal.' Heavy tread closer. Is he trying to approach the pen again? 'Forget it,' calls his friend. 'They're not in there.'

'C'mon then.'

'We'll be back for that goose. Make sure you've caught it.'

The women stay quiet. The sound of steps retreating. I let my breath out very slowly.

God bless that poor goose.

64

Lenny and I stay inside the coop all the rest of the day. The soldiers don't come back. But we jump every time we hear a noise. Bridey brings us water, stays tight-lipped. Takes away one of the geese. Hannah checks on us, pale-faced. At last, when it's dark, we come in.

An eerie feeling settles over the house, like a thunderstorm's brewing. It starts to rain, hard, fast. No lightning. We wait, darn clothes, turn steaming laundry in front of fires. The evening drags. Where's Tarquin? Is he safe? We wait for the miners to come. Will he come too? No one will recognise him covered in coal dust, stooping like the rest, will they?

We get the news as soon as the men arrive. Two of them come into our kitchen.

'The soldiers have enforced curfew. They've put a stop to night shifts. Albert's furious.'

Immediately everyone's worried. Hannah sinks into a chair. She's so pale. I fetch her water.

'How will we mine the coal then?' says Bridey.

'Won't be able to,' replies the miner, an old man called Topper. 'There won't be enough output to fill the orders.'

'They won't lift curfew till they find the runaways,' adds Colin.

'You're not thinking of scabbing,' says Bridey, suddenly dangerous.

'Nobody's thinking of that,' says Colin. 'We're just going to have to stay down there twenty-four seven.'

'But you can't,' says Hannah. 'You'll get ill. Nobody can stay down mine without coming up.'

'We did when we needed to – back then,' says Topper.

'We'll go out on the spoil tips and collect shale and slack, rather than see you stuck down there,' says Hannah.

'You'll not go near them slag heaps,' says Topper. 'They're unstable.'

The four of them stand there, chins in hands, backs bent, faces frowning. Lenny snuggles up to Bridey, puts a hand in her apron pocket, tugs her arm. 'Don't be sad, missus,' he says. 'I'll help you. I can carry things.'

I slip outside, hoping to find Tarquin. The rain's pelting down. I hover under the back porch. Nothing but problems. *It's you they want.* A blessing and a curse. *You should walk up to the barracks. Hand yourself in.*

I make a dash through the rain to the greenhouse, slide open the door, get inside.

Tarquin's there, grimy, drenched, coal dust in every pore. He struggles to stand straight. He's wet and tired and in pain. He wants to leave this place right now. I can see it in every angle of his body.

'I can't go down again,' he says. 'And they're gonna try and get Lenny there tomorrow.'

'We can't go,' I say. 'There're patrols everywhere.'

'We're going,' he says. 'Tonight.'

I tell him about hiding in the coop, about Lenny cooing, the goose attacking. How it was all right. How even the animals were on our side.

He shakes his head.

'They've searched the houses now. Let's wait till the soldiers go? Lenny needs to eat, put on some weight?'

He shakes his head again. 'Spring's coming. If we reach the cottage, we can still plant and get a decent harvest in. Len can eat all he wants then.'

'Since when were you a farmer?'

'I love the countryside, Melissa. Imagine me, the city ganger, loving the countryside.' He tries to brush the coal dust off him. 'I can't go down that mine again.'

'When the soldiers don't find us, they'll give up.'

I look into his eyes, try to let mine speak for me. *Just a bit longer.*

'We're going. That's final.'

I'll have to tell him. I take in a deep breath.

We hear footsteps. Two men. '*You there?*' they hiss.

Miners. 'You heard the latest?'

'No,' answers Tarquin.

'We're passing it down the rows, through the back yards.'

'If we don't make the orders there'll be food penalties.'

'*Merde!*' explodes Tarquin.

'And another special's on its way.'

65

We look at each other. *Another special's on its way.*

'That clinches it,' says Tarquin. 'I'm not waiting around until this town is heaving with soldiers. We're getting out now.'

'Lenny's asleep,' I say. 'We can't.'

'He can wake up.'

'Tarquin,' I plead.

He takes my hand in his. 'I'm sorry, but we are.'

I pull my hand away. I'll tell him then.

'Tarquin?'

He takes my hand again, folds it in his. 'Yup?'

The time has come. *This is it.* My heart's thumping so hard I'm turning dizzy.

Then I just say it. 'There isn't a cottage.'

It's out. I've done it.

His hands drop away from mine. 'Pardon?'

'No cottage.' I think I'm going to faint.

He steps away. Can't seem to take it in.

'*No cottage?*'

I nod my head. My throat dries up.

'The valley?'

'*I'm sorry,*' I whisper.

'I don't understand.'

'*I tried to tell you.*'

His eyes are confused. He shakes his head. 'The hazelnuts and the blackberries and the wild rabbits?'

The storm breaks overhead. Rain slashes down, beats the glass roof. A bolt of lightning. His face. Drawn. Deathly.

'*But the key . . . ?*' He wipes his hand over his forehead, says something – thunder drowns out his voice.

'Was – Nan's key . . .' I shout. I think he hears.

He sinks on his heels, bewildered. Looks up at me. It registers.

There's a silence. A long silence. Even the rain pauses. I sit down on a stack of logs. His face like a corpse. I turn away. Suddenly I'm so cold. I'm shivering. Then the rain starts again. Ferocious. Drumming out all sound. Did he speak? Another flash of lightning. Jagged. Blinding. Tarquin as still as stone.

When the thunder passes, I say, 'We'll tough it out here, make a plan, even if there're more soldiers.'

He stands as if turned to ice.

'Tarquin? There's shelter and warmth and food and work and shelter . . .' My list falters out.

Only the beating of the rain.

'I should have told you before.'

The pounding overhead and his silence.

'But I was scared you'd leave me, and there was never the right time.' My voice trails off. *I wish he'd say something.*

Water streams down the windows.

'I'm sorry.'

Trickles and drips through cracks in the ceiling.

'And there was no need.'

'*No need?*'

At last. I hide my face. 'Lenny can have a future here.'

'*A future?*'

'There's fires and electricity and . . .'

'*Down a mine?*'

'There's nothing else.'

'*Nothing else?*'

'There's no cottage. I made it all up. *Everything.*'

'No.'

'I did.'

'No. There *is* something else.'

I look at him.

'There's hope, Melissa.'

'There was never any hope.'

'And a dream.'

'You can't eat hope, Tarquin. We need food, beds, warmth.'

'And the dream. Our dream.' He grabs my shoulders, shakes me.

'It's over.'

'You and me and Lenny and the cottage and the ducks and the fish in the pool.'

'Stop it.'

'I can't.'

'Without a dream, life ain't worth it. *I have to dream.*' His hands fall away from me.

'Will you tell Lenny?'

'I'm going.' He clenches his jaw. A muscle down the side of his face flexes.

'*You're going?*'

'Come too? We won't tell Lenny.'

'You're not listening, Tarquin. *There's nothing there.*'

'You're wrong. There *is* something there. And I ain't giving it up.'

'I won't let you.'

'You can't stop me.'

'I won't go.'

'So be it.' He looks up and raises his chin. 'Melissa – I've loved you from the minute I pulled you out the river. When I brought you back to life, I brought myself to life too. I've believed in you. I've followed you. I've wanted you. Hour after hour I've dreamed of holding you, of kissing you, of being with you in our hidden cottage. But I'm gonna leave you. *I swear to God.* If you don't wanna come with me, I'm gonna bloody leave you.'

I stare at him.

'We started like this – we'll end it the same.'

Suddenly he steps forward, drags me upright. Pulls me to him. He yanks me from that dim place where everything is terrible. My shoulders hurt. My arms ache.

Hot lips press on mine. Hot hard lips. Just like that time on the brink of the river. The aching and the fear and the guilt. His lips hurt. I feel his chest against mine. He crushes me to him. His lips move, my lips move. My throat hurts. My chest hurts. The blood pounds in my legs.

He lets go. He looks up at the sky. 'God forgive me,' he says. 'But I've wanted you so much.'

And he kisses me again. And again. And he keeps on kissing me.

Then he lets out a groan and pushes me away.

'That was goodbye,' he says.

'*Goodbye?*'

'*Adieu.*'

He crosses the yard. And I can't stop him. And I can't reason with him. He won't listen. He pushes open the back door, goes through the kitchen.

'At least, leave it till tomorrow,' I plead.

'No,' he says.

'But you don't know the way.'

He just laughs. He climbs the stairs. Nobody tries to stop him. Bridey takes one look at him and goes to her room. Shuts the door. I try to hold him. He shakes me off.

Gently he lifts Lenny, gently he wakes him. 'Hi, Quinny,' says Lenny sleepily.

'We're leaving,' says Tarquin.

Lenny smiles.

'We going to the cottage?'

'Yup,' says Tarquin.

'Good,' says Lenny.

I sink onto the other bed.

'Collect up your stuff.'

I rouse myself. I get together Lenny's bits and pieces. The new tops, the jeans. *Think*. One yellow duck from the bathroom. I run downstairs. *Bread*. *Water*. I take carrots. I push them into a bag. I hand it all to Tarquin. '*Please?*'

Lenny sees I'm not coming.

'You ain't coming with us, Missa?' he says, confused.

'Yes, she is,' says Tarquin hoarsely. 'But she's gonna stay

here for a bit.'

'*Please, Tarquin?*'

'OK,' says Lenny.

Tarquin takes his hand. They go back down the hall, out the front door. I follow. My arms slack against my side. I can't believe it. He'll see sense. He'll turn back.

'Bye, Missa,' calls Lenny. He hugs me, kisses me.

I put my hand on Tarquin's arm. He casts it off. 'We'll wait for one night, until daylight at Hadrian's Wall,' he says hoarsely. 'That's all.'

'*You can't go,*' I say.

'See you at Adrian's wall,' calls Lenny.

'But the curfews, the patrols . . .' I plead.

'Pulleese,' says Tarquin. 'Me an' Lenny are gangers. No patrol ain't gonna stop us.'

'And it's raining . . .'

He looks at me and shakes his head.

And they leave.

They simply walk down the street, and round the corner, and are gone.

And I stand there.

66

When Bridey comes down, I'm sitting by the fire, shivering, staring at the embers.

'You should be in bed,' she says. She's pale, shaky.

'Tarquin and Lenny've gone.'

'I know.' She sits down. Like me, she stares into the fire. 'You can't keep them as wants to go,' she says.

I think of Lenny's tiny face and Tarquin. Tarquin saying he loved me. His lips on mine.

And now they're not here.

'So why d'you stay?' asks Bridey at last.

I tell her. I can't stop myself. I tell her everything. I don't leave out any of my guilt.

She doesn't answer quickly. At length she says, 'He's right, though, pet.'

I don't understand.

'Without a dream there's nought to wake up for each morning.' She pauses. 'I dreamed of Lenny growing up here, in my house, of sharing him with you, of being his miner granny.' She smiles so sadly.

We both stare at the fire. The embers are dying, turning

black, then silvery white.

'And now I can't shield him. I'll have to tell Albert they've gone. They'll not be under the mine's protection any more. We can't hold a picket line for them as is gone.' Her voice breaks. 'It's harsh, I'll grant you, but the mine comes first.'

I don't say anything.

'But I won't tell him till tomorrow – they'll have tonight to get as far away as they can – before the soldiers get to know.'

She picks up a poker and stirs the ashes. 'The soldiers will get to know once the picket's gone.' She screws up her face like she's trying to think a way out of it. She gets up, goes out, comes back, blows her nose.

We both sit there in silence.

'Can you live here without them?' she asks.

I shake my head. Shrug my shoulders.

'Can you marry one of the lads here? Make a home with us? Bear children to go down the mine?'

I bring my head up abruptly. *I can't.* I know it with a certainty that's like ice on bare skin. I look at her wildly.

Is that the only option left?

I could have stayed here with Tarquin. Been with him. Raised Lenny. But without them everything's meaningless.

'I thought as much,' nods Bridey. 'When you know your own heart, you got to follow it, pet, wherever it takes you.'

I can't live here. *Not without them.* I can't love *anyone* else. *Not like I love Tarquin.*

'If I was a beautiful young lass like you, I'd go. I'd follow that boy and be with that child.'

'*I must go,*' I say wildly. '*I must follow them.*' I jump up from the chair, panic stricken.

'Aye,' nods Bridey. 'Look into your own heart, it'll always tell you what needs doing.'

I understand.

I thought he wouldn't leave me. I thought once he knew there was no cottage he'd stay. We'd be together. He'd forgive me.

I didn't know I'd found my Orpheus.

I didn't know I loved him.

67

Suddenly there's this great clanging. Bridey straightens up. Something like alarm seems to spike through her. 'It's Old Maria, the Throckley bell,' she says, her face as white as a sheet. 'They're summoning us up to the football stadium, by the pithead.'

I sit up.

I wait for her to do something, say something. Tell me why. *Oh God, don't let anything have happened to Tarquin.*

Hannah bursts in. 'We're needed up at Old Maria,' she says.

I don't say anything. I stand up. I'm going with them to the stadium then. *What if it's Tarquin?* Hannah nudges Bridey. 'C'mon. Her too?'

'What's wrong?' I ask. *What if they've caught him?*

'Don't know.'

'I'm scared.' Suddenly I'm petrified.

'It's nothing. It's nothing,' says Hannah. 'It'll be all right.' Both women look terrified.

'*What is it?*' I say.

'They only ring Throckley bell when there's been a disaster down mine,' whispers Bridey.

I'm stuck in the underworld. I tried to hold Tarquin back. He told me he can't stay underground. He told me to follow him. Nan was right. I should have listened.

'Let's go,' says Hannah, wrapping her shawl around her shoulders. 'Let any bloody curfew try to stop me. I'll tell them what for.'

I don't know what to do. Go to the stadium by the pithead? Follow Tarquin. *What if they've caught Tarquin? What if they're summoning us there to watch a flogging?*

'Wear this,' says Bridey. She passes me her long dark cloak. 'Keep the hood closed. You might be recognised in your own. Leave your nan's coat here.'

Follow Tarquin. I must find him. Before he reaches the light and turns back to wait for me.

Hannah takes my hand, leads the way. Her hand's trembling.

We stumble through the dark, taking cuts through alleys that only the women know. There's no sign of soldiers. No noise of army boots marching. Only the bell tolling.

We hurry through the night in silence. Up to the stadium by the Old Maria pithead. Others are on the move. They slide noiselessly out of side streets, all heading the same way.

'What's happened?' Bridey whispers.

Nobody knows. Hannah crosses over to a group of miners. They talk in low voices, but I catch some of it.

'They've lifted curfew for tonight,' whispers one man.

'Another special's got in.'

We don't see any soldiers. I grope along the streets. It's very dark between the houses. I miss my footing. Bridey catches my elbow. I steady myself.

Please don't let it be Tarquin.

Hannah comes back, takes my other hand, grips it tight. 'Careful,' she says.

'What's it all about?' I whisper.

'Don't know.' She's not happy. After a few moments she adds, 'I think it's the special.'

'Praise the Lord, it's not the mine,' breathes Bridey.

Praise the Lord it's not Tarquin.

'More soldiers?' asks Bridey. 'Why ring the bell for more soldiers?'

If they've lifted the curfew . . .

I glance up at the moon. It's waxing, soon be full. I remember little Lenny when he first saw it. The way he said, *New beginnings.* My heart catches, as if something's sliced it open.

'Which way is it to Hadrian's Wall?' I say. If Tarquin's OK, I'll leave the stadium and just keep going.

'Head for Heddon-on-the-Wall, that's the nearest bit,' says Bridey. 'Only two and a half miles.'

Lenny used to hold my hand. He used to say, 'It's gonna be OK, ain't it, Missa?'

But it's not OK. The bell tolls on. I bite my cheek.

Please watch over them, Nan. Please.

'I'll show you the road, if I'm not needed at the pithead,' whispers Bridey. 'Let's get to the stadium and find out what's wrong first.'

And then I hear it. In between the peal of the Throckley bell. A distant clanging. It sends ice into my chest. I freeze. I listen. The noise stops. *It can't be. Not here. Not so far north.*

I must be imagining it.

At that moment we turn in through the old gates to the football stadium. The place glows with an oddly familiar light. A huge fire has been lit in the centre of the playing field. The flames lick up at the air. Smell of burning. Wood. Plastic. Thick smoke. With a shiver I remember the Olympic Stadium in London, the night they chose Lenny. I pull my cloak in tighter. *Thank God he's far away now.*

We're not the first there. Figures trickle in through the players' entrance. They stand a little back from the flames, gathered in a wide circle.

Together we inch closer. Bridey lets go of my arm. 'Wait here, pet,' she says. I can tell by her voice she's worried. 'Stay in the shadows.'

I peer through the gloom. Outlined against the fire crouch miners. Stooped and grimy. They look a lot older in the dark, like lean stick figures bent with age. Bone thin, like twisted wire. Their working gear still tied round them. Smell of smoke. Of coal. That dusty metalled scent.

Then I hear the sound again. And this time there's no mistake.

Instantly my blood runs cold. Hannah lets out a squeal, clutches my hand tight.

It can't be.

Oh my God. It is.

It comes again, clanging over the air. Pans banging. *Steel on pans.* There's no mistake.

The sound of the Blah-Blah.

385

Everyone strains forward, trying to see. I feel my heart pounding. My knees dissolving. *Who can be banging out the Blah-Blah?* In the centre of the field two groups face each other. *Oh my God, it can't be.* We crowd forward. Tense. Terrified.

'Don't be seen,' hisses Bridey.

I pull the cloak tighter. Drag the hood lower.

Suddenly Bridey turns to me, grabs hold of my hand. Her palm's slick with sweat. 'I don't know what's happening,' she says. 'They never ring Throckley bell unless it's bad. If anything happens, get out of here, then follow me.'

The pan banging reaches a crescendo. I make out the two groups by the fire. On the far side, lit up in a dull red glow, a battalion of soldiers, all in uniform, rifles at the ready, lined up in ranks.

At their head, the General.

Beside them, in front of the flames, armed with every kind of weapon going, is a tiny crew of gangers. Just three. Two hang back. But there's no mistaking them. They hold dogs, a pack of street dogs. More than ten cross-bred Staffs, on short, tight leashes.

And at their head, silhouetted in his long black coat is Careem.

68

Careem steps forward. His gangers bang their tin pans. There's a hush. Everyone strains to hear his business.

Careem raises his hands. In each one is a long bone. He waits till the noise subsides. 'Careem, of Bone Cross Bone Crew, salutes you miner people,' he says. He knocks the bones together. He makes the word 'miner' sound like 'minor'.

He waves the bones at the two gangers with him. 'My main mans, Kaylem Hardcore and Nailey Smiles, greet your peeps.'

Careem knocks the bones again. 'Times is hard and it's Dog's Law, but we're better off working as allies. So we come up here on account of our mainer man, General Hammond.' Big banging of pans from Kaylem and Nailey. 'We're joining up with these soldier mans to retrieve a little lost property what got lost up here.

'Yeah,' continues Careem. 'So me and my boys from Games City, us Bone Cross Bone Boys, gonna get up a horde with them soldiers, and use our tracker dogs to hunt that bitta lost property down. And we gonna mash up any of yous that's hiding it.'

An intake of breath goes through the crowd.

'Jesus help us,' whispers Hannah.

Careem waves the bones again. A hush falls. 'Now give me and da General and him soldier-brothers a cheer,' he says.

There's no cheer.

'I expect a better greeting than that,' says the General, his voice low and dangerous.

There's a few coughs and then silence.

'I've entered into a deal with these men,' he says. 'If anyone impedes the progress of our search, I will take them down to the prison farm.'

Deadly silence. Everyone knows, at the farm they'll be flogged half to death. Everybody knows he's lifted the curfew to come and tell them that: personally.

'If anyone wilfully hides an escaped convict, or aides and abets them in any way, I will take them down to the prison farm. If anyone fails to inform me of what they know concerning the whereabouts of escaped convicts, I will take them down to the prison farm.'

He raises his arm. Lets his message sink in. 'These are no idle threats.' He brings his arm down. The soldiers fire a round of shots into the night.

'Right on,' joins in Careem. 'We's allies, innit, so we're going to start up the hunt here and now – so you peoples can see. My dogs is trained – I brought them with me all the way from my ends. And they knows who they's looking for. They'll know if you been with them. They'll sniff up their scent on your clothes.' He holds up something, a piece of cloth that hangs wispy, frail. 'My main man, Nailey, gonna be coming round your houses. So you better think 'bout that, and what you're gonna tell my mainer man, the General, when we catches you.'

Careem pulls the dogs forward, gives them something to smell.

And then I realise what it is.

The green dress, the one I wore when I was taken to the General.

The first dog sniffs it. The second lifts its muzzle and howls into the night air.

And immediately the stadium is filled with a wild baying.

69

Hannah gestures: Go! Go!

Bridey's on her feet. She hurries me back down the alleys. '*Quick!*' She brings out a bag. 'There some bits of food in here,' she says. 'I packed them in case we were stuck waiting at the pithead for our men. Let's get going.' She gives me the bag, drags me into a half run. 'I'll come as far as the outskirts with you, get you on the Hexham Road, show you the way to Heddon-on-the-Wall. That's where your boys will head for. We need to hurry.'

I know we do. Already I can hear the pans banging, the dogs howling. I can imagine them sniffing the air, searching for my scent.

'Let's get to the back streets.' Bridey moves quickly for her age. Underfoot the road is uneven. I jog beside her, trying to keep up.

'You keep my cloak,' she says. 'It's good you have it. Less scent to give you away.'

I drag her cloak tight around me. 'Thanks,' I whisper.

'Down here.' She drags me through narrow streets lined with houses.

'Your nan's coat'll be safe with me, pet. I'll be like your nan now. I'll wash it and darn it and hide it. Always keep it for you.' She leads the way round the next corner.

I grab her hand. 'What makes you so good?' I whisper into the darkness.

'Love, my pet,' she says, wiping the back of her hand over her eyes. 'And hope. Never give up on it.'

We cut across old fields. Scrub-covered with thick bushes at the back of semidetached houses. Most of them ruined: ceilings fallen in, front drives crumbled. They rise threateningly beside the road, still enough of them left to house robbers. Behind us the sound of the pans.

I'm trembling. I swear the blood in my veins is trembling. My legs feel like mashed potato. I try to get a grip.

Bridey crosses the road. I run stumbling after her. 'Careful at the end here. Sometimes stones drop,' whispers Bridey. 'Don't walk directly below the ledges of buildings.'

'OK,' I whisper, straining to look up.

'The kittiwakes used to nest there long ago. Their droppings loosened the stonework.'

Fleetingly I wonder what kittiwakes are, what it was like so long ago.

We scramble through the playground of what was once a big school, tripping over loosened turf. Rusted swings creaking in the night. The pans sound closer. I stop wondering about anything except moving as fast as I can. The wind picks up, the first thin blowing of rain starts again. The moon goes behind a cloud. It's dark. If we get caught in another rainstorm, we'll be soaked. I think of Lenny out in only his little jacket.

We turn our faces away from the wind; push our hands deep into our pockets. Through the dark I see a flash of lightning.

We cut into the back garden of a house. We pause and listen. Except for the pans, everywhere's quiet. Not even the rustle of dead grass. They sound so much louder than before. 'Listen for a change in the rhythm,' I say. 'They use the pans to talk to each other when they're out hunting.' We strain our ears. The panning rises and falls like some savage drumbeat. Behind that the baying of dogs.

They're out there, testing the air, finding my scent, tracking the way we've come.

Aristaeus chased Eurydice along a river bank, hunted her with dogs.

We struggle through the garden. Old rose bushes tear at my cloak, I trip on a flowerpot. Like shadows we pass along the side of the semidetached house. Must once have been beautiful. A ruined conservatory. Broken glass.

We pass it all, picking our way as fast as possible, through the shards of glass. Then quickly on, until we are at the road. We stand panting on what must once have been a dead-end street.

'Down there is the Hexham Road,' whispers Bridey, glancing back. Anxious face. Pinched cheeks. 'It's straight and quick, but easier for them too.'

'You ought to go back,' I say.

'I'll come just a little further, see you onto the road.'

'I'll take it,' I say. 'Maybe Tarquin went that way.' *Please wait for me. Please be there waiting.*

We reach the main highway. Deserted. Overgrown. The pan beat is much closer. There's another noise too. I can't quite place it. We scan the road behind. I settle the bag across my shoulder. Look out over the dark country. The road's empty. A long way off, the shiny skin of the river. Lying so still.

I think of that other river.

Oh Nan, are you still there waiting for me in the green hollow? If it hadn't been my birthday, none of this would have happened.

And it seems as if I hear her voice . . .

Your birthday was important, because you were born for a purpose, Melissa. That is why you bear your name, honeybee. The Gods are waiting. The underworld must be held back. The sacrifice must be made. The bulls must be slain. Aristaeus must be defeated, and the bees freed.

'Please go back,' I say. A sudden feeling of doom.

'I'll take you just a bit further.'

Then the rhythm changes. An insistent drumming. A great clamouring, like all the dogs in England are on the scent.

'They've found our trail!' I say.

We start to run. The rain settles into a thin drizzle. The road is slippy underfoot. My side aches. 'Go back,' I tell Bridey.

'I may be old but I can run a mile or two,' she pants.

We settle into a fast jog. The ruined houses on our right get larger, more spaced out. Soon we hit open road. Ahead is a patch of woodland.

'It's going to storm,' gasps Bridey.

We cross over a narrow footpath, a toppled pole, a bank of undergrowth and into the woodland. We crouch under branches. Suddenly the rain slashes down, fast. It hammers on the twigs overhead. We shelter beneath the trees, panting.

'The rain will wash our scent off the road. From the

woodland we can cut out into fields,' she wheezes.

Trees sway under fierce gusts. God bless Bridey.

For the first time since I left the farm, I hear rustling in the trees. Not just leaves rattling in wind and rain, but scuttling. The sound of something racing for shelter.

Something living in the woods. Does it mean the wild things are back?

We stand there catching our breath and listening. As soon as the downpour is past, we cut into the woods. Head west. It's not long and we're into fields. Thick growth underfoot. The way is hidden by surrounding banks, and by what once must have been shrubbery.

We cross an old road and stick to the fields.

'This once was an extension of the Wylam Waggonway, built to carry the coal to the riverside,' pants Bridey. 'My family worked these seams for centuries. It was used by the first steam train, the Wylam Dilly.' She's sweating; her face is shiny in the darkness.

Such old, odd bits of information. Who needs them now? Who logs such things in the great book of history?

'You *must* go back,' I say.

But we jog on. The clouds lift a little, a glimpse of moonshine on trees, a far bank, an old wind farm above the tree line. The rain stays.

'When I get back I'll have to tell.' She's slowing down.

'I know.'

'If you'd stayed, we'd have protected you, whatever the General threatened.' She holds her sides. Her breath comes in great spasms.

'I know.'

'Alfred'll lift Scabs' Law. We can't tell our men they should suffer all the curfews, stay silent – not now you've left.'

She's right. The General won't stop till he gets me. He'll make everyone's life a misery.

'But I'll go with you a little further.'

'What about *you*?' I ask. 'Will you be safe?'

'Hannah's gone on home. She'll scrub the room you used, wash your things, especially the coat. She'll hide it. She'll let the geese into the yard. Light fires and smoke the place clean. No street dog will trace you there.'

God bless Hannah. They'll be safe.

'We suffered for the mine, you see. And it's taken care of us. When it happened we all went down underground. We stayed there for nearly a year. We let the women go out to forage for food. The old women first, those that couldn't bear children. When they got sick and died, the younger women went. We did it to keep the men strong. For the future. We paid the price with our children.'

'Please go back. I'll be OK,' I say between great gasps.

'But the mine saved us. And the mine comes first.'

'I'm sorry we brought all this on you. Tell them I'm sorry.'

'But you brought Lenny too,' she says.

Yes. Lenny. *Where are you now? Pray God you're OK.*

She catches hold of my hand. A cloud rolls aside and a ray of moonshine lights up her face. She looks at me. 'One day, maybe . . . when you come back for your coat . . .' Her voice trails off.

We come to an abandoned roadside petrol station. The sound of the dogs is much louder. And the pans too. We race across the tarred entrance, past the old pumps. There's that other noise too. It sounds like a horn or a trumpet. The rain slashes down again, suddenly faster. We crouch in the porch of the shop building.

We leave the petrol station, get to a crossroads. We're very near.

Bridey stops, doubled over. 'I can't,' she wheezes. '. . . Can't run any more . . . I'm holding you up . . . have to stop. Go back now.'

Through the night air the horn sounds again. Weirdly chilling. Much closer.

Bridey tries to straighten up. 'That's like a view-halloo,' she puffs out.

'View-halloo?'

'In the old days – the call of the hunter . . . when his prey breaks cover.'

'Hunter?' I gasp.

'In the long ago,' she says. 'The fox hunt.'

I search my memory. Did Nan ever tell me about fox hunting?

'Someone is out there on a horse,' she says. 'They're out hunting, following the dogs . . . enjoying the chase.'

70

I make Bridey go. I hug her close. Tell her I'll be OK. Tell her we'll meet again. I stand at the crossroads. Water running in the dark. I can't hear anything over the trickle of water. *Where will Tarquin be?* I must move. *Find him.* I'm very near the Wall. Bridey pointed the way. *Find the stream. Wade through the water. How far should I wade? Will it cover my scent?*

So the General is out hunting after all.

I set off again at a run down a long stretch of bank. Into another field. The footpath is smaller, harder to follow. The rain stops. The clouds clear. The moon shines out. Scarily bright.

Let Bridey get back safely. How long have I got? As if in answer, the howling of the dogs breaks out. A great din of barking and growling. The horn rises above it.

The Wall must be here somewhere.

In my mind I hear what Bridey told me. 'Wylam Waggonway. George Stephenson was born near here.'

'George Stevenson?'

'The trains.'

'Oh.'

'Follow the track till you come to the Wall. It's on your left.'

The wind whips down from the north. I tug Bridey's cloak tight about me.

On my left.

There's a tearing noise. Something crashes through undergrowth. I twist my head round, strain into the darkness. And then I see them. About two fields away. Large dogs streaming out of the trees. The moonlight shines on the white patches of their coats, glints on their yellow teeth, catches the fire in their eyes.

They're here. They've found me.

I turn and run. I leap towards the village, burst through the hedge on the far side, don't bother about thorns or bramble. I'm into the next field like a bullet. I pull at saplings and those tall weeds, leap the ruts, race through a patch of nettles. I tear through the undergrowth, swerve boulders, rip through air like I'm an arrow.

A thudding crashes behind me. The dogs? Careem?

The horn sounds again. Deafening. My heart races. My legs shake. Up ahead is the village. I can see ruined buildings. *Reach it*. Weave inbetween lampposts, ducking, leaping, twisting. *How close are the dogs?* No time to look. Ground's covered with wet bracken. *Can't slip. Can't fall*.

A pounding shakes the road. *What the hell is after me?* I twist my head. Snatch a glimpse of something larger, behind the dogs, bursting into view. A horse.

Holy shit! On its back a rider, a shape I recognise. *Holy shitting shit*. The General, bent low against the horse's neck, whip in hand, spurring the creature on.

My only chance is to get off the road. If I stay, he'll catch me. I look for another chance, a gap in the embankment. My lungs can't make it.

Get to the village, barricade yourself in a building. Pray for a miracle.

I drive myself forwards. I race down the road, jumping stones, tearing across shattered tarmac. Stones skitter, chunks of crumbling road surface fly out.

No time to look back. No time to think. Just run. The dogs howl. The thud of horse hooves racing. It's no use, I can't outrun a horse. *Where did he get a horse from?* No need to answer. No time to think. Just run. And breathe. And pray I can find some place to hide.

And as I run I think of Lenny. I think of Tarquin. *Rescue me. Tarquin, where are you? Save me.*

But what if the dogs pick up *their* scent? Panic seizes me. *What if I'm leading the dogs straight to Tarquin and Lenny?*

I can't do that.

I won't do that.

So I skid to a stop.

71

I turn around. I put my shoulders back. I bring my chin up. I'm not going a step further. I'll hold my ground right here. Without me, Lenny and Tarquin may get away. If I lead the General and the dogs to the Wall, they may not.

Tarquin may be waiting. Not knowing what's coming.

No, better to die here. There never were any Gods. No escape. No cottage. No happy ever after. So I stand my ground in the centre of a patch of empty land, by the road. I wedge my foot up against a broken piece of stone.

And I crouch low.

And then the dogs come.

Big thick-set pitbulls, cross-bred Staffs. All of them feral, all of them starved, eating whatever they can hunt.

There are ten or so of them. I watch them race towards me. The lead dog is squat and dirty white. His flank's scarred, his jaw drools open. He's an old survivor. Like that dog by the river. Flecks of spittle speck his chest.

I know how to fight dogs. Everyone learns that, sooner or later.

I crouch and wait. I flex my bare hands. I wedge my foot

tight against that crevice. I stare at the lead dog. And I prepare myself.

This one doesn't care. He doesn't care about my crouch. He doesn't care about the staring. The thrill of the chase has hold of him. He doesn't even try to turn his head to meet my gaze. He doesn't waver. He just lets out a series of short barks, cranks his tail round and charges.

I crouch lower and shake my head in that strange sideways warning motion, like a bull before a charge. Behind him the pack stream. If he goes down, they will still come.

He draws back his maw. His fangs shine in the darkness: short, stub, long canine incisors.

And he springs towards me, paws reaching, muzzle open.

I grab his front legs and rip them apart.

With a cracking sound, he goes down.

He drops like stone.

The next dog lunges.

I can't fight them all. I raise my arm to guard my throat.

Don't show you're afraid. Time his moves. Don't lower your arm. If he springs again, thrust forward into the jaw. Grab the back of his neck. Push down on his spine. Body slam into the bite.

Jab at his eyes.

Break his neck.

Hold your ground. Don't let them wear you down.

Suddenly the horse is there. Huge. Looming above me. Nostrils flaring. Outlined in a ghostly glow of moonlight. The General, silhouetted in black, towers over me. Cracks his whip. Reins his horse in. Slicing hooves drive back the dogs. One dog, bolder than the rest, still races on. A foreleg slashes out. The dog rolls, is caught under the horse, whines, shrill, terrified. Is trampled underfoot.

'Let's play,' hisses the General.

Then he spurs his horse forwards. The dogs scatter, desperately trying to escape the horse hooves. The horse shies. Rears up. Twists and leaps over the body of the fallen dog.

And crashes down. I throw myself sideways.

It gives me a split second. I'm on my feet and sprinting across the ground. *Tarquin. Lenny. Can I double back? Lead the horse away from the village?*

But I've come too far. Right in front of me are houses, boarded up, burnt out. *I'm in the village.* I swerve again. There's a strip of grass and behind that, low bushes. I see pale stones shining dull in the moonlight, like a low causeway. *Hadrian's Wall.* I swerve again. I don't want to draw the General here. The dogs regroup, howling, unsure. *Keep away. Where's Careem?*

The horse crashes through the houses towards me.

No further then. *Maybe Tarquin hasn't got here yet, hasn't waited?* I try to think.

I stop, unsure which way to head. *Here. I'll stay here.* I wedge my foot against another piece of stone.

The horse is nearly on me. It's just another dog, I tell myself. *Think of a way to take it out. It's skittish. It's scared.*

It rises above me. Looms closer. *I can't take it out. Its legs are too thick.* Its nostrils flare. Its breath comes in grunts. Large, open teeth. Froth covered mouth. Ears laid back. Its movements wild. Mane flying. It's crashing towards me. Its eye rolls white. I spin away. Its muzzle sprays out foam.

The General brings the lash down across the horse's flank.

Poor creature, it must be as scared as me. It's going at such speed. At the last minute I jump aside. I can't wrench out one of those legs. They're too huge. I throw myself on the ground and roll. The slashing hooves miss. The General's whip hits empty air. My head knocks against the wall.

With a cry the General brings the horse back round. He raises his whip again. Turns to rush me for a third time.

The knock on my head hurts. I stand back up, dizzy. But the knock helps too. I didn't see the stones there. Screened by the bank of brush. Quickly I check. Yes, an outcrop of the wall, shining low in the moonlight. Hadrian's Wall. A metre of it exposed. A metre long. A metre high. Two metres broad.

And in front of it, thicket. Low bush. You'd never know it was there.

Suddenly I see what I must do.

The horse is wild with fright, can barely see. I saw how its eyes rolled as it galloped towards me. It's blind with panic. And it's dark. Quickly I'm on my feet. I jump forward and stand again, crouched low.

But this time the thicket is right behind me.

And behind that is the solid stone wall.

A metre long. A metre high. Two metres broad.

The dogs howl, anxious to get their teeth into something. They're tired of circling and doubling back to avoid the deadly hooves.

Just a little longer, I whisper. And you will have your kill.

72

This time I'm ready. The General reins in his mount, charges again. Flies towards me at a terrible speed. I crouch like before, waiting for the horse to be right on top of me. No chance for it to swerve.

I hear Nan's voice. 'Hold your nerve. Learn to take things to the very brink. If you give up before you have to, nobody will spare you.'

I wait until the final second when those slicing hooves are about to pound into my face, then with every ounce of strength I have, I throw myself aside.

The horse has no time to swerve. Does not see the need to swerve. Blunders on through the thicket and hits the wall.

It lets out a terrifying neigh. Agonised. Nightmarish.

Then over it goes. Catapulting the wall, its momentum forcing it forwards, crashing into more solid stone.

I hear bone snap and the thud of flesh. A shower of gravel. Branches flying. A snowstorm of twigs and leaves and blood.

It must've broken a leg. Or its neck.

Above the thicket a body flies. The General, pitching high, twisting, paddling the air, thrown clear over the wall.

I'm on my feet, watching.

The General crunches into the ground on the far side of Hadrian's Wall, limp like a broken doll. His limbs twitch for an instant and then the horse, shrieking, jerking in its death throes, balanced in agony on the broad stones, rolls in terror off the edge of them and smashes down.

Right onto him.

One thousand five hundred pounds of horseflesh.

Then the dogs are streaming straight past me, tearing through the thicket, scrambling over the wall.

There's a crunch of teeth on bone, a grunt, a whinnying cut short, screaming, and then the satisfied growling and slavering of feeding animals.

I've barely time to stop trembling before I hear them.

Pans banging.

And the sound of feet running this way.

73

I drop to my knees, roll and drag myself into the thicket.

Careem and Kaylem.

Hide. Escape in the confusion. The horse. The snarling dogs. The General . . .

Which way to go? Get away from the dogs. With shaking legs I try to stand. Look for a chance.

And there, racing from the far side of Hadrian's Wall, is Tarquin.

Dear God, couldn't you have spared him?

I forget all thought of escaping. I stand up and scream. *'Get back! Hide! Careem!'*

But he already knows. He heard the pans banging, didn't he? *Thank God he's hidden Lenny.* He heard everything.

The rain stops. The moon sails out. Tarquin vaults up onto a long outcrop of Hadrian's Wall. Stands silhouetted. His figure dark against the skyline. My heart contracts. *Tarquin.*

'Come on then, man,' yells Tarquin. 'Dog's Law. Let's see who's the dog.'

Careem smashes through the trees and bears down on us. In one hand a metal bar, in the other a machete. Long black coat flying.

Tarquin has no weapon, but he doesn't seem afraid. He walks along the top of the wall, as sure-footed as ever. I'd forgotten how tall and slender he was. How broad his shoulders.

Oh, Tarquin.

He stands and waits, his face lit up in moonlight.

Kaylem skulks down the side of the wall, stooping, sly and quiet. I look around for Nailey, but see no one else. Maybe's he's still doing house-to-house searching. In the distance, very faintly, I hear a bugle.

Holy shit. This is just the advance party, the dogs and the General, Careem and Kaylem. Soldiers are coming, maybe less than half a mile away.

I step back into the thicket, catching my breath, trying desperately to think. Careem vaults onto the wall too. He's not going to give Tarquin the advantage. He swaggers along towards Tarquin, machete in hand. *I must do something. Help him.*

Kaylem circles round to the back of my patch of thicket. He shuffles about behind the wall. Tries to drive the dogs away from the horse, away from the body of the General. But the dogs are starving. They won't let him near. I can hear him cursing. I peer out, watching. He's looking for something. He doesn't get it. The dogs turn ugly and fly at him. He backs off. I look back at Tarquin.

Tarquin. Dear God, let him be OK. I search around, looking for any weapon – a loose bit of stone, anything.

Kaylem skirts down the edge of the field, so that he comes out beside Careem. With one easy vault he's on the wall too. Careem passes him the iron bar. The two of them stand there, filling up the two-metre breadth of wall. Tarquin backs off, but there's nowhere to go. The wall ends in a drop down onto rugged terrain. If he gets off the wall, there'll be the dogs to worry about.

Oh God, he's trapped.

'We got you now,' jeers Kaylem. He winds the iron bar round and round above his head. Careem sways with him as if they've done this manoeuvre many times before.

'Wanna come quietly?'

Tarquin doesn't answer. Instead he crouches down, steadies himself and then launches forward. His fist flies out.

Careem steps back, lifts up his forearm, his tattooed skin flashing through the moonlight. He blocks the punch. With his other hand he wields the machete. It swishes through the air. The hiss of steel.

Tarquin.

Tarquin twists, dodges sideways, totters on the edge of the wall. The blade passes, misses him.

I taste blood. I've bitten into the inside of my cheek.

'You can't beat the dog,' sneers Careem. 'First, I'm gonna cut you into little pieces, then your baby brother next and after that, me and my main man, Kaylem, gonna have a little fun with your ho.'

'You talk too much,' says Tarquin. 'Always did.' He lunges forwards, driving his fist into Careem's stomach.

There's a distinct rush of air and a grunt, but Careem only staggers slightly. Before Tarquin can steady himself, Kaylem is on him. He swings his iron bar and it smacks into Tarquin's side.

Dear God, no.

Tarquin staggers back. Misses his footing and falls backwards, spread-eagled on the wall.

Careem gets his breath back.

'Well, *you* won't be saying anything soon,' sneers Careem. He steps alongside Kaylem.

Tarquin tries to kick out, but Careem stamps on his leg and pins him down while Kaylem raises the iron bar to smash it into Tarquin's head.

I bite down on my lip, scream out. *What can I do? I must do something.*

'No-oo,' shouts Lenny, and suddenly his little figure streaks from its hiding place by the edge of the wall.

Kaylem pauses.

'Wait,' says Careem. 'Let's entertain big brother, shall we? Let's slit little Lenny's throat first, and let him watch.'

'Get back, Lenny,' screams Tarquin, struggling to escape from the boot pinning him. 'Run!'

But Lenny doesn't listen, he's scrambling up onto the wall, rushing at Kaylem, fists flying.

Careem flicks out his machete. *Oh God, not Lenny.*

I shake myself into action. I'm on my feet. I'm moving. No time to think. From the corner of my eye a see a dog bound onto the wall too.

'Lenny!' I shout. I'm climbing over my end of the wall. Jumping down, landing on rocky stones the other side, scraping my knees. There, on the far side of the wall, the rest of the dogs are gorging themselves on the horse. A few metres off is the General, one dog still tugging at his booted leg, trying to drag him away. His face is half gone, his exposed, still-bandaged arm mauled beyond recognition. He moans. *Holy shit, he's still alive!*

But I don't care about blood and gore. I don't care about him. *Bastard*. If I had time I might put him out of his misery. But I haven't. I've realised what Kaylem was after, what he failed to get. I jump, hit the ground running, roll, and suddenly I'm down there, stamping and kicking that dog. I'm going to get the one thing that I need right now.

A gun.

For a split second the dog backs off. Before it rushes back to maul me too, I snatch the gun from the General's belt. I'm rolling over onto my stomach and raising myself up, and smashing that dog in its muzzle with the butt end of the gun. Then I'm on my feet again. I'm racing down the side of the wall towards Lenny. The dog goes back to savaging the body, rips again at the General's face.

Careem sees what I've done. He charges forward, machete in hand. He reaches Lenny, grabs his hair, twists his head back. 'If you shoot,' he hisses, 'I'll slit his throat.'

And there's the machete in his hand, glinting silver in the pale light. Pressing right against Lenny's neck.

74

I take aim.

I hold the gun steady. I've never shot one before. I'm not even sure what to expect, or if I can hit him at this distance and not Lenny. But I don't let any of that show.

Nan always said, 'Remember, nobody knows the truth about you, unless you tell them. Make them believe what you want them to believe.'

'I can take a flea off a dog at this range,' I say. 'One false move and you're dead.'

'Shoot and he dies too,' snarls Careem.

I inch forward. From the corner of my eye I see a shadow move. *Don't get distracted.*

Careem twists Lenny in front of him.

Don't look at Lenny's face. Don't see the fear there. Look at Careem. Hold your bluff.

'Drop the machete,' I say.

Tarquin is on his feet, crouching, a look of fury across his face. Kaylem sidles towards the edge of the wall, eases himself away, slides down towards me. There's something else behind him. Can't see it clearly. I don't look.

'Can't shoot both of us,' Kaylem hisses, and step by step he starts to creep towards me.

Kaylem coming closer. Careem with Lenny at knifepoint. *Oh God what do I do?* I waver. *Help me, Nan. Help me.*

But at this moment, Lenny lets out a cry. And from the corner of my eye I see that shadow streak forwards. A dog.

It's the brindled bitch from Games City. The one Lenny fed his little pieces of meat to. The one who rested her scarred and hurt muzzle in his lap.

Like a bullet straight from hell, she streaks past, bounds in airy leaps along the wall, sprints forward, scattering loose stones and, like a demon, flies straight at Careem's throat.

Too late, Careem realises this new danger. He twists Lenny round again. Tries to body shield himself. Swings the machete wide. Shoves Lenny at the dog, hoping the animal will attack him instead.

But the dog doesn't hurt Lenny. She doesn't waver one millimetre.

And Careem's too slow. There's one look of utter surprise. No time to shout, no sound again from Careem's lips. The jaws of the brindled bitch snap to.

The machete clatters to the ground.

Lenny picks himself up, runs towards Tarquin.

Careem struggles.

But pit bulls never let go.

And I wheel round, gun in hand, and shoot.

The gun explodes, jolting my arm.

And like a stone Kaylem drops dead.

On the top of Hadrian's wall, under the waxing moon, with the first streak of daylight in the east, I find them. Tarquin hugging Lenny, the two of them fused together. Their arms open as I scramble up beside them. I'm held in their tight embrace. Lenny's hand slips into mine. He squeezes it under the winter stars.

Tarquin's lips find mine. He kisses me in the fading darkness.

AFTERWARDS

Out of the eater came forth meat, and out of the strong came forth sweetness. And they could not in three days expound the riddle.

Judges 14:14

It took us three days to cross Northumberland. We took the dog, the brindle bitch. She was heavy with pups and Lenny said, 'She ain't going back to no Games City. I don't want them pups being hit and hungry.'

I don't think she would have gone anyway. She stuck to Lenny like glue.

'Having a dog along ain't such a bad idea, anyways,' said Tarquin.

Of course we didn't wait for the army to find us. We left everything behind, even the gun. We put it near what was left of the General's arm, so it'd look like he shot Kaylem. That's if anyone could work out anything, after the dogs had finished with them.

We wiped out every trace of ourselves.

Lenny said that was a shame seeing as 'Nobody ain't gonna get the big picture now.'

'What picture was that again?' said Tarquin.

Lenny tried to explain. 'How Missa's changed everything,' he said. And how the farm was 'gonna be different with Harold in charge, 'cos he can do magic,' and how 'now Careem's gone and that General too, maybe people gonna share out the food, and not just keep it for their own little boys and girls.'

Tarquin hugged him and said maybe that was gonna be true.

And then we set out.

And it looked like Nan was right. The world, when it's left to itself, does recover. Up there by the Scottish borders there's wild rabbit. And where there's one living thing, you can be sure there's another.

We caught enough to eat and Tarquin skinned them. I rolled the pelts up between dry grass, and told Lenny, 'We got one sleeve of your new coat already.'

I don't think the dog ever had so many bones to crunch on.

When we came down off the moors, it was a clear day, the whole of Scotland stretched ahead. We could see misty mountains rising up to blue skies. A warm wind blew.

I remember it, like it was yesterday.

'We nearly there yet?' says Lenny.

I look at Tarquin.

'Yep, we're nearly there,' he says.

'Must be just behind them hills,' says Lenny.

He looks at me.

I don't know what to say.

'Cos that's just the place for a secret valley.'

Lenny and the brindle dog run up the hill and disappear round a bend, out of view.

Tarquin takes me in his arms, seizes the chance to kiss me. 'Spring's coming,' he says.

'There's nothing there,' I whisper. 'When're we gonna tell him?'

'You really should learn to believe in things,' says Tarquin.

I think of Nan. I believed in her. I never gave up, Nan. I got tougher. I fought back. I defeated the underworld. I found my Orpheus.

Tarquin grabs my hand and we run up the track after Lenny. We round the bend and there, stretched before us, is a narrow glen.

It's full of sunshine. A stream runs babbling down to a tiny tarn at the end of the valley. Lenny's rolling over in the long grass, tickling the dog's tummy, playing at counting how many pups are inside.

I sit down on a pile of tumbled rocks that was once a little croft. Tarquin sits beside me. He kisses me again.

'There's nothing here. I told you.'

He laughs. 'We better get to work then, innit?'

Tarquin picks up a rock beside us, examines it closely, sets it on another, steadies it.

Then he hands it to me. It's big and very heavy. I nearly drop it.

'Careful,' he says. He takes the stone off me again. 'Gotta hold on to that. It's gonna be the cornerstone of our cottage.'

Lenny runs back. He's doing a little dance, all knees and feet and elbows.

'Look, Missa! Look what I found.'

He throws himself into my arms, twists round, cups his hand over mine and very, very gently, he releases his.

And there, still sleepy from her long winter's rest, is a bee.

Lenny smiles and taps his chest where he keeps the Torch.
'*I told you it was gonna be OK, didn't I?*'

Acknowledgments

Minty Barnor
Sakky Barnor
Joy Coombes
Ruth Eastham
Sophie Hicks
Annie Hadley-Stone
Jane Howard
Jenny Jacoby
Caroline Johnson
Maurice Lyon
Melissa Murawski
Georgia Murray
Sarah Odedina
Jet Purdie
Και σε όλους τους θεούς του Olympus

Thank you all

Sarah Mussi

Sarah was born in Cheltenham and raised in the Cotswolds, and received a BA from Winchester School of Art and an MA from the Royal College of Art. Sarah spent over fifteen years in West Africa as a teacher and now teaches English in Lewisham.

Sarah has written three previous books, has donated a story to an Amnesty International anthology, has given workshops for the SCBWI, and is the current Chair of the Children's Writers and Illustrators in South London society. THE DOOR OF NO RETURN won the Glen Dimplex New Writer's award for children's literature in 2007 and was shortlisted for the Branford Boase. Sarah is also the author of ANGEL DUST and SIEGE. Visit Sarah at www.sarahmussi.com and on Twitter: @sarahmussi

BREAKDOWN

Age Assessment

See also **Unaccompanied Asylum-seeking Children.**

Assessment is the bread and butter of social work; assessment of need, assessment of risk, assessment of behaviour, assessment of resources, assessment of individuals, of families, even communities. These are conducted in formal and informal ways with a purpose, generally to inform the nature of the intervention necessary within the resources available. Assessment involves making judgements by gathering and evaluating information. All assessments will ask questions about age and at times there may be an age dimension to the process, for example, assessing the age appropriateness of behaviours or services, but generally there is no debate about the *actual* age of a person, it is fixed, a certainty, written in black and white on innumerable forms of official documentation. However, for those subject to **immigration controls** where documentation may be missing, incomplete or subject to challenge, the fixing of age may become a more difficult process.

Age assessment in this arena is in reality largely concerned only with determining the point at which a person becomes 18. There may very well be good reason to determine age, for example, in securing rights and entitlements in our age-stratified society or placing a person in the right school or residential setting. However, in asylum and immigration terms, the role and function of age assessment has more worrying features. It has emerged as part of the social work role with unaccompanied asylum-seeking children and other young people arriving in the UK separated from family or other carers. This group are the clear responsibility of local authority social services departments having rights to assessments and services as children in need under the Children Act 1989.

Straightforward enough if there is clarity about age, but in many cases this is not the situation. Those young people considered adults either by the **Home Office** or social services departments will enter different systems, being supported and managed through **National Asylum Support Service (NASS)**. Similarly, those young people considered to have turned 18 while resident may also become the responsibility of NASS, resulting, for example, in dispersal to other areas. Research by the Save the Children Fund (Stanley, 2001) found the single most worrying thing for this group of young people was what would happen to them when they turned 18.

Unpacking this further, then, determining the point at which someone turns 18 is of considerable importance. Social workers are, as key childcare professionals with sophisticated assessment frameworks, ideally placed to help in this determination. The tension emerges when we contextualise this process within immigration, not child-centred systems. In 2004 2,990 unaccompanied minors applied for asylum, at the same time some 2,345 cases were 'age disputed' (Home Office, 2004). As the **Refugee Council** has pointed out, we are seeing rising numbers of unaccompanied minors, an estimated half of all applications, being challenged about their age (Craig Kenny: *Community Care*). Where the dispute involves their alleged status as a child, they will be treated as adults, the onus being on the applicant to prove otherwise. In reality, then, we have a vulnerable group of young people placed in adult systems, sometimes facing **detention** and removal without the protection of the Children Act. Added to this there are funding implications for local authorities where these children are not identified as such. One consequence of this has been to draw the enormously stretched resources of social services departments into age-assessment processes.

It would be difficult to find another present-day example where children are so routinely disbelieved and forced to prove the unprovable. The culture of suspicion that permeates all immigration controls and demonises all those attempting to enter or stay in the UK is alive and well in our management of this group of young people. While there are strong arguments for the social work profession to identify all these children as children, a more detailed look at the process makes for more uncomfortable reading. First, does a young person in this position really understand the difference between an immigration official judging their age and a social worker questioning them on the same subject, particularly given the circumstances from which many of them are fleeing? Second, the frameworks being used are Immigration and Nationality Directorate (IND) led (see **Home Office**) and not necessarily commensurate with principles of good practice in work with children. The current age assessment pro forma focuses on physical appearance, demeanour, interaction during interview, social history and family composition, developmental issues concerning age-appropriate roles and activities, education, self-care skills and health/medical history. While some of these themes are not a million miles away from questions routinely asked in assessments of children, applying them to asylum-seeking children exposes their Eurocentric nature. For example, how can we judge the level of self-care and independence of a parentless child fleeing a war zone against numerical age? How do we ask questions concerning family composition to those who have lost so much? How can we even make judgements about physical appearance and age given the diversity of ethnic origins and experiences in countries of origin? Even the Home Office accepts the 1999 Royal College of Paediatricians' advice that there can be a five-year error in assessing age and that there is no definitive scientific way of defining age at present (cited in Home Office/ADSS, 2003). What we do know is that the 'Separated Children in Europe Programme' which includes the United Nations High Commissioner for Refugees (UNHCR), as well as the Refugee Council and Save the Children (SCEP, 2000; Ayotte and Williamson, 2001), states that children should be given the benefit of the doubt in age determination and if an assessment is thought essential it should be done by an *independent* paediatrician who has expertise and familiarity with the child's ethnic/cultural background. The current UK position institutionalises the opposite: the presumption is to locate the child in adult systems until they prove otherwise using assessors who fulfil none of the above criteria.

So the key question in conducting age assessments remains: are social workers conducting a valuable exercise in protecting the interests of unaccompanied minors and securing them full packages of care as *looked-after* children? Or are they instead simply replicating a culture of disbelief that exists around these children, which may result in placing them in adult systems? At present there is no available research or information concerning any divergence between Home Office determinations and social work age assessments. A recent joint protocol between the IND and the Association of Directors of Social Services (ADSS, 2006) formalises the use of the pro forma previously referred to and encourages a culture of persuasion and agreement between the two parties. In the event of a disagreement the case will apparently be referred to the 'Asylum Policy Unit' to attempt a reconciliation. The Refugee Council and Save the Children are clear, 'No judgements of age should be carried out by Local Authority staff' (Ayotte and Williamson, 2001, p. 62) and the British Association of Social Workers is increasingly concerned about the ethics of the profession being compromised by involvement in immigration systems (BASW, 2004). What we can certainly see is a worrying drift into immigration systems by **social work** and **healthcare** professionals, which raises questions beyond the experiences of this group of young people. We are now seeing a move towards specialist social workers located at main ports of arrival and screening units, the first a pilot in 2006 at Liverpool **Asylum Screening Unit**. A consultation process is underway which is concerned to make systems more efficient and consistent and is considering the usefulness of medical and dental checks in age assessment. The alternative would be to simply accept the young person's word.

[DH]

Appeals

In some respects, the system of appeals against immigration decisions, for the most part refusals to grant asylum and refuse UK entry visas for family members, is the most visible part of the process of migration to the UK. (As the only category of visa refusals that is appealable is that for entry clearance for family members, I will confine this discussion to the appeals system as it affects people seeking asylum in the UK.)

In 2005/06, immigration judges determined 28,025 appeals. The proportion of appeals dismissed was 76 per cent (Home Office, 2006a).

The body that administers immigration appeals is the Asylum and Immigration Tribunal (AIT). A visit to one of its hearing centres throughout the UK offers the opportunity to study its procedures and protocols closely and to hear the stories and testimonies of those who wish to be recognised as refugees under the terms of the **UN Convention on the Status of Refugees** of 1951.

The AIT has been in existence since April 2005, when the previous two-tier structure of the Immigration Appellate Authority (IAA) and Immigration Appeals Tribunal (IAT) was replaced by the single-tier AIT. Under the old system, an unsuccessful appeal heard before an adjudicator could be referred to the Appeals Tribunal for leave to appeal on points of law that may have caused an erroneous decision. Refusal of leave to appeal was often the subject of recourse to **judicial review**.

Under the present system, unsuccessful appellants whose case is heard by the newly-designated 'immigration judges' may apply for a reconsideration of their appeal by the AIT, which, if leave is granted, may be 'remitted' for a fresh hearing before two immigration judges. A request for a reconsideration will only normally be granted if it is clear that the judge hearing the original appeal made an error of law and there is a real possibility that the AIT would decide the appeal differently on reconsideration (JCWI, 2006, p. 1135). Requests for reconsideration must be made within five days or 28 days if the appellant is not in the

UK on the date on which the appellant is deemed to have received the immigration judge's notice of determination of the original hearing. This extremely tight deadline produces many problems for unsuccessful appellants, mainly due to the near impossibility of finding a legal representative who will cast an expert eye over the appeal determination and ascertain the likelihood of a reconsideration request being successful. Because of the restrictions on legal funding, many practitioners will simply not advise on this matter and many non-legal voluntary organisations may be faced with requests from unsuccessful appellants to help them complete the necessary form to request a reconsideration. This is sometimes possible, but it may not be within the competency of social care staff to present coherent and persuasive grounds for reconsideration.

For many unsuccessful appellants, the appeals process stops here; this is where the hope of settling in the UK starts to unravel. It is useful, I think, to confront head-on the likelihood that the unsuccessful appellant might never be granted asylum in the UK under the narrow terms of the Refugee Convention and adopt a position of realism with the individual concerned. Hard on the heels of an unsuccessful appeal will follow withdrawal of **National Asylum Support Service (NASS)** support for single people and enforced destitution among the swelling ranks of the UK's undocumented migrants.

This is difficult for many people to accept.

I attended the funeral of an asylum seeker at which his pastor expressed a rather over-optimistic view of the system. 'Sometimes', he said, 'you aren't given asylum the first time you ask for it.'

Nor the second or third time in all probability and it is sometimes necessary for those advocating for or befriending asylum seekers to accept that the accounts they have given simply do not add up to a claim to be recognised as a refugee. The issue then becomes one of the continued welfare of the unrecognised applicant who, if single, must survive without state support and accommodation. Retrospective discussion of the ethical rights and wrongs of the asylum system seems a frothy luxury by comparison.

Refusals to grant reconsideration are now more usually challenged by recourse to **statutory**, rather than **judicial**, review.

However, we are getting ahead of ourselves and becoming unduly pessimistic where we would be better looking at what happens at appeal hearings, which are, as I have said, open to the public in most cases (for exceptions, see JCWI, 2006, pp. 1099-1100) and presumably, therefore, transparent and open to scrutiny with nothing to hide.

....

The following description applies for most non-detained or non-**fast track** appellants. Within ten days of being served with a notice of refusal of asylum the applicant, or more usually their legal representatives, must give notice of an appeal to the AIT. If the appeal is accepted, there will follow a 'Case Management Review' (CMR) hearing at the AIT, which is to ensure that the appeal is ready to go ahead. Both parties, that is the appellant's representatives and the Home Office officer who will present the Home Office's case for the non-granting of asylum, should attend this hearing; the entire appeal may be determined in the absence of the appellant.

Voluntary agencies meet many people who state that they were unaware of the date of the CMR or even of the full hearing, which normally takes place several days after the CMR. Sudden and enforced changes of NASS accommodation address can leave appellants confused and forgetful of reminding their representatives of the new location. It has even been known for some asylum seekers to be unaware that their asylum claim has been refused, an appeal granted and heard – thus without their knowledge and presence at any of the proceedings. It is therefore important for all advocates and befrienders to ensure that their service users maintain close contact with their solicitors or legal caseworkers in order to prevent such disasters from occurring and avoid a largely unfruitful process of blame and accusation.

If it is felt that such matters are the fault of the legal representative, a complaint may be made to the **Office of the Immigration Services Commissioner (OISC)** who will be able to request files of correspondence and check on known addresses filed with the representative. This is unlikely to help the appellant, precisely because of their unknown whereabouts, and who will by now also have forfeited the right to a reconsideration application within the prescribed time limits.

Section 19 of the AIT (Procedure) Rules 2005 states that the Tribunal must hear an appeal in the absence of a party or their representatives if it is satisfied that the party has been 'given notice of the date, time and place of the hearing and has given no satisfactory explanation for his [sic] absence'.

It may well be the Home Office Presenting Officer who is absent. In this case there is no cause to breathe a sigh of relief or celebrate prematurely since the same rules apply to ensure fair conduct of the hearing. In the case of MNM, heard by the then IAT in 2000, guidelines were drawn up as to judges' procedural conduct in such cases where representatives were absent, most notably stressing the need to read all the evidence in the papers before the hearing and not taking over the role of the Home Office by acting as the appellant's opponent (JCWI, 2006, p. 1103).

It may seem bizarre, to say the least, that hearing asylum appeals in the absence of one or more parties could be conducive to the upholding of an appellant's human rights: does not Article 6 of the European Convention uphold the right to a fair trial? However, decisions of the European Court of Human Rights indicate that asylum and immigration matters do not relate to 'civil rights and obligations'. Macdonald and Webber (2005, p. 360, para 8.17) maintain that:

> the legislation on immigration and asylum appeals, and the procedure rules are clearly intended to reflect Article 6 requirements of due process, openness and fairness. In cases involving human rights, the appellate authorities and the courts thus have a dual function: to review the decision of an immigration officer or the Secretary of State, or of a lower court or tribunal, for compatibility with the Convention, *and to act compatibly with the Convention themselves* (emphasis added).

The AIT is thus a self-policing body as far as its compliance with human rights legislation is concerned, but the taste of injustice and lack of fair consideration for all appellants must remain in those instances where appellants, relatively powerless with regard to the determination of the quality of their representation, are often now obliged to appear at AIT hearings unrepresented because their solicitors have been unable to access sufficient funding to appear for them. It is as if the Legal Services Commission has already partly decided the outcome of such appeals or has at least laid down serious obstacles in the way of a just outcome.

In such cases, social workers and other non-legal advocates could inform the AIT in writing of the reasons for non-representation and ask the judge to consider an adjournment so that a further search for legal advice may be made. Ultimately, of course, the individual immigration judge will decide the issue for themselves, and will be permitted to continue with the appeal if so minded. In all appeals, consideration will be given as to whether a case falls within the UK's obligations under the European Convention on Human Rights and/or the **UN Convention on the Status of Refugees**.

....

The effect of lodging an appeal with the AIT is usually to suspend any further actions against the appellant; they may not be removed from the UK, for example, and will continue to receive NASS support, although, when reconsideration requests are granted, communication between the Home Office and NASS itself can break down and NASS support can cease until appropriate action by professionals or volunteers is taken to remind NASS that appeals procedures are continuing. Appeals are thus said to be 'suspensive'.

Asylum claims from nationals of certain countries which are certified by the Home Office as "clearly unfounded" may be subject to a "non suspensive" appeals procedure. In 2006 the list of such countries was:

- Albania
- Bolivia
- Brazil
- Bulgaria
- Ecuador

- India
- Jamaica
- Macedonia
- Moldova
- Romania

- Serbia and Montenegro
- South Africa
- Sri Lanka
- Ukraine

The Home Secretary can order any country to be added to or removed from this so-called 'white list' of safe countries. Any appellant from these countries may apply for judicial review to have the certificate removed from an appeal, but if unsuccessful, will only be allowed to appeal against a refusal of asylum from outside the UK – effectively enforcing a return to the country from which they have sought protection in the UK in the first place. Such appeals are therefore 'non-suspensive' in that an appellant could be removed from the UK before the outcome of an appeal is known.

It is difficult to know what the countries on this list have in common, apart from the fact that the Home Office considers them to be 'safe' and free from blatant records of human rights abuses. Two were potential **European Union accession countries**; one has an unenviable record of systematic discrimination against gay people; one has one of the highest rates of HIV and AIDS infection in the world; two are among Europe's poorest and least developed countries and several have glaring discrepancies between the wealth and power wielded by oligarchies and the abject poverty of the majority of their citizens.

But none of these circumstances could give rise to a Convention claim for refugee status, so they must be safe after all, or safe within the confines of media and academic debate about the effects of globalisation at the very least.

....

So, we have been refused asylum in the UK; we have not been fast-tracked; we have a representative who believes in the validity and credibility of our case, and whom we have kept informed of our changes of address; we are lucky enough not to belong to a safe country as defined by the Home Office. What next?

Most appeals are won or lost at the preparation stage. Preparation should be careful and comprehensive. By the time of the hearing, not only should all the documentation have been served in accordance with the directions, but the appellant's representative needs to have a thorough knowledge of the case and the evidence. Hearings dash by and it is easy to miss points. Representatives need to be able to point the immigration judge quickly to evidence dealing with particular points that may arise during the hearing. They should be able to answer all the points raised in the letter of refusal and anticipate additional questions that they may be asked by the immigration judge. (JCWI, 2006, p. 1105)

Immigration appeals are civil procedures and the burden of proof, which is on the appellant, is low: the appellant must establish a reasonable fear of persecution under the terms of the UN Convention on Refugees if they were to be returned to their country of origin.

Nevertheless, the above comments taken from the Joint Council for the Welfare of Immigrants' *Handbook* are extremely pertinent: credibility of asylum appellants is the key to a successful appeal and due consideration should be given to the fact that appeals do have a forensic and adversarial character, forming a template into which evidence must fit to the satisfaction of the judge who is deciding the case. The appeal, and especially preparation for it, is a major opportunity to rectify any shortcomings of the Home Office's interviewing procedures and to set forth coherent and credible responses to any discrepancies and inconsistencies that may have entered the applicant's account at the initial interviewing stage due to confusion or trauma.

One observable feature of AIT hearings is the degree of emphasis placed upon chronological exactitude: whether incident A occurred before or after incident B. Whether it occurred on such-and-such a day according to the Gregorian calendar is often the source of much confusion and exploited by Home Office Presenting Officers with the result that appellants find it difficult to appear anything other than confused, forgetful or devious. Cultures that are unused to the recounting of narratives in strict chronological order, and which do not understand the sequencing of events as being particularly important, sometimes have great difficulties with this aspect of oral evidence. If the judge is equally confused it will certainly be noted in their subsequent determination and may be an element in the dismissal of the case. The interpreter, who will be present at the hearing, may find it impossible to render certain nuances of meaning from one language into English. Many languages do not express the time continuum of past, present and future in ways that accord with the need of the Refugee Convention to establish credibility.

Again, there may be occasions when the nature of events may sound implausible to European ears, but which need to be understood within their cultural context. For instance: the ease with which appellants state that they or their relatives bribed prison guards in order to effect their escape; the fact that the doors of public buildings where political meetings were being held were kept open during the meeting; addresses of key localities that are unknown by the appellant, and so on. It may be too late for many appellants, but those with experience of Africa might volunteer the information that security in some African prisons does not reach that of British standards with expensive electronic monitoring equipment, and that access to prisoners and their guards is easier than in the UK; without open doors, meetings and church services would become intolerably hot and stifling; many addresses in African cities are described according to district or neighbourhood, rather than being a particular number in Acacia Avenue, for example.

I appreciate that these examples are anecdotal, but there is continuing evidence that such apparently minor considerations are not appreciated by immigration judges and that a number of such apparent lapses in memory or of intimate knowledge of Kinshasa or Khartoum may add up to a rejection of the appeal.

Part of one such determination letter received by an asylum seeker reads as follows:

She [appellant] said that she did not know the name of the friend who told her that the plane had been shot down. He knew they were responsible by the way they were talking at the airport. He was satisfied they had a plan and that the plane had been sabotaged. (personal communication to author)

Home Office Presenting Officer submitted that the Appellant had not provided a coherent account of what had happened to her. She claimed that she feared the authorities in ___ but she said that her husband had been killed because ___ and his friends did not wish the authorities to have the information which he had gathered. She said that her husband had been working for the government as an anti-corruption officer. There was no explanation as to why they should have sent him on this task if they were intent on suppressing information about corruption. Putting it at its highest level, the Appellant's claim was that she feared a section of those working for the government. There was no reason why she should not seek redress through the proper authorities.

[HOPO] suggested that the Appellant's evidence was confusing and vague. She has spoken of her husband's friend being present when the plane took off and assuming from the way people were talking that they intended to sabotage it. [HOPO] pointed out the discrepancy between her reply at question 43 at interview when she said that she did not know if her husband's friend had been at the airport and her comment in the rebuttal statement. Her friend had taken her from the house to the airport.

[HOPO] pointed out that none of the documents produced by the Appellant referred to any particular crime [for which the appellant claimed that she would be apprehended if returned to her country of origin]. The wanted poster appeared to be produced on a word processor. There was no explanation as to why it should have been pushed through her door.

The Appellant apparently did not have the documents which she claimed the authorities were seeking. She had not demonstrated any political opinion. There was no reason to think that she would be recognised if she returned to ____.

The judge's confidence in the unreliability of this appellant is almost palpable. Could she have been better prepared to answer the Home Office's questions? Perhaps so, but there must be a limit to the extent that what comes across as confusion and incoherence can be overcome by patient preparation within the five hours' time limits now in force for asylum representation.

One presumes that the expert oral and written evidence on questions such as disputed ethnic identity, language and information on issues related to specific countries or regions might fare better at hearings, and especially so when specialist medical reports are presented concerning evidence of torture and other forms of mistreatment. However, this is not always the case and much still depends on the appellant's ability to get under the skin, as it were, of an alien judicial system and act out the part of someone whose case is fully formed, coherent and credible to an extent which is hardly compatible with the chaotic situations arising from persecution and forced flight.

And persecution is what this is all about. The pastor I quoted earlier was misguided in his assumption that all of his flock would eventually be given leave to remain in the UK as refugees. The present asylum system is not, and cannot be, a means of regulating the undocumented migration of the world's poor to the world's wealthy countries and somehow regularising their status (Van Kessel, 2001). It requires those requesting asylum to prove that the persecution that they face is political, religious or ethnic in nature and only such proof will do. It is a collaborative effort on the part of representative and appellant that will help to achieve this – often the appeal has been lost before it has begun.

[PF]

Further information

Home Office (2006) Asylum Statistics: 1st Quarter 2006
United Kingdom. Available online at:
www.homeoffice.gov.uk/rds/pdfs06/asylumq106.pdf

Further reading

Good (2007)

Application Registration Cards (ARCs)

While the debate on compulsory identity cards for UK citizens continues, asylum seekers have had the dubious privilege of being issued with **Application Registration Cards (ARCs)** since 2002.

These cards are a credit card-sized piece of plastic containing the asylum applicant's name, date of birth, nationality, place and date of issue, information regarding dependants, a photograph, and, in most cases, the legend 'Employment Prohibited'. They also contain fingerprint information and a secure updateable chip with address information. They are usually issued after the applicant's screening interview.

ARCs serve the dual purpose of providing easily verifiable ID for each individual adult asylum seeker and as the means by which they can access their weekly **National Asylum Support Service (NASS)** allowances at post offices by means of the inbuilt microchip (for families, only the 'principal claimant' can use the ARC for this purpose, which can give rise to difficulties in cases of family break-up and separation, for example). Unaccompanied minors also receive an ARC to confirm that their asylum application has been made. Minors are not fingerprinted, however, and receive financial support from the agency responsible for their welfare.

If there is some reason why the weekly allowance cannot be issued, post office equipment will issue a code slip with a number for all eventualities from withdrawal of support to an unreadable card. Asylum seekers are then expected to contact NASS for an explanation. This is an area where support workers can assist on behalf of those who do not speak English. If the fault lies with NASS or the **Immigration and Nationality Directorate (IND)**, then emergency support tokens should be issued to the claimant and delivered to their NASS-registered address by courier. The problem of an unreadable card can often be resolved with a clean cloth being applied vigorously.

For asylum seekers whose claims are ongoing, regular attendance at IND reporting centres is now a condition for continuing to receive NASS benefits. In the event of a prolonged failure to report, post office equipment can be programmed to refuse payment when the ARC is presented.

It is important that loss of the card is reported immediately to the police, a crime reference number obtained and the loss also reported to NASS. NASS should then arrange for emergency support tokens to be issued.

There is currently no section of the UK population whose material well-being relies so heavily on the technology of identity as does that of asylum seekers.

[PF]

Asylum

Normally associated with terms like, 'shelter', 'refuge' or 'sanctuary', the word 'asylum' has had a place in immigration history for decades. It has come to refer to the right to enter or remain given to a person recognised as a **refugee** under the **UN Convention on the Status of Refugees 1951.** The asylum seeker is a person requesting asylum or refugee status whose application has not yet been decided. They must show that they have a well-founded fear of persecution on the grounds of race, religion, nationality, membership of a particular social group or political opinion.

In every day terms, however, the meanings associated with asylum and in particular *the asylum seeker* are consistently negative. A powerful discourse has emerged at the heart of which is an assumption that many seekers of asylum are not fleeing persecution at all, rather they are using such mechanisms to enter countries like the UK for less deserving reasons. The asylum seeker has been persistently constructed as 'bogus', 'illegal', costly, antisocial and burdensome (Refugee Council, 2005a) and to understand this requires an overview of the history of immigration control in the UK.

Controlling entry to the UK is a relatively recent historical process and the first substantial controls were a direct response to a group seeking asylum. At the turn of the 20th century Eastern European Jews fleeing persecution in Russia and Poland began to cross into parts of Western Europe. After a period of intense lobbying and media panic, which constructed 'Aliens', or in the popular mind 'the Jew', as responsible for all the social ills of the day, the Aliens Act 1905 was passed in the UK in an attempt to respond to this perceived crisis (Hayes, 2004). The Act gave powers to newly created Immigration Officials and Medical Inspectors to identify and reject those undesirables, the diseased, the insane, the criminal and those thought likely to be a burden on the public purse. For just a hundred years then we have had mechanisms in place to weed out those whose entry to the UK is considered problematic even when fleeing accepted catastrophic global events. In short, a culture of questioning and judging the legitimacy of such claims has been enshrined in law for a century. What has prevailed has been machinery that judges the usefulness or costliness of a person to the UK, which removes our gaze from the global context and fixes it on the individual.

Racism has been central to this development of **immigration controls** because controls rely on an idea of *Nation*, which assumes *we* must protect *our* resources and *way of life* from *outsiders*. All lobbies for controls have been posed in racist terms, targeting different groups at different times. A further dimension to this racialised nationalism is the UK's Colonial history. While those *aliens* or *outsiders* initially controlled were not British subjects, the size and scale of the British Empire meant automatic rights of entry technically existed to large parts of the globe up to and beyond the Second World War. This was useful in times of labour shortages, but less palatable as longer-term settlement became a consideration. In short, developed economies need migrant labour but resist family reunification and the acquisition of long-term settlement rights. Like many other Colonial powers, the past 30 to 40 years have seen the withdrawal of automatic rights of entry to former citizens of the UK. Starting with restrictions to former Commonwealth citizens in the 1960s, this process has relentlessly reconstructed citizens as outsiders, in short, today's asylum seeker could have been yesterday's Commonwealth citizen.

Asylum, then, has assumed a new importance as the only available route of entry as other legitimate avenues closed. It began to enter the legislative vocabulary in the 1990s, the category *asylum seeker* being formalised in the **Immigration and Asylum Act 1999**. The current 'top ten' countries generating asylum seekers who enter the UK are Iran, Eritrea, China, Somalia, Afghanistan, Iraq, Pakistan, Zimbabwe, DR Congo and Nigeria (Home Office, 2005a). Each of these tells its own story regarding the displacement of people and its causes. That the majority of these (88 per cent) will fail in their attempts to gain refugee status or even be allowed temporary protection seems to indicate the complete failure of asylum as an avenue to safety from the most catastrophic of global events.

[DH]

Asylum and Immigration (Treatment of Claimants, etc) Act 2004

The third major piece of asylum and immigration legislation since 1999, this Act contains a number of provisions aimed at controlling and penalising some of the characteristics of irregular migration to the UK. It creates new offences of assisting unlawful immigration; entering the UK without a passport; forging immigration documents and trafficking people for exploitation. It legislates for the one-tier appeals system in the form of the Asylum and Immigration Tribunal (see **Appeals**). The Act also specifies a number of conditions that may affect the consideration of an asylum claim as credible, which include such factors as destroying one's passport before arrival in the UK and whether an asylum claim has been lodged as a last resort following other negative immigration decisions (Section 8).

Further sections of the Act cover the ending of back-dated benefits claims for persons granted refugee status; the introduction of a refugee integration loan and the conditions under which persons subject to immigration controls may marry – in effect, non-European Union (EU) nationals without valid leave to remain in the UK are not free to marry, which means all asylum seekers whose applications have failed. All other non-EU citizens wishing to marry in the UK need to apply to the Home Office for a 'Certificate of Entitlement' before they are free to marry lawfully (Sections 19 and 20).

This is an interesting example of the British state's ever-increasing attempt to regulate the private, indeed, intimate sphere of the lives of those it considers to be outside normal, regulated society and whose very wish for a legally sanctioned union cannot be allowed because it may be a bogus attempt to undermine the immigration laws and rules (see **Marriage of Persons Subject to Immigration Controls**).

However, the most notorious part of the 2004 Act is its Section 9, an amendment to the 2002 Act, which adds a 'Fifth class of ineligible person: failed asylum seeker with family' – 'ineligible' here meaning that a person whose asylum claim has been unsuccessful is no longer entitled to National Asylum Support Service (NASS) support. Before the 2004 Act, only single people without minor children had their NASS support removed following a negative decision on their case. Families with children continued to receive full NASS benefits and housing, based, presumably, on the belief that children should not be made deliberately destitute by the act of a government department. This could be seen as a benign residual echo of the welfare state still reaching out to those who were not British citizens but who could not be impoverished and placed at risk in a civilised society.

These proposed legislative changes were the focus of much media frenzy from all shades of the political spectrum, with a widespread assumption that families who failed to take steps to comply with removal directions would have their children removed by social workers and 'taken into care' when their NASS support ceased. It would therefore be the fault of the asylum-seeking parents if this happened, having been given a clear choice by the inexorable logic of the legislation: *your asylum claim is unfounded, your NASS support will cease, your children will become at risk through your inability to house, feed and clothe them through the decision which you have made to remain in the UK without any legal basis to do so.*

The Home Office piloted the Section 9 legislation with 116 families in London, Greater Manchester and West Yorkshire in 2005. In February 2006, the Refugee Council reported that:

> So far, only one of these families has left the UK. Four families have signed up for **voluntary return** and at least 32 families (more than a quarter) have gone underground. 80 per cent of parents taking part in the process have also reported that mental health conditions have been aggravated by the policy. (Refugee Council, 2006)

In the event, the Association of Directors of Social Services (ADSS) called on the government to repeal the legislation, and frontline social workers found themselves in an acute professional dilemma in being called upon to enact legislation that ran counter to the practice enshrined in the Children Act 1989 that the interests of a child are paramount in all proceedings and decisions that may affect their welfare. Procedures relating to Section 9 differed in detail between local authorities, but there seemed to emerge a consensus which saw families' accommodation and support of their children being maintained by recourse to Section 17 of the Children Act 1989, with the parents themselves being supported with the help of voluntary sector agencies. In this way, good social work practice in the maintaining of intact family units was made to prevail counter to the provisions of legislation that, by the end of 2005, had lost all credibility and was quickly becoming a lame duck and an embarrassment to central government.

There is no doubt that individual social workers found themselves under pressure to act as agents of the Home Office in carrying out Section 9, and it is to the immense credit of the profession that ways were found both to act ethically and to draw attention to the inherent unworkability of Section 9. The British Association of Social Workers (BASW) undertook to support any of its members who refused to carry out duties under Section 9.

It was good to see a measure of positive local support for the families involved, such as the well-publicised S family of Bolton, Greater Manchester. The eldest daughter of this family, already enrolled in further education at the time of her family being made subject to Section 9, became a spokesperson for young people embroiled in a situation not of their own making.

Section 9 is based on a relatively simple premise whereby the seeking of asylum is understood as being a contract between the asylum seeker and the UK government: You claim asylum, your claim is assessed and if it is rejected, you return to your own country. *If you linger in the UK, there must be a form of leverage that will encourage you to return to your own country. In the case of single people, this lever is enforced destitution; if you have a partner and a family, we will make all of you destitute – you will not wish to see your children forcibly removed from you by social workers, therefore you must co-operate with us. Is that not reasonable?*

For the factors that prevent people from returning voluntarily, see **Destitution** and **Voluntary Return**. However, it is a great cause of concern that the drafters of Section 9 could be so out of touch with accepted practice in contemporary social work. Although the legislation itself does not make provision for social work involvement with destitute families, it is (or was) inevitable that social services departments were at the receiving end of the consequences of this law in carrying out their statutory duties to care for children at risk and in need. The whirlwind of images thrown up in the media, such as the bundling of asylum-seeking children into cars by kindly social workers, belong to a bygone age of unannounced swoops by the 'rescue men'. One wonders if such legislation is, in fact, written by presumably highly educated Whitehall personnel, or whether it is dreamt up after reading the latest anti-immigration article in the tabloids or a conversation with the 'bloke in the pub' who will offer you his thoughts for the price of a pint.

Like most barroom philosophy, Section 9 and its companions in the 2004 Act are crude, reactionary and impulsive. They do not represent an attempt to address the real situation and problems of asylum seekers in the UK in humanitarian terms.

[PF]

Further reading
Cemlyn and Briskman (2003)
Community Care (2004)
Cunningham and Tomlinson (2005)
Refugee Council Information Service (February 2006)

Asylum Interviews

There are usually two levels of interviewing of asylum applicants: the first interview will take place either at the port or airport of arrival or one of the **asylum screening units** if a so-called 'in-country' application is being made some time after actual arrival in the UK.

At this level 1 interview, the immigration service will ascertain basic data about the applicant's identity, nationality and/or ethnicity, how they got to the UK and their reasons for claiming asylum. The applicant is also photographed and fingerprinted. They may be issued with an **Application Registration Card (ARC)** at this stage.

It is quite possible for an advocate to accompany an adult asylum seeker to this interview, but it is obviously easier in the case of in-country applications as the applicant may have already been able to contact sources of support by this stage. In the case of unaccompanied minors, it is vital that they are accompanied by appropriate statutory workers at all stages of the interviewing process as disputes about claimed age can arise even at level 1 interviews. A teenager who claimed to be seventeen was told she was actually eighteen years of age by an immigration officer who simply looked at her for a few seconds! Matters of **age assessment** can be addressed in more detail by statutory authorities at a later stage of the application process.

At the conclusion of a level 1 interview, it is likely that an applicant will require **National Asylum Support Service (NASS)** support and accommodation and they should be directed to the local agency such as Refugee Action or the Refugee Council who can arrange this. They will also need to access legal representation for help in completing the **Statement of Evidence Form (SEF)**, which will have been given to them by the immigration officer who conducted their initial interview and which will need to be returned to the Home Office by a certain date in order for the 'substantive' interview to take place.

If there are particular circumstances which make it undesirable for this interview deadline to be met – for example, if there are detailed medical examinations to be carried out and reports to be produced – it is essential for legal representatives to communicate these facts to the Home Office before the substantive interview takes place.

....

Ever been a member of a political organisation?
I don't like politics.

So you've never been a member of a political organisation – correct?
I'm not a member of a political party.

Ever been a member of a political organisation – yes or no?
No.

What event was it that caused you to leave ____?
We had a tribal/ethnic war. An ethnic war.

When was this?
It started a few years ago.

What one specific event caused you to leave ____?
If I left ____ it was because they wanted to kill me.

Did anything actually happen to you?
Yes.

What?
They destroyed my farm.

When was this?
3.12.2002.

Did anything happen to you personally?
After they destroyed the farm, they came the next day to kill me at the house.

Who destroyed the farm?
The [illegible], I told you that.
Tell me again who destroyed your farm?
The men from the army.

[several questions later]

How busy was your farm?
I had more than a hundred pigs. 150 head of cattle. So it was busy.

How many hectares?
The land was very big. I couldn't estimate the hectares, it was vast in my case.

You owned your own farm yet don't know how much land you owned?
[Applicant draws box] 150 hectares by 300 hectares approx.

Gestation period of a pregnant cow?
I can't say. Nine months like a baby.

Gestation period of a pregnant pig?
Five months, at least four months. And for the first time a pig can deliver two, the second time it can be four, and for the third time it can be eight. If a pig delivers one we have to kill them.

Where were you born?

....

Readers may be tempted to discover for themselves the respective gestation periods of cows and pigs, but they may be assured that these fine details of animal husbandry did not, in the event, play any part in the applicant's being refused asylum in the UK.

However, this transcription from an actual interview record gives some notion of the detailed questioning which the Home Office considers necessary in order for it to judge the credibility of an asylum claim.

In the case of applicants who are highly vulnerable, such as those who have undergone torture and other forms of mental and physical abuse, the asylum interview could prove traumatic in its insistence on a fine level of detail. The Home Office's own instructions to its staff recognise that it may be extremely difficult for an asylum seeker to discuss torture or traumatic experiences with an immigration officer.

Nevertheless, it continues to be the case that non-disclosure of information at the interview is taken as a sign that the application may be 'unfounded'.

The reliance on a strictly detailed and chronological approach to eliciting the 'facts' of a particular asylum claim may be inappropriate with some applicants whose cultures may not express experience in linear terms, and the undeniably forensic approach of the asylum process as a whole leads to a quasi-adversarial scenario where the applicant is posited as a 'suspect' who needs to prove the facts of their case before a sceptical administrative machinery.

As Asylum Aid found several years ago:

> Most asylum-seekers are deeply unhappy about their interview, and tell their legal representative so (if they have one). Indeed many are amazed to discover that the interview on arrival is their only chance to put their case in person before a decision is reached. Dissatisfaction with the interview surfaces later, at every stage of the procedure up to and including the appeal. Indications of poorly conducted interviews are a feature of a disturbing number of refusal letters, and should set off alarm bells. (Asylum Aid, 1999, p. 64)

Following the case of **Dirshe v Home Secretary** (2005) EWCA Civ 421, asylum interviews are now taped in the absence of an Legal Services Commission-funded representative (JCWI, 2006, p. 660), which should remove some areas of contention about what was or was not said at interview. However, the format of close questioning and the implicit agenda of attempting to 'catch out' the interviewee still exist and it remains the case that many asylum seekers, especially those whose appeals have been refused and have reached the end of the processes available to them, are profoundly dissatisfied with the process.

The quality of interpreters is also variable and many asylum claimants dispute details of the English version of their interview.

At the end of the interview, the applicant is asked to sign the interview record. But as this is usually never read back to the interviewee, it seems reasonable to decline to do so, and many legal representatives have often instructed their clients to withhold their signature.

The current constraints on legal funding for work with asylum seekers means that legal representatives are effectively barred from attending asylum interviews, but this may not prevent a non-legal advocate or trained befriender from attending and persuading the interviewing officer, as I have done, that the interests of fairness might be served by a reassuring presence in the interview room. This is particularly important when any interview might appear to the asylum applicant as another form of interrogation conducted by hostile authorities.

[PF]

Asylum Screening Unit

As at 2006, there are two Asylum Screening Units (ASUs) in the UK, which process in-country asylum applications, that is, those made after arrival in the UK after passing through immigration controls, as opposed to those made directly to an immigration officer at the port of entry. They are situated at Lunar House in Croydon and Reliance House in Liverpool.

In-country asylum applications must be made in person at one of these two offices of the Immigration and Nationality Directorate (IND). Screening interviews are carried out in order to gather information about the person applying for asylum, such as:

- basic details about their identity;
- their travel route to the UK, how long was spent in each country and whether or not asylum applications were made there;
- details of any visas used to travel to the UK and previous visa applications to the UK or another country;
- details of the applicant's family, including those who may be considered as dependants of the principal asylum claimant;
- the type of documentation used to travel to the UK; whether it is false or has been destroyed, and the role of any 'agents' used to facilitate the journey to the UK;
- details about the timing of the claim, which may be used to decide if **National Asylum Support Service (NASS)** support can be granted;
- education and employment details. (JCWI, 2006, p. 649)

The ASU is thus a processing agency designed to categorise and test out the validity and credibility of an asylum claim at a basic level. Even at this primary stage of asylum application, the information given to the interviewing officer could form a major element in the subsequent decision making (see **Asylum Interviews** for further remarks on the interviewing process).

In 2005 the ASU at Lunar House was the subject of scrutiny by South London Citizens, 'an alliance of institutions and organizations from across South London' (South London Citizens, 2006, p. 7) concerned about the treatment that asylum applicants were receiving at Lunar House, and also about the way in which IND staff conditions and training impacted upon the quality of service provided to some of those whom their report describes as 'mobile citizens'.

> … moving for many reasons – to find new opportunities for work, to travel, to embrace the promise of a new future through study and Higher Education, or to seek refuge and asylum. (South London Citizens, 2006, p.6)

On the subject of the culture of the ASU and the quality of service which its 'customers' receive, South London Citizens note that:

> There is a common thread in our research which suggests a 'culture of suspicion' and a 'culture of indifference' operating throughout the system. This affects communication, procedure and outcomes. One minor whose parents had been brutally killed in her country of origin heard an interviewer at the next desk shouting repeatedly to an interviewee 'Your parents are not dead!'. The young woman became convinced that she would not be believed and having no means of proof became too nervous to tell the truth in her own interview.
> (South London Citizens, 2006, p. 34)

The report later quotes from a Home Office staff survey of 2004:

> … 50 per cent of staff are dissatisfied with the training and development they have received in the last 12 months. This is below the Government Benchmark. IND staff were

also more negative than other Home Office staff on the subject of training and development … Staff were asked to handle asylum cases with, in our view, a basic level of training – and certainly less than the German and Dutch Immigration departments give their staff. Furthermore, turnover of staff, drawn by promotion to better paid jobs elsewhere in the Directorate and some outside the Civil Service, meant that the Department was putting more recruits into the 'frontline'. (South London Citizens, 2006, p. 60)

Whether the 'culture of suspicion' demonstrated at Lunar House is a matter of policy or the result of poorly trained staff confronted with situations which they are poorly equipped to handle is a matter of debate; the conclusion might be drawn that there is, indeed, an increasingly suspicious and punitive overlay to the successive phases of UK asylum and immigration legislation since 1999 (see references to specific Immigration Acts), which, combined with hostile media coverage, must make the prospect of 'frontline' asylum interviewing increasingly unattractive to those civil servants who might be best equipped to deal intelligently, objectively and sympathetically with the complex issues presented by those applying for asylum in the UK.

[PF]

Further reading
South London Citizens (2006)

Bail

See also **Detention**.

In everyday terms, bail is understood as being granted liberty while a case is pending, generally a criminal case. Dictionary definitions refer to 'the accused' being granted temporary release from custody. In immigration terms, there may not in fact be a criminal offence; the accusations may therefore refer not to crimes but to their immigration status.

Bail is a legal procedure whereby almost any person who is detained by the Immigration Service can ask to be released under certain conditions. When a detainee asks for bail they are brought to the Asylum and Immigration Tribunal where an independent Immigration Judge makes a decision. (BID, 2006)

Conditions of bail can involve conditions or sureties, for example, moneys to be paid in the event of absconding, the requirement to live at a particular address or report regularly to police station. If bail is granted it is usually for a limited period and further court attendance will be necessary. Research by South Bank University on behalf of Bail for Immigration Detainees (BID) between 2000 and 2002, which followed up around 100 bailees, found over 90 per cent complied with their conditions within the community (Bruegel and Natamba, 2002). All of these cases were originally disputed by the Home Office as having an above average risk of absconding. It also found inconsistencies in decisions to bail or detain including breaches in **immigration rules**. The report calls into question the justification for the increased use of detention for this group. Once again we see an exaggerated understanding of risk, which relates to the culture of suspicion and dangerousness surrounding asylum seekers.

[DH]

Further information
www.biduk.org

Befriending

See also **Campaigning**.

Susan and her family met Baptiste at their local church. As a recently arrived asylum seeker he had been 'dispersed' under the **National Asylum Support Service (NASS)** scheme to a small town in the north west of England. He had turned up at the church one Sunday, speaking little English and obviously isolated and bewildered.

He shared a NASS house with three other men from the African country he had been forced to flee following torture by a militia that was seeking to impose its rule over the locality where Baptiste had been a student. As Susan got to know Baptiste, it became evident that his distress was not simply due to an enforced move to a strange English town where people spoke an incomprehensible language and where, as an asylum seeker, he had to report regularly to the police station as one of the conditions of his 'temporary admission' to the UK.

Baptiste was withdrawn and his church attendance seemed to be his only contact with people other than his housemates. Susan began to invite him back to her house after church for a meal and she and her family began to know him better. It was during one of these occasions that he produced a photograph of his sister after the conversation had turned to Baptiste's family 'back home'. This was no ordinary family photo: in it, Baptiste's sister lay with her eyes closed and her face covered in scars and bruises. She was dead. The photograph was the only picture that Baptiste had of her and it had been taken at a mortuary following her rape and murder. The militia had visited his house and tried to find out his whereabouts while he was in hiding and shortly before his escape to the UK. His sister had refused to tell them anything.

Susan became increasingly concerned about Baptiste's health and accompanied him to his General Practitioner (GP) who referred him for a psychiatric assessment.

Baptiste eventually attended an interview at the Home Office in

Croydon where he was questioned about the facts of his asylum claim. About two months later he heard that his application had been rejected and his case went to appeal.

The adjudicator who heard his appeal rejected his claim on the grounds of credibility, as did the second-stage appeal tribunal. By this time, Baptiste had been diagnosed with post-traumatic stress disorder and clinical depression. He was an outpatient at the psychiatric unit of his local hospital and was taking medication for his illness, supported by Susan and her family who had now virtually adopted him as one of their own. Occasionally Susan would contact a local voluntary agency involved in asylum-seeker support and take their advice as to the best course of action and the probable outcomes in Baptiste's case. She also contacted her local Member of Parliament (MP) for support who, while unable to intervene in the case directly, wrote several letters to the Home Office, asking for a reconsideration of the case on humanitarian grounds.

Inevitably, the time came when Baptiste was forced to leave his NASS accommodation and his financial support was terminated. At this point, Susan invited him to come and live with her family. They had a spare room and it seemed to be a logical step in their support of a vulnerable man whose mental health continued to deteriorate, exacerbated by the lack of belief in his story and having to live in constant fear of arrest and removal.

Such was Susan's determination that she arranged a short visit to Baptiste's country and was able to obtain a visa even though travel there by Europeans was considered inadvisable by the Foreign and Commonwealth Office.

Baptiste had given her the names of some contacts who he thought would be able to find documentary proof that he would face danger, probably death, if he was forcibly returned there. Susan had some success in locating contacts who, although they made promises, failed to produce anything of substance.

Eventually, with the help of a local law centre and a series of specialists' reports, new evidence on the serious nature of Baptiste's mental health was used to persuade the Home Office to grant him

Discretionary Leave to remain in the UK.

He was safe.

....

This story is an example of what may be achieved through determined and informed befriending. The offering of unconditional friendship and the security of a quasi-family no doubt provided Baptiste with the knowledge that someone cared for him and was determined to obtain a just outcome to his asylum claim.

Because of the NASS dispersal regime, asylum seekers have been present in most urban areas of the UK for several years. They are often a visible minority in areas that may have not seen the first and second generation black and Asian Commonwealth migrants of the 1950s and after.

They have stories to tell of escape from brutality and torture, which speak directly to the values of compassion and hospitality that many 'ordinary' people, both within and outside faith communities, share as an expression of belief in a common humanity. These stories also resonate on a quasi-mythical level since the themes of capture, imprisonment, escape and the conquering of evil form part of the collective unconscious of many cultures.

The befriending process implies that friendship is offered purposively to someone who is perceived to be 'worse off' than the befriender. The befriender has personal resources or access to sources of assistance that the person being befriended does not have. (It is interesting that the English language does not have a term that, in a single word, describes this relationship: if we offer each other friendship, then we are both 'friends' and are on an equal footing, but if I befriend you, then who are we? Protector and victim? Comrades in a struggle? Mentor and mentee? Perhaps we are just friends after all.)

Informal, but informed and careful befriending of asylum seekers can be quietly and gently subversive of the immigration laws, as in the case of Susan and Baptiste. Or it can lead to anger and frustration if the full implications of a befriending relationship are misunderstood and there is a temptation to be a rescuing hero, snatching someone from the jaws of fate (or the Home Office) without recourse to readily available support and advice from lawyers and specialist voluntary agencies. It may become an exploitative relationship (on either side), fulfilling emotional needs or fantasies and creating a dependent link from which it is difficult for either party to break free.

It can end in tears, or worse.

One example of good practice in the area of befriending is the refugee mentoring programme operated by such agencies as **Refugee Action**. Here, people who have been granted refugee status are assigned on a one-to-one basis to a trained mentor who guides the refugee through the minefield of benefits, housing, training and employment that they must negotiate when they are granted leave to remain in the UK. This is valuable in that it provides not only practical help but establishes a symbolic relational bond between the refugee and a member of the welcoming UK community which is vital for the psychological well-being of a person who will previously have experienced many forms of dislocation and loss in their attempts at becoming a recognised refugee.

[PF]

Further information
www.ecsr.org.uk/cm – the website of Enabling Christians in Serving Refugees is a good resource for all befrienders, Christian or otherwise.

The following websites contain a large amount of updated information on all asylum seeker and refugee issues:
www.ncadc.org.uk
www.refugee-action.org.uk
www.refugeecouncil.org.uk

Campaigning

See also **National Coalition for Anti-Deportation Campaigns (NCADC).**

Social work and related professions have a long history of voicing concern over issues of social injustice, discrimination and oppression. It has felt entirely appropriate that through our work with *individuals* we should be aware of and articulate those social and economic inequalities that impact upon them most. Indeed, the early welfare reformers who spawned our profession lobbied not only around the behaviour of the poor, but the social and economic conditions under which it occurred. Throughout this history then is an engagement with what might be described as elements of campaigning, for example, in pressure groups or religious organisations concerning child labour or child poverty or the condition of prisons, or the denial of liberty to mental health patients. From the Joseph Rowntree Foundation to the Child Poverty Action Group through to Shelter or Mind, organisations of this kind have informed our work, educated government and lobbied for change. Modern social work remains attached, influenced and informed by such organisations and is comfortable being aligned with a great many. Indeed, the British Association of Social Workers (BASW) in the *Code of Ethics for Social Workers* (BASW, 2003) states that social workers have a duty to:

> Bring to the attention of those in power and the general public, and where appropriate challenge ways in which the policies or activities of government, organisations or society create or contribute to structural disadvantage, hardship and suffering, or militate against their relief.

That the social work profession extends this position to those subject to **immigration control** would seem entirely appropriate then. Certainly the profession's support for organisations like the **Refugee Council**, Amnesty International, Oxfam or more specific campaigns around the detention of children or against deportation is evidence of this sustained tradition of opposition to injustice.

However, there is another history of campaigning that needs to be considered here. (We will look further at the specifics of individual campaigning shortly.) That is, a sustained and relentless history of campaigning *for* ever restrictive immigration controls, which has gone on for a period of not much more than 100 years and has reached new depths today through the 'war on asylum seekers'. Agitation for controls began in response to the first significant wave of Jewish refugees fleeing persecution in Eastern Europe (see Cohen, 2001). The thread that runs through this period to the lobbying for the control of Commonwealth citizens in the 1950s to the 1970s, to today's relentless calls for more control of asylum seekers, is a virulent campaign of hostility. The press has been used throughout to problematise these *outsider* groups as burdensome, costly and undesirable. This constant demonising has included mythologies around disease, sexuality and criminality as well as sustained attempts to deny the reality of flight from persecution and to construct migrants as 'economic', as scroungers, as beneficiaries of things that aren't rightly theirs. There is here a direct link with welfare delivery because the nationalism at the heart of immigration control demands that welfare is *for our own.*

This is of relevance to this entry because this is the terrain upon which individual anti-deportation campaigns have to be fought. Any campaign in support of a fight to stay will be inherently swimming against the tide, forced to justify, account for and expose someone's life story as a last throw of the dice. Campaigning has become such a feature of the asylum landscape in the present day, simply because of closed and restrictive policies and reduced appeals available to applicants. In the asylum game now, it is often all that's left. This resistance, however, is of vital importance to both the individuals at risk of deportation and the ideological battle being waged. Such protests force a different reality into the public domain and in connecting with others, forge a unity between asylum seekers and the rest of the community, which cuts through the media lies and distortions. Campaigns are and can be successful (see **National Coalition for Anti-Deportation Campaigns (NCADC)** and professionals such as social workers can provide invaluable support. There are rich examples such as the Okolo campaign in Manchester, which united social care professionals with school children and community members in a successful fight for the family in the case to stay (see Gibbons, 1999).

Current campaigns, for example, around Section 9 of the **Asylum and Immigration (Treatment of Claimants, etc) Act 2004**, are similarly galvanising and educating professionals concerning their involvement in immigration systems. They have become a focus for discontent from social workers and their managers at the prospect of the removal of children from their families as a result of **destitution**. Campaigns can slow down legal processes, strengthen legal representation and open up new avenues. For a full and practical overview of how to campaign, see www.ncadc.org.uk. Social workers do perhaps have something to contribute in commenting upon the detrimental effects of immigration controls on children, families and communities and should be encouraged, in line with the statement of ethics, to do so.

The bigger asylum project may have different plans for social work, for example, as guardians of the state's resources, as part of the local machinery of welfare delivery or as helpful partners in applying and enforcing government policy. The nationalism at the heart of welfare will continue to force us down that path. The drift into immigration machinery outlined elsewhere in this book, for example, in **NASS** teams, in the **age assessment** of children, in **detention** centres or generally through offering differential services is part of this. Resistance is more crucial than ever now in halting this shift and remaining grounded in that alternative history, a history of opposition to injustice. For those at risk of deportation back to Iran, Iraq, Afghanistan, Somalia, Pakistan, the Congo or wherever, there may be no choice but to expose your story to the world with all that goes with it. As a profession our choice is much easier; put simply, it is a choice between being part of the solution or part of the problem.

[DH]

Further information
www.basw.co.uk
www.ncadc.org.uk

Community Care Assessments

The **Immigration and Asylum Act 1999** made significant care in the community functions dependent on immigration status. The creation of the separate Asylum Support Service, which removed asylum seekers from mainstream benefits, significantly excluded them from areas of community care provision. However, it is important to separate myth from reality because many asylum seekers are continuing to be denied access in situations where they do have entitlement.

First, refugees, and those with other forms of temporary settlement, for example **humanitarian protection** or **discretionary leave**, have the same entitlements as UK citizens. Second, the exclusions apply only to three provisions in the Community Care statutes. These are residential accommodation under Section 21 of the National Assistance Act 1948, services promoting the welfare of older people under Section 45 of the Health Services and Public Health Act 1968 and services for the social and after care of the ill under Section 8 of the NHS Act 1977. Asylum seekers are, therefore, entitled to 'other' community care services under Section 46 of the NHS and Community Care Act 1990. In addition, the exclusions described above only apply when the asylum seeker's needs for assistance arise 'solely as a result of destitution' (Darnbrough, 2004). In practice, therefore, if the asylum seeker's needs arise because of **disability**, physical or mental illness or old age, they have an entitlement. A House of Lords ruling in 2002, which has come to be known as the Westminster ruling, affirmed the local authority's responsibility in such cases rather than that of **NASS**, which provides support for destitute asylum seekers.

In such situations where NASS support is inappropriate, applications need to be made to the local authority social services department for a community care assessment under Section 47 of the NHS and Community Care Act 1990. These assessments should involve the applicant and include an interpreter if necessary. The 'care plan' arising from the assessment should outline the services to be provided by either the local authority or other care providers and be reviewed regularly.

However, there is a growing body of research (Roberts and Harris, 2002; Refugee Council, 2005b) that indicates that this is simply not happening. The Refugee Council research found only a third of their sample with an entitlement to a Community Care assessment received one and of those a half were still awaiting services. The causes for delay were largely disagreements between NASS and local authorities concerning responsibility, despite the Westminster ruling. Many of these asylum seekers were in completely inappropriate emergency accommodation for lengthy periods and some had unmet needs arising from previous experiences of rape and torture.

[DH]

Counselling and Therapies

I do not intend to give an overview of the current state of therapeutic work with victims and survivors of torture: Blackwell (2005) provides a concise account of the relevant issues for practitioners and clients based on his practice with the Medical Foundation for the Care of Victims of Torture.

I believe that the value and meaning of counselling and therapy with asylum seekers and refugees is problematic. Ironically, without 'problems' presented by clients seeking help, there would be not much need for counselling. However, what I have in mind is not, and could never be, of the same order as the problems faced by asylum seekers and refugees who arrive in the UK after having undergone, in some cases, unspeakable trauma involving murder of their closest family members, rape, war and all of the other events that are the common currency of the refugee experience in the 21st century. It is this: What functions do counselling and therapy perform in the refugee experience in its extended form as seeking asylum in the UK?

One way of addressing this issue may be to view counselling and therapy as 'plausibility structures', to use the phrase of Berger and Luckmann (1971). These authors elaborate on the term by describing it as

> a social base serving as the 'laboratory' of transformation. This plausibility structure will be mediated to the individual by means of significant others, with whom he [*sic*] must establish strongly affective identification ... These significant others are the guides into the new reality. (Berger and Luckmann, 1971, p. 177)

In other words, counselling and therapy cannot be understood simply at the micro-level of the application of various paradigms of practice: person-centred, cognitive-behavioural, psychodynamic, group therapy, (and we should perhaps include the various 'alternative' practices such as massage and aromatherapy in our list). Rather, their importance for the asylum seeker could be understood as extending beyond the purely therapeutic and curative healing of trauma, which is the hoped-for outcome of the encounter with the therapist or counsellor; their importance also lies in their symbolic value as legitimate means of healing within the culture where the refugee finds themselves and as a legitimate and legitimising source of evidence to support the patient's or client's asylum claim.

Thus, the talking therapies are precisely the laboratory of transformation suggested by Berger and Luckmann (1971) in that they may provide a powerful reframing mechanism of the individual's experiences. Being accepted by a recognised agency such as the Medical Foundation starts the process of giving form and identity to an individual's narrative of abuse and torture. In recounting experience, a 'case' consisting of clinical notes, opinions and reports can be constructed in parallel with the therapeutic interaction with the professional practitioner.

However, there are different levels of legitimacy and plausibility.

Many potential clients of such agencies as the Medical Foundation are deeply disappointed when, following assessment, they learn that their case is inappropriate for them to receive counselling or therapy. It may be that their needs are better addressed through medication or social support, leaving their perceived traumas unrecognised and therefore unlegitimated by high-status agencies who are seen to lend considerable evidential weight in the area of asylum appeals. It may, of course, turn out that agencies are unable to provide such evidence of trauma where none is perceived to exist (see **Medical Matters**).

Some asylum seekers may have to be content with GP referrals to counselling services provided by Primary Care Trusts where they can receive short-term help alongside the general UK population who almost certainly will not have experienced the same kinds of trauma as those inherent in the experience of some refugees and asylum seekers (see **Healthcare**).

....

At their 2003 Annual Meeting, the Royal College of Psychiatrists heard that:

> Psychiatrists are in danger of unconsciously [*sic*] undermining the ability of asylum seekers and refugees to integrate into British society and move on by medicalising their experience and labeling them as suffering from 'depression' or 'post traumatic stress disorder'. (Royal College of Psychiatrists, 2003)

It is easily possible that the legitimising of experience, which the therapeutic professions may justly provide, can also have the effect of maintaining their clients within a closed circle of 'victimhood': legal representatives can be so eager that their client is able to amass as much evidence as possible that the client's life becomes an endless round of appointments with counsellors, psychiatrists and social workers. There is little space for them to lead a fairly 'normal' life that does not involve constant reminders of past traumas. It is important for there to be access to other types of social support in which a trained befriender or advocate may work with a particularly vulnerable person in order to foster recreational activities, for example, which offer some insight into what life might be like after a successful asylum claim and to begin to help an individual to construct an identity other than that of 'client' or 'patient' (see **Advocacy** and **Befriending**).

Collins (2000, p. 75) offers this definition of counselling:

> Counselling involves a paid or voluntary worker offering specifically to give time, space, care and attention which focuses upon the concerns of another – the client. Clients have the opportunity to explore and clarify their strengths and weaknesses, to improve the quality of their life and to move towards greater well-being.

We should ask what form this 'greater well-being' would take in the case of someone whose asylum case is dismissed, and who is effectively made destitute if they are a single person. Does this state of affairs not make a mockery of any attempts at therapeutic intervention? In which direction can a counselling client move when they are effectively imprisoned within state-sanctioned rejection and all of the loss of identity that this involves?

I recently accompanied an unsuccessful asylum seeker to a psychiatric outpatient department over the course of several months. He had a diagnosis of post-traumatic stress disorder: he had been allocated one identity within the current psychiatric model of the society in which he sought refuge. He had been given a second identity as an asylum seeker whose claim had been judged as without foundation. I suppose he had another identity as a service user of the voluntary agency that provided him with bus fare and food each week, thus stemming his slide into total destitution.

At each appointment, his psychiatrist would ask the same series of questions: *How are you feeling? Are you eating? What is your social situation?*

The answers were equally predictable: *My head doesn't feel good and I'm afraid every time I see the police. I am in exile here and I have family back home. I need a solicitor to re-open my case, but I am told that I have to pay.*

The doctor would write and rewrite this information and finally had to admit defeat and discharged his patient into the care of his GP with continued medication. Neither he nor I, nor anyone else for that matter, apart from the Home Office, could provide what our service user wanted – the peace of mind guaranteed by permission to stay in the UK and in circumstances that might permit a move to greater well-being.

Without this, the potential freedoms promised by counselling and therapies cannot be realised and the positive relationship established between client and therapist cannot be actualised because of the client's inability to self-determine their life.

[PF]

Deportation

See also **Removal**.

Immigration controls do not simply operate at borders; to be effective they must include *internal* mechanisms to expel those who for a variety of reasons become subject to removal. This has been the case since the inception of controls in the UK through the Aliens Act 1905. Not only would 'undesirables' be turned away at the point of entry as a result of disease, insanity, criminality or being thought likely to become a burden on the public purse, but having gained entry would become subject to deportation if they became convicted of a criminal offence or were found to have been in receipt of parochial relief. A hundred years later the commission of offences remains a route to deportation for those subject to immigration control who may be considered 'not conducive to the public good' as a result (see also '**Double Punishment**'). The strong link between welfare control and immigration control is also explored elsewhere in this book (see **Immigration Controls**) and it remains the case that having recourse to public funds can be a route to expulsion.

People become subject to expulsion when they have breached the conditions of their entry or stay or they are involved in behaviour not conducive to the public good. I have now used the words expulsion, deportation and removal almost interchangeably and it is important to understand that the **Immigration and Asylum Act 1999** abolished most appeal rights against deportation. The **Home Office** can now use the speedier 'removal' procedures in most cases and there is no separate appeal right against removal. The effect of the creation of one-stop appeals and rapid removal procedures has been serious in speeding up the process of expulsion. I have chosen to use 'expulsion' as it encompasses these shifts. The Home Office had been fully aware of the 'slowing down' of decisions and expulsions through appeal processes and has acted accordingly. The consequence has been that legal advisors are struggling to find ways through this, and it is clear that contesting expulsion is becoming more and more difficult and demoralising. Opportunities to build a case, gathering professional reports from medical professionals and welfare professionals such as social workers are reducing. Home Office statistics are also complex and difficult to understand as a result of reclassification in 2003 regarding enforcement action and **voluntary return**. In 2004, almost 57,000 people were removed or left the UK, however, 58 per cent of these were removed after being refused entry at port. 37 per cent were removed as a result of enforcement action and 4 per cent left under Voluntary Assisted Return Programmes (Home Office, 2004).

Where 'compassionate grounds' have been argued there are further problems. The effect of presenting individuals and families and their horror stories has been pathologising and dehumanising. Presentations of ill-health, disability, mental ill-health, domestic violence and other features of people's lives to try to avoid expulsion has served to reinforce victim-like images of the largely black families subject to immigration control. Stereotypes regarding countries of origin can further problematise black people by presenting 'Western' systems and values as superior. Current constructions of asylum claims present overwhelmingly terrible stories which, though largely true, can leave us desensitised as to their true meaning. As long as we have immigration controls we will be forced into these corners in the fight to let people stay, being left to call upon notions of deservingness and desirability. The problem with this is that if some people are deserving, some people simply are not.

Such representations are a problem for campaigns against expulsion (see **Campaigning** and **National Coalition for Anti-Deportation Campaigns (NCADC)**. Campaigns are important in humanising the experiences of asylum seekers and others subject to controls, in telling the truths the media seems to struggle to present. They provide support networks and encourage activity that keeps the brutality of the current situation visible. It has been through such campaigns that we have all been educated about the horror of expulsion when our friends have been taken. The realities of forced ejection, the handcuffs, the physical restraint, the panicked fear of return, all takes place in airports and on normal passenger flights. Resistance through campaigning makes us stronger and begins to break through the dehumanising process 'as part of a movement for demanding rights as opposed to free standing pleas for mercy' (Cohen, 2001, p. 298).

[DH]

Further information

www.ncadc.org.uk

Destitution

The Penguin English Dictionary describes destitution as 'being extremely poor or lacking the basic necessities of life'. It is a situation in which an increasing number of unsuccessful asylum seekers find themselves.

When an asylum application is deemed by the Home Office to be 'fully determined' – when it has been unsuccessful and all appeals have been heard and been refused – single adults without dependent children lose the financial support and housing that they have received from National Asylum Support Service (NASS) while their asylum claim has been ongoing. The situation for families with minor dependants is that they continue to receive support and housing even though their asylum claims have been unsuccessful (but see **Asylum and Immigration (Treatment of Claimants, etc) Act 2004**).

The choice given to those refused asylum is stark: they receive a standard letter from the Home Office informing them of the date on which their NASS support and accommodation arrangements will be terminated. They are also informed that they must make arrangements to leave the UK and that advice and assistance with doing so may be obtained from the International Organization for Migration under the Voluntary Assisted Return and Reintegration Programme. In other words, there is no basis on which an unsuccessful asylum seeker can legally remain in the UK. They are unwanted people and have become non-citizens overnight.

As their material well-being has been strictly bound up with their status as asylum seeker, they are washed up in a kind of welfare limbo: with NASS support withdrawn they are unentitled to any of the state benefits that can act as a safety net for UK citizens and are left to fend for themselves, relying entirely on charity and friendship for sources of food and accommodation, possibly for an indefinite period of time.

In the coldly logical discourse of the **Home Office**, it becomes the responsibility of the individual to remove themselves from these shores as soon as possible following a decision. It is possible, of course, that the Immigration Service could forcibly remove a failed asylum applicant to their country of origin. The necessity for most asylum seekers to report regularly to the police or Immigration Service makes it likely for some people to be arrested at their signing-on place, detained and removed. Others may find themselves the subject of early morning visits to their home by the Immigration Services Enforcement Unit.

However, to remove an unsuccessful asylum seeker from the UK requires the Home Office to draw up **removal** directions, and this requires the co-operation of foreign embassies in the issuing of a travel document for the destination country. Most asylum seekers will have arrived in the UK using invalid documents provided by the agent through whom they arranged their journey here. Without any form of internationally recognised identification, overseas travel becomes impossible. The unfortunate minority who may have used a valid passport to reach the UK will have had it confiscated by the Immigration Service on claiming asylum, and it may then be used to effect removal if it is still valid.

Many foreign representations in the UK may refuse to issue travel documents for various reasons: they may not recognise those who have left their countries 'illegally' as *bona fide* citizens; international relations between the UK and particular countries may not be conducive to co-operation; there may be doubt cast upon the veracity of an individual's identity as a citizen of a particular nation state.

For all of these reasons, unsuccessful asylum seekers may find themselves unmolested by the enforcement of immigration controls for an indefinite period. Obviously, the longer and further an individual travels in time and distance away from the point where their NASS support ended (they will no longer be living at their NASS accommodation address and may well be living in a different part of the country), the greater their chances of eluding detention, providing that they do not bring themselves to the attention of the authorities in some other way, through the committing of an offence, for example. In this regard, the understandable desire to work clandestinely, and under current asylum regulations, illegally, may be an opportunity that many are willing to risk (see **Employment**).

Single people whose asylum claims have not been recognised but who are still eking out some kind of existence in the UK are a growing group who exist truly at the margins of civil society. Some are separated from family in their country of origin; some are suffering from chronic illness, physical and mental. All have been denied the identity of refugee that they sought on arriving at the UK, and many will find unbearable the lack of a definable identity within the society in which they are forced to exist. They have become, to use the French phrase, the *sans papiers*, the undocumented, unwanted and undeserving of welfare since, according to government logic, they should not be here.

What kind of life is this? The Refugee Council's Report 'The Destitution Trap' (Refugee Council 2006) gives many insights into what it terms 'Asylum's untold story', but there is still a need for extensive research into the scope and levels of destitution. It seems clear, however, that most unsuccessful asylum seekers who are not eligible for **Section 4 support** have taken a tacit decision to exist in relative poverty in the UK rather than return to their countries of origin voluntarily where they may face penury or persecution, and may be scorned and stigmatised by their fellow citizens.

In certain areas, Greater Manchester for example, the involvement of local voluntary organisations in the financial support of destitute asylum seekers has been developing steadily since 2004. Food parcels and a small amount of money are being provided with the support of the Red Cross. However, the extent to which the voluntary sector can meet the demands of the increasing numbers is uncertain (see **Healthcare**).

The provision of housing is more problematic: undocumented asylum seekers are ineligible for housing benefit and other welfare provision, which might encourage providers of temporary accommodation to shelter them, and friends, acquaintances and religious groups are being forced to step in. There are clearly issues of risk involved in offering makeshift long-term accommodation available, both for the providers and for asylum seekers and such projects will need to be properly managed if undertaken by churches or other organisations with a community profile (see **Befriending**). The vulnerability of unsuccessful asylum seekers to criminal or sexual exploitation in return for shelter should also be borne in mind.

The *Living Ghosts* campaign initiated by Church Action on Poverty in 2005 aims 'to change government policies that make refused asylum seekers destitute by raising awareness of the reality of life for destitute asylum seekers'. Fifty church leaders signed a letter published in several UK national newspapers on 3 December 2005. Among its statements was one that 'the threat of destitution is being used as a way of pressuring refused asylum seekers to leave the country.' There are therefore encouraging signs that this issue is acquiring a higher public profile, although there is a long way to go before destitute asylum seekers reach public awareness, as the French *sans papiers* have done. On the downside, greater public awareness can evoke sympathy and resentment in equal measures.

The restoration of the right to work for asylum seekers would no doubt alleviate much of the hardship that undocumented asylum seekers currently face. It would enable them to be self-supporting and to regain some sense of identity as a socially useful individual. This was one measure advocated by Refugee Action.

There remains the question of the extent to which any British (or European) government would dare to take the step of regularising in some way the status of refused asylum seekers. By refusing to do so, it could be suggested that they are avoiding responsibility for a situation, which is of their own making, and ignoring its potential social consequences.

In the meantime, it is left to the fragile voluntary sector to provide some hope and support for the equally fragile lives of destitute asylum seekers.

[PF]

Further information

www.church-poverty.org.uk/campaigns/livingghosts.htm
www.gisti.org/dossiers/sans-papiers/

Detention

Dictionary definitions of detention generally associate the word detention with *custody, imprisonment, confinement, arrest, incarceration or locking up.* Before exploring the mechanics of this process, it is perhaps timely to remind ourselves of the context within which we are considering this term. The countries of origin currently heading the list for asylum applications to the UK are Iran, Somalia, Zimbabwe, China and Pakistan (Home Office, 2005a). Time does not allow an examination of each of these, but the scale of traumatic events experienced in these regions is well documented. War, civil war, massacre, persecution, political instability and severe economic crisis, being just some of them. Asylum seekers in the UK may be no strangers to detention and may carry with them many scars from their previous lives. Important, then, that as a *civilised* nation we adopt the highest possible standards in international terms.

According to the organisation Bail for Immigration Detainees (BID) (see BID, 2006), over 2,000 people were detained under Immigration Act powers in the UK in 2005. The majority of these are male and the figure includes around 75 children under the age of 18. Around 1,700 of the people had claimed **asylum** at some point. Most of the detainees are held in one of ten Immigration Removal Centres (IRCs) in the UK, with over 10 per cent held in prison establishments. Prisons are designed to punish and manage offending behaviour and it is questionable whether they are appropriate for immigration detainees. Unlike in criminal cases where there is a right to be released on **bail** unless there are good reasons for detention, there is no similar right for immigration detainees. Asylum seekers can be detained at any stage in their application and there is no maximum period of detention. While some experience short stays in IRCs, hundreds find themselves detained for months. There are a number of family units housed within specific detention centres to accommodate the children referred to earlier. According to BID, while some people such as pregnant women or those with serious mental or physical disabilities should only be in detention in exceptional circumstances, there is evidence to suggest detention is being used in such cases.

That such worryingly low standards of care apply, should be understood within the context of the history of immigration control. The negative discourse around asylum seekers shares a great deal of resemblance with that experienced by other *outsider* groups historically. Jews at the turn of the last century were also constructed as undesirable, socially costly and burdensome, as well as promiscuous, diseased and criminal (see Cohen *et al.*, 2002). There has been a culture of *illegality* around groups of perceived outsiders, which has allowed and legitimised treatment well below that of acceptable standards. Add to this a heightened association with dangerousness and it is easy to see why there is a general acceptance of the use of detention for asylum seekers. Significantly though, just like internment, detention can occur without the commission of a *criminal* offence. To be clear then, the vast majority of those in detention are *not* criminals and have not committed criminal offences. International law is clear: the right to liberty is fundamental and detention should only be used in exceptional circumstances.

The UK Government sees detention as crucial to its strategy of removals. In line with this, Oakington Reception Centre was opened in 2000 not to house those likely to abscond, but to deal administratively quickly with certain cases. Detention places have increased rapidly since 2001, leading to heightened concerns. Amnesty International believes we are seeing an increased and arbitrary use of detention in the UK, which falls outside of international law. The perception is that detention is being used as a punishment and deterrent to others. Research by South Bank University on behalf of BID (Bruegel and Natamba, 2002) seems to support this, showing disproportionate detention when asylum seekers come from parts of the world in crisis at any particular time. For example, in 2001 Zimbabwe and the Middle East featured heavily in detentions. Amnesty International is particularly concerned about the detention of children and other vulnerable groups, as well as the increased use of so-called 'fast track' processes, which result in immediate detention. As it rightly says, seeking asylum is not a crime. Along with Save the Children and BID it is campaigning to stop the use of detention particularly for children through the 'No Place for a Child' campaign. This highlights the physical and mental impact of detention on children, the lack of time limits on detention in the UK and the probable contravening of international law.

[DH]

Further information

www.amnesty.org

www.biduk.org.uk

www.noplaceforachild.org

Disability

There are two themes running through the history of immigration control in the UK that are relevant to this discussion. First, the long-term construction of the refugee as costly, burdensome, needy and undesirable, and connected to this, the idea that those who do gain entry should be socially useful and productive. Flowing from this is:

> a powerful ideology concerning welfare and nation, producing immigration controls which consistently place at their centre the need to access welfare as grounds for refusal of entry, and a welfare state which ensures provision is restricted to 'its own'.
> (Cohen *et al.,* 2002, p. 30)

Early immigration controls such as the Aliens Act 1905 had a clear purpose to refuse entry to the unproductive and undesirable, which included the poor, the 'insane', criminals and those with 'any disease or infirmity appearing likely to become a charge on the rates' (Cohen *et al.,* 2003, p. 34). Evidence concerning the early rejections under the Aliens Act suggests that ill-health and disability did indeed make individuals and their families unfit for Britain. Steeped in eugenicist notions concerning maintaining the superiority of the British stock, the first controls rejected many Jewish refugees seeking safety on these grounds. These themes have continued to run through immigration rules to the present day, preventing entry to anyone who may have 'recourse to public funds'. Definitions of public funds, which now include disability benefits, illustrate this strong link between the welfare state and the internal control of immigration. Applicants must show that they can maintain and accommodate themselves 'without recourse to public funds' which will clearly impact on individuals and families where disability may increase the costs involved. This also has implications when applications are made for other family members or dependants to join their families in the UK should they have needs arising from disability. For those subject to immigration control, then, the experience of living in divided families and the long, hard battles to reunite are compounded should disability be a feature of their lives.

While those granted refugee status (and also those receiving the former exceptional leave to remain, **humanitarian protection** and **discretionary leave to remain)** gain the same rights and entitlements as British citizens, including disability benefits such as Disability Living Allowance, Attendance Allowance and Carers Allowance, the position of asylum seekers is somewhat different. Differing also from those others subject to immigration control described above, their location in the completely separate and inferior welfare system established after the **Immigration and Asylum Act 1999**, has created other problems. To replace mainstream support, the **National Asylum Support Service (NASS)** was established. That subsistence support described elsewhere, includes dispersal to 'no choice' accommodation. While those applications invite information about particular needs, a picture is emerging of inappropriate and inadequate accommodation and support for those asylum seekers with disabilities. Research by Roberts and Harris (2002) showed unmet personal care needs, inadequate accommodation, extreme isolation, poorly informed social care professionals and a failure on the part of those professionals to assess and articulate the size and scale of the problem. It is worth contemplating that this group may well also have higher than average needs regarding physical and mental health, given their experiences and reasons for seeking asylum.

Asylum seekers since 1999 have been excluded from **community care** services where their needs arise 'solely from destitution'. However, where their needs, for example, because of physical disability or mental health problems or old age, are beyond destitution, they are entitled to local authority support. Disabled asylum seekers in this situation are entitled to assessment from their local social services department under Section 47 of the NHS and Community Care Act 1990 (see Darnbrough,

2004). Research indicates, however, that disabled asylum seekers continue to experience difficulty in accessing those assessments. Additionally, even where assessments are carried out, the local authority may argue that they cannot provide the required services because of resource limitations (Roberts and Harris, 2002). That many of those services are now the subject of charges further compounds the experiences of this group and there is continued evidence of unmet need. Poor communication and ill-informed practitioners persist in batting this vulnerable group of asylum seekers back and forth between NASS and social services. A study by the Refugee Council (2005b), showed that although those interviewed qualified for Community Care Assessments, only a third had received one, and half of those who had received one were waiting for service provision. The main reason cited for delays was disagreements between NASS and the local authority concerning who was responsible for their social care needs (Refugee Council, 2005b). While asylum seekers remain locked into a separate and inferior 'welfare' system it seems likely that we will continue to ignore the needs of this group. The firmly entrenched ideology constructing disabled 'outsiders' as unwanted and socially burdensome is alive and well in the 21st century UK.

[DH]

Discretionary Leave

UK immigration law subsists in the triangular structure of the various Acts of Parliament, the **Immigration Rules** and the executive decisions of the Home Office and Home Secretary. The notion that the Home Secretary can exercise discretion over individual cases seems at variance with a statutory, rule-bound and impersonal system that appears to be applied rigorously in the determination of immigration status. However, in the granting of discretionary leave (DL) (for a detailed discussion of criteria for its use, see JCWI, 2006, p. 864-8), the sources of the Home Secretary's powers to act according to his/her discretion may appear to 'cause some difficulty' in the words of Macdonald and Webber (2005, p. 33, para 1.45). These are powers to overrule decisions made by immigration officers and grant leave to remain in the UK contrary to the prescriptions of the Immigration Rules whose purpose is to stipulate how a particular individual should or should not enter or remain in the UK. The same applies to the recognition that a particular group or class or nationality should be allowed to remain, and, indeed to the granting of amnesties (see **Family Amnesty**).

Macdonald and Webber (2005, p. 33, para 1.45) reach the following conclusion:

> Our view is that [discretionary power] derives from the Secretary of State's and immigration officers' statutory powers, and, in particular, from the discretion under section 4(1) of the Immigration Act 1971, which is a very broad discretion, not made subject to the Immigration Rules. The Secretary of State can, therefore, waive a requirement of the Rules in an individual case as a matter of statutory discretion.

Section 4(1) of the 1971 Act makes it clear that it is immigration officers who make decisions as to who shall be given or refused *entry* to the UK, but it is the Home Secretary who decides who shall be given leave to *remain* or to vary the conditions of existing leave to remain.

In other words, what appears to be the exercise of individual freedom of choice in particular cases is actually provided for by statute and elaborated further by the Asylum Policy Instructions (JCWI, 2006).

Requests for the granting of DL, for reasons not within the scope for granting leave permitted by the Immigration Rules, are often the preferred next move by legal representatives whose clients have exhausted all appeal rights following the rejection of an asylum claim. It is a strategy resorted to by the desperate, and because of the often flimsy nature of the evidence offered to support such a claim, usually involves destitute people having to find money for the request to be made outside the scope of Legal Services Commission funded work.

If a request for DL is successful, it is usually granted for three years and is subject to extension until DL has reached a total of six years (JCWI, 2006, p. 868). DL is only granted to those who do not qualify for full refugee status or **humanitarian protection**.

Although the Home Secretary's prerogative powers are derived from statute and not merely the result of personal inclination, the very existence of such powers does seem to highlight the arbitrary nature of immigration controls and, as forms of temporary protection, both DL and Humanitarian Protection can only exacerbate feelings of insecurity once the initial euphoria of being permitted leave to remain in the UK has passed. The granting of such additional forms of protection on the basis of finely gradated criteria of rights and risks inevitably calls into question the ability of **immigration controls** to defend the most vulnerable. Either one is a refugee or not.

[PF]

Dispersal

The formal dispersal of asylum seekers to particular locations or more specifically *away* from particular geographical areas has become a feature of 'managed migration' in the UK and in most of the West (see Robinson *et al.,* 2003). This 'common-sense' approach to **asylum** is premised upon a number of ideas, which need unpacking further. At its heart is the idea that asylum seekers are a 'burden' to be spread, that they are inherently problematic and costly both financially and socially. Connected to this has been a sustained ideological offensive, which overplays the scale and size of asylum seeking and concludes that in the interests of social order and 'good race relations' we must adopt such strategies.

While it is certainly the case that central government in the UK failed to support properly those local authorities in London and the South East where asylum seekers more spontaneously settled, there is also considerable evidence that the *perceived* problem was based on a set of often racist distortions. The media response to asylum in the 1990s in the UK has been well critiqued as consistently negative and scare mongering (see Refugee council, 2005a). Alongside the idea of an uncontrollable 'wave', 'tide' or 'flood' with the potential to 'swamp' has been the idea that asylum seekers are 'bogus' and not genuine in their flight from persecution. Connected to this notion of dishonesty is a whole set of other ideas around illegality and criminality as well as a propensity to 'sponge' or 'scrounge' from the British welfare system. This vitriol reached fever pitch in late 1990s in Dover, despite the fact that there were only 750 asylum seekers resident there, an estimated 0.4 per cent of the population (Robinson *et al.,* 2003, p. 16). Local politicians were also quick to pursue the position that their region was being expected to carry a disproportionate amount of the 'burden'.

This, then, is the context within which dispersal became articulated as a modern response to a modern problem. A brief historical analysis though serves to improve our understanding of the forces at work here. Similar distortions have occurred before, for example, around Jewish refugees fleeing persecution in Eastern Europe at the turn of the 20th century. The linking of disease, criminality, promiscuity and a host of other social ills to the Jewish newcomers again sat alongside claims of unfair access to British hospitality. Similarly numbers were exaggerated with claims of uncontrollable 'hoards' (see Cohen *et al.*, 2002) and once again the geography of settlement became an issue. The areas where Jewish migrants tended to settle for historical and economic reasons, places such as the East End of London or parts of Leeds and Manchester became a focus for lobbyists who wanted immigration restricted. Jewish migration was then blamed for an array of pre-existing social problems rooted in poverty. A comparison of quotations, which span a hundred years, tells its own story:

> Not a day passes but English families are ruthlessly turned out to make room for foreign invaders ... Out they go to make room for Rumanians, Russians and Poles ... It is only a matter of time before the population becomes entirely foreign ... The rates are burdened with the education of thousands of children of foreign parents ... The working classes know that new buildings are erected not for them but for strangers from abroad. (Conservative MP in Parliament, 1902, cited in Cohen, 2003, p. 81)

> Illegal immigrants, asylum seekers ... bootleggers ... and the scum of the earth drug smugglers ... have targeted our beloved coastline. We are left with the back draft of a nation's human sewage and no cash to wash it down the drain. (*Dover Express*, 1 October 1998, cited in Robinson *et al.*, 2003, p. 16)

In the period in between, attention was of course focused on Commonwealth immigration. Again, numbers and the geographical location of those numbers became a source of agitation for ever restrictive controls. Riots and disorder in the late 1950s in Nottingham and Notting Hill focused attention on the parts of cities where Commonwealth immigrants had been forced to settle. The language of *integration* stressed that controls would be necessary to ensure we continued to be a welcoming nation. As Thatcher later stated: 'If you want good race relations, you have to allay people's fears about numbers' (Hayter, 2000, p. 56). So, today's strategy of dispersal draws from a much older set of ideas, which problematise outsider groups by their very presence. This logic proclaiming as sensible race relations – the control of those who come, the numbers who stay or where they reside while present here – is flawed. A set of ideas that places the responsibility for hostility and racism on those arriving is distorted and distracts our attention from reality. As long as we construct these groups as a problem to be managed we are sowing the seeds of racism. We also add credence to the idea that the 'host' community has something to fear, is somehow at risk or is somehow being disadvantaged by the asylum seeker's presence. This is quite at odds with a set of ideas that welcomes refugees and asylum seekers, describes them in terms of what they add, bring or contribute; acknowledges, believes and accepts their histories and genuinely strives integration.

Before the year 2000 in the UK, there are examples of what might be described as dispersal, for example, the use of 265 military camps, largely based near centres of industry to house Poles after the Second World War. More recently, Bosnian refugees were dispersed to resettle in what were described as *cluster* areas, though there were elements of choice around destination and accommodation (Robinson *et al.*, 2003, p. 119). The current dispersal project was formalised through the **Asylum and Immigration Act 1999**. The removal of asylum seekers from normal welfare arrangements meant that any financial support came on condition that they would be dispersed. In line with this the **National Asylum Support Service (NASS)** was set up to facilitate dispersal from London and the South East. Once relocated, asylum seekers would be given housing on a no choice basis and 70 per cent of subsistence-level benefits. Regional Consortia were created to provide services, the main provision necessary being housing. In a relatively short space of time, then, we have witnessed significant change in the arrangements for asylum seekers. Critics of the dispersal programme talk of the separation of supports that would come naturally if asylum communities could cluster where they choose, the failure to develop the infrastructure necessary, for example, adequate health and education in dispersal zones, the use of inadequate housing, and an abject failure to respond to the individual needs of asylum seekers (Refugee Council, cited in Robinson *et al.*, 2003, p. 137). The removal of the right to work from asylum seekers since that time calls into question the pretence that dispersal is about better integration. Being thrust into ill-prepared communities, often on the impoverished margins of cities and receiving allowances well below subsistence level, unable to work and estranged from their own language and culture is not a recipe for integration. Instead, it has often been a recipe for violence, harassment and increased levels of racist attacks and murders. Further changes to the law and reduced rights of appeal have also brought complete destitution for many when their claim is refused. Despite claims that asylum seekers are scroungers on the welfare state, many, in fact, choose not to receive NASS support and rather go it alone to face the prospect of illegal or undocumented employment in dangerous, sometime lethal circumstances as the cockle pickers of Morecambe Bay illustrate. It is likely that dispersal itself has created a larger pool of those choosing to go underground, the benefits of visibility often seeming marginal.

The asylum machine, particularly since the significant changes created by the Asylum and Immigration Act 1999, is an expensive machine to run. No one really knows the true cost of detention, dispersal and removal, but it seems safe to say that it is significantly more than could have been spent effectively supporting those communities where asylum seekers choose to go.

[DH]

'Double Punishment'

'Double Punishment' refers to the practice of deporting those subject to **immigration controls** when they commit a criminal offence, essentially punishing twice for the same offence.

Historically, since the introduction of immigration controls via the Aliens Act 1905, it has been possible to deport non-citizens when they commit criminal offences (see Cohen, 2001). The practice is firmly linked ideologically to the idea that 'outsiders' are only welcome in the UK if they behave appropriately. This confirms their position as different and inferior, as it is usually a principle of English law that a person cannot be punished twice for the same offence.

It is important for practitioners to be aware that this can apply to *all* those subject to immigration control, including many long-term residents here legally. Often described as *foreign nationals*, the Prison Reform Trust estimated in 2004 that there were 8,937 prisoners in this category in UK prisons (Prison Reform Trust, 2004). Worryingly one in five women in our prisons are categorised as foreign nationals. Some of these will have been arrested at the point of entry and will have no direct link with the UK, but many will have been long-term residents. Jamaicans currently form the single largest group, further illuminating the shifting boundaries in immigration control in the UK. Residents with a clear historic link, and often family and work connections, are then considered outsiders and may become subject to deportation in the event of the commission of offences. Historically, this has impacted most on black prisoners who are not British citizens even though they may have these firm roots here. In some cases this can mean the splitting up of the family or partners and children making the decision to move to countries they may never even have visited. This is referred to as *constructive* **deportation**. In 2006 a media frenzy erupted in the UK concerning the failure to deport *all* prisoners in this category following the completion of their criminal sentences. Once again, images of dangerousness have been used to heighten concern and increase panic regarding the presence of this group, leading to calls for tighter restrictions and more use of deportation.

In the case of asylum seekers the commission of offences is likely to result in a failed asylum claim and subsequent removal. For all those subject to controls, offences considered serious, for example, drugs offences, sexual offences and offences of violence, are more likely to trigger deportation procedures. There are two routes to deportation, one initiated at the point of sentencing on the criminal matters and one where there is no court recommendation and the **Home Office** subsequently initiates expulsion on 'conducive to public good' grounds. Depending on the route being taken, the appeal procedures differ and the potential role of the worker will be different. Practitioners can intervene effectively in appeal procedures, for example, by writing reports that positively locate the defendant/prisoner within their family and community. These prisoners may find it difficult to secure early release into the community as a right like UK citizen prisoners. An 'Early Removal Scheme' established in 2003 means that prisoners can be released early in order to be deported. Many foreign national prisoners will find they remain detained at the end of their prison sentence, awaiting deportation.

It is also important to acknowledge that *all* immigration control criminalises in the sense that non-citizens are constructed as *illegals* and **detention** of this group is commonplace even when there have been no criminal charges.

[DH]

Further information
www.prisonreformtrust.org.uk
www.NCADC.org.uk

Dublin Agreements

If someone seeking asylum in the UK passes through a third country that is deemed to be 'safe', and is a signatory to the UN Convention on Refugees of 1951, the UK government may wish to know why asylum was not claimed in that country. The question is a valid one, although the reality dictated by local knowledge may well deter an asylum seeker from Iran to linger awhile in Iraq and ponder the question of claiming asylum in that country, for example.

In 1990, the Dublin Convention was signed by European governments and came into force on 1 September 1997. It was designed to settle questions of which European Union (EU) member state should be responsible for dealing with asylum applications in cases where there is doubt on this matter. In 2003 it was replaced by the Dublin II Regulation, an EU regulation similar in scope to the original Convention.

Since 1997, asylum seekers in the UK have been given a screening interview, part of whose purpose is to decide which state is responsible for processing a particular asylum application. If the Home Office believes that an applicant can be returned to a third country, it will attempt to obtain the agreement of that country before attempting to remove the applicant. (For the criteria for assessing responsibility, see JCWI, 2006, pp. 748-9).

There can obviously be complexities arising from the dispersal of family members over different European states, and despite the Dublin Agreements, such dispersal can encourage further irregular migration between states in order for families to be reunited. Dissatisfaction and frustration with the length of time taken to process an application could lead to a family member undertaking a clandestine journey to the country where their family have already been recognised as refugees and declaring themselves as asylum seekers in that country, with the additional complications that further 'illegal' entry may pose.

Or one family member in country A may be recognised as a refugee, while a family member in country B may have been refused status even on the basis of an identical claim. In such cases, the impetus to join the other family member by clandestine means may be irresistible.

In these cases, the Dublin rules could be engaged by the state assessing the claim. Even a few days spent in a third EU state 'en-route' could mean insistance on a claim being pursued there rather than the UK.

In February 2000, a hijacked Afghan airliner landed at Stansted Airport having been diverted during an internal flight in Afghanistan. Many of the passengers claimed asylum in the UK and Home Office ministers announced that they were seeking alternative countries of reception for them. Presumably, close study of the aircraft's new flight plan would have revealed which countries were overflown by the aircraft and decisions made on which of these countries it would have been possible for the plane to have landed in and advantage taken of the asylum laws pertaining there. However, none of the would-be asylum seekers were returned to safe neighbouring countries.

In May 2006, a judicial review upheld a decision to give nine of the 'hijackers' leave to remain in the UK, following a Home Office challenge.

[PF]

Further information

For details of the Afghan plane incident and subsequent developments:

http://news.bbc.co.uk/1/hi/uk/1768974.stm

http://news.bbc.co.uk/1/hi/uk/4757523.stm

Education

The connection between education and immigration status has existed for some time, in particular since the Education Act 1944, which excluded from educational grants students 'not ordinarily resident'. Even before this there are recorded examples of 'children of aliens' being refused scholarships in the 1920s and despite the fact that admission to school should not be affected by immigration status, there have been examples, particularly in the 1980s, of attempts to do so (Cohen, 2001, pp. 230-1). In fact, local education authorities have a duty to provide full-time education for all compulsory school-age children (five to sixteen years of age) in their authority (Education Act 1996, Section 14). The Education Act 2005 makes it a statutory responsibility to prioritise school admissions for children cared for under Section 20 of the Children Act 1989, some of whom are asylum-seeking children (see **Unaccompanied Asylum-seeking Children**). These children should have an education plan as part of their care plan and, for example, should not be moved geographically until education is secured. Unsurprisingly, the reality strays far from this and many asylum-seeking children, particularly those over fourteen, find it difficult to secure a school place (Free, 2005). For asylum-seeking children in families, again while enough school places should be available in **dispersal** areas, this has proved not to be the case, nor have specialist supports such as language classes been adequate (Robinson, *et al.,* 2003, p. 134).

Schools are important sites for integration into communities. Schools provide networks for both children and their carers and so have a significance beyond simply education. They are places we learn about difference, about *others*, they are places where myths about the asylum seeker can be exploded. Schools, for this reason, play an important role in **campaigns** against **deportation**, they can evidence settlement and attainment, as well as draw school children and teachers together in resisting expulsions. Gibbons (1999) describes the successful four-year campaign for the Okolo family to stay in Manchester, where the whole school united in supporting the family. Schools are also particularly important for unaccompanied children in providing structure and support. Research among that group shows education to be the most important feature of their lives, hopes and aspirations (Stanley, 2001). Interesting, then, that government plans have been mooted to educate the children of asylum seekers separately. The 2002 White Paper *Integration with Diversity in Modern Britain* contained a vision to house more asylum seekers in Accommodation Centres. These centres would provide education themselves, thus excluding asylum-seeking children from mainstream education. While these plans have not come to fruition, their existence in a White Paper tells us something about governmental thinking.

With regard to further and higher education, the picture is a complex one. In higher education 'home student' fees link to immigration and residency status. To be classed as 'home' the student must have been 'ordinarily resident' in the UK for three years and there are settlement requirements to access the lower fees. Since the introduction of tuition fees in 1998, many long-term residents who do not fulfil these criteria will be charged the overseas student rates, which are prohibitively extortionate. Where tuition fees are outstanding, universities are, in my experience, no longer allowing progression and award. The consequences for those classified 'overseas' are therefore serious. While those with refugee status and other forms of stay are entitled to be classified 'home students', those seeking asylum and awaiting decisions are classified 'overseas'. Universities, however, could opt not to charge them the higher rates and there is differential practice occurring. In terms of applications for grants and loans from local education authorities, refugees can apply as soon as they are granted refugee status; others with other forms of stay must meet the three-year 'ordinarily resident' criteria. Asylum seekers are not eligible to claim grants and loans for higher education.

With regard to further education there are other complicating features. Asylum-seeking children are more likely to turn eighteen during this period of study and this is precisely the point at which their status and entitlements change; sometimes this might include geographical moves. College funding is dependent on completion rates so some colleges will not accept young people who will turn eighteen during the period of the course. Again, refugees and those with other forms of stay are classified 'home students' with regard to further education fees but asylum-seeking young people may not be, unless, for example, they have been assisted under the Children Act 1989. All are entitled to free adult literacy, numeracy and English as a second language (ESOL) courses, but only those with refugee status or other forms of stay can apply for Education Maintenance Allowance (EMA).

Not only are such complex patterns of entitlement obstructive, they also place the institution of education firmly in the middle of immigration controls. The internal operation of controls, which focuses particularly on controlling social costs, now requires poorly equipped workers in education to make assessments regarding eligibility. Not only are we denying access to education to many who want it, we are part of the web of information sharing around the lives and circumstances of those subject to immigration control. The Code of Practice regarding school admissions includes the Immigration and Nationality Directorate's address and phone number, which encourages the reporting of pupils. Similarly, further and higher education institutions, in making decisions about who is 'home' or 'overseas', are implicated in immigration machinery.

[DH]

Employment

Before July 2002, asylum seekers in the UK who had not received an initial decision on their claim within six months of application were entitled to apply to the Home Office for permission to seek employment. Now that this concession has been withdrawn, all forms of paid employment are barred and **Application Registration Cards (ARCs)** bear the stipulation 'Employment Forbidden'.

Article 23(1) of the Universal Declaration on Human Rights states:

> Everyone has the right to work, to free choice of employment, to just and favourable conditions of work and to protection against unemployment.

However, the extension of the right to work to those seeking asylum in the UK and who are not, by definition, citizens of a sovereign state, is a tangible sign of their status as *others*, as outsiders who do not enjoy the benefits available to citizens, whether of the UK or of wider geo-political groupings such as the European Union (EU), whose citizens have community-wide employment rights.

The restoration of employment rights to asylum seekers with temporary admission to the UK would greatly alleviate the destitution to which those without dependent children must succumb when their claims are rejected. Even for the adult members of such families, there must surely come a time when the independence and dignity supplied by reasonably paid employment will become a desirable goal.

However, being able to support oneself through work brings with it too many tangible signs of self-determination and independence for any British government to risk restoring employment rights to asylum seekers. Being in legal paid work implies inclusion in the fabric of a society to a degree which is at odds with the non-status of unsuccessful asylum seekers. Denying employment is yet another lever in attempts to force 'failed' applicants to quietly leave the territory of the UK.

In accordance, however, with Article 11 of Directive 2003/9/EC of the Council of the European Union, which lays down common 'reception conditions' for asylum seekers, in member states of the EU, 'access to the labour market' should be granted to any applicant whose initial application has not been decided within one year, and where the delay is not due to the applicant. Given the UK's desire to speed up most asylum applications, it is unlikely that this clause would ever be enacted with any but a few UK applicants.

For those who are lucky in the refugee lottery and win the right to live in the UK either indefinitely or on restricted terms, access to the employment market is offered as if by magic.

Yet the road is still difficult, and depends largely upon the prior training and experience that the newly-minted refugee had gained prior to arrival in the UK. For many, lack of competence in English may result in university graduates being offered jobs stacking supermarket shelves or office cleaning while undergoing training in English and other skills as part of schemes offered by the Department for Work and Pensions, for example.

Many refugees are drawn, as they always have been, to work with organisations that support other refugees and asylum seekers. Here they bring enormous benefits in terms of language skills and cultural awareness and empathy to well-established organisations such as **Refugee Action**. Others may choose to set up groups representing particular national or ethnic groupings, which may then seek public funding if they are constituted in a way acceptable to potential funding bodies. As with all voluntary sector organisations, some of these associations may lead a precarious existence, and a proliferation of narrowly-defined groups may fail to address effectively larger issues, such as relieving the increasing **destitution** of unsuccessful asylum seekers.

Given the difficulties of finding employment generally among the refugee population, the impulse to set up such organisations which serve to reaffirm ethnic identities, is understandable, but can set up divisions between those with and those without their 'papers'.

Other refugees will be attracted to further and higher education or the wider job market, initially having to settle for low-paid employment in socially useful sectors such as the care of elderly people, and school teaching assistants. Such posts can lead on to retraining and regaining previous employment status as nurses and teachers, for example, in a hopefully, not-too-distant future of settled well-being and safety in the UK.

[PF]

Further information

www.refugeesintobusiness.org.uk

www.bma.org.uk/ap.nsf/Content/refugeedoctorslinks

European Union Accession Countries

On 1 May 2004 ten countries joined the European Union (EU): Poland, Hungary, the Czech Republic, Slovenia, Slovakia, Estonia, Latvia, Lithuania, Cyprus and Malta. In January 2007 they were joined by Romania and Bulgaria. The citizens of these countries now enjoy the same privileges of unrestricted cross-border travel and access to employment across the EU as do the existing member states. In one sense, however, the enlargement of the EU could be seen as widening the frontiers of 'fortress Europe': while freedom of movement is granted to EU citizens within this conglomerate of – mainly – Western European nations whose original impetus for union in the Treaty of Rome of 1957 was to prevent a reoccurrence of warfare between France and Germany, access to Europe from those outside its borders, especially from the poorer nations of Africa and Asia, will no doubt become increasingly restrictive.

It would seem that, for freedom of movement across borders to exist, there must be a prerequisite trade-off whereby a supreme decision-making body – in this case the European Council of Ministers – promotes the eventual harmonisation of social and economic policies to the supposed benefit of all those residing within the EU's borders. Those residing outside must beg for access and demonstrate, through the **visa** system, that they are eligible for a seat at the banquet of the relatively rich if they wish to work or study.

In the case of the 'new' EU countries, the UK has imposed restrictions on the degree to which these brand-new Europeans can have access to social security benefits (Cyprus and Malta are excluded from this arrangement, presumably on the basis of affiliations with the British Commonwealth and hence the possession of a pre-existing identity, which makes them less 'other' than the countries of the former

Communist bloc, which constitute the remainder of the accession nations).

Potential workers from these countries are expected to register under a workers' registration scheme once they arrive in the UK and remain registered until they have been in continuous employment for a period of twelve months. During this period of registration, there are entitlements to certain state benefits, while others are excluded (Willman *et al.*, 2004, pp. 71-2). The UK thus wishes to demonstrate that it, not EU directives, has the final say on the treatment of people from the EU accession states, in the same way that the British government reserves the right not to enter fully into the Schengen agreement on the complete abolition of border controls within the EU.

While the fanfares were sounding in Dublin, where the enlargement of the EU was celebrated in 2004, people from, for example, the Czech Republic, who had claimed asylum in the UK prior to this date, suddenly found themselves in the position of being EU citizens residing within another EU state. If their asylum claim had been refused, as applied to most of the Roma people from the Czech Republic, the new state of affairs meant that they could not be forcibly removed to their country of origin. It was, and presumably is, still possible for someone from these countries to make an asylum claim, but such a claim will be 'clearly unfounded' and refused in the same way as a claim from the countries on the so-called 'white list' of safe countries outside the EU is still treated. After all, it is obviously a well-known and verifiable fact that all citizens of the EU enjoy a uniformly affluent lifestyle and live peaceably and in harmony with their fellow citizens with their democratic freedoms guaranteed by stable democracies and the rule of law that knows no favoritism and is immune from corruption.

The Z family, of Roma origin, came to the UK to claim asylum on the basis of persecution as a social and ethnic minority in the Czech Republic, where gratuitous violence against Roma was commonplace. Their asylum claim was refused, and all of their appeal rights eventually exhausted. The oldest daughter of the family became pregnant and claimed asylum in her own right. This claim was also rejected and the family decided to leave the UK and return to their country of origin. This they did, but decided to return when the Czech Republic became a member of the EU. They became employed in low-level, poorly paid jobs in the service sector and are barely surviving as a result.

M, a woman in her fifties, also from the Czech Republic, came to the UK, claimed asylum and also had her claim rejected. On the enlargement of the EU she obtained work as a domestic employee and duly registered under the work permit scheme. She was assisted in this by a voluntary agency who simply downloaded the appropriate information in Czech from Work Permits UK.

She was befriended by a couple from the church that she attended who let her stay with them until she had accumulated enough money to afford a small flat. She is now hoping to undertake training as a school support worker, which is a step towards regaining the profession of teacher, which she held in her homeland.

Asylum seeker one day, EU citizen the next? As these examples seek to illustrate, the effect of immigration controls resides solely upon arbitrary and contingent political arrangements, which are not shaped by considerations of justice or welfare, or even rights, but on the delineation of borders and decisions on who shall be deemed eligible to pass through those borders and who shall be repulsed. M did not undergo a transformation between 30 April and 1 May 2004. Her molecular constitution was the same; her desire to be useful in the society that had formally rejected her claim for asylum was the same; her tenacity and unwillingness to bow to the stresses of survival in an alien environment were the same and, if anything, were doubled by the status that had been conferred upon her.

All that had changed was that she was now able to partake, imperfectly at first, of a set of guaranteed freedoms conferred by the stroke of a pen, steel drawn over sumptuously bound velum, which happened to confer upon her what is still denied to the vast majority of those who seek asylum in Europe and whose only mistake is not to have been born in the right place at the right moment in history.

[PF]

Family Amnesty

In Home Office language, the 'Family **ILR** Exercise', was announced in February 2003. At that time it was estimated that there were 15,000 asylum-seeking families whose asylum applications fell into one of three categories:

- applications that were under consideration;
- applications that had been rejected but which were awaiting an appeal;
- applications for which there was no further right of appeal, but whose applicants had not been removed from the UK.

In addition, families must have had at least one dependent child under the age of eighteen.

Consideration for what became known generally as the 'amnesty', giving **Indefinite Leave to Remain** (ILR) in the UK, had to satisfy various criteria, the most limiting of which was that asylum applications had to have been made before 2 October 2000.

Initially, there were additional criteria regarding dependants who were defined as being under eighteen years of age on 2 October 2000 or 24 October 2003 and who was or is 'financially and emotionally dependent on the main applicant', that is the parent in whose name the asylum application was made.

There were a number of exclusions to those eligible for consideration under the amnesty, including persons with criminal convictions; those with anti-social behaviour or sex offender orders; those who had made or attempted to make multiple applications for asylum in the UK under different identities; those who should have their applications for asylum considered by a third country (see **Dublin Agreements**); those who present a risk to security; those who have committed a crime against humanity; and those whose presence in the UK is not 'conducive to the public good'.

Some of these criteria were subsequently modified: in 2005, the Home Office announced that families where the youngest child turned eighteen before 2 October 2000 could be included. Later amendments included the eligibility of minor children who had joined the family unit after 2 October 2000 and modifying the criminal convictions exclusion criteria to allow certain minor convictions as not preventing consideration in the amnesty.

....

News travels quickly and those who thought they might qualify sought advice from agencies who helped them apply for the ILR exercise. Inevitably there were many more who were excluded simply because of the October 2000 cut-off point. Others who may have been excluded at first, because their families were 'incomplete' at that date, have since found themselves included due to the shift in criteria and constant revision of closing dates. Indeed, at the time of writing in mid-2006, the backlog of applications is still being processed. At 31 March 2006, 58,800 main applicants had been 'identified for consideration', 22,925 had been granted ILR, 7,505 were considered on 'another ILR application' (presumably this refers to the number admitted on the revised criteria), 17,245 were refused and 8,420 were 'found to be ineligible'. There were ten main applicants awaiting an initial examination of their case and 2,700 awaiting a decision (Home Office, 2006).

The number of cases found not to qualify for the exercise under any of the criteria is significant: 14 per cent of applicants apparently believed, or had been advised, that they were, in fact, eligible, and went ahead with their applications on this basis. One could draw two conclusions from this figure: either the level of professional advice-giving is highly incompetent or ineffective, or both; or, many applications were made in the hope that there might be a chance of success, anyway, a chance to grab at what, after all, must seem like a heaven-sent opportunity to regularise one's situation in an increasingly desperate climate of non-belief and rejection.

In June 2006, the Home Office announced that continued consideration would be given to granting ILR under the exercise, providing the basic criteria were met, but only under exceptional circumstances.

It is not clear what the motives of the Home Office were in instituting what seems to constitute an unusually magnanimous gesture in the context of UK immigration controls.

Is it possible that the cost of providing **National Asylum Support Service (NASS)** support to families and continuing that support following the rejection of their asylum claims was becoming an unacceptable burden on the Treasury? Or was the ILR exercise a truly humanitarian exercise in removing doubt and fear from families who would otherwise face an uncertain future as undocumented non-citizens?

In either event, there are bound to be winners and losers in such an amnesty. The criteria for eligibility were very careful to welcome only those who, in general terms, had displayed model behaviour during their spell as asylum seekers. If you wanted to be included in an exercise which might be a first step in the process of naturalisation and citizenship, it was important for the Home Office to do some rigorous pre-selection. If, after all else had been considered, your presence in the UK was not considered 'conducive to the public good', the doors remained shut.

Rather like the holding of referenda to decide constitutional issues, the granting of amnesties to sizeable sections of the population previously considered 'irregular' or even 'illegal' seems peculiarly un-British. By contrast, Spain, for example, completed its *fifth* regularisation programme in May 2005 (IPPR, 2006, p. 20).

According to the same IPPR report on irregular migration in the UK, 'regularisation', 'normalisation', 'legalisation' or 'amnesty' of those with irregular immigration status has both positive and negative consequences.

The advantages of such regularisation are that it:

- increases regulation of the labour market and collection of tax revenues;
- reduces the scope for exploitation and abuse of irregular migrants;• can help bilateral relationships with sending/transit countries;
- can provide valuable information about the demographics and labour market participation of migrants, and, in theory, help countries plan to control future irregular migration.

On the other hand:

- it may encourage further irregular migration if there is an expectation of further regularization;
- if only temporary regularisation is granted, it may lead to a reversion to irregular status;
- it poses considerable operational challenges;
- some employers may not want to pay higher wages to regular workers, thus fuelling continued demand for irregular migrant workers;
- it might lead the public to see it as a reward for criminal behaviour (that is, entering a country without valid travel documents). (IPPR, 2006, p. 15)

It is notable that no mention is made of 'asylum seekers' as such, the majority of whom, as is mentioned elsewhere in this book (see **Destitution**, for example), arrive in the UK using false documentation. The UK currently has no other means of processing, let alone regularising the status of undocumented migrants except through the asylum machinery, which results in a rejection rate of approximately 80 per cent each year (for figures for the first quarter of 2006 see 'Further reading').

One could propose a tautologous and risk-laden argument, which would run something like this:

- People from the poorest countries of the world need to be 'invited' to work, study or settle in the UK for various purposes through the visa system.

- When people from these countries arrive in the UK (and other European countries) without valid documentation, they have two choices: either to remain in a state of 'illegality' and work and live without formal documentation, or to claim asylum.

- To claim asylum, one must prove that one is in need of international protection under the terms of the Geneva Convention of 1951.

- If one cannot prove this, then one's claim must consist of reasons not recognised by the Convention and protection and leave to remain is not given.

- Who, therefore, are those not recognised as asylum seekers?

There is no answer to this question that could embrace the totality of the 'push' and 'pull' factors that motivate people to migrate in desperation and which are only known to the hearts and minds of the individuals concerned; there is certainly no point in re-engaging with the fallacious 'genuine/bogus' dichotomy so beloved of conservative journalism in the UK at the beginning of the present century. All that can be objectively stated is that, under present UK policy, there is no alternative, parallel system to which those refused leave to remain as asylum seekers could be offered the alternative of staying as regularised migrant workers.

Such a policy would no doubt have the advantages and disadvantages discussed above and would most certainly involve some kind of reciprocal agreements with the countries from which most irregular migrants originate. This would also work towards removing the involvement of **people traffickers and smugglers** in the currently chaotic and inhumane world of unplanned and unwelcomed migration to the UK and other European countries.

....

Someone (the father of two children who are being supported by social services following the withdrawal of his partner's **Section 4** support) asked me regularly in 2005 and 2006 (and will probably still be asking me by the time this book is published), 'When will they pass a new law?' What he means is, 'When will there be a new family amnesty so that I, my partner and children can look forward to some kind of stable life in the UK?' I choose not to tell him that there *has* been a new law passed (the Immigration, Asylum and Nationality Act 2006) but that it doesn't mention anything about regularizing the situation of families who came to the UK since October 2000, and is, as we have come to expect in UK asylum legislation, more restrictive than lenient, offering war measures rather than reconciliation.

[PF]

Further reading

Home Office (2006) *Asylum Statistics: 1st Quarter 2006* United Kingdom. London: Home Office. Available at: www.homeoffice.gov.uk/rds/pdfs06/asylumq106.pdf

For information on Spain's regularisation programmes, see Arango and Jachimowicz, (2005).

Family Reunion

During the flight from oppressive circumstances, there may be many reasons why family members become separated.

If a parent involved in political activity in opposition to the ruling factions feels compelled to seek refuge abroad, it can be very difficult to arrange for all of their family to accompany them on what is usually a complex and sometimes hazardous undertaking. If an 'agent' or trafficker is involved, there may be reluctance on the agent's part to arrange passage for several family members at once due to the lack of available false documentation for a person of the appropriate age and sex. Some smugglers are reluctant to facilitate the passage of entire families with children because of additional risks posed by the trafficking of small children. Often, the predominant factor is that of money: it simply costs less to buy the passage to Europe for one person than for a family of several people.

If an overland route is the only option of reaching Europe, it is questions of safety which prevail. When the Sangatte Red Cross camp was operating in Calais, it housed an overwhelmingly male population of migrants desperate to reach the UK. Some of these men will no doubt have left their families behind, thousands of miles away, in search of a better life in the UK. Once established in the UK, their hopes revolved around employment and being able to remit part of their earnings to their families 'back home'. Even after the closing of Sangatte, a largely male transient group was still to be found in Calais entertaining the same desperate aspirations (Channel Four, *Dispatches,* 27 March 2006).

In the chaos of forced departure, the family members who cannot secure an immediate passage to Europe may have no other option than to pass clandestinely across the border to a neighbouring country. If they are fortunate – and this word carries a heavy burden of relativity – they may be able to enter a United Nations (UN) refugee camp and remain there awaiting word from the husband, wife, father or mother who has preceded them in the uncertain venture of claiming international protection. They may have to wait several years.

In the UK, when someone is recognised by the Home Office as a refugee within the terms of the 1951 Convention and is granted **leave to remain**, immediate family members still living in the refugee's country of origin may apply for visas to enter the UK (paragraphs 352A-F of the Immigration Rules [HC 395]).

In this context 'family members' are defined as the pre-existing spouse and dependant minor children of the refugee. Children who are over the age of eighteen will be considered to have formed a life which ceases to make them dependent on their refugee sponsor, but this point may be arguable.

For example, Samuel had been granted indefinite leave to remain in the UK. His wife and two of his children were living with him and had been his dependants in his asylum claim. Therefore, both Samuel's wife and children were also accorded refugee status. However, two of Samuel's children were living in a refugee camp in an African country that bordered Samuel's homeland. One was fourteen and one eighteen. They both applied for entry clearance (that is, **visas**) to rejoin their father at the British High Commission in the country where the refugee camp was situated. The younger child was granted entry clearance under the Immigration Rules, but the older one was refused because of her age.

A social worker employed by a voluntary agency argued that it could not be in the interests of the children if they were separated in this way. They had been living together for two years in the camp and were emotionally and practically dependent on each other for day-to-day survival. The social worker had formed a good working relationship with the entry clearance officer over the course of several weeks of faxes, emails and telephone calls, and it was eventually agreed that the older child should be granted a visa on the same basis as her younger sibling, leading them to be reunited with their parents in the UK.

People granted **humanitarian protection** will have to wait for three years until they can make an application for family members to join them; persons given discretionary leave must wait for six years. In both cases the maintenance and accommodation requirements have to be met.

There is thus a recognisable hierarchy in operation in the question of who or who may not apply for family reunion. The granting of full refugee status carries moral obligations for the state to facilitate the bringing together of families divided through persecution and conflict. Chapter six of the UN *Handbook* for the determination of refugee status (UNHCR, 1992) makes this obligation explicit:

181. Beginning with the Universal Declaration of Human Rights, which states that 'the family is the natural and fundamental group unit of society and is entitled to protection by society and the State', most international instruments dealing with human rights contain similar provisions for the protection of the unit of a family.

182. The Final Act of the Conference that adopted the 1951 Convention:

Recommends Governments to take the necessary measures for the protection of the refugee's family, especially with a view to "Ensuring that the unity of the refugee's family is maintained particularly in cases where the head of the family has fulfilled the necessary conditions for admission to a particular country."

Those granted leave to remain for a limited time under the provisions of humanitarian protection or discretionary leave therefore are considered less in need of the presence of immediate family members. There exists the possibility, however, of requesting entry clearance on compassionate grounds, for example when the person granted temporary protection may become gravely ill and require the support of and contact with their separated family.

Difficulties can arise resulting from differing concepts of 'marriage'. In many African societies, for example, marriage is deemed to exist upon the giving of a dowry by the prospective husband to the family of his prospective wife, and by the exchange of promises. Such a couple would consider themselves married without recourse to the formal solemnisation through a civil ceremony conducted before an appointed representative of the state or local community. In the same way, 'proxy' marriages conducted without the presence of one partner may be deemed to be binding in a way that is not recognised in the West.

In these circumstances, the 'married' partner will be treated by the entry clearance officer as a fiancé under the immigration rules, and the refugee will have to satisfy maintenance and accommodation requirements as well as the proofs required that a genuine relationship exists in order to be reunited with their significant other.

Separated partners of the same sex may apply for entry clearance, but will obviously not be considered to be 'married' as that term is defined by English law and will therefore be in a similar situation to heterosexual couples whose contractual ceremonies do not have the force of marriage for purposes of family reunion (Immigration Rules, para 295AA, concerning entry clearance for same-sex couples who can prove the 'cohabitation threshold' of a relationship 'akin to marriage' of two years). It yet remains to be demonstrated how the separated same-sex partner of a refugee who, before separation, underwent a form of civil partnership ceremony, would fare under the Immigration Rules. One might suppose that cultural taboos on same-sex relationships are so entrenched in many of the countries that produce refugees that state recognition of such relationships is virtually non-existent.

Assuming that a person has been recognised as a refugee in the UK and has been given leave to remain, there then arise practical considerations.

It may be that the refugee has maintained fairly close contact with their spouse or family while in the UK and knows where they are living and what their current circumstances are with respect to support and accommodation. In this situation, the refugee will need to obtain the appropriate entry clearance forms from the Immigration and Nationality Directorate (IND) internet site, partially complete these on behalf of the relevant family member and send them, preferably by courier service, to the appropriate home address of the person or family requesting entry clearance. Visas can only be requested at the British Embassy or High

Commission (the latter in a Commonwealth country) in the country in which the family member resides. Although, as I have suggested, the refugee may assist in the completion of the form, photographs of the applicants and other documents such as birth and marriage certificates will be required by the entry clearance officer. These will have to be provided in-country and the principal applicant will need to sign the form requesting entry clearance. The person making the application will also need to obtain passports issued by the country of their nationality if they do not already have them, as the visas, when they are obtained, usually take the form of a stamp or vignette affixed to a page of the applicant's passport.

It is not strictly necessary to engage the services of an immigration lawyer to undertake the process of visa application, but it may be advisable to do so unless the refugee can find assistance from a voluntary agency with experience in such matters. However, a lawyer may charge for this service.

If entry clearance is granted, with a visa giving the holder leave to enter, there is the question of financing the travel to the UK. It is unlikely that the refugee will be able to afford this: some voluntary agencies may fund the whole or part of this cost, especially if they have been involved with the refugee for many months and have given other forms of support throughout their application for asylum.

The British Red Cross will also consider requests for travel assistance, although their procedures may be lengthier as each request has to be considered on its merits at a high level within that organisation.

The Red Cross also operates a tracing and messages service, which helps to locate family members who may be dispersed in a war zone or in refugee camps and whose current location is unknown.

The sudden coming together of family members who may have been separated for a considerable time, perhaps several years, may on one level be a completely joyous affair as established affective bonds are renewed and reinforced. It can also be a moment of stress and difficulty as attempts are made to adjust to and compensate for the 'missing' time during which family members have grown and developed independently and without the supposedly nurturing support of intimate relationships. Children have grown up and those who were very young at the time of separation may not recognise the person they have been asked to call 'father' or 'mother'. Spouses may be shocked at the appearance of their partner if the latter has undergone severe hardship since the forced separation. Intimate relationships may be difficult to re-establish after a lengthy separation, compounded by the uncertainty and unfamiliarity caused by new surroundings.

In one family, the children's unwitting revelations about a partner's extra-marital liaisons during the time of forced separation gave rise to a second separation when the refugee partner found it impossible to cope with what she had discovered.

The housing of the sponsoring refugee will inevitably prove too small for changed circumstances and there begins a search for more suitable accommodation, together with the finding of school places for children, access to benefits for a partner or older children and the wholesale adaptation to what is usually perceived as an alien environment by the newly arrived family members – one whose social and cultural values may be greatly at odds with those taken for granted in the country of origin.

In the initial period of resettlement, both voluntary and statutory agencies, and possibly more so, churches and other community organisations, have an important role to play in ensuring that reunited families are enabled and empowered to benefit from this sudden transition from separation to unity. Those who assist families in such a situation do not need to romanticise them and assume that the sole fact of renewed physical proximity is the final goal: in many ways the journey is just beginning and the process of resettlement is at an early stage with many difficulties, depressions and setbacks still to be encountered.

[PF]

Fast Tracking of Asylum Claims

The applicant fled Iraq and arrived at London Heathrow Airport on 30th December 2000. On arrival at the immigration desk he spoke to an immigration officer and claimed asylum. He was granted 'temporary admission' by the immigration officer and was asked to return to the airport at 8.00am the following morning. Overnight, the applicant was permitted to stay at a hotel of his choice. On the morning of 31st December 2000 he reported as required and was again granted temporary admission until the following day, 1st January 2001 at 10.00am. When the applicant again reported as required he was (for the third time) granted temporary admission until the following day, 2nd January 2001 at 10.00 am. Again the applicant reported as required. On this occasion the applicant was detained and transferred to Oakington Reception Centre.

This is the opening paragraph of a judgment (Saadi v. The United Kingdom ECHR 13229/03) handed down in July 2006 by the European Court of Human Rights (ECHR) after consideration of an application by an Iraqi national, which tested the legality of detaining asylum seekers in the UK under the so-called fast-track system for administrative purposes.

In May 2005 the Home Office produced a Fast Track Processes Suitability List (JCWI, 2006, p. 675), which, not surprisingly, includes virtually all countries that are the most frequent sources of asylum seekers who arrive in the UK, including Afghanistan, China, India, Nigeria, Pakistan and Zimbabwe.

Apart from the country of origin, the basic criteria for deciding who shall be fast tracked is the likelihood of a quick decision being made on the asylum application. One might be tempted to interpret this as 'a quick negative decision', using the historical outcomes of applications from certain countries on the suitability list to indicate the continuing likelihood of negative decisions being made in the future.

Although Oakington may have been closed by the time this book appears in print, similar facilities will probably still be in force at Harmondsworth and Yarls Wood removal centres.

The essence of fast tracking is essentially just that: the speed with which asylum applications are processed while their applicants are detained pending the outcome of the procedure.

In 2006, the timetable for processing claims through Oakington was as follows:

Day 0:   Arrival

Day 1-2: Consultation with legal representatives

Day 3:   Asylum interview

Day 4-5: Submission of further evidence and representations. Further consultations with legal representatives.

Day 6:   If not certified as 'clearly unfounded', then a decision is served.

Day 7-9: Senior caseworker to review a decision that it is proposed to certify.

Day 10:   Service of decision if it is certified and removal directions. (JCWI, 2006, p. 677-8)

At Harmondsworth and Yarls Wood the process was even speedier, with all stages being completed within five days (JCWI, 2006, pp. 678-9).

Cases that are certified as clearly unfounded will only be appealable from outside the UK as non-suspensive **appeals**.

Cases that were deemed by the **Home Office** not to be suitable for fast tracking were those in which a quick decision could not be reached; those involving unaccompanied children and age-disputed cases; those involving disabled applicants or applicants with special medical needs; cases where there were disputes as to an applicant's nationality; and where the asylum seeker was violent and uncooperative (ECHR 13229/03, para 19-20).

In connection with this last category of detained applicant, one is bound to mention the highly damaging impression of Oakington's ability to fulfil its role given by the BBC TV programme *Detention Undercover – The Real Story*, broadcast in March 2005. This programme showed clear evidence of some of the staff of the security company contracted to run Oakington racially abusing detainees.

However, it is the speed of the process and the potentially harmful effects of prolonged detention on vulnerable people, including families, who have suffered torture and other degrading treatment, which must raise concerns over the ability of fast tracking to humanely and fairly deliver considered decisions on asylum claims.

In a written parliamentary answer of September 2004, the then Minister of State for Immigration, Des Browne MP, set out the government's policy on detained fast tracking, which made it clear that 'fast' could be interpreted as 'as fast or slow as is necessary in the circumstances':

> The fast track process has scheduled days set aside for specific activities (interviewing, serving the decision and so on) but we intend this to be a guide as to how the process will generally operate. There will always be occasions when for operational or other reasons it is not possible to undertake certain activities. This may be because the claimant is temporarily unwell, there is an interpreter problem, the claimant requires longer to obtain further evidence or wishes to submit late representations for example. The process must be flexible enough to accommodate such circumstances. We would not necessarily release people from detention or from the process or move them to another place of detention simply because the timetable cannot be adhered to, if the indications are that we can make and serve a decision within a reasonable time-scale. However, the period of detention for making a quick decision will not be allowed to continue for longer than is reasonable in all the

circumstances. We will aim to make decisions within 10 to 14 days, but there will be occasions where it is quicker – for example, at Harmondsworth or a non-NSA decision at Oakington. However, we will continue to detain for the purpose of deciding the claim quickly, even beyond the 10 to 14 day time-scale, unless the length of time before a decision can be made looks like it will be longer than is reasonable in all the circumstances. *Continued detention may also be merited in some cases irrespective of decision time-scale, where our general detention criteria apply.*

We may also detain claimants after we have made and served a decision in accordance with our general detention criteria. (Hansard, 16 September 2004, Column 158WS, emphasis added)

In Saadi v. The United Kingdom, Mr Saadi's contention that his seven-day detention at Oakington was contrary to Article 5 (1) of the European Convention on Human Rights, the right to liberty and security of person, was dismissed by the European Court on the grounds that it was a *bona fide* application of the policy on fast-track decisions. Neither was it found to be arbitrary simply because of a need to fulfill administrative necessity based on a list of nationals whose citizens could or could not be detained at Oakington (ECHR 13229/03, para 45).

As the European Court also pointed out, Mr Saadi had also had an opportunity to seek redress through the English courts, which had upheld the legality of his detention prior to his seeking redress at the European level.

However, Mr Saadi won a small victory when the court decided in his favour under Article 5(2): Mr Saadi was not informed in a language that he could understand of the true reasons for his detention, namely that an immigration officer had decided that his case could be treated under the fast-track system.

Thus, the expedited method of detaining asylum applicants looks set to continue: some of its features, other than secure detention, have been incorporated into the **New Asylum Model**. The criteria on which people are detained according to nationality continue to appear arbitrary, and the notion of fast tracking and the interests it serves highly problematical.

It is perhaps best analysed as a bureaucratic response to the putative problems posed by risk in a society supposedly saturated by risks. The message is this: where there is a perceived risk to the stability of the UK as posed by asylum seekers from particular countries (read 'from asylum seekers' *tout court*), then to rid the nation of the problem, and to be seen to be doing something about it, everything shall be speeded up, the film wound on until the unpleasant bits have passed in a blur which prevents a considered analysis of events from ever having to lodge itself in official discourse and which pleases the crowd no end.

[PF]

Gateway Protection Programme

The vast majority of the world's uprooted people remain in developing nations. The 2005 statistics show five nationalities accounting for nearly half of the total population of concern to UNHCR [United Nations High Commission for Refugees]: Afghans (2.9 million), Colombians (2.5 million), Iraqis (1.8 million), Sudanese (1.6 million) and Somalis (839,000). With more than two million internally displaced, Colombia hosted the largest population of uprooted people of concern to UNHCR, followed by Iraq (1.6 million), Pakistan (1.1 million), Sudan (1 million) and Afghanistan (912,000). (UNHCR, 2006)

We need to keep this fact in mind, and that those people who reach the world's developed countries to seek asylum with the eventual aim of being recognised as refugees are a minority in comparison. The burden of the refugee situation is being borne by the globe's poorest countries, not by the wealthiest. According to the UNHCR (2006), asylum seekers – those seeking refugee status in a 'safe' country that is of necessity outside their country of origin – constitute only 3.7 per cent of the 'population of concern' as defined by the UNHCR, a category that includes refugees, stateless and internally displaced persons.

Since 2004, refugees from the Democratic Republic of Congo (DRC), Liberia and Sudan have arrived in Bolton, Bury and Hull to be resettled in the UK under the Gateway Protection Programme. In having been given 'assisted' passage to the UK, they differ from their compatriots from the same countries who have arrived by different means, usually involving the services of an 'agent' or smuggler, to achieve their journey to the UK (see **Trafficking and Smuggling of People**).

Those received by the UK under the scheme were living in UNHCR refugee camps on the borders of their home countries, displaced there by war or famine, or both. The Congolese resettled in Hull, whose numbers included 48 children, had been living for several years in Zambian refugee camps after being forced to flee their homes by the war in Eastern DRC. Like previous arrivals under this programme, the group was given full refugee status in the UK and **leave to remain**, allowing them to take up employment, education and training, or claim benefits if necessary. **The Refugee Council**, in its Bulletin of April 2006, reports that some of the Congolese were formerly nurses and teachers who were keen to rejoin their professions in the UK.

The Home Office (2006b, p. 8) explains its criteria for the resettlement of refugees in the UK as follows:

The refugee must be in one or more of the following:

- in danger from forcible return to their country of origin;
- in fear for personal safety because of attacks from government agents of persecution;
- a victim of trauma and violence who is exceptionally at risk and in need of specialist care;
- in need of specialist care not available in the country of asylum;
- a dependant, whose head of household is in another country;
- an elderly refugee who has children in other countries willing and able to care for them;
- a woman who is left isolated and vulnerable, in particular if she has children to care for;
- in a situation where basic human rights are threatened.

Applicants for resettlement are referred to the Home Office by the UNHCR and are assessed by Home Office staff to determine whether they are refugees and have no possibility of safe return to their home country. The Home Office also assesses whether a person's human rights are at risk in the country where they have sought refuge and whether they have any long-term security in the country where they are currently living. (Home Office, 2006, p. 10). The Gateway Protection

Programme operates on a quota system agreed with the UNHCR, which in 2003/04 was set at 500 people per year (JCWI, 2006, p. 698).

Australia, Denmark, Finland and Norway are amongst other countries which participate in the scheme (Home Office, 2006, p. 6).

The local authorities of the receiving towns in the UK are closely involved in the Gateway Protection Programme and work in close co-operation with regional refugee support agencies, such as **Refugee Action** who provide designated workers to assist with the practical needs of the newly arrived refugees. Bolton Metropolitan Borough Council, for example, was keen to build on its positive experience of previous planned resettlement schemes involving Somali, Bosnian and Kosovan refugee groups, believing that integration into the community was made easier by co-ordinated and focused local authority and non-governmental organisation services (Home Office, 2006, p. 14).

....

The criteria for resettlement listed above are derived from the **UN Convention on the Status of Refugees** of 1951 and the UNHCR *Handbook* on **Procedures and Criteria for Determining Refugee Status** (UNHCR, 1992) (see **Refugee**). They are what everyone aspiring to the status of refugee must be able to prove and which so many who arrive in the UK claiming asylum are apparently unable to prove. I do not know how an unsuccessful asylum seeker living in one of the UK's resettlement towns would view their newly arrived compatriots who seemingly have been granted all the advantages of refugee status at a stroke. The Gateway Protection Programme is, by its nature, a scheme of managed refugee migration in which checks and evaluations of individual refugee status are carried out prior to entry to the UK and is probably how the Home Office would like to manage all such migration.

There are refugees and there are refugees.

The messy, chaotic business of 'irregular' migration, using invalid documentation and false identities, is an inevitable concomitant of forced departure and the restrictions imposed by **visa** regimes on those wishing to travel, for example, from Africa to Europe. And if you cause chaos and uncertainty, you are not welcome and must pass through increasingly restrictive asylum regimes to be afforded some kind of civil status in the country of arrival. You will probably be unsuccessful.

On the other hand, it is entirely right and just that those whose only means of escape from war, poverty and oppression is a squalid camp in a neighbouring and probably equally unstable country should be given a chance of international protection in the managed way of the quota schemes.

If what counts as reality is defined and maintained by those who wield the biggest stick (Berger and Luckmann, 1971) then the defining and granting of refugee-hood could be seen as an act performed by the wealthy and powerful nations towards the dispossessed of the world who are often as they are because of economic and political realities brought about by a world order which sustains that very wealth and power.

It is an exquisite, but deadly, paradox.

[PF]

Healthcare

see also **Medical Matters**.

The connection between health/ill-health and **immigration control** is a complex one. It has two main dimensions, first, the construction of 'outsiders' as a health problem and connected to this the place of ill-health and disease in the 100-year history of lobbying for controls. Second, it concerns the operation of controls in restricting access to free healthcare for those subject to immigration controls.

The first controls in the UK outlined in the Aliens Act 1905 were a response to largely Jewish refugees fleeing persecution in Eastern Europe. In Parliament and the media, Jewish refugees were consistently portrayed as diseased and dirty and responsible for a range of diseases, particularly those experienced by the urban poor. Anti-alienists would use these images regularly in their calls for controls. Particular diseases such as trachoma became racialised to the point where they were seen only as Jewish diseases despite their prevalence among the poor generally. It is no coincidence, then, that the 1905 Act had health grounds as one of the major categories for rejection at the port of entry. Along with the criminal, the 'insane' and those thought likely to be a burden on the public purse, disease was grounds for 'undesirability' and importantly Medical Inspectors were the only other officials to work along side Immigration Officers right from the start. Early medical rejections under the Act indicate a conflation of eugenicist ideas around undesirability and health. For example, those thought likely to be unproductive or a social burden because of disease or disability or old age were routinely rejected (for a fuller discussion, see Cohen *et al.,* 2002).

When debates around control heightened in response to black migration in the 1950s, disease re-emerged with Commonwealth immigrants being consistently portrayed as a threat to the physical health of the nation. The medical establishment were powerful lobbyists for strengthening controls and once again, a single disease, this time tuberculosis (TB), became racialised in the popular mind. TB was, of course, prevalent among the poor but became perceived as a threat from the *outside*. The Commonwealth Immigrants Act 1962 denied entry to anyone 'undesirable for medical reasons'. Connected to this again, we see the idea that those undesirable on health grounds are also likely to become a social burden. Ever since the creation of the NHS there have been debates about its usage by *outsiders* and attempts to control access to it. Indeed, it has often been seen as the very reason why immigrants want to come to the UK. Eventually the NHS Charges to Overseas Visitors regulations were imposed in 1982, which restricted free treatment to those 'ordinarily resident'. While their impact on longer-term residents was minimal, they are significant in marking the start of a process of assessing access to free NHS treatment on the grounds of immigration status. Alongside the 'no recourse to public funds' requirements within **immigration control**, they come together to create significant obstacles to family reunification for those subject to them. For example, should a family member with particular health needs wish to gain UK entry, they would need to prove they could pay for any medical treatment required.

These themes emerged most notably in discussions concerning HIV/AIDS from the 1980s. Again debates around a specific condition had a racialised dimension and though HIV/AIDS is not grounds for refusal of entry, the need to provide evidence of the ability to pay the costs of medication and treatment can be prohibitive. HIV/AIDS and TB continue to have a significant place in the construction of outsiders as posing a threat, both to the physical and moral health of the nation. They have been regular themes in the demonic presentation of the asylum seeker as the current-day target for controls. Despite the centrality of migrant labour in the history of the NHS, asylum seekers have been persistently constructed as a *drain* on the resources of the NHS. The concept of the 'health tourist' is further used to give the impression of large numbers of asylum seekers targeting the UK specifically for the NHS. Today, while refugees and those asylum seekers awaiting decisions are entitled to the full range of NHS provision, we are seeing an increasing tinkering at the edges of this universality. For example, since 2004 those asylum seekers at the end of the asylum process will have to pay for non-urgent in-hospital care. Those who may for whatever reason be undocumented or those who have exhausted rights of appeal will no longer qualify for free treatment. This affects those, for example, with long-term conditions such as diabetes which require medication. The **Refugee Council** reported recently that it has worked with numerous women now denied access to maternity care and cancer patients turned away unless they paid money up front (Boseley, 2006). While there are many exemptions to charging, for example treatment in accident and emergency units, treatment of certain communicable diseases and sexually transmitted diseases and compulsory psychiatric treatment, in practice, we will see increasing numbers of asylum seekers in this position at their most vulnerable time, the point at which they face removal.

Further to this, refugees and asylum seekers may suffer a range of health problems relating to their past experiences. The experience of destitution once in the UK along with continued separation from family and homeland has also been shown to impact greatly on health (BMA, 2002). In short, their needs are higher but the provision poorer. The Refugee Council reports evidence of poor attention to health needs in the **National Asylum Support Service (NASS)** dispersal process and problems accessing primary healthcare services such as GP registration for asylum seekers (Refugee Council, 2005c). What is clear is that the NHS along with the other major players in the welfare state now has mechanisms for checking immigration status and rights to free treatment. Once again, we see an army of unsuspecting welfare professionals becoming enmeshed in the operation of immigration control. Indeed it is becoming a *requirement* rather than an afterthought that such professionals become key players in the internal workings of immigration.

[DH]

Home Office

The Home Office is the Government department responsible for immigration. Its stated aims regarding immigration are that 'migration is managed to benefit the UK, while preventing abuse of the immigration laws and of the asylum system' (Home Office, 2006(a) p. 10). The central thrust, therefore, that migration should actively *benefit* the UK poses a problem in terms of **asylum** applications. These rely and call upon a more humanitarian starting point and are requests for safety from the threat of persecution (see **UN Convention on the Status of Refugees**). Asylum seekers are consistently portrayed as a problem or drain, rather than a *benefit*, and in fact are actively barred from making an economic contribution through employment. The task of implementing this policy around immigration and nationality falls to the Immigration and Nationality Directorate (IND) of the Home Office. Its remit includes:

- managing controls at UK borders;
- enforcing immigration rules and taking action against those who break them;
- managing work permits, student applications and other requests to visit or reside;
- managing the asylum system and providing support for *genuine* refugees;
- helping refugees and those granted asylum to integrate into communities.

The process described elsewhere in this text that has removed most legitimate entry to richer parts of the globe such as the UK and left asylum as the only route, means this part of the IND's work has increased enormously. The government's strategy reflects the tensions for most rich nations in their continuing need for migrant labour but their desire to avoid the cost of absorbing global crisis. The preoccupation is now with the latter and the entrenched dichotomy between fleeing persecution or having the skills/attributes required by countries such as the UK is serving to deny, detain and deport the majority of applicants now, despite the serious economic and social situations from which they are fleeing.

This is evidenced most clearly in the Home Office's own statistics, which indicate that some 88 per cent of asylum applications fail despite the major applicant countries such as Iraq, Afghanistan, Somalia and Zimbabwe suffering severe crisis (Home Office, 2005a).

It is interesting to consider the work of the Foreign and Commonwealth Office alongside that of the Home Office. Its purpose to 'work for the UK's interests in a safe and prosperous world' (FCO, see Further information) includes a concern with global terrorism, weapons of mass destruction, crime, drug trafficking, prevention of conflict, supporting the UK economy abroad and supporting British nationals abroad. A sensible strategy, it would seem, in attempting to reduce those globally in need of safety and protection. Unfortunately a closer look at the statistics tells us that the largest groups who have asked for such protection in recent years have come from precisely those parts of the world (for example, Iraq and Afghanistan) where the UK and other global powers have intervened supposedly in the interests of global harmony.

[DH]

Further information
www.ind.homeoffice.gov.uk
www.fco.gov.uk

Housing

We've heard that asylum seekers in Britain live in paradise!

These words were spoken to me when I visited a refugee support project in one of South Africa's largest cities in 2004. Post-apartheid, South Africa had become a magnet for those fleeing central African countries to seek: asylum, work or healthcare. If they were lucky, they could live in a freight container adapted for human habitation by a Church-based relief agency, or in an old warehouse without heating or lighting and in a dangerous state of repair run by a local entrepreneur, himself a refugee.

The 'paradise' that my informants referred to was, I suppose, the support system for asylum seekers by the **National Asylum Support Service (NASS)**. DH, in her entry on the National Asylum Support Service in this book, has already rehearsed a critique of NASS and I do not wish to go over the same ground which questions the existence of a parallel welfare system for a significant segment of the UK's (temporary) population. Neither do I intend to examine the operation of NASS, nor the varying quality of its sub-contracted accommodation.

However, I would like to draw attention to two aspects of the asylum support system in the UK, which rarely, if ever, receive any attention.

First, the provision of support and shelter to those seeking asylum in the UK is both just and justifiable in humanitarian terms. However, the system has the effect of cocooning asylum seekers in an artificial reality, which bears little relation to their actual status and is an inadequate preparation for life in the UK for those granted refugee status.

One arrives in the UK; one applies for asylum; one is granted NASS monetary benefits and housing – at this point, asylum seekers could be forgiven for thinking that they have arrived in the best of all possible worlds. They have made it to the UK with its advanced systems of medical and social care, and functioning infrastructures. The self-evident virtues of their asylum claim can be left in the hands of their legal representative. If the claim is initially refused, they can argue the case before an immigration judge on appeal who will no doubt be convinced by the force of their unassailable evidence and grant them asylum.

For a small minority, fortunately, this is the way things do work out; for families with dependent children, support does continue and longer and firmer roots are put down in the communities where asylum seekers are now virtually settled, with varying degrees of acceptance by their neighbours, but with the shadow of enforced removal always hovering. For the remainder, the single, the rootless, paradise has ended and they are cut adrift, relying on their own informal networks, if they have any, for charitable support.

Second, for those granted refugee status, there begins the long and often frustrating process of accessing their own accommodation, usually in the social housing sector. I recommend a day attempting to find temporary accommodation for a refugee as essential for anyone training as a social worker. Endless telephone calls to social housing 'teams', homeless persons units, the Salvation Army, whoever. Eventually, a social landlord will be convinced of the responsibility to house someone given refugee status and we can all go home, all that is, apart from our refugee service user who will probably be packed off to temporary accommodation for the night.

It is at these transitional moments at the juncture of asylum seeking and refugee status that advocacy and befriending can be vital: for previous NASS tenants who have had to pay no rent, utility bills or Council Tax, the change to having sole responsibility for these matters can be overwhelming. Without advice, rent and council tax arrears can mount up and spiral out of control, taking the shine off the enormous achievement of being recognised as a refugee in the UK in the 21st century and substituting further anxiety for what should be a time of celebration and renewal.

Welcome to Britain!

[PF]

Humanitarian Protection

When asylum applications are lodged in the UK the applicant will only be granted **refugee** status if they meet the criteria laid down in the 1951 **UN Convention on the Status of Refugees**. Following an initial decision, only 7 per cent of applications in 2005 resulted in such an outcome (Home Office, 2005a). If applicants do not meet these criteria they may qualify for **humanitarian protection (HP)** or **discretionary leave**. HP may be granted if the Home Office accepts that there is a real risk of death, torture or other inhuman or degrading treatment, which falls outside the 1951 Convention but falls within the scope of the European Convention for Human Rights (see **Human Rights Act 1998)**. Those granted HP are given leave to remain for five years and also have rights to family reunion. Additionally, they are allowed to work and access normal welfare arrangements. At the end of this period they may apply for **indefinite leave to remain**; alternatively, if they are considered to no longer be in need of protection they may be refused leave and will be expected to return.

When considered alongside the erosion of the complete and indefinite protection afforded to refugees (since 2005 this is also granted only for five years and is then subject to review), this is a worrying shift towards temporary rights. While refugee status and HP allow access to work and welfare benefits as well as family reunification, their temporary nature will contribute to insecurity and inevitably impact upon life choices. Getting a mortgage, starting a degree course or other education or training, planning a family, and so on, are all examples of the 'normal' choices many of us take for granted, but which will be more difficult for those in these categories. The government's own 'integration strategy' as outlined in **Integration Matters: A national strategy for Refugee Integration** (Home Office, 2005b, p. 6) describes integration as:

the process that takes place when refugees are empowered to achieve their full potential as members of British society, to contribute to the community, and to become fully able to exercise the rights and responsibilities that they share with other residents.

Whittling away at the edges of refugee status does not seem to be compatible with such a strategy.

[DH]

Human Rights Act 1998

The Human Rights Act incorporated into UK law the human rights that had been protected by the European Convention on Human Rights (ECHR). The ECHR was originally conceived after the Second World War when concerns about fascist and communist states and their impact on individual rights were at their highest. The European Court of Human Rights sits in Strasbourg, France and makes decisions about whether complaints are admissible, making final rulings where they are. The rights incorporated into the Human Rights Act include the right to life, prohibition of torture and other inhuman or degrading treatment or punishment, the right to liberty and security, the right to a fair trial, respect for private and family life and the right to marry and form a family, to name but a few. 'Public authorities', courts, tribunals and Parliament should operate in ways that are compatible with these principles.

In the light of this, we are left contemplating how such rights seem to be consistently violated for those subject to **immigration controls**, both in the challenging of their reasons for flight/migration and in their treatment upon reaching countries such as the UK. Part of the answer is that there are restrictions and limitations on these rights and states can enter 'reservations' about any of the Convention rights when signing up to them. In times of crisis, such as war, states can also suspend rights. Some rights are absolute, for example the right to life, and some are not. The right to liberty, for example, can be restricted where someone has been convicted of an offence. The actual exercising of many human rights is, therefore, much more limited than it first appears.

In practice, human rights claims can be made in conjunction with asylum claims; the rights most relevant to immigration and asylum cases often involve claims for protection. In these cases the risks of return are most likely to be under Article 2, the right to life and Article 3, regarding torture or inhuman or degrading treatment. Another common theme concerns family connections and Article 8, the right to family and private life. The requirements in these human rights cases are, however, extremely stringent, for example regarding the right to life, it must be almost a certainty that they would lose their life. The leave granted to those successful has also changed significantly. Since 2003 applicants get **humanitarian protection (HP)** or **discretionary leave (DL)** rather than the previously used exceptional leave to remain (ELR). These are now temporary protection measures. Those entitled to HP, being those facing serious risk to life or person under Articles 2 and 3, are now normally given the protection for five years. DL is for shorter periods ranging from six months to three years. While 7 per cent of initial decisions were to grant asylum in 2005, 10 per cent were granted HP or DL (Home Office, 2005a). That 83 per cent of cases in 2005 resulted in refusal on all fronts seems to indicate once again that these time-consuming and costly mechanisms are systematically failing to offer protection to displaced people globally.

[DH]

Immigration and Asylum Act 1999

In the history of **immigration control** in the UK and the raft of legislation it has produced there is one piece which requires special attention: the Immigration and Asylum Act 1999. This Act is significant in a number of ways and is discussed regularly throughout this text in both operational terms, for example through **dispersal**, and in the ideas which underpin it, for example regarding **asylum**. Prior to the 1990s, asylum was hardly mentioned in legislation, though the *process* of restricting welfare entitlements for those subject to immigration control was, as described elsewhere, firmly established (see **Immigration Controls**). The 1999 Act was the first major piece of immigration legislation brought in by the Labour government elected in 1997. It established the completely separate and inferior welfare arrangements for asylum seekers and created the **National Asylum Support Service (NASS)** to implement this. In order to be assisted, those asylum seekers faced compulsory dispersal and would then receive 70 per cent of Income Support subsistence rates and housing. Initially that support was by way of vouchers, though sustained lobbying by Oxfam and refugee organisations concerning the dehumanising effect of a non-cash system led to their partial withdrawal. The creation of the NASS machine, and the regional consortia that would become significant in the implementation of the new procedures, have been subject to intense criticism. Providers of services, for example private and social housing providers, enter into contractual arrangements with NASS in those dispersal areas, creating a new relationship between local authorities, the voluntary sector and immigration systems.

The creation of this separate and inferior 'welfare' system is the culmination of a century of creeping exclusion for those subject to immigration control and evidences that strong ideological link between welfare and immigration. The almost unchallenged notion of outsiders as a costly burden to be controlled, policed and removed is central to the purpose of the Act. Those who find themselves within NASS systems are subject to many other controls which curtail their liberties, for example, reporting at police stations, not being able to have others stay or be away from their property for periods of time. The 1999 Act has systematically excluded asylum seekers from many aspects of mainstream life and forcibly located them in poverty-stricken areas in substandard housing in often hostile communities. It has been a blueprint for increased racial tension, increased racial violence and racist murder and when considered alongside the refusal of the right to work, must call into question the government's strategy of 'integration'.

There are a number of other features of the Act worthy of attention. As mentioned earlier, it has formalised the relationship between local authorities and immigration systems and it has left those parts of the voluntary sector choosing to contract with NASS complicit in this oppressive machinery. They are, in short, not neutral or independent in their advice and support roles and in many cases have become dependent on being part of these systems for their very survival. At a time when the voluntary sector is facing a fight for its survival, this is a serious matter. Other organisations have found that if they work in ways the Home Office disapproves of they will have their funding cut (see **National Coalition for Anti-Deportation Campaigns (NCADC)**. The Act also allows for a greater flow of information about asylum seekers between agencies, creating tensions for welfare agencies of all kinds. Marriage registrars, for example, must now report marriages to the Home Office if they consider them to be a 'sham'. This strengthening of the *internal* control of immigration is one of the most important shifts for welfare agencies and workers within them. Unions supporting workers in those agencies, for example, UNISON and NATFHE are beginning to acknowledge the contradictions and ethical dilemmas this is producing for their members.

[DH]

Immigration Controls
– the legislation in context

> It is no coincidence that controls are a twentieth century phenomenon. This was the century of mechanised transport allowing for rapid international movement. It was also the century of imperialism and world markets which demand the availability of cheap labour. Immigration laws are not there necessarily to prevent the movement of this labour. They are there literally to control and regulate it. (Cohen, 2001, pp. 32-3)

To understand how and why immigration controls exist and their role in both stopping entry and controlling the conditions under which some enter, requires unpacking. They have throughout their existence been articulated in racist ways from early restrictions on Jewish refugees fleeing persecution in Eastern Europe, through to attacks on black Commonwealth migration after the Second World War, to present-day attitudes to asylum seekers. Those who believe immigration controls can be non-racist are missing the point because all controls are about reinforcing notions of *us* and *them*, of *insiders* and *outsiders*, which are steeped in racism. Today many 'foreigners' who are nationals of the European Union or have British parentage/grandparentage are free to enter, and are largely of white racial origin. The others who are not so welcome are largely black and overwhelmingly poor. Immigration controls are based on the premise that those of us within the nation share common interests that would be compromised by outsiders who are different. In richer parts of the globe this means constantly reinforcing negative constructions of the *other* as a burden, a problem, a drain and certainly not our responsibility.

Despite a century or more of positive contribution, economically, culturally and socially, the debate about migration is almost always articulated negatively. Racism is integral to that and for this reason controls will always be racist. The Irish and the Jews in the nineteenth century were characterised in the media, in Parliament and in the popular mind in ways startlingly similar to today's attitudes to asylum seekers. Being lazy, criminal, diseased, dirty and a threat politically, socially and economically is a thread throughout. Significantly, later controls targeting black migration in the 1960s had to reconstruct Commonwealth citizen *insiders* as *outsiders*. This was done again through racism as black people were held responsible for crime, disease and poverty in British cities. The racism informing attitudes to asylum seekers today is complex and vicious, capable of constructing the Roma as beggars and thieves, the Muslim as the terrorist or the African as the carrier of disease.

The controls resulting from this have two important dimensions that have existed from the start. First, the control at borders, keeping out the undesirables and second, the *internal* mechanisms which ensure that difference continues to be marked. This is done through lesser rights and entitlements for those we reluctantly let in or economically require. The Aliens Act 1905 targeted the poor Jew, disallowing entry to those without means, or the criminal, the 'insane' and the diseased. It also established internal controls by allowing deportations of those who, once here, behaved in undesirable ways, through the commission of offences for example, or through claiming Poor Law relief. We are beginning to see here a connection emerging between immigration control and welfare, which flows naturally from the ideology of immigration control. Namely that *we* cannot afford *them,* those who do enter must be socially and economically useful and not a burden on the rates. Welfare systems become, therefore, integral to the internal functioning of immigration controls and need mechanisms for assessing eligibility. This theme continues to the present day with 'no recourse to public funds' requirements in Immigration Rules.

After the Second World War, Britain looked to its Commonwealth to provide labour at a time of labour shortage. These workers were, of course, at that point citizens and consequently had citizenship rights. As return became less and less an option as people became trapped by poverty or the economic crisis at home, other family members came to settle. The next wave of controls in the 1960s, therefore, were about reconstructing and reinforcing this group as outsiders. Automatic rights of entry were to be eroded through immigration legislation. The Commonwealth Immigrants Act 1962 made entry conditional on work permits and differentiated between skilled and unskilled workers, producing different categories for entry that inevitably discriminated in racist ways. In the 1960s we begin to see a system of entry clearance established in sender nations to investigate applications and attack family reunification. Spouses from the Indian subcontinent, in particular, experienced long delays and obstructive, intrusive systems.

The Commonwealth Immigrants Act 1968 starkly demonstrates the role and function of immigration control. This subjected all holders of UK passports to controls unless they had a parent or grandparent born, adopted or naturalised in the UK. Kenyan and Ugandan Asians with UK passports found them meaningless overnight and were left at the mercy of a voucher system in their flight from persecution. Those with parents and grandparents born, adopted or naturalised were, of course, largely white. The Immigration Act 1971 effectively brought primary migration from the black and Asian Commonwealth to an end by introducing the concept of 'patrial' and 'non-patrial'. Patrials were not to be subjected to controls and consisted of those British or Commonwealth citizens born in the UK or with parents and grandparents who had been. Shifting previous citizens to the role of guest worker, temporary work permits did not bring residence rights to workers and their families. The 1980 Immigration Rules introduced the 'primary purpose rule', which only allowed spouses and fiancés entry if they could prove the primary purpose of the marriage was not the desire to live in Britain. The Nationality Act 1981 reinforced patriality through parentage, removing birth on British soil as access to citizenship and replacing it with access via the bloodline.

At the same time as these developments we have seen a strengthening of relationships among the richer parts of the globe. The

European Economic Community from 1957 has allowed the free movement of both capital and people within Europe. In contrast to the experiences of the largely black former Commonwealth citizens, migrants within Europe would have full social and family rights. By the 1980s we can see a dichotomy between the rights of those within Europe and those not. Those *outsiders* within Europe, third country nationals and migrant workers without settlement rights were to be excluded from the unrestricted rights of European nationals. As the spectre of the asylum seeker began to replace the black immigrant as the perceived source of all social ills, the richer parts of Europe began to unite and harmonise in their attempts to control borders. The last 15 years have seen **asylum** as the only realistic source of entry to richer nations and in this process the asylum seeker is the new target for immigration controls. That many of the countries which produce asylum seekers in large numbers were previously colonies of rich nations is scarcely mentioned.

Since the 1990s, waves of legislation have therefore attacked the asylum seeker and enshrined in law the idea that many seekers of refuge are bogus, illegitimate, problematic, costly and a threat to British life. Again this is not done simply at borders by turning away undesirables but also through ever elaborate internal mechanisms designed to control and deter. Central to this is the idea that this group are less deserving than insiders and so should be treated differently. The **Immigration and Asylum Act 1999** institutionalises differential and inferior welfare for those human beings who happen to fall into this category. It takes to a whole new level the involvement of other professionals and agencies in the policing of immigration and evidences clearly this inherent link between immigration control and welfare. **Section 55 of the Nationality, Immigration and Asylum Act 2002** established the denial of support from those asylum seekers whose claims were judged not to have been made during a reasonable period and led to widespread **destitution** and a voluntary sector swamped with the need to feed and clothe people at the most basic level.

The **Asylum and Immigration (Treatment of Claimants, etc) Act 2004** extended this enforced destitution to families, leaving social workers precariously close to the removal of children from asylum-seeking families in order to protect them. Additionally, 'hard case' support for such end-of-the-line cases is dependent on promises of return and may be conditional upon community activity. This has proved difficult to implement as organisations likely to run such activities have grasped the uncomfortable resonances. Wave after wave of legislation, each more draconian than the last, has left us with a very expensive enforcement machine, increased use of **detention**, institutionalised destitution, high levels of control and surveillance for those seeking refuge and a charged racist atmosphere, which continues to discredit genuine flights from both persecution and economic crisis. The government's current strategy indicates very much more of the same.

[DH]

Immigration Rules

Section 3(2) of the Immigration Act 1971 gives the Home Secretary powers to:

> lay before Parliament statements of the rules, or of any changes in the rules, laid down by him as to the practice to be followed in the administration of this Act for regulating the entry into and stay in the United Kingdom of persons required by this Act to have leave to enter …

> If a statement laid before either House of Parliament under this subsection is disapproved by a resolution of that House passed within a period of forty days beginning with the date of laying … then the Secretary of State shall as soon as may be make such changes or further changes in the rules as appear to him to be required in the circumstances …

The Immigration Rules thus amplify the provisions of the Immigration Acts, but also have a life of their own to the extent that they constitute an operations manual for entry clearance officers deciding on the merits of **visa** applications to the UK, deciding, in the words of Shakespeare's *King Lear* (Act 5, Sc. 3):

> Who loses and who wins, who's in, who's out.

And we notice that these rules are simply presented to Parliament whose members may or may not disagree with them and bring their substance to public attention (or those who read *Hansard*) by doing so.

So there is something faintly arbitrary and unaccountable about the way in which the Immigration Rules change, which they do frequently.

The Immigration Rules are often referred to by their number in the series of orders laid before Parliament, in this case HC 395. Strictly speaking, this number refers to the 'Statement in Changes in Immigration Rules' presented to Parliament on 23 May 1994. All subsequent changes to the Immigration Rules are given their own HC number, but it is to HC 395 to which they refer and into which they are incorporated.

The Rules cover the various categories of people who might wish to obtain visas to enter the UK and the conditions that must be fulfilled in order for them to be granted entry clearance: workers, students, working holidaymakers, highly skilled migrants, and so on.

One of the most frequently used section of the Rules is Part 8, which governs the conditions on which family members of a person settled in the UK may apply to join their spouse or parent. There is a clear pyramidal hierarchy of applicants, descending from relationships that can be legally validated and attested to the more clouded issues of who and who cannot prove their identity as a significant individual in the visa applicant's bloodline:

Spouses (and civil partners)
Victims of domestic violence
Fiancé(e)s
Unmarried partners
Children
Parents and grandparents and other dependent relatives

The emphasis on forms of marriage or civil partnership that are recognised by the Home Office, that is, having undergone a civil ceremony in the UK or the country of the spouse's origin, causes great difficulties in countries where 'customary' unions are the norm. Partners whose marriages are recognised as valid within particular cultures or which are recognised by foreign states, but which have only involved the exchange of promises and the payment of a dowry, may face enormous difficulties in convincing entry clearance officers that they have contracted a valid, legally binding contract in the sense that marriage is understood in the West unless the appropriate documents can be produced.

In cases such as these, the UK and other Western states deem it perfectly legitimate to intervene in a couple's intimate sphere and demand proof that they are acquainted with each other; that they have communicated regularly and have proof such as letters and telephone bills and that the applicant can be supported by their spouse without recourse to public funds and has adequate accommodation in which to do so.

[PF]

Further information

The Immigration Rules may be accessed online at:

www.ind.homeoffice.gov.uk/lawandpolicy/immigrationrules/

All visa applications should be made preferably with the advice of a representative regulated by the Office of the Immigration Services Commissioner.

Joint Council for the Welfare of Immigrants (JCWI)

JCWI is a national independent voluntary organisation offering a range of services in the **nationality**, immigration and **asylum** field. The organisation began in the 1960s in response to a wave of legislation that began to erode the rights and entitlements of Commonwealth citizens. The impact of those changes was absorbed most by black Commonwealth citizens, in particular in their ability to unite their families in the UK. Attacks on family reunification have been a feature of **immigration controls** since the 1960s because family reunification equates to long-term settlement. Immigration controls have never simply been about who is or is not let into the country, they are also concerned with the conditions under which non-citizens reside. Advanced economies will at various times require migrant labour; the immigration project since the 1960s in most of the West has been to facilitate the use of such labour while reducing long-term settlement and its perceived social costs. The right to family reunification has been a central plank of JCWI's work throughout its existence. It has made a strategic decision throughout not to accept government funds in order to be truly independent.

Since the 1960s JCWI has operated on a number of levels. Offering free advice and casework in immigration, asylum and nationality, it has been an invaluable resource for law professionals. Connected to this, it is the most important provider of training for caseworkers in this arena, offering a range of courses in different parts of the country. JCWI also produces the *Immigration, Nationality and Refugee Law Handbook,* the most accessible and comprehensive book available to caseworkers and advisors. The most recent edition of this was published in 2006 (JCWI, 2006). Its other role has been to lobby and campaign around the welfare of those subject to immigration controls and its independence has been crucial in this. Most recently its campaigning has been around marriage rules, identity cards, healthcare for migrants and the issue of legal fees within immigration and asylum systems.

[PF]

Further information

www.jcwi.org.uk

Judicial Review and Statutory Review

Although neither of these procedures forms part of the asylum and immigration appeals process as such, they have had and will continue to play an important part as checks and balances on the decisions made by the Home Office and the Asylum and Immigration Tribunal (AIT).

As we have stated in our preface, this book is not intended as a step-by-step guide to legal practice, and I will confine my description of statutory review and judicial review procedures to a brief outline. (Detailed descriptions can be found in the relevant sections of JCWI (2006) and MacDonald and Webber (2005).

The statutory review process can be initiated in order to challenge the decision of the AIT not to allow a reconsideration hearing (see **Appeals**). Under Section 103A of the Nationality, Immigration and Asylum Act 2002:

> a party ... may appeal to the appropriate court on the grounds that the Tribunal made an error of law for an order requiring the Tribunal to reconsider its decision on the appeal.

For appeals decided in England and Wales, the 'appropriate court' is the Administrative Court department of the High Court; in Scotland, the Court of Session.

Many anxious asylum seekers whose claims for a reconsideration of AIT decisions have been refused now present themselves and their court forms to voluntary support agencies, having been refused further representation by their solicitors or other accredited advisors on the grounds that there are no discernible grounds for attesting that the AIT has made an error of law in its refusal. Since the time limit for submitting claims to the High Court is a mere five days in most cases, there is very little that untrained befrienders or other social care workers can do in these cases to assist would-be applicants to the High Court apart from offering guidance as to how the forms might be completed in acceptable English. It is important to note that, at this stage, we are not dealing essentially with matters of factual inaccuracy that may not have been addressed at an earlier stage of an appellant's case, or at least only in so far as a complete and utter misinterpretation of the appellant's narrative may have led the AIT to have made an erroneous decision in which the proper interpretation of the applicable legislation was rendered impossible.

So we are not concerned entirely with the current situation in country X,Y or Z; we are not concerned whether the immigration judge was having a bad day or whether the interpreter was lazy or incompetent; the entire issue is whether there has been an error of law at the appeal stage and whether the Administrative Court believes that there is a real possibility of the AIT reaching a different decision if it were to reconsider the appeal.

This is one of the decisions that the Administrative Court could reach; it could also dismiss the application or it could refer the case to the Court of Appeal, if, in the wording of Section 103 of the 2002 Act, 'it thinks the appeal raises questions of law of such importance that it should be decided by the appropriate appellate court'.

The Civil Procedure Rules (CPR) state that the High Court's decision is final and that there is no further right to a hearing in the Court of Appeal (JCWI, 2006, p. 1143).

This statutory review procedure is, therefore, an application made to the High Court 'on the papers' alone, and has largely replaced the route to judicial review that was, when I first started working with asylum seekers in 2001, something of a holy grail: a kindly, wise (and learned) judge would review a negative decision of the statutory appellate bodies and immediately discern the incompetence and befogged judgments that had led to even the most unfounded of asylum applications being refused. Then, as now, the route to independent review was open in theory, but costly and time-consuming in the preparation required for an application and only likely to be considered by legal representatives under the most compelling circumstances.

According to JCWI (2006, p. 1216), among the grounds on which the judicial review route may be used are cases certified by the Home Office as 'clearly unfounded'; cases where the Home Office refuses to accept that a fresh claim giving rise to an appeal has been made; decisions about removal to safe third countries; and challenging unlawful decisions about detaining persons under immigration powers.

'Illegal', 'irrational', 'procedurally unfair': aside from being the terms in which most unsuccessful asylum applicants might describe the decisions on their cases, these are the instances in which the High Court may intervene in judicial review cases (JCWI, 2006, p. 1215).

Let us read them again, this time with emphasis: *illegal, irrational and procedurally unfair.*

If those who drafted the Bill that eventually became the **Asylum and Immigration (Treatment of Claimants, etc) Act 2004** had had their way, there would have been no independent judicial examination of asylum decisions at all.

We need to go back to 2003, when, at the Labour Party Conference of that year, Tony Blair spoke of cutting back a 'ludicrously complicated appeal process' and of removing those who fail in their claims 'without further judicial interference' (Rawlings, 2005, p. 378).

Rawlings describes the measures introduced in the Bill as a 'revenge package' to counter what was seen by the government as:

> A burgeoning of asylum cases in courts and tribunals, which in ministers' eyes has been an unwarranted obstacle to the application of a firm and robust immigration control ... a 'revenge package' ... designed to pre-empt or drastically reduce a whole activity of formal legal challenge and by necessary implication to neuter the judicial role in the constitution. (Rawlings, 2005, p. 378).

There were three main ways in which asylum seekers were to be denied full access to a just consideration of their cases: first, a restriction on the supply of publicly-funded legal services to asylum seekers; second, the abolition of the second tier of appeal in the form of the Immigration Appeals Tribunal, thus 'halving the formal rights of appeal for many asylum seekers' (Rawlings, 2005, p. 379). The third element was a so-called 'ouster' clause, 'an attempt at whole scale exclusion of court jurisdiction in the vital matter of status determination in asylum and immigration cases' (Rawlings, 2005, p. 379).

To 'oust', to supplant an existing institution, usually illegitimately, by another according to whim or superior force – this was the government's intention in a move that caused intense outcry within the legal profession and Parliament and which eventually led to the suppression of this cause from the ensuing 2004 Act (which still contained provision for the enforced destitution that proved so unworkable that it had to be repealed by the 2006 Act).

Such proposals are not redolent of a seriously considered and just process of responding to reality; rather they seem infantile and spiteful, to reduce their import to basic and base elements.

> *We, the government of the United Kingdom, have noticed that all you unsuccessful asylum seekers are using the appeals procedures, including judicial review, to which you have a right. We do not like this as it takes up too much time and is giving too many of you the right to remain as refugees in our country when you plainly deserve not to do so. So we will restrict the amount of legal help to which you are entitled and abolish one of the appeal bodies. And then we will remove your right to access the High Court and allow an independent judge to review your case. So there, see if we care!*

In the event, the clause was defeated by a huge majority in the House of Commons (Rawlings, 2005, p. 379) and this challenge to the rights of the courts to challenge administrative decisions went away quietly into a corner where it probably still sits, waiting for a more opportune moment to restrict the human rights of those who have come to the UK precisely because these rights are not respected in so many parts of the world.

Illegal, irrational and procedurally unfair?

[PF]

Leave to Enter/Remain

The right to decide who shall enter the UK, and indeed any other country, could be seen as the defining characteristic of sovereign states throughout the world. The control of borders is deemed necessary in order to prevent the entry of those whom it might be undesirable to admit on account of the danger that they may pose to the security of the state or its identity as an homogenised national entity with certain characteristics such as ethnicity.

To enter the UK, permission must be obtained from the British Embassy, High Commission or other diplomatic post in the country from which entry is sought. It is the job of the entry clearance officer to decide eligibility for admission based on the criteria listed in the **Immigration Rules**. No one may enter the UK without this leave except, principally: British Citizens and Commonwealth citizens who have the 'right of abode'; persons arriving from Ireland; members of another member country of the European Union.

Limited leave to enter is given subject to restrictions on employment and requiring the holder of such leave to support themselves without recourse to public funds. Indefinite leave to enter is not made subject to any conditions.

The families of refugees recognised by the UK are permitted to apply for leave to enter, subject to the conditions of the Immigration Rules. If entry clearance is granted, their **visa** will be stamped 'Leave to Enter'. The meaning of this phrase is, in effect, that the person is free to leave and re-enter the UK at will and is coupled to the fact that, as a refugee, their sponsor will have been granted Leave to Remain in the UK.

Leave to remain is granted only following entry to the UK. It is a means of regularising the immigration status of those who may have entered the UK through illegal, or in stigmatising terminology 'irregular' means.

The nature of forced migration is that it is usually impossible for those fleeing persecution to apply to a foreign diplomatic post in their own country for a visa for entry to a foreign 'safe' country. There are no internationally recognised means of refugee status being requested within the country that one wishes to leave. Therefore those seeking asylum must have recourse to traffickers who supply false visa documentation in order for their client to gain access to another territory (see **Trafficking and Smuggling of People**).

In the UK, people claiming asylum are given temporary admission so that their case may be decided. If their asylum claim is accepted and they are recognised as a refugee in the terms of the Geneva Convention, this temporary state of affairs is converted into **Leave to Remain** for five years, since 2006 (see **Discretionary Leave**, **Humanitarian Protection**).

In 2005, the UK government announced that, under proposed legislation, indefinite leave would no longer be granted to refugees, but that they would be subject to limited leave of five years, pending a review of conditions in their country of origin. This legislation can only be seen as giving flesh to a culture of fear, doubt and suspicion concerning both the numbers of refugees whom the UK is apparently 'forced' to recognise through inconvenient international legislation and whether these refugees are 'genuine' or not.

[PF]

Legal Help for Asylum Seekers

'I_____, of_____, write to confirm that
_____(solicitors) have advised me that my case has
less than a 50 per cent chance of success and I cannot
therefore get Legal Aid. They have informed me that I can
go to other solicitors who may take a different view and
proceed with my case on Legal Aid.

However, I am willing to instruct_____to deal with my
case on a private basis. I agree to pay their charges of
£75.00 per hour attendance and preparation. Letters and
telephone calls will be @ £7.50 each. Hearing £100 per
hour. Travelling to court £32 per hour. Interpreter charges
£15.00 per hour plus any translation charges. I also
understand that VAT will be payable in addition to these
charges.

I also agree to pay £300.00 on account.

(Signed and Dated)'

This, in 2006, is the state of affairs for asylum seekers whose claims
have been refused, and who continue to seek some kind of expert legal
help, perhaps for a 'fresh' asylum claim based on new evidence not
available at the time of their original hearing, perhaps for representations
to the Home Office to request **discretionary leave**, and so on. Quite
where someone whose **National Asylum Support Service (NASS)**
support has been terminated is expected to find the sums of money
demanded is hard to fathom: it is hardly likely to be covered by the small

amounts given to destitute asylum seekers by charitable organisations and is possibly an incentive to work clandestinely for employers unwilling to pay even the minimum wage.

The issue of Legal Aid funding for asylum cases is complex and readers are referred to JCWI (2006, pp. 67-73) for a comprehensive overview. However, the situation as it affects non-legal advisors and advocates, and obviously asylum seekers themselves, whether pursuing their initial claim or attempting further judicial paths, is as follows.

In June 2003, the Department of Constitutional Affairs (DCA) proposed changes to limit the amount of time that immigration advisors could spend on cases, and hence the amount of money they would get paid by the Legal Services Commission (LSC). This appears to be the direct result of an ideological position expressed by the Prime Minister, Tony Blair, when he spoke of 'derailing the gravy train of legal aid' at the Labour Party Conference in September 2003 (JCWI, 2006, p. 68). Put crudely, the British government was getting sick and tired of the extent to which unsuccessful asylum claims were being dragged out by appeals and further representations to the Home Office. Can we not also discern a subtext which would read:

> *About 80 per cent of asylum claims fail anyway – funding these 80 per cent beyond the minimum amount of time which we can get away with is pointless. We will let the Legal Services Commission be the ultimate arbiter of whether a claim appears to have any chance of success, and this will limit the resources which might otherwise be squandered on this undeserving group of bogus claimants who are wasting everybody's time.*

'Legal Help', defined as initial advice with asylum and immigration matters, is capped at a limit of five hours' work for asylum matters and three hours for non-asylum work, such as **visa** applications. In the case of detained asylum seekers, the limit is extended to fourteen and fifteen hours respectively (JCWI, 2006, p. 70).

It may be feasible to complete the interviews required for the completion of an applicant's **Statement of Evidence Form (SEF)**, for example, but in the case of more complex cases and those requiring the production of medical reports, the five-hour limit seems punitive. Any extension of funding must satisfy criteria set by the LSC that further work is 'reasonable and necessary' and not in cases where the aim of application for further funding seems to be to 'delay a case where the delay itself will make the application more likely to succeed' (JCWI, 2006, p. 70).

Any notion of justice in the preparation of asylum cases has been lost in a maze of suspicion and cost cutting. Why asylum seekers should be subject to limitations of this kind when those accused of the most serious of crimes against the person, for example, are assured of legal representation at every step of the judicial process, can only be due to a spiteful and infantile assumption that people seeking asylum in the UK are, by their very nature, unworthy of just treatment.

Turning now to appeals against refusal of asylum, 'Controlled Legal Representation', the term for legal aid at this level, turns around notional 'prospects of success', which must be more than 50 per cent in order to qualify for funded work. Examples of circumstances in which the likelihood of success is deemed to be poor are where:

- reasons for asylum claims are outside the criteria of the 1951 **UN Convention on the Status of Refugees**;
- the conditions in the client's country of origin have changed since the original application to the extent that an asylum appeal made on the basis of human rights would be likely to fail;
- the client's credibility is significantly in doubt and the client is unable to provide a satisfactory explanation for any discrepancies or provide relevant corroborative evidence of their statement. (JCWI, 2006, p. 72)

Here, we have the extraordinary situation in which legal representatives are directed to a set of descriptive criteria, which are used to justify funding for legal aid even before the substance of an appeal has been evaluated on the facts that are peculiar to the case itself. It is as if the result of an appeal has been decided in advance and is, moreover, the reason why increasing numbers of appellants are appearing at their hearings without any representation. In concrete terms, their appeals have been decided in advance by a system that is ideologically skewed and whose criteria are based on preventing calls on public finance and not fairness, and with which most representatives must collude, either willingly or otherwise.

[PF]

Further information

Details of new contractual criteria imposed on immigration advisors by the LSC from 2 October 2006 are available online at:
www.legalservices.gov.uk/public/cls/index.asp

Marriage of Persons Subject to Immigration Controls

Marriage is here understood as it is defined by English law: essentially, a contractual union freely entered into by a man and a woman who are over the age of sixteen and who are not already married to another person.

Until 1 February 2005 it was possible for those subject to immigration controls to marry another such person provided that the above conditions were met and that each party to the marriage had resided for at least seven days in the registration district in which it was proposed that the marriage should take place.

However, the **Asylum and Immigration (Treatment of Claimants, etc) Act 2004** introduced restrictions on the rights of persons subject to immigration controls to actually marry at all.

These restrictions apply if all of the following three conditions are met:

(1) Notice to marry is given to a registrar after 1 February 2005.

(2) One of the parties to the marriage is subject to immigration control. For these purposes, this means that they are not an EEA [European Economic Area] national and that they require leave to remain in the UK (even if they have an existing grant of leave).

(3) If the marriage is in England and Wales, the marriage will be solemnised by a Registrar of Marriages. (In England and Wales, the procedures do not apply to marriages conducted according to the rites of the Church of England, whose clergy have devolved powers to act as de facto registrars in the solemnisation of marriages). This exception does not apply to marriages solemnised in Scotland or Northern Ireland. (JCWI, 2006, p. 296)

If the party to the marriage subject to **immigration controls** does not have entry clearance (that is, a **visa**) specifically for the purpose of marriage in the UK, he or she must obtain permission from the Home Office in the form of a 'certificate of approval', which is subject to a fee (£135 in 2006). This form asks a number of questions not dissimilar to those asked on the forms for entry clearance for fiancés wishing to enter the UK from abroad: length of relationship, whether there are any children from the relationship, and so on.

These regulations seem to preclude the possibility of marriage for asylum seekers, either those whose cases are still pending, and, most definitely, those whose applications have failed but who are still present in the UK. It appears highly unlikely that the Home Office would give approval for a former asylum seeker to marry a British citizen, for example, since the whole purpose of these regulations has been described by the government as a measure to deal with the supposedly increasing numbers of 'sham marriages' (JCWI, 2006, p. 299).

What is meant, of course, is the use of marriage by a person without leave to remain in the UK to a British citizen in order to gain some kind of leverage against the threat of removal. However, the marriage of, for example, an asylum seeker to a UK citizen, does not in itself guarantee protection against removal to the country of origin in the event of an unsuccessful asylum application; neither does the marriage of an unsuccessful asylum seeker to someone with refugee status or other forms of leave to remain. In both cases, removal could be threatened or carried out with the justification that the removee would need to apply for a visa to rejoin their spouse in the UK once returned to the country of origin. This is plainly bizarre and serves no useful purpose other than maintaining the UK's sovereignty in controlling its borders.

Although Article 8 of the European Convention on Human Rights seeks to guarantee the right to private and family life, administrative removal that separates spouses and families *is* carried out and is presumably justified by paragraph 2 of the same Article, which states:

> There shall be no interference by a public authority with
> the exercise of this right except such as is in accordance
> with the law and is necessary in a democratic society in the

interests of national security, public safety or the economic well-being of the country, for the prevention of disorder or crime, for the protection of health or morals, or for the protection of the rights and freedoms of others.

The restriction on marriage rights for persons subject to immigration controls could be read as an unwarranted intrusion into the very heart of intimacy and identity: the freedom, within the law, of men and women to choose with whom they wish to make intimate relationships and to celebrate the long-term commitment of that relationship by entering into marriage. One wonders what will be next on the agenda of immigration controls as they increasingly become life-controls.

[PF]

Medical Matters

The powerful role of medical professionals in elucidating and legitimating the experience of refugees and asylum seekers has already been the focus of another entry in this dictionary (**Counselling and Therapies**). The importance of obtaining thorough and authoritative diagnosis of conditions relating to torture, rape and other forms of degrading treatment, in order to substantiate claims made under Article 3 of the European Convention on Human Rights, is paramount and self-evident.

Of equal importance is the need for such medical reports to be objective in nature and to have been carried out by recognised specialists in the effects of trauma and torture. It is not sufficient, as I have occasionally experienced, for a sympathetic GP to write a few lines of diagnostic remarks that conclude with a statement along the lines of 'this person should therefore not be removed from the UK' or even a personal opinion about the unfairness of the UK's asylum policy.

Obtaining specialist reports has inevitably become more difficult following the restrictions on publicly funded **legal help** for those pursuing an asylum claim. A degree of pre-screening by the Legal Services Commission will need a convincing case to be made by the individual supplier of legal services in order for an extension of funding to be obtained, and this, in turn, will hinge on the initial impression of credibility formed by the legal representative when interviewing the asylum client, based on the client's ability to give a coherent account of painful events of recent memory.

Guidelines to legal representatives issued by the Medical Foundation for the Care of Victims of Torture advise that clients should be referred only when:

> a report from ourselves is likely to make a significant contribution to the evidence for your client's application.

> We are interested in documenting all torture cases, but because of resource limitations, we have to prioritise, limiting ourselves to such cases where such evidence, if positive, is absolutely necessary.
> (Medical Foundation, circular of September 2003)

The Medical Foundation is undoubtedly the best-known source of aid for torture survivors in the UK. Founded in 1985, it receives clients who have:

> experienced torture and/or organised violence such as ethnic cleansing which has left them physically and/or psychologically vulnerable.
> (Medical Foundation, 2006, p. 8)

Following consultation with one of its doctors, a medico-legal report can be produced which documents:

> the injuries, and in some cases the psychological condition of a client, in order that the information can be presented as evidence in an asylum claim ... Scars will be scrutinised, with doctors also on the look out for other injuries such as badly healed fractures, burns, crushing on the soles of the feet from repeated beatings ... damaged ligaments or chronic bone infection. Only in rare cases can the doctor state that a scar or other injury could not have been caused in any other way than torture.

> In line with the UN's Istanbul Protocol on the subject, the doctor indicates the degree of consistency between the injury and the client's account of how it occurred.
> (Medical Foundation, 2006, p. 9)

Such is the recognition of the Medical Foundation's diagnostic standards that any negative asylum decision including one of its medico-legal reports has to be scrutinised and endorsed at a senior level within the Home Office and there are guidelines concerning the time to be allowed for production of such a report before appeal hearings can proceed.

The Medical Foundation also offers counselling and psychotherapy, and the services of clinical psychologists and psychiatrists for those with more complex needs.

The Medical Foundation and the other independent consultants providing diagnosis and reports, are all responding to what Moorehead (2005, p. 209) characterises as the 'illness of exile'. This illness has a name: post-traumatic stress disorder (PTSD), a bundle of symptoms and behaviours which attracted increasing medical attention in the 1980s and which 'seemed to be triggered by a single specific event' (Moorehead, 2005, p. 216).

> Patients, it seemed, appeared to alternate between re-experiencing, and then avoiding, their traumatic memories. They were using different defence mechanisms to keep away what felt so acutely painful, to lock into the unconscious what they could not bear to experience. But then the moment would come when the conflicting need to integrate this information into their existing cognitive world became too powerful and it would break through these defences and into the conscious again.
>
> (Moorehead, 2005, p. 216)

I have already borrowed Berger and Luckmann's (1971) term 'plausibility structure' to designate a set of quasi-ritualised interactions that confer legitimating value on the raw data of unframed experience. Counselling, social work and medical consultations might be understood as interpretive encounters, which confirm one's status as a traumatised refugee, child in need or suffering from a sprained ankle respectively. Whatever the specifics, the encounter has the effect of confirming our identity, or at least that bit of our identity that is causing us problems or pain and which we know can be addressed, banished or reframed by the wise person to whom we have turned for help and who probably has letters after their name to prove that they themselves have the legitimate capability of helping us.

We have to believe, or be encouraged to believe, that our problem has an independent existence from ourselves, and that it can be described, attributed to some recognised category and then nailed and zapped so that we can continue to enjoy our 'normal', pre-traumatic existence, if we are lucky.

The need for survivors of torture to receive such legitimation of, and healing from, their traumas, and the need for the asylum system to recognise that torture has indeed taken place and that to return such a person to their country of origin where they might be subject to further such treatment is the whole point of medico-legal reports produced by reputable, even prestigious, sources. However, as I have been hinting at in the last few paragraphs, notions of 'trauma', or 'illness', or 'mental health' are also socially constructed concepts that should be viewed in their relevant contexts.

> *Thus, if I am the latest corrupt despot in a long line of corrupt despots who can only hold on to my tenuous power by torturing x, y and z to find out who my enemies are, then I will do so. It will be carried out in secret so that only I and my trusted associates will know about it. In any case, most of them are HIV positive anyway and won't last a few years at the most. The last time the UN [United Nations] inspectors toured our country, we managed to put on a good show by pointing to our constitution, which specifically forbids torture.*

The context changes when a torture victim reaches the comparative safety of the West, with its liberal systems of care and response to trauma:

> Collectively held beliefs about particular negative experiences are not just potent influences but carry an

element of self-fulfilling prophecy; individuals will largely organise what they feel, say and do, and expect to fit prevailing expectations and categories. Underpinning these constructs is the concept of 'person' which is held by a particular culture at a particular point in time. (Summerfield, 2001, p. 96)

In the same article, which problematises the notion of PTSD, Summerfield (2001, p. 96) also notes:

Once it becomes advantageous to frame distress as a psychiatric condition people will choose to present themselves as medicalised victims rather than as feisty survivors ... In the West, positivism and instrumental reasoning (that is, reasoning based on supposed empirical proof) are privileged modes of persuasion: to show that you have been wronged you seek to show that you were not just hurt but impaired. The diagnosis of post-traumatic stress disorder is the certificate of impairment.

And it is this 'certificate of impairment' that the would-be refugee needs to produce to convince the Home Office of its duties and responsibilities to protect them according to international law. Victimhood is the necessary first stage in the putative construction of a new existence in conditions of safety, healing and freedom.

....

However, the 'illness of exile' does not consist solely of trauma experienced in the pre-exilic state: the long-drawn-out procedures of the asylum system can also provoke uncertainties in those who wait for an answer to their asylum claims.

The worst-case scenario is that, in spite of substantial medical evidence of torture, the immigration judge, and subsequently the Home Office, decides that, because of changed circumstances in the country of origin, it would be possible to return a person without flouting the UK's duties under the UN and European Conventions. Anxiety, clinical depression, and somatic conditions associated with disturbed psychological states and loss of hoped-for identity as a refugee – all are now familiar to GPs and consultants who have sizeable populations of asylum seekers among their patients.

However, these manifestations of post-exilic conditions in the receiving country are extremely difficult to use as the basis of further representations to the Home Office in cases that have been refused without further rights of appeal. Furthermore, unless there is severe physical or mental impairment present, it is similarly difficult to use such symptoms as depression or PTSD to gain community care support for asylum seekers whose cases have been rejected and who have lost **National Asylum Support Service (NASS)** support.

In cases where accounts of pre-flight trauma have been judged as lacking in credibility, both from the judicial and medical aspects, it seems to me that the difficulty of the further medicalising of an asylum claim resides in the degree to which diagnosis of conditions such as PTSD, clinical depression and non life-threatening physical illness can justifiably be used as an argument that x should not be removed to his country of origin. This is either because adequate medical treatment is not available in country y, or because the threat of removal might exacerbate the existing condition. As far as I am aware, there are no clear data that demonstrate the incidence of, for example, PTSD among asylum seekers as compared to sub-groups of the resident UK population, such as those adults and children who have experienced bullying and harassment at school or in the workplace; or comparative data for depression among those who have poor housing, are unemployed or live in poverty. I would suggest that for many unsuccessful asylum seekers, there comes a point when the push factors leading to flight and exile are relatively unimportant compared to the daily struggle to survive in the UK as undocumented migrants. This struggle will lead to medical problems that have inevitably arisen through conditions experienced while in the UK.

The main difference, of course, between 'aliens' and 'citizens' is in the extent to which the latter, including asylum seekers, have access to medical treatment and other services such as outpatient care. Some non-urgent primary care services are now, in theory at least, chargeable to unsuccessful asylum seekers who have lost their NASS support, although assistance with the completion of HC2 forms should ensure that even NASS-less asylum seekers should continue to benefit from free prescriptions and other NHS services overseen by the Prescription Pricing Authority. It is difficult to see how destitute asylum seekers can be expected to pay a bill of £3,000 for a few days of in-patient care, as was the case with one of my service users in 2006, nor how payment could be enforced by a debt collection agency.

As Schuster (2003) remarks, it is difficult to 'conceive of a nation state that is anything but exclusive and particular'. She goes on to say:

> ... given states as they are currently constructed, and the system of which they are part, providing welfare to any non-citizen who might enter a state and claim it would be challenging. In part, this is because, as representative democracies, political representatives are convinced that the electorate's votes can only be purchased by direct appeals to its particular interests. Few are prepared to risk those votes by appeals on behalf of those who are not considered to have contributed to the nation, the welfare state or the polity. These difficulties are compounded by the coincidence of the boundaries of these entities at the borders of the state ... this is the condition of statehood that is most significant in the construction of asylum seekers as a multifaceted threat. (Schuster, 2003, p. 266)

In this analysis, the granting of refugee status to those who have credibly demonstrated that they have been the victims of terror, persecution and trauma is an entry ticket which guarantees 'inclusivity' within the nation state and thus automatic access to its welfare provision of all types. Those who do not must remain notionally in a condition of exclusion. Even though they may be physically present within a territory, their inability to meet the criteria for admission bars them from permanent welfare rights, and whatever their medical condition, it will not, except under exceptional circumstances, shield them from removal from the UK.

....

The 'coincidence' of welfare provision with state boundaries is perhaps nowhere better demonstrated than with the case of 'N', heard by the House of Lords in 2005 [2005 UKHL 31]. (All references are to the reported judgment in this case.)

N was a Ugandan woman, born in 1974, who arrived in London in March 1998. Within hours of her arrival she was diagnosed as HIV positive and later developed Karposi's sarcoma (para 2).

She had made a claim for asylum in the UK, which was initially refused and went to appeal. In July 2002, N's asylum appeal was dismissed, but allowed on the human rights grounds that return to Uganda would breach her rights under Article 3 of the European Convention on Human Rights. The Home Office appealed against this decision, which it won, and then N appealed to the Court of Appeal, where her appeal was dismissed on the grounds that it did not fall within the 'extreme' class of cases that could be covered by Article 3 (paras 5-6).

The House of Lords in turn dismissed N's appeal, and the judgments handed down by the five Law Lords who deliberated make interesting reading in terms of the responsibilities of the UK for the health of 'aliens' (and this term is used frequently by their Lordships) who find themselves within the territory of another sovereign state.

Lord Nicholls of Birkenhead:

> Sadly the appellant is not a special case. In its overall shape the appellant's case as a would-be immigrant is far from unique. As everyone knows, the prevalence of AIDS worldwide, particularly in southern Africa, is a present-day

tragedy on an immense scale ... The AIDS illness of the would-be immigrant is currently under control by treatment received here while the immigration process is being completed, but his [sic] medical condition will deteriorate rapidly and fatally if he [sic] is deported and in consequence the necessary medication is no longer available ... (para 9)

Lord Hope of Craighead:

The function of a judge in cases of this kind is ... not to issue judgments based on sympathy ... The argument, after all, is about the extent of the obligations under article 3 of the European Convention on Human Rights ... It is about the treaty obligations of the contracting states. (para 21)

(There follows, in Lord Hope's judgment, much argument about the jurisprudence emanating from the European Court of Human Rights, and in particular about the case of D, a citizen of St Kitts who was jailed in the UK for drugs offences and whose removal to his country of origin was deemed to be contrary to Article 3 due to his AIDS-related condition being life-threatening – in fact D was on the point of death [24 EHRR 423]. D has been used since as a touchstone for the extremity of medical conditions which needs to be established in order to engage the UK's Article 3 duties. The argument about N hinged on whether allowing her appeal would constitute an 'extension' of the precedent set by D.)

He continued:

[such an extension] would have the effect of affording all those in the appellant's condition a right of asylum in this country until such time as the standard of medical facilities available in their home countries for the treatment of

HIV/AIDS had reached that which is available in Europe ... This would result in a very great and no doubt unquantifiable commitment of resources which it is, to say the least, highly questionable that states party to the Convention would ever have agreed to. (para 53)

Lastly, I will quote Baroness Hale of Richmond:

The humanitarian appeal of this case is very powerful indeed. None of us wishes to send a young woman, who has already suffered so much but is now well cared for and with a future ahead of her, home to the likelihood of an early death in a much less favourable environment ... In my view, therefore, the test, in this sort of case, is whether the applicant's illness has reached such a critical stage (that is, he [sic] is dying) that it would be inhuman treatment to deprive him of the care which he is currently receiving ... It is not met on the facts of this case. (paras 67/69)

If you have read patiently, thus far, you will probably have anticipated that N's appeal was dismissed.

Cases like N's rarely progress to the level of the House of Lords and raise many complex ethical and moral questions, which, frankly, it is easier to pose than to answer here with a level of analysis that meets their challenge.

- To what extent is the UK responsible for compensating for inadequate medical facilities, especially with regard to HIV/AIDS in sub-Saharan Africa and other areas?
- What is the reason for the low availability of anti-retroviral drugs in 'poor' countries and what is the global role of drugs manufacturers in maintaining this situation?
- Was not N one of the lucky ones who was able to afford a journey to the UK?

- What will happen to the thousands who suffer from advanced HIV/AIDS who cannot afford to travel for advanced treatment in the West?
- Is not the present asylum system an inadequate instrument for processing requests for leave to remain in the UK for medical treatment?
- Are not cases such as this better dealt with by an independent body as humanitarian issues without the need for lengthy progression through the courts?
- Is it not time for a new world order?

The future of those not given leave to remain in the UK and who do contract serious chronic conditions thus remains uncertain, although there is a likelihood that such conditions may give rise to community care support, which is still often subject to a struggle on behalf of voluntary organisations to convince statutory authorities of their duty of care.

I have raised the question of plausibility and legitimacy several times in this section. All of those raising questions of torture, ill-treatment or serious illness of any kind have to pass through the hoop of credibility before being allowed access to healing and health.

[PF]

Further information
The 'Opinions' (judgments) of the House of Lords are available at:
    www.publications.parliament.uk

Further reading
Burnett and Peel (2001a)
Burnett and Peel (2001b)
Refugee Council (2006)
Taylor (2006)
Williams (2004)

Mental Health

see also **Medical Matters**.

There is growing evidence that asylum seekers and refugees experience poorer mental health than settled populations (CPPIH, 2006). A study of asylum seekers with special needs (Refugee Council, 2005b) found that 82 per cent of asylum seekers in their sample reported 'mental health issues' as a feature of their lives. Depression, insomnia, anxiety, fear and flashbacks were the most common concerns. Of course, the circumstances from which many have fled and the journeys they have endured are part of this, for example 30 per cent of the Refugee Council sample were rape victims and 64 per cent had suffered torture. Political persecution, war and imprisonment take their toll on mental health. However, it is increasingly clear the **asylum** *process* once in the UK is contributing to their worsening mental health. BMA (2002) research found that health generally deteriorates rather than improves once in the UK. The Commission for Patient and Public Involvement in Health (CPPIH, 2006) research cites housing, poverty, separation from family and destitution as major causes of mental health problems among this group. Added to this, anxiety about the outcome of their asylum claim and the legal process is identified as a significant factor. In short, the fear of return is a persistent cause of anxiety, helplessness and despair. Since the changes in the support arrangements for asylum seekers in 2000 (**Immigration and Asylum Act 1999**) outlined elsewhere, poor accommodation, lengthy stays in inappropriate emergency accommodation, poor access to healthcare generally and destitution have become regular features in the lives of asylum seekers. While others subject to immigration control may not face the brutality of the **National Asylum Support Service (NASS)** system, living in divided families and being separated from loved ones, homeland, cultural roots and all the other features of life we take for granted can impact on the mental health of this group.

In terms of accessing help, the picture is also worrying. Poor access to healthcare generally, problems accessing **Community Care Assessments** and inappropriate and inadequate mental health provision mean that there is significant unmet need. Additionally, asylum seekers at the end of the line, that is, who have been refused and have exhausted rights of appeal, are no longer exempt from healthcare charges, leading to untreated physical and mental conditions. Organisations such as MIND are beginning to develop strategies and expertise along with specialist organisations such as the Foundation for the Care of Victims of Torture to work with this group. There are, however, some dangers arising from Western psychiatric constructs. For example, reducing the story of an individual's search for refuge to 'post-traumatic stress disorder' (PTSD), which is defined by symptoms such as nightmares, flashbacks and insomnia, focuses the solution within the person's own mind. Such individualist concepts are beginning to be challenged as it is acknowledged that solutions need to include the social and the global (Bracken and Petty, 1998). These are, in short, resilient people made unwell by the nature of the asylum process.

[DH]

Further information
www.MIND.org.uk
www.torturecare.org.uk

National Asylum Support Service (NASS)

see also **Housing**.

NASS was set up in 2000 under Section 4 of the **Immigration and Asylum Act 1999**. Its significance was that it disentitled asylum seekers and others from welfare benefits including accommodation previously possible under the National Assistance Act 1948 and the Children Act 1989. Alternatively to this previously local authority-delivered support, NASS now provides support to asylum seekers while their applications are being considered. It is part of the Immigration and Nationality Directorate (IND), which is part of the **Home Office**. IND's stated brief 'to strengthen our borders, fast track asylum decisions, enforce compliance with immigration laws and boost Britains economy', further evidences the tensions of its role in providing support within an immigration system largely concerned with deterrence and cost (www.ind.homeoffice.gov.uk/aboutus). NASS was charged with deciding upon entitlement to benefits and providing those benefits outside mainstream welfare systems. It has been the mechanism for implementing the **dispersal** programme and providing accommodation and 70 per cent subsistence rates to those applicants on a no choice basis.

Consortia were established regionally to provide the range of services needed by asylum seekers as well as to consider the longer-term integration of those who gain **refugee** status. NASS is not involved in the decision making about the asylum application but as stated earlier its neutrality is questionable in that it is part of IND machinery. One aspect of this is the increased level of control and surveillance experienced by asylum seekers within NASS systems, for example, in reporting changes in their personal relationships, moving, sharing accommodation or visiting others. Compliance with a range of other restrictions will also apply including weekly or daily reporting to the Immigration Service, use of voice recognition and the compulsory wearing of electronic monitoring devices. Non-compliance will lead to the withdrawal of supports. NASS was initially charged with supporting asylum seekers through the voucher or non-cash system, which was eventually removed after successful lobbying, but which has made an unwelcome return under the regulations for **Section 4 support**. Where claims are not successful, NASS has responsibility for the removal of asylum seekers from support, including accommodation. As appeal procedures are exhausted we have witnessed a growing number of such destitute asylum seekers left without any support whatsoever. Indeed **destitution** has become the issue dominating the work of welfare organisations for this group, leaving the poorly resourced voluntary sector to pick up the pieces or the prospect of local authority intervention where children face destitution.

What have also been significant have been the operational relationships established through contractual arrangements with NASS. For example, housing providers including local authorities enter into contracts to provide accommodation. Consortia are multi-agency fora where refugee organisations, social and private housing providers and the voluntary sector work alongside each other in the provision of support services. Once again, welfare agencies find themselves on terrain fraught with ethical contradictions. We have to remind ourselves that this is a no choice, compulsory system with below subsistence levels of support and high levels of surveillance. It is also a system with endings where destitute individuals and families are removed from help and support if their claims fail. The quality of support, particularly housing standards, has been the subject of some criticism and we have noted elsewhere (see **Disability)** the failure of NASS to consider individual need in their dispersal programme.

In 2006, a large-scale redistribution of NASS housing contracts led to the forced uprooting of many asylum seekers into new areas. This particularly affected the most vulnerable who had to seek new facilities for the treatment of chronic physical and mental health problems.

[DH]

Further information

www.ind.homeoffice.gov.uk

National Coalition for Anti-Deportation Campaigns (NCADC)

See also **Campaigning**.

In 2006 the NCADC faced an uncertain future. Set up in 1995 by asylum seekers, refugees and activists who had been involved in anti-deportation campaigns, it has helped countless individuals and families and led 134 successful campaigns in that 10-year period. The living proof of that success lies in the personal stories of those families and individuals who have gained the right to stay in the UK and are therefore safe.

NCADC is a voluntary organisation that has offered realistic, practical help and advice in how to set up and run an anti-deportation campaign. Some of this has involved the practicalities of producing leaflets, petitions and letters of support, using the press effectively, lobbying MPs and so on. Its other strengths are the wealth of experience in running campaigns, understanding what is likely to produce success, connecting campaigns together in mutual support and its unerring stance of opposition to immigration control.

As well as helping those refused asylum who have no other avenues to pursue, the organisation has been most concerned about the division of families through **immigration controls** and the impact on gay and lesbian couples. It has had an educational role well beyond the focus on individual campaigns through lobbying, use of the press and through newsletters, which inform and connect asylum seekers and activists nationally. Archives of these are all available online and will remain useful to anyone facing deportation or indeed social care professionals who may come into contact with them.

Although NCADC had a small number of paid coordinators, its work was largely conducted by volunteers and it had to fight for its survival throughout its existence. The hostile climate towards asylum seekers and a particularly virulent and sustained attack by the press upon asylum seekers has undoubtedly impacted on this organisation. In 2002 the *Daily Mail* highlighted NCADC's grant from the Community Fund (part of the National Lottery) and stirred up a nasty series of press attacks. These included allegations that NCADC was a 'political organisation', was employing staff who didn't have permission to work and was encouraging people to break the law. The continued demonising of, not only asylum seekers, but those attempting to help them, led to death threats being received at both NCADC and the Community Fund (NCADC, 2003). The hysteria that followed this led eventually to 'strings' being attached to the part of its funding that came via this source. While this was resolved satisfactorily in 2002, the events illustrate the very grave difficulties of campaigning work within the voluntary sector. For example, NCADC had not registered as a charity because charity commission rules would have constrained its work. Similarly, many funders who would consider supporting such work would prefer to give to registered charities. The principled stance taken by NCADC, which has been part of the very reason for its success, it seems has also led to its demise.

There are bigger issues for the voluntary sector here. The introduction of the market into social care and the role of the statutory sector as gatekeepers of the state's resources have changed the landscape for the voluntary sector. Increasingly, the state purchases and the voluntary (and private) sector provides, leading to contractual arrangements and funding implications. It has become difficult in this climate for that sector to remain truly independent or not be *drawn* into government agendas. The current government has, for example, wanted to nurture a particular relationship with the voluntary sector and has encouraged its involvement in many elements of the asylum process. Particularly since the **Immigration and Asylum Act 1999** and **dispersal**, the input of the voluntary sector has grown enormously and is often contracted to provide help and advice services which at first glance seem entirely benign (see Cohen, 2003b for a fuller discussion).

The experience of NCADC should serve as a warning that true independence comes at a price and those organisations that want to operate without constraint and with asylum seekers/refugees central to delivery, will struggle in the scrap for government and charitable handouts.

[DH]

Further information www.ncadc.org.uk

Nationality

Nationality is a major signifier in the construction of our identity. It is seen as a natural state that forges our commonality with some and our difference from others. In fact, nationality can only be understood in relation to the historical development of nation states. This has been a *process* taking place over hundreds of years, in particular in the increasing centralisation of states. Nation states have become entities where the population is said to share common characteristics, for example language or religion.

Historically, people within a nation state have been encouraged to share a *nationalism*, an identification with those common characteristics, as opposed to those of *others*.

Inherently, this has posed problems for those inside nation states who do not share certain characteristics. In Europe in the forging of nation states in the fifteenth century, certain religious and linguistic communities were displaced, for example Jews from Spain and Portugal and Protestants from France. In short, nationality is not a natural state and exists because of this forming and reforming of nation. Who should be included and excluded in the forming of nations, and consequently who has rights afforded to them, is a political question that has been grappled with across time. From eighteenth-century revolutionary France to the modern-day reconstruction of Eastern Europe, notions of national belonging have been used to unite some and divide others.

The idea that those within a nation share common interests has another dimension that is important for this book. **Immigration controls** formally exclude on the grounds of nationality and that justification is expressed in racialised terms. Throughout the history of controls, racial stereotypes and assumptions have been used both to *exclude* some and to *control* others who do cross borders. As industrial capitalism has always needed migrant labour it cannot simply exclude all; what it *can* do is decide who to let in and when, and the conditions under which people reside if they are let in. Racism is a key component in this process.

Possessing British nationality, then, is not as straightforward as being born within the borders of Great Britain and Northern Ireland.

There is, in my experience, often a very confused understanding in Britain regarding nationality rights and an assumption, particularly by those unaffected by immigration controls, that birth on British soil affords nationality or citizenship rights. In fact, the concept of *ius soli*, that birth within the English realm allows you to be an English subject, no longer exists. As an Imperial nation that English realm has at times been extensive and just what constitutes British soil is not fixed or certain but a historically shifting entity through control of territory, war and independence. For example, someone coming from Jamaica before its independence would have travelled on a UK and Colonies passport but after independence would have had a Jamaican one. Up to 1981, citizenship was acquired through birth in the UK but since the British Nationality Act 1981 it is acquired through parentage. Since that time, then, many born in Britain are not British at all and the 1981 Act expressed most clearly the racialised nature of British nationality. *Ius sanguinis* or citizenship through bloodline allows, for example, many white residents abroad with British ancestry access to the nation, which is denied to many black residents within British territory. Narrowing notions of nationality sit alongside increasingly restrictive immigration controls that have essentially closed the door of long-term settlement to the UK. This process has occurred in all rich nation states, leaving **asylum** as the only route of entry. The asylum seeker has now, therefore, become the main threat to Britishness or the British way of life. Calling upon racial stereotypes once again, current expressions of nationality pose the asylum seeker as *different*, as *other,* an unwanted inconvenience to be controlled within our borders and expediently removed from them.

[DH]

New Asylum Model

The UK government's proposal to develop a New Asylum Model (NAM) was contained in the five-year strategy for immigration and asylum published in February 2005 (Home Office, 2005c). The emphasis of the proposal is on increased managerial efficiency: decisions would be reached more speedily and the whole process would be 'tighter', a term beloved of New Labour's velvet fist approach to 'tackling' (another New Labour buzz word) contentious social issues with an appropriate degree of macho rhetoric combined with an apparently caring attitude to 'genuine' cases of need. Grant Mitchell meets Mother Teresa in the struggle to restore order to the streets and borders of Albion.

The three main features of NAM are 'segmentation', fast-track processing and case ownership.

At the stage of the screening interview (see **Asylum Interviews**), immigration officers assign a case to one of seven asylum processes or segments, based on the nature of the asylum claim. This procedure determines the way in which each case is progressed according to various pathways available:

- the speed at which cases are processed;
- where initial interviews will be held;
- whether they will be assisted in obtaining legal help;
- the type of accommodation that is allocated (for example, highly supervised accommodation blocks as in Liverpool, which was the trial area for NAM), or other types of housing;
- the frequency of reporting to the Immigration Service and whether personal visits to a **reporting** centre will be replaced by voice recognition or tagging.

The seven segments were defined as follows (ICAR, 2006):

(1) Third country cases: the Home Office believes that a person could have applied for asylum in a third country other than the UK.

(2) Accompanied and unaccompanied children: people under eighteen who require social services and Immigration Service assessments and are accommodated either by social services or with their own families.

(3) Non-suspensive **appeal** cases: people from one of the designated safe countries to which applicants may be returned before any appeal has been heard in the UK.

(4) Late and opportunistic claims, with low barriers for **removal**: people already having leave to enter the UK, that is, are in possession of a **visa**, and who have had their visa extension refused and subsequently claimed asylum. This segment may also include people found to be working unlawfully in the UK, have been arrested and subsequently applied for asylum.

(5) Late and opportunistic, high barriers to removal.

(6) General cases, low barriers to removal.

(7) General cases, high barriers to removal.

In mid-2006, the criteria for segments 5-7 had not been clarified and the definition of 'general' remained unclear. There will need to be a much higher level of decision making at an initial level if the narrative of an asylum claimant is to be accurately channelled into one of the seven segments and the task will have to attract an extremely high calibre of interviewing officer, since one other important feature of NAM is that cases will be 'owned' by the same officer who will be responsible for all decision making from initial interview to grant or refusal of asylum.

An example of the reduced timescale inherent in NAM is the process for late and opportunistic cases trialled in Liverpool and Croydon from October 2005 (the Home Office expected NAM to be fully operational throughout the UK by the end of 2006).

The whole process from screening interview to initial decision was expected to take no longer than a month. In Liverpool, the speed of the process was facilitated by the accommodation of **National Asylum**

Support Service (NASS) supported claimants in a former student residential block, with support agencies such Refugee Action and legal services being available on site.

In its March 2006 Bulletin, the Refugee Council reported that:

> the success rate of asylum applications being processed under the pilots is significantly higher than positive decision rates under any of the old processes. Under the pilot in Liverpool, 50 per cent of decisions made so far have been positive. The success rate in Croydon is lower, but still well above normal decision rates. 64 cases out of a total intake of 213 have received a positive decision under the pilots ... 31 were granted on initial decisions and 34 on appeal.

These results are interesting, given that a major concern about NAM's speedier processing was precisely that there would be insufficient time for an applicant to brief a solicitor or legal caseworker. However, as under the 'old' asylum system, it is the credibility of individual cases that remains of crucial importance to success. Perhaps the concentrated nature of NAM is also concentrating the minds of legal representatives in preparation of cases, both at an initial level and on appeal and ensuring a higher quality of work. However, such an assertion remains speculative until further evidence about the functioning and fairness of NAM becomes available.

....

On 5 July 2006, Abiy Fessfha Abebe, an Ethiopian asylum seeker, was found hanged in his accommodation block in Liverpool following news that his claim for asylum, made under NAM, had been refused.

[PF]

Further reading

Home Office (2005) *Controlling our Borders: Making Migration Work for Britain – Five-year Strategy for Asylum and Immigration*. Available online at: www.archive2.official-documents.co.uk/document/cm64/6472/6472.htm

Office of the Immigration Services Commissioner (OISC)

The OISC was established by the **Immigration and Asylum Act 1999**. Section 83 of this Act states that the Immigration Services Commissioner must ensure that providers of immigration advice and services are 'fit and competent to do so; act in the best interests of their clients; do not knowingly mislead any court ... in the United Kingdom; and do not seek to abuse any procedure operating in the United Kingdom'.

Subsequent sections of the Act specify that immigration services may only be provided by a 'qualified person' who must be specifically registered by the OISC or be exempt from registration due to their membership of another regulatory body such as the Law Society or Bar Council.

It is therefore a criminal offence for an 'advisor' (but not a solicitor) to provide immigration services or advice unless they or their organisation are either registered with the OISC, have been granted exemption from registration (for the criteria for this, see the OISC website: www.oisc.gov.uk), or are regulated by another body.

In one respect, the creation of the OISC can be seen as another example of the increasing move to regulate certain professions set in motion by the Conservative governments of the 1980s and 1990s. For example, teachers, and more recently social workers have been forced to seek registration with newly created regulatory bodies in order to legitimate their activities within a market-driven economy and to supposedly eliminate all risk to their 'clients'.

However, in the field of immigration advice work, there was, before the 1999 Act, a growing culture within which advice and representation was being undertaken by persons who were not legally qualified and not always supervised by a solicitor, and it is likely that some of those who sought advice on immigration and asylum matters were poorly advised and misrepresented.

From this point of view, the creation of the OISC can be seen as a consumer-friendly move, although the objective of preventing 'abuse of procedures' seems to indicate a subtext of suspicion that unregulated advisors were not only misleading their clients but also subverting and circumventing the UK's immigration laws in the process.

For those working as non-legal advocates with people subject to immigration controls, one of the most useful services of the OISC is its complaints procedures.

For example, there is a widespread belief among asylum seekers whose claims have been refused that payment for further legal services is a method of re-opening their case and guaranteeing success the second or perhaps third time round. Sums in the region of £500-£800 have changed hands for an advisor to make representations to the Home Office by stating grounds on which their client should be considered for leave to remain in the UK on compassionate or humanitarian grounds outside the **Immigration Rules** or to enter a new asylum claim on the basis that the client now possesses new evidence about their claim that was not previously available.

This places a considerable financial burden on asylum seekers who are destitute because of the withdrawal of their **National Asylum Support Service (NASS)** support following an unsuccessful case and who then have to rely on the borrowing of money from within their communities to fund this legal advice, which is often rudimentary in nature. Voluntary agencies meet many people in this situation, which often resembles a bizarre pantomime of claim and counter claim, dragging on for months and even years without a satisfactory outcome and raising false hopes at every turn. The OISC may be able to give some redress to clients whose representatives have not taken the promised action in such cases. The likelihood of investigation may cause money to be returned to dissatisified clients.

[PF]

Further information

www.oisc.gov.uk

Refugee

A term generally used to denote anyone escaping persecution, natural disaster or famine, and doing so by crossing the borders separating them from their own country, or region of origin into another, safer, territory. (Thus, in 2005, people escaping the effects of Hurricane Katrina were routinely described as 'refugees' by the world's media.)

In the conscience and consciousness of Western Europe the classic paradigm of the refugee condition is that of the Jewish emigration from Central Europe following the rise to power of the Nazis in the 1930s: a political power constructs a particular ethnic group as its enemies and carries out systematic persecution and annihilation of that group, some of whom, if they have the means to do so, escape to a safe place beyond the reach of the hostile agents of destruction.

The **UN Convention on the Status of Refugees** of 1951 enshrines this transnational characteristic of refugees when it emphasises that recognition as a refugee is given to persons 'outside the country of … nationality' and who are 'unwilling to return to it' due to a fear of subsisting fear of persecution.

Therefore we need to understand that the primary meaning of the term is that of designating someone who has been recognised as a refugee by the state whose protection they have sought. And this is why we distinguish 'refugees' from 'asylum seekers' in the contemporary discourse and debate around this subject in the UK. Those who flee persecution and reach the UK may all be refugees in a general sense, but only those who successfully claim political asylum here and are recognised as refugees by the British government under the terms of the UN Convention are, strictly speaking, refugees. Those who wish to be recognised as refugees and who have applied to the British government for international protection are in the *process of seeking asylum* in the UK but have not yet been granted it.

According to the United Nations High Commissioner for Refugees (UNHCR), Britain hosts less than 2 per cent of the world's refugees. Those fleeing famine and natural disaster will never get further than another region of their country, becoming 'displaced persons', or the border areas of a neighbouring country. Those who reach Europe will have made a determined effort to do so, helped by the dubious services of people smugglers and traffickers, and often with uncertain or disastrous results (see **Trafficking and Smuggling of People**).

The definitions of who may attain the status of refugee as laid down in the UN Convention (Article 1A[2]) are specific: they must have a:

> Well-founded fear of being persecuted for reasons of race, religion, nationality, membership of a particular social group or political opinion ...

This definition embodies fundamental elements of individual identity, both given and acquired, and those who drafted the UN Convention consider the granting of refugee status as an act of a high moral and ethical order. Those calling upon a sovereign state to exercise its powers of protection must, however, prove that their fear of persecution is 'well-founded'. There thus seems to be a type of contractual relationship at work in the process of becoming a refugee: if I seek refugee status, I must understand that it can only be given if I can prove to the satisfaction of those charged by each sovereign state with deciding my case that my fear is based upon evidence that I can substantiate and is not merely subjective or opportunistic.

It is worth quoting in detail the relevant sections from the UNHCR (1992) *Handbook on Procedures and Criteria for Determining Refugee Status*.

> Para 38. To the element of fear – a state of mind and a subjective condition – is added the qualification 'well-founded'. This implies that it is not only the frame of mind of the person concerned that determines his [sic] refugee status, but that this frame of mind must

be supported by an objective situation. The term 'well-founded fear' therefore contains a subjective and an objective element, and in determining whether well-founded fear exists, both elements must be taken into consideration.

39. It may be assumed that, unless he seeks adventure or just wishes to see the world, a person would not normally abandon his home and country without some compelling reason. There may be many reasons that are compelling and understandable, but only one motive has been singled out to denote a refugee. The expression 'owing to well-founded fear of being persecuted' – for the reasons stated – by indicating a specific motive automatically makes all other reasons for escape irrelevant to the definition. It rules out such persons as victims of famine or natural disaster, unless they also have well-founded fear of persecution for one of the reasons stated. Such other motives may not, however, be altogether irrelevant to the process of determining refugee status, since all the circumstances need to be taken into account for a proper understanding of the applicant's case.

40. An evaluation of the *subjective element* is inseparable from an assessment of the personality of the applicant, since psychological reactions of different individuals may not be the same in identical conditions. One person may have strong political or religious convictions, the disregard of which would make his life intolerable; another may have no such strong convictions. One person may make an impulsive decision to escape; another may carefully plan his departure.

41. Due to the importance that the definition attaches to

the subjective element, an assessment of credibility is indispensable where the case is not sufficiently clear from the facts on record. It will be necessary to take into account the personal and family background of the applicant, his membership of a particular racial, religious, national, social or political group, his own interpretation of his situation, and his personal experiences – in other words, everything that may serve to indicate that the predominant motive for his application is fear. Fear must be reasonable. Exaggerated fear, however, may be well founded if, in all the circumstances of the case, such a state of mind can be regarded as justified.

It is therefore not sufficient for those claiming asylum to rely upon assertions such as 'conditions in my country are bad' or to produce evidence obtained via the internet, for example, which attests to persecution of particular ethnic, religious or political groups. An individual must prove that they as an individual are at risk of persecution and it is a constant source of amazement to those working closely with those whose claims for refugee status have been rejected that applicants from many countries whose regimes are violent or unstable are told that their claims are unfounded and that it would be possible for them to relocate to another area of their country where they would be free to go about their daily lives unhindered. Nevertheless, this is an inevitable state of affairs in cases where individual fears do not add up to 'persecution' that can be objectively verified.

Although I have suggested that broadly ethical principles underlie the criteria of the UN Convention, it may be said that they are, in fact, narrowly restrictive and in need of redrafting to reflect contemporary realities.

Readers will be familiar with the campaign against 'bogus asylum seekers' conducted by the right-wing British press in the early years of the 21st century. In October 2003 the Press Complaints Commission found it necessary to issue guidelines to newspaper editors pointing out that 'bogus' or 'illegal' asylum seekers, or indeed, refugees, do not exist as all asylum seekers are simply awaiting decisions on the validity of their cases, and that refugees have been afforded international protection by the UK government.

The moral panic about those who apparently claim to be refugees but who are in fact 'economic migrants' seems to lean upon the moral principles of the UN Convention, but distorts them in a quest to differentiate between the 'deserving' and 'undeserving' among those who arrive in the UK and seek asylum. The fact is, however, that approximately 80 per cent of applications for refugee status are rejected as unfounded, including those rejected after appeal. The only justification for rejecting an asylum claim is that it does not fit into the criteria listed in the UN Convention, or that it has not been proved to do so and that the UK's obligations under the European Convention on Human Rights are not affected by doing so.

What, then, does the UN Convention, and the British Home Office, who decides asylum claims, NOT consider to constitute persecution?

- Poverty.
- Lack of economic opportunity.
- Poor health, including the prevalence of HIV and AIDS in a particular country.
- Threats by local chiefs, mafias and non-state militias.
- Being ostracised by a family following failed marriage or reneging on promises of marriage.
- Violence in intimate relationships of marriage or other forms of partnership.
- Cultic practices involving physical harm to the initiate.
- The practice of certain spiritual activities not considered to be religious in nature, for example Falun Gong in the People's Republic of China.

This is, of course, an arbitrary and incomplete list, but is based on the experience of one voluntary support agency. Most of the above could possibly be subsumed under the contentious Convention category of 'particular social group'. The case of Shah and Islam (2 AC 629, HL) defined women as a 'particular social group' in the context of two women who sought refuge in the UK from domestic violence in Pakistan. In October 2006, the House of Lords ruled that a family may be considered to form a 'social group' within the UN Convention's definition under certain circumstances.

> The original evil which gives rise to persecution is one thing; if it is then transferred so that a family is persecuted, on the face of it that will come within the Convention. (UKHL, 2006, 46:14)

However, it is increasingly the case that 'non-Convention' reasons for claiming asylum are virtually bound to fail.

The UN Convention cannot therefore be used to grant status to and regularise the position of those who claim asylum for reasons other than those which it explicitly recognises. It cannot be used by governments to regulate 'irregular' movements of migrants from relatively underdeveloped countries in Africa and Asia, for example, to Western Europe. The current position in the UK is that the asylum system and its accompanying **National Asylum Support Service (NASS)** system are the only mechanisms through which those who flee to the UK can attain temporary admission and support. The minority whose claims are adjudged to meet the ethical criteria of the UN Convention are admitted as refugees with the chance to become citizens if they so choose. The rest are left in limbo.

[PF]

Refugee Action

Founded in 1981 Refugee Action describes itself as an independent charity offering a range of services to asylum seekers and refugees. Its main contribution has been in the area of reception and settlement of refugee communities, its early work assisting, in particular, Vietnamese, Bosnian and Kosovan arrivals. This early experience has been put to good use since the more formalised **dispersal** process began in 2000 following the **Asylum and Immigration Act 1999**. This Act completely changed the landscape regarding the entry and support of asylum seekers and led to the formation of the **National Asylum Support Service (NASS)** and the dispersal of asylum seekers away from the South East of Britain and London. The significance of this was the removal of asylum seekers from normal welfare delivery to this separate and inferior provision via NASS. This involves a no choice offer of accommodation and 70 per cent subsistence-level support. Regional Consortia would be responsible for managing these 'supports'. In line with this, Refugee Action since 2000 have offered a reception service to new arrivals to help them through these NASS processes and receive their entitlements. Refugee Action is funded partially by the Home Office because of this invaluable work and it has had a pivotal role in the development of effective reception services. Other organisations, for example, the **Joint Council for the Welfare of Immigrants (JCWI)** and the **National Coalition for Anti-Deportation Campaigns (NCADC)** have chosen not to take funding from the Home Office or to be as enmeshed in the infrastructure of dispersal, so the question of *independence* is not without contention.

Refugee Action has played a significant role in the development of refugee communities and works hard to assist hundreds of refugee organisations. It attempts to put centre stage the voices of those communities, believing such development is the key to successful settlement. It is also an important source of information and publications in the asylum and refugee arena.

More controversially, Refugee Action has a 'Choices' project, which offers advice on voluntary return to asylum seekers and refugees. This is run in conjunction with the 'International Organisation for Migration' and offers confidential, impartial advice so that informed choices can be made about possible return. This project has an absolute position of opposition to forced or involuntary return but believes through their close relationship with refugee communities that such a service is needed. The tension here is the general direction of Home Office policy regarding the return of 'failed' asylum seekers and the 'starving out' of that group through the withdrawal of NASS support. Under these circumstances it is difficult to judge what is or isn't genuinely voluntary. They are, however, one of the few organisations actively engaged in a dialogue about the reconstruction of countries from which asylum seekers come in order to foster the conditions under which they may make realistic decisions to return.

Whether to work *within* oppressive asylum systems or stand outside of them will remain an important debate within the delivery of welfare. Whichever side of the line the reader falls on it is important to acknowledge that organisations such as Refugee Action have advised thousands of new arrivals at their most vulnerable time. Low-paid workers or often volunteers in fact, face the daily pressure of trying to remain humane in an inhumane system and of trying to help people in a monolithic machine designed to deter and remove, not assist to settle.

....

In memory of Israfil Shiri 1973-2003, a destitute Iranian asylum seeker who poured petrol over his body and set fire to himself in the offices of Refugee Action in Manchester in 2003.

....

[DH]

Further information

www.refugee-action.org.uk

Refugee Council

The Refugee Council is the largest organisation in the UK working with asylum seekers and refugees. It is of central importance in the infrastructure of advice and support services to this group. Its work at this level is done via four regional offices, namely London, East region, West Midlands and Yorkshire and Humberside. In addition to this crucial work the organisation works hard to include and involve refugee community organisations through its Community Development Team.

The organisation has a particular role with **Unaccompanied Asylum-seeking Children**, offering specialist advice and support to this group as they work their way through asylum procedures. This Children's Panel of Advisors and the important work they are doing has contributed to an increased awareness among social care professionals of their needs. In fact, the Refugee Council's commitment to research and policy development, which includes the refugee voice, is a major contribution to the immigration, asylum and refugee landscape in the UK. All its briefing papers, research reports and policy documents are freely available via its website (www.refugeecouncil.org.uk). Its monthly briefings, available on subscription, provide an invaluable reference source on the latest developments in refugee and asylum issues. It also provides a variety of training courses for volunteers and professionals throughout the UK.

This all continues to provide a focus for campaigning and lobbying on behalf of and alongside this vulnerable group.

[DH]

Further information
www.refugeecouncil.org.uk

Removal

see also **Deportation**.

'Removal' is the term used for the forcible ejection of someone from the territory of the UK. It is sometimes referred to as 'administrative' removal since it results, in the words of Section 10 of the **Immigration and Asylum Act 1999**, from directions given by an immigration officer: in other words, removal directions are given on the basis of administrative decisions reached with regard to certain classes of persons no longer having leave to remain in the UK. Asylum seekers whose claims have been refused, for example, clearly fall into the category of people who 'having limited leave to enter or remain, (remain) beyond the time limited by the leave'.

The temporary admission granted to asylum seekers so that their claim can be examined is deemed to expire once their case has been fully determined and all appeal rights have been exhausted. They are therefore liable to be removed from the UK, but only when and if removal directions have been given which specify the time, means of transport and place to which they are to be removed. In theory, all asylum **appeals** are appeals against the Home Office's intentions to remove the appellant to their country of origin. Removal, then, is a lawful process that can be applied to all those whose asylum claims have been refused, and to those who have overstayed the terms of their **visas**.

A person can, generally speaking, only be removed to a country of which they are a national or to a country that has provided them with a passport. It is not unknown for someone to be removed to a particular country only for that country to refuse to accept them for reasons of disputed nationality, which then entails return to the UK and a lengthy period in immigration detention while nationality or ethnicity is decided, if it ever can be. In addition, travel documents need to be obtained to effect removal and this can often be impossible if a person's nationality is disputed (see **Destitution**). If an individual entered the UK using a passport that is still valid and held by the Home Office, removal could be relatively straightforward. For removal to be effected, it is obviously necessary for someone's whereabouts to be known by the Immigration Service: families are often more at risk because of their continued residence in **National Asylum Support Service (NASS)** accommodation; single people may be more mobile and find it easier to disappear into large cities, providing that they do not come to the attention of the police, for example.

It is a lawful process, but the means by which it is carried out can be far from benign and often appears to be operating at the limits of humane treatment and often oversteps them. In July 1993, Joy Gardener, a Jamaican-born woman, died from suffocation during an attempt to arrest and deport her made by the Metropolitan Police. There are frequent reports on the **National Coalition for Anti-Deportation Campaigns (NCADC)** website alleging disproportionate measures being taken by the Enforcement Unit of the Immigration Service in the arrest of persons subject to removal directions. There is the disruptive effect on schools, for example, when two or three children are suddenly missing following their and their parents' enforced departure. There are the lingering doubts that asylum cases have been handled ineffectively and that people who should have been afforded refugee status have been denied it and have been sent back to further persecution. In 2005-06, Zimbabweans seeking asylum in the UK were subjected to a bizarre game of musical chairs played out between the Home Office, the Asylum and Immigration Tribunal and the Court of Appeal who, between them, could not decide whether it was safe to return failed asylum seekers to Zimbabwe. At the time of writing, it has been decided that state authorities of Zimbabwe do not, after all, pose any threat to forcibly returned persons.

Jenny Cuffe, a reporter for the BBC World Service, described her first-hand experience as she tried to discover the fate of former asylum seekers removed from the UK to the Democratic Republic of Congo:

> At the very back of the plane, a young African woman was moaning quietly and pleading monotonously in a low,

intimate voice, 'Laissez-moi, laissez-moi'. Like a child wearing down a parent. She wasn't crying. The escorts at either side of her looked straight ahead impassively. Two police officers in the aisle made it clear there was to be no interference from any curious or kind-hearted passengers. (Cuffe, 2005, p. 97)

In the Congo, failed asylum seekers are regularly taken aside into a small airless room for questioning … Most arrive empty-handed or with just a small amount of money, but officials insist on a bribe of 100 US dollars or more before releasing them. If they cannot call family or friends to bail them out – an option only for those with connections in Kinshasa – they are at risk of a long stay in detention. (Cuffe, 2005, p. 99)

Of course, this is precisely what the traffickers and smugglers who charge you to take you to the West do *not* tell you. Would-be asylum seekers are oblivious to the contractual nature of the process: you claim asylum only if you can prove that you suffer persecution as defined by the **UN Convention on the Status of Refugees** – if you cannot do that, you are likely to be ejected and forced to go back with nothing, where, even if the secret police are not interested in you, then the smugglers may get to you to ensure that their methods remain secret (see **Trafficking and Smuggling of People**).

Fekete (2005) lists a gruesome catalogue of torture and death that has befallen forced returnees from many European countries once they have arrived in what can only be ironically termed 'home'; another author who is implacably opposed to all forms of immigration controls, assimilates the very term 'removals' to the 'newspeak' endured by the denizens of George Orwell's novel *1984*:

Some immigration newspeak is now so well used by all sides of the political debate that it can take a feat of intellectual willpower to be able to stand back and understand the real, hidden, agenda behind it – namely the dehumanization of the undocumented. Take the word 'removals'. This, until recently was confined to issues of furniture (as in 'furniture removals') and perhaps cargo commodities generally. Now it is used daily to apply to unwanted human beings, as a form of deportation or expulsion ... So a vocabulary that was once confined mainly to the transportation of inanimate objects is now best known politically for the forced expulsion of sentient humans (Cohen, 2006, p. 66).

....

Whichever term is used, the effect on the lives of individuals is the same:

the forcible expulsion of non-citizens from national territory by the state is a power that has traditionally been seen to flow from the state's right to control immigration: just as states are entitled to prevent aliens from entering their territory, so they claim a correlative right to expel aliens who have entered or remain on state territory in breach of immigration laws. In some respects, the right to deport is more revealing of the capacity of states to exercise control over the lives of individuals than almost any other aspect of state power. The deportation of an individual severs permanently and completely the relationship of responsibility between the state and the individual under its authority in a way that only capital punishment surpasses. (Gibney and Hansen, 2005, p. 127)

Furthermore, the ability and capacity to remove the undesirable and those who have outstayed their welcome is the king-pin of all governments' immigration policies. In its paper *Fair, Effective, Transparent and Trusted* the British government refers to a 'tipping point', by which is meant 'removing more failed asylum seekers than make unfounded claims' and:

Deal(ing) with the legacy of older cases that have yet to be fully resolved. We plan to do this within five years or less. We will prioritise those who may pose a risk to the public *and then focus on those who may be more easily removed.* (Home Office, 2006a, p. 9, emphasis added)

This is the most blatant kind of populist window dressing, assuring the public that its government is on the case with its sleeves rolled up and ready for the task of clearing our shores of both terrorists and those who have innocently applied for asylum. (As an aside, it seems that the Home Office may be in danger of running out of convincing adjectival titles for its discussion papers, titles which strive to convey connotations of both justice and toughness, but which are in grave danger of descending into the kind of antonymous Orwellian newspeak decried above by Cohen.)

A study of the numbers of persons forcibly returned by Canada, Germany and the UK between 1993 and 2000 (the year range varied slightly depending on country), reached the following conclusion:

While large numbers of asylum seekers arrive, and few are given refugee status, fewer still are forced to leave the country. Deportation remains a singularly rare occurrence. Indeed, the striking feature of the data is that it shows that deportations have in no way increased in a manner commensurate with overall asylum applications … In short, deportation only touches a small minority of those whom the state has formally forbidden from remaining on its national territory. (Gibney and Hansen, 2003, p. 4)

If we assume a continuation of this trend, then we might suggest that those most likely to be removed are indeed the 'easy' targets hoped for by *Fair, Effective, Transparent and Trusted.* They are the most visible: families with dependent children who are to some extent settled in their NASS accommodation and continue to use their **Application Registration Cards (ARCs)** to access NASS support, and those in detention or those who have been convicted of criminal offences and serving prison sentences and thus already located within the supervisory gaze of the state. For, as Gibney and Hansen (2003, p. 11) also conclude:

> Deportation is above all expensive. Tracking down individuals who have gone underground is time consuming and resource-intensive, involving the use of scarce public resources. Removal is particularly difficult in countries, like the UK and Canada, without national systems of identification that enable the tracking of members of the public.

....

Social workers and other professionals working with people subject to immigration controls do, no doubt, find themselves in a dilemma when confronted with families on the verge of removal. Removal is a lawful process: it could, however, be viewed as an arbitrary construct and single out certain groups of people for the process of severance from their aspirations for a new and safe life in the UK. The question of whether **immigration controls** differ in essence or effect from other statutes that social workers, for example, may be routinely asked to enforce is not, in my view, easily answered. The Children and Mental Health Acts, for example, both combine elements of protection with elements of coercion. The UK's adherence to both the **UN Convention on the Status of Refugees** and the European Convention on Human Rights implies provision for international humanitarian protection for those who can demonstrate their need for such protection. The concerted resistance of frontline social work staff to the provisions of Section 9 of the **Asylum and Immigration (Treatment of Claimants, etc) Act 2004** in 2005-06 was based on a belief in the rights of children being paramount over the rights of the UK to police its borders.

Indeed, the focus of social work in the statutory and voluntary sectors must surely continue to be with the needs of human beings as they present themselves to us in our various work situations. The supposed needs of the state to protect its borders are irrelevant to the essential relationship of professional care. If we wish to resist immigration controls, this is one way, quiet, persistent and radical.

> There is no true word that is not at the same time a praxis.
> Thus, to speak a true word is to transform the world.
> (Freire, 1996, p. 68)

[PF]

Reporting Conditions

Dallas Court is an unremarkable grey building that could easily be the base for one of the numerous service industries located in the regeneration zone of Salford Quays in Greater Manchester.

On weekdays there is a constant procession of people to its front entrance where they show a letter to the security personnel on duty and are then admitted. They then pass through airport-style metal detectors and are searched, given a number and sit down in a waiting area, which resembles any one of a number of agencies whose function is the bureaucratic processing of those who are seeking a service of some sort. We could be at a Job Centre, a local government housing office or social services. We are, in fact, at one of the eleven reporting centres in the UK operated by the Immigration and Nationality Directorate (IND).

What is there to report? As one of the conditions of being given Temporary Admission (TA) into the UK while an asylum claim is being assessed, most asylum seekers, unless prevented from doing so by acute medical conditions, must attend on a weekly or monthly basis at one of the centres in order to confirm their continued presence in the UK at the address that has been assigned to them by the **National Asylum Support Service (NASS)** (see JCWI, 2006, pp. 653-4 for the criteria for frequency of reporting). If the asylum applicant lives more than 25 miles from a reporting centre, they are required to report at a designated police station.

When their number appears on the waiting room screen they go to the next available booth and present their **Application Registration Card (ARC)** to the officer who will check the asylum applicant's name against computer files, record the visit and, if all goes smoothly, issue a date for the next reporting visit.

Access to NASS cash payments is linked to continuity of reporting, and missed visits without prior explanation can result in the denial of payment at the next visit to a post office to collect the weekly

NASS allowance.

It is fair to say that many asylum seekers find the visit to a reporting centre a fairly arduous experience. While many people seeking asylum may willingly accept the imposition of what could be a long journey made difficult by inadequate public transport as part of the necessary inconvenience of the pursuance of asylum in the UK, for others, this can be extremely stressful. They may recall conditions in the country from which they have fled, the uncertainties and serendipities of living in a quasi police state where the rules are unknown and every move could be a false one. I have often accompanied particularly vulnerable people to their signing-on, and while front-line staff have generally provided a courteous and efficient service without any signs of undue hostility, the fear and uncertainty engendered by being present in a building whose officers potentially have the power to restrict individual freedoms can be daunting for both worker and client.

'Reporting', as such, is the most obvious function of Dallas Court and its ilk. However, the reporting centres are also the location for various types of interviews to which asylum seekers, especially those whose cases are found to have been unfounded and whose appeal rights have been exhausted, may be asked to attend.

Under Section 35 of the **Asylum and Immigration (Treatment of Claimants, etc) Act 2004**, unsuccessful asylum seekers are expected to co-operate with their removal from the UK by 'attend[ing] an interview and answer[ing] questions accurately and completely' (Section 35 [2g]). It is on these occasions that the presence of a legal representative could be useful, to say the least; however, given the current restrictions on legal funding for asylum work, it is becoming increasingly rare for this to happen. Other advocates from the field of social care obviously have a role to be played here, although it can sometimes be extremely difficult to gain access to a reporting centre to undertake effective support and accompaniment. Security personnel may have to be persuaded that their 'customer' has no intention of entering the building without their advocate, and, if this ploy is successful and the advocate's appearance and demeanor do not give rise to any suspicions as to the likelihood of anarchy or mayhem being unleashed by one's presence, one will probably succeed. Entry will certainly not be gained if an aggressive and hostile attitude is presented by the advocate towards low-paid staff who are simply implementing government legislation as part of their regular employment. One may discuss further with the interviewing officer, that, as a non-legal advocate, one will not take any active part in the proceedings and simply be present as an observer.

This does not mean, of course, that social advocates will not have discussed beforehand with their service users the implications of the 're-documentation' interview. In any event, the process of questioning, fingerprinting and taking of photographs leaves little doubt as to the purpose of these interviews. The process can be especially distressing when the primary purpose of the interview is to update IND records in the case of children who may have been born to an asylum seeker since their claim was first registered.

Refusal to co-operate is an offence under Section 35 (4a and b) of the 2004 Act and may be punishable by fine or imprisonment. I have been present at an interview where this penalty was mentioned at a point where the interviewee refused to sign her interview form, but I am not aware of any threatened prosecution in this case. In its March 2005 bulletin, the Refugee Council stated that it was unaware of any prosecutions under this section of the 2004 Act.

The question of continued reporting becomes problematical when appeal rights have been exhausted. If **removal directions** have been set, it is possible that an asylum seeker could be detained during a reporting visit, which, unfortunately, happens with some frequency and forms the basis of the fears which many people harbour about continued reporting after they have received the standard Home Office letter notifying them that they should 'now take steps to leave the UK'. If people have been denied asylum and their NASS support has been terminated, there seems little purpose in continuing regular visits to a centre or to the police. On the other hand, if there is the remotest likelihood of a particular case being resubmitted to the Home Office on the basis of new evidence being obtained or because of changed conditions in the country of origin, there may be justification in continued reporting, which would demonstrate a willingness to comply with temporary admission requirements, no matter how tenuous the benefits of this course of action might appear. For families, NASS support may be suspended for reasons of non-reporting.

Decisions on this matter can only be made, ultimately, by the individual asylum seeker who must weigh up the situation as best as they can. Many have and will continue to relinquish all contact with the Home Office and IND and go 'underground', becoming untraceable by the authorities and existing in a state of limbo, and usually remaining unmolested unless they bring themselves to the attention of the police by the committing of an offence, for example.

For example, Richard entered the UK using false documents and obtained employment for a number of years. He had not claimed asylum and was quite open in describing himself as coming to the UK to work. He had obtained a flat from his local authority, voted in elections, paid income and was a model citizen in many respects. After a few years he decided to do something about his irregular status in the UK and believed that the best way to do this was to obtain a UK driving licence. He applied to the DVLA using a birth certificate which was not his own, having no form of 'official' identity document. When this fraud was discovered he received a caution from the police, who then found out that he was in the UK illegally and brought him to the attention of the IND.

Unknown to Richard, Section 36 of the 2004 Act had introduced the availability of electronic monitoring or 'tagging' as a method of enforcing the residence restrictions imposed as a condition of Temporary Admission to the UK. When Richard was interviewed at his local reporting centre he was offered the option of being tagged as an alternative to being detained and was obliged to spend three days of each week at home as part of his reporting conditions.

In Richard's case (and he was fortunate to obtain the paid services of an immigration solicitor to plead for him) the tagging option was no doubt offered on compassionate grounds as he had become a father while in the UK and was living with the child's mother.

Home Office guidelines indicate the risk assessment criteria under which tagging (or voice recognition technology or tracking by global positioning satellite) can be used. Included in these are:

- The person is not removable to their country of origin.
- No travel document is available for the potential removee.
- The person has criminal convictions.
- There is a previous history of 'non-compliance' with immigration law. (JCWI, 2006, pp. 953-4)

Thus, Richard became an unwitting participant in the Home Office's pilot electronic monitoring scheme. He does not (yet) face an uncertain future in immigration detention, but his movements have been restricted, he can no longer work and he, his partner and their child have no recourse to public funds of any kind. His future in the UK is bleak.

The electronic signals emitted by his tagging device report that he is *here*, physically present within range of the IND's receiver; the regular personal reporting of asylum seekers similarly says that they are *here* through their mark made on the IND's documents.

But they are *here* and not yet, if ever, truly *here* in the sense that they may become citizens and not aliens whose very existence *here* has to be proved in case they slip away from the watchful eye of the state, which probably wishes, anyway, that they were *anywhere but here*.

[PF]

Section 4 Support

This section of the **Immigration and Asylum Act 1999** gives the Home Secretary powers to 'provide, or arrange for the provision of, facilities for the accommodation of a person if a) he was (but is no longer) an asylum seeker, and b) his claim for asylum was rejected' (para 2).

At a first glance, this measure seems to be very generous. When a claim for asylum is dismissed and all rights of appeal have been exhausted, **National Asylum Support Service (NASS)** support is withdrawn, and if the claimant is a single person without minor dependants, they are effectively made destitute (see **Asylum and Immigration (Treatment of Claimants etc, Act) 2004** and **Destitution**). However, government generosity usually depends upon the fulfilment of certain conditions, and this is the case with Section 4 support.

The Immigration and Asylum (Provision of Accommodation to Failed Asylum Seekers) Regulations 2005 set out who may be entitled to this so-called 'hard cases' support.

The essential condition is that the failed asylum seeker must appear to be destitute, which is interpreted as meaning that a person must be without adequate accommodation, food and other essential items.

In addition, one or more of the following criteria must be met:

- The applicant for Section 4 support must be taking all reasonable steps to leave the UK. This might involve in co-operating with Home Office attempts to obtain a travel document for them to be able to leave the UK.
- The applicant is unable to leave the UK because of 'a physical impairment to travel' or a medical condition which prevents travel.
- There is no viable route of return to the applicant's country of origin.
- The applicant has made an application for judicial review of a decision relating to their asylum claim.

- The applicant needs to be provided with accommodation in order to prevent a breach of their human rights under the European Convention.

The experience of many support agencies is that it is often extremely difficult to obtain Section 4 support, even when the relevant criteria are being met. Women in the late stages of pregnancy are usually granted support, but sometimes only within a few days of the due delivery date.

In instances where no 'viable' or safe route of return exists, the case of Iraq is salutary and demonstrates the arbitrary nature of decision-making on issues of Section 4 support.

In January 2005, and following a test case, NASS announced that there were significant risks involved in a journey to Iraq and that it would not demand that Iraqis agreed to return before they could access Section 4 support. Large numbers of Iraqis thus became eligible for support. However, in August 2005, NASS announced that there was a safe route of return for Iraqis and that applicants would have to satisfy one of the above criteria in order to be eligible for 'hard cases' support.

In 2006 many Iraqis were receiving Section 4 support while they awaited individual appeal decisions as a result of the case of *Baktear Rashid v. the Home Secretary*, which decided that the possibility of relocation to the Kurdish Autonomous Zone should not be used as a basis for refusing asylum to Iraqi Kurdish people.

Following the case of *AA v. the Home Secretary* in 2005, the Home Office considered that unsuccessful Zimbabwean asylum seekers who were forcibly returned were at risk from the Zimbabwean Central Intelligence Organization and Zimbabweans could thus apply for Section 4 support on the basis that they were prevented from returning to Zimbabwe through a UK government decision. It was no means certain, however, that support would be provided in every case.

In 2004/05, there was a sustained campaign against a NASS proposal to make the provision of 'hard cases' support subject to the undertaking of 'community activities'. This would have led to the further stigmatising of unsuccessful asylum seekers with the association of such activities with those persons convicted of certain offences and serving community punishment orders. The YMCA, which had emerged as the likely manager of the community activities, decided, as a result of the campaign, to withdraw from this scheme, which expired quietly in 2005 and has not been resuscitated since.

Section 4 support is provided in the form of accommodation and vouchers, which made an unwelcome reappearance in 2005 after having been replaced as the main form of support for all asylum seekers by 2003.

The use of vouchers was originally criticised because of their stigmatising effect. They signify that the person using them is 'other' and outside of the mainstream means of exchange for goods and services carried out by the civil population by means of recognised monetary currency. Their message to the person receiving 'hard cases' support is: *you are here in the UK, but you are not really here – you are only here because we have taken pity on you because of your impossible circumstances.*

Perhaps we remember playing monopoly or pretending to run a toy post office or bank when we were children: infantilisation and dependency are inherent when adults are forced to use a currency whose value resides in ideological intent rather than the freedom and responsibility that the spending of 'real' money conveys on the spender.

In purely practical terms, the nature of the vouchers dispensed varied between accommodation providers. Some applicants were given luncheon vouchers, others vouchers issued by major supermarkets. Mothers of babies were finding it particularly difficult to buy essentials items such as nappies and powdered milk. Accommodation providers were expected to have a designated worker for such women who would ensure that these items could be purchased by the issuing of appropriate store vouchers.

In 2006, one provider of Section 4 accommodation started to issue its residents with supermarket gift vouchers with an electronically stored value which could be used for any type of in-store purchase This had the advantage of allowing the purchaser access to a wider range of necessary items. However, there also developed an undercover trade of exchanging vouchers for cash, at a rate that was always disadvantageous to the Section 4 recipient.

Travel is made impossible in this symbolic economy and is a restriction which seems to embody the essentially punitive nature of the voucher regime.

The duration of Section 4 support depends on the reasons for which it has been granted. For example, women who are pregnant and thus unable to travel because of physical impairment may find that NASS requires proof of resumed or continuing efforts to leave the UK voluntarily, or of actual destitution itself when their children reach the age of about six months. However, there does not seem to be any consistent policy on this issue and some applicants may continue to receive support for longer periods without NASS investigation into their current circumstances.

The reluctance of many unsuccessful asylum seekers to avail themselves of Section 4 support because of the imposed obligation to seek voluntary return means that many thousands are standing their ground and preferring relative poverty in the UK rather than revisiting unknown, insecure and possibly dangerous circumstances. The use of Section 4 to, rightly, support nationals of countries whose internal circumstances are recognised by the UK government as making forced return undesirable implicitly devalues the experience of asylum seekers from the many countries whose human rights records are equally deplorable but which do not seem to attract the attention of government at the level of foreign policy-making.

[PF]

Section 55 (of the Nationality, Immigration and Asylum Act 2002)

In 2003, this piece of legislation was the focus of great concern among those working to maintain the right to welfare of asylum seekers.

It was part of an Act which, as part of a now familiar process, tinkered and added to existing legislation with the aim of 'getting tough' with those claiming asylum in the UK by attempting to enact punitive measures designed to prevent and deter those whom the government deemed bogus and opportunistic.

The essence of Section 55 is that it gave powers to the Home Office to deny **National Asylum Support Service (NASS)** support to asylum seekers if their claims were not made 'as soon as reasonably practical after the person's arrival in the United Kingdom' (para 1b). However, the same section contains an escape clause in the shape of a statement that a decision to deny support should not entail a breach of someone's human rights (para 5a).

How soon is soon and how reasonable is reasonable? Seeking asylum is neither an entirely rational nor ordered activity, adhering to some kind of typical timescale. Asylum seekers may arrive in the UK in a state of confusion and may know little, if anything, about the concept of 'asylum', and will certainly know nothing of the current UK asylum legislation that is in force on the particular day they arrive.

According to the Refugee Council's Information Service (September 2004):

> When these measures (Section 55) went through Parliament, MPs and peers were assured that they would only apply to those who had been in the country for a

significant time before claiming asylum – illegal workers, (visa) overstayers, individuals making multiple asylum applications or students whose visa had expired.

However, from the outset, Section 55 was interpreted in the strictest possible terms by the Home Office, resulting in the denial of support to 9,000 asylum seekers, regardless of actual need, resulting in a sustained campaign by the voluntary and public support sectors, the legal profession and politicians. A spate of legal challenges followed, and in May 2004 the Court of Appeal found the Home Office to be in breach of Article 3 of the European Convention of Human Rights – the article forbidding inhuman and degrading treatment – for denying support under Section 55. In June 2004 the Home Office was forced to concede that support could only be refused to asylum seekers if there was positive proof that an alternative source of help was available to the applicant.

In the first quarter of 2006, 875 asylum applicants were referred to NASS for a Section 55 assessment. Of these, 205 were deemed to be ineligible for NASS support on the grounds that the 'Secretary of State was not satisfied that their claims had been made as soon as reasonably practicable'. The remainder were granted NASS support as their claims had been made as soon as practicably possible, or they had dependants under 18, or a failure to support might have led to a breach of their human rights (Home Office, 2006c).

It is difficult to comprehend how the Home Office could have proceeded to apply this legislation in a way which contradicted one of its own provisions as mentioned previously (para 5a), and thereby inviting judicial challenge. One can only conclude that, in the sphere of operational policy, there prevailed a 'starve them out' mentality which has more the characteristics of revenge rather than that of a rational and humane response to human distress.

Two years later, a similar mindset was to emerge in the denial of support to families under section 9 of the 2004 Act. No lessons, apparently, were learned.

[PF]

Social Care

A broader concept than **social work**, social care refers to a range of welfare provision for those with particular needs at particular times. This might include caring needs that arise as a result of age or disability or mental health. Popular understandings of the 'welfare state' are that it is there to do just that, to provide help, support and services to people who have such requirements, whether temporarily or permanently. This provision has, in fact, never been universal and throughout the history of welfare intervention there have been conversations about just who should be entitled to it and where restrictions should apply. When it comes to the question of immigration status, attitudes over a century of welfare provision tell us that there is a powerful set of ideas at work here, which link entitlement to status. In short, welfare provision is 'for our own', to improve the lives of those who belong and not those considered outsiders. The negative discourse discussed elsewhere in this text, which constructs outsiders as burdensome and dangerous both financially and socially, is at the heart of this connection between immigration control and welfare control (Cohen *et al.*, 2002). In the modern context conversations about immigration and asylum more often than not end up concerned with cost. *We* can't afford *them*, *they* are not *our* responsibility and in fact *their* very presence is an attempt to access *our* welfare. Similar discussions occurred over a century ago regarding Eastern European Jewish refugees entering Britain. Unsurprisingly, the Old Age Pensions Act 1908 and the National Insurance Act 1911 both contained residency and citizenship requirements, which excluded those Jewish refugees.

Throughout the history of welfare delivery in the UK then, there have been elements of exclusion. The idea of *public funds* needing to be protected from those undeserving of them is a constant theme. Those subject to immigration control must show they can live without 'recourse to public funds', affecting the ability of many families to unite or for individuals to marry. Public funds now include Income Support, social fund payments, local authority housing, Housing Benefit, Council Tax Benefit, Child Benefit and Disability Benefits (Seddon, 2006, p. 309). Many of the features of social care we take for granted, therefore, are not available to those subject to immigration control. It is also useful to point out here that where families are divided, as many subject to immigration controls are, the care usually provided within that institution will be diminished. Without family support, many may have increased, not reduced, needs in social care terms. Also of significance here is the inclusion of social care systems in the *internal* control of immigration. If eligibility depends upon immigration status then those systems need to make decisions regarding entitlement, drawing workers in social care into checking status. Workers in housing, welfare benefits, healthcare and education systems are now firmly entrenched in such information gathering, which raises important issues about professional roles.

It is important to note the significance of the **Immigration and Asylum Act 1999**, which removed entitlement to most non-contributory benefits from 'persons subject to immigration control'. The removal of asylum seekers from state benefits and local authority assistance was intended to place them at the mercy of the newly created 'support' system, **National Asylum Support Service (NASS)**. This has institutionally separated this group from normal social care provision and placed them in this inferior system. This has reinforced their position as outsiders, as undeserving interlopers and unfortunately has resulted in social care providers absolving themselves, sometimes inaccurately, of any responsibility (see **Community Care Assessments** and **Disability**). The consequences have been disastrous for those asylum seekers with specific needs not met by NASS, leaving large numbers in dispersal communities dangerously unsupported.

[DH]

Social Work

The British Association of Social Workers (BASW) provides a definition of social work as a profession which,

> promotes social change, problem solving in human relationships and the empowerment and liberation of people to enhance well-being ... Principles of human rights and social justice are fundamental to social work.
> (BASW Code of Ethics for Social Work, 2003, p. 2)

Flowing from this BASW describes the social work role as helping individuals, families, groups and communities to overcome suffering and hardship through the provision of appropriate services and resources. The five basic values it sees as intrinsic to social work are human dignity and worth, social justice, service to humanity, integrity and competence.

Exploring this further in the asylum and immigration arena exposes some contradictions. These contradictions are perhaps not exclusive to this arena; many commentators have noted the historical role of social work in the policing of the behaviour of the poor and in the gatekeeping of resources to that group (see Jones and Novak, 1999).

Essentially, then, social work has never been entirely benign and has occupied a dual position regarding responses to social problems, being engaged in both *care* and *control*. While this contradiction can be said to run throughout the history of social work, the last 30 years have brought significant shifts in the meanings and construction of welfare. Humphries (Hayes and Humphries, 2004) describes this process from the 1979 Conservative administration to the current New Labour project as fundamentally affecting the role and function of social work. Sitting alongside a particularly virulent moral agenda regarding some social groups, the social work profession has become overwhelmed with ascertaining eligibility for services and controlling behaviours. These social groups, whether young offenders, drug users, single parents or indeed asylum seekers face commonalities in their poverty as well as in the generally hostile attitude to their very presence.

Unsurprisingly, then, social work has found itself in an uncomfortable position regarding asylum seekers and others subject to **immigration control**. The state has been quick to see the usefulness of an army of local officials who can check status, provide information about, decide and act upon questions of eligibility and withdraw resources from the 'undeserving'. Add to this the creation of a completely separate and inferior 'welfare' system for asylum seekers via the **Immigration and Asylum Act 1999**, and it could be argued the profession has become enmeshed in the machinery of oppression rather than liberation. More detailed examples of the role of statutory social work can be found elsewhere in this text but include **age assessment**, **community care assessment** and involvement in **detention** and **National Asylum Support Service (NASS)** systems.

Statutory social work is, of course, only one part of the profession and it is useful to explore the role of the voluntary sector here. The voluntary sector historically has occupied a different space, responding to gaps in services, giving a voice to oppressed groups and communities, campaigning for change and challenging mythologies around service user groups. The changes in the delivery of welfare described earlier and the introduction of the market has impacted greatly on this sector. On the one hand the state has encouraged the growth of the voluntary sector in this new world, leading to huge expansion and funding, but on the other hand this sector is now hugely integrated in delivering the government's welfare policy. The autonomy of the voluntary sector is now heavily compromised as funding is often dependent on working within government agendas. In the context of asylum and refugee work the voluntary sector has grown dramatically particularly since **dispersal** in 2000. For some organisations, for example **Refugee Action**, this has meant entering into contractual arrangements with NASS. For others, for example the **National Coalition for Anti-Deportation Campaigns (NCADC)**, standing outside government policy has led to withdrawal of monies and imminent collapse.

The dichotomous position of social work described above does, however, provide us with some hope amidst the despair. An alternative history of standing alongside the oppressed, challenging government policies, fighting for services and defending services sits more neatly with the BASW definition above. There is evidence of a growing voice within the profession to reorientate around issues of social justice and questions are being asked about social work involvement in oppressive immigration machinery (Hayes and Humphries, 2004). It will remain to be seen whether the profession drifts further into this machinery or engages in more effective resistance to it.

[DH]

Statement of Evidence Form (SEF)

When someone applies for asylum in the UK, they will undergo an initial 'screening' interview, either at the airport or seaport at which they arrived, or, as is most likely to be the case if they apply 'in-country', having already passed through immigration controls, they will be interviewed at Home Office units in Croydon or Liverpool. This interview is mainly concerned with questions of identity (including age when dealing with unaccompanied asylum-seeking children), ethnicity and means of travel to the UK.

If they are not selected for a **fast-tracking** procedure, they will be given a Statement of Evidence Form (SEF), which has to be completed and returned to the Home Office within ten days. The form must be completed in English and the timescale for its return must be adhered to, otherwise the claim may be refused on the basis of non-compliance with the need to provide supporting information.

An asylum applicant will almost always require the help of an English speaker to complete the form, and, if possible, this should be done by their legal advisor.

The SEF requires the applicant to state the basis of their claim under the various categories of the **UN Convention on the Status of Refugees**: to describe what has happened to them in detail; who was responsible for any ill-treatment they may have suffered; whether there is a safe area to which they could return; if there are any outstanding criminal charges against them; and whether they are subject to the obligations of military service.

After the SEF has been considered, applicants will be invited to a 'substantive' interview and asked questions to amplify information given in the SEF (see **Asylum Interviews**).

This SEF procedure is liable to further modification or replacement as the **New Asylum Model** is rolled out in 2006-07.

[PF]

Trafficking and Smuggling
of People

There is no 'legal' method by which people who wish to flee their home country because of persecution can pre-arrange their travel to a safe destination. **Visa** controls mean that entry, for example to the UK, can only be given to those in categories recognised by the UK government as satisfying entry requirements under the **Immigration Rules**. Requests for asylum do not constitute such a category.

If we accept that the prospect of immediate personal danger is the main determining factor in an individual's decision to flee from the causes of danger, then it is unlikely, and in fact impossible, for someone to go through the lengthy procedures of obtaining a passport from their national authorities and then using this to transit to another neighbouring country. For those with a high political profile, this procedure would, in itself, draw unwelcome attention.

However, as United Nations statistics demonstrate, the vast majority of those recognised as refugees get no further than a neighbouring territory. If those escaping from persecution wish to get further afield, the most effective means of doing this is to engage the services of a trafficker or smuggler.

It is useful, at this point, to make a distinction between the two terms, although such a distinction is probably easier to make from the standpoint of end results rather than point of origin.

Briefly, *trafficking* may be defined as effecting the transit of persons across national boundaries in a clandestine manner, without the use of valid international travel documents, in order to exploit these persons for financial gain once they have reached their destination. Such examples as the trafficking of women for prostitution are well known. *Smuggling*, by contrast could be seen as the same facilitation of illicit travel, either openly or clandestinely, but with the difference that the smuggler is indifferent to the fate of the 'client' after arrival at destination. More sophisticated methods of smuggling, using air transport for example, require that the agent accompanies the client to the destination and through border controls at which point false travel documents are retrieved from the client for re-use at a later date with a new client.

Victoria Climbié, the nine-year-old child who died in London in February 2000 as a result of malnutrition and hypothermia caused by the abuse of her aunt and her aunt's partner, was a child who had been smuggled to Europe, first from the Ivory Coast to France, and then from France to the UK, again using false documents.

As this case demonstrates, it is relatively easy, given knowledge of, and access to the trafficking networks, to smuggle a child across thousands of miles for exploitative purposes, and all those involved in social care should be aware of the sad fact that, every day, throughout Europe, children are arriving by clandestine or irregular means. Some may have been smuggled by families with leave to remain in the UK who have grown tired of the delays imposed by the Immigration Rules; some may be arriving for malevolent purposes such as cultic abuse or domestic slavery.

However, I wish to concentrate on the role played by traffickers. I prefer this term to the more general one of 'smugglers', because the object of the operation of facilitating clandestine transnational travel is that of profiting in vulnerable people. This may be either as an end result of forced labour in the country of origin, or at the point of origin in the receiving of fees from those who simply wish to be transported to a Western country where they feel that their chances of freedom are better than in a neighbouring country where conditions may not be much better than those of the country which they wish to leave.

This belief may be an answer to the question frequently asked by the Home Office of asylum seekers who transit through a third country – 'Why did you not seek asylum when you arrived in X?' A more accurate answer is that X was merely a staging post in the trafficker's plans and the would-be asylum seeker may have seen no more of X than the inside of one of its airports while awaiting transfer to a flight to a European destination.

In research commissioned by the Home Office (Robinson and Segrott, 2002), the role of trafficking in the processes leading to the claiming of asylum in the UK is examined in detail. (The common euphemism of 'agents' is used to denote those who traffic human beings for the purpose of profit.)

> [I]t is important to note that agents were critical determinants of the destination eventually reached by asylum seekers. Overall, 42 of the respondents had been assisted by agents, but this was true of nearly all the Sri Lankans and Iranians that were interviewed. Respondents said that agents often offered the only means of escaping the country of origin and reaching a place where asylum could be sought. Consequently if individual asylum seekers wanted to leave their home country they had to give over control of migration decision-making to these paid facilitators. In some cases agents were in a position to impose their will upon their clients about destinations and routes, but in others, agents and asylum seekers negotiated, with the outcome depending on the ability of the latter to pay and the former to deliver chosen destinations. (Robinson and Segrott, 2002, p. 19)

The imposition of final destination on the asylum seeker in some cases is a measure of the control exercised by traffickers and gives the lie to the media myth about the UK being targeted deliberately by vast hordes of asylum seekers who wish to exploit the 'generous' provisions of the welfare state (which, incidentally, they cannot benefit from at all until given some form of leave to remain).

Robinson and Segrott's findings about the services provided by traffickers are worth quoting in detail:

> This research has found that, in simple terms, agents provided three types of services to asylum seekers:

The first of these was the provision of travel documents, including tickets, visas and passports. One of the respondents, for example, used an agent to flee from Sri Lanka. She paid 600,000 Sri Lankan rupees, for which she received a false passport and air tickets to London via Singapore and South Africa. Another Sri Lankan woman was provided with passports for herself and her daughter, and travel from Jaffna to Trincomalee, Trincomalee to Colombo, Colombo to Moscow, where they stayed over for two days and then Moscow to Heathrow. For this the agent charged £20,000. A Yemeni simply bribed a Saudi Arabian agent to arrange an exit visa for him.

The second type of service offered by agents was the actual facilitation of journeys. In certain cases, agents even travelled with asylum seekers, often so that they could re-possess false documentation before arrival in the UK. One of the respondents (an Afghan male) for example described how he had left Afghanistan on foot through the hills to find an agent recommended to him by his cousin. This agent then transported the asylum seeker in stages by road to Moscow, travelling only at night in lorries, a journey that took some two and a half to three months. Another respondent, an Iranian male, contracted an agent to take him from Iran, through Iraq to Turkey. This cost him $400 and involved being transported by car, lorry and donkey. He then paid another agent in Istanbul to take him to the UK in the back of an articulated lorry, for which he paid a further $3500.

The third type of service was the channeling of asylum seekers towards particular destinations, either through limiting the possibilities available to them, offering a choice of migration destinations, or giving advice on specific countries. One Iranian man described how he had asked an agent in Turkey about the possibility of travel to various countries, and explained that he would prefer to travel to Australia, New Zealand or Canada. The agent told him that these destinations were difficult to arrange and very expensive. The respondent then enquired about the Netherlands and Germany, but was told by the agent that these were 'not good places to go to'. The agent recommended the UK instead, suggesting that it was easier to get into, and easier to get asylum there because Britain needed and respected cheap labour. Another respondent, a Sri Lankan female, approached a trusted agent (a 'good man' in her words) and was offered France, Switzerland, Germany and the UK as possible destinations, from which she picked the latter. Each destination had a different price, and direct travel to a country was more expensive than travel via third countries. A Sri Lankan female described how the agent she approached in Jaffna was offering a variety of destinations (France, Germany and England) but how he was selecting destinations for his clients according to the languages they spoke and where they had friends and relatives resident. He chose the UK for her because she spoke English. (Robinson and Segrott, 2002, pp.19-20)

Robinson and Segrott's research is one of the few studies – another is Morrison (1998) which gives an excellent overview of the subject – to illuminate the necessarily secretive nature of international people trafficking, and I suggest that it is the availability of such services which is the immediate cause of the presence of asylum seekers in the West. Only those who can afford to do so can undertake such long and sometimes dangerous journeys from their homelands.

Bilger *et al.* (forthcoming), in a study of human smuggling as a 'transnational service industry', draw attention to the personal risk that migrants may have to bear:

> Attempts to reduce the amount of risk involved normally result in higher costs for the migrants. Air and sea journeys leading directly from the country of origin to the country of destination are safer, more convenient and of shorter duration, but naturally a lot more expensive than the longer more exhausting and more dangerous journeys via land routes (where) migrants are much more likely to find themselves in dangerous, in many cases even life-threatening situations, for instance when being transported across borders hidden in containers, under ceiling linings in trains, or between goods in trucks without sufficient air supply, in the freezing cold, or in extreme heat. (Bilger *et al.,* forthcoming, pp. 21-2)

The deaths of 58 Chinese people being smuggled into the UK in June 2000 tragically illustrates the potential fate of desperate people who put their future in the hands of those who exploit hardship of every kind.

In addition to the monetary expenditure and personal risk involved in trafficking, there is also the possibility that severe penalties may be exacted by the traffickers if their clients reveal any details of the identity of the traffickers. A report in *Le Monde* in March 2006, detailing the role of Mauritania as a staging post for clandestine migrants travelling between sub-Saharan Africa and Europe suggests that, for onward transit from the western Sahara region, between 10-15,000 migrants were being asked to pay 1,000 Euros (about £700). Any identity papers that the migrant might possess would be destroyed and there would be a death threat in operation against the migrant and their family as a deterrent against revealing any information about the traffickers and their routes.

This last factor is undoubtedly a major reason why unsuccessful asylum seekers choose not to leave the UK of their own volition (see **Destitution** and **Voluntary Return**). Trafficking is an additional form of oppression, which, paradoxically, must be used by those fleeing both political and economic oppressions in their country of origin.

Though it cannot be proven, it is doubtful that individuals who have gone to great effort to circumvent the modern state's sophisticated (and at times severe) battery of immigration controls; who have often risked their lives in unsafe travel; and/or have paid traffickers thousands (if not tens of thousands) of dollars will simply leave their destination countries once all forms of legal appeal have been exhausted. They are most likely to disappear into the anonymity of Europe's and North America's large cities. (Gibney and Hansen, 2003, p. 17, n. 22)

The Dutch organisation *United* has documented the deaths of 3,750 clandestine migrants in transit since 1993. It calls these 'deaths by policy', the policies in question being the increasingly restrictive asylum and immigration policies of 'Fortress Europe'. However, it is far from clear whether an open borders policy on the part of the European Union directed at migrants from countries subject to **visa** controls would remove the need for recourse to trafficking as the only viable means for those from the South to reach the North. Open borders may, in the end, only benefit the West whose economies have an insatiable desire for labour at the lowest price. Those seeking international protection from political persecution must, of necessity, use the same trafficking networks if they wish to reach a place of safety.

[PF]

Further reading

www.united.non-profit.nl

'Les routes de l'émigration clandestine subsahrienne passent désormais par la Mauritanie'. *Le Monde*, 11 March 2006.

UN Convention on the Status of Refugees, 1951

UK asylum law stems from the UN Convention on the Status of Refugees, 1951. Arising in the Cold War period following the Second World War it was the first coherent international statement on refugees and reflected the period's concern with political persecution. It has remained an inadequate mechanism since, given the type of global events that have produced large numbers of displaced peoples. Particularly since the 1990s there has been a tendency to narrow interpretations by receiving states and define movements previously seen as refugee flows as 'economic'. Much flexibility has been given to governments, particularly in terms of definitions of a 'well-founded fear of persecution'. It became a firm part of British law in the Asylum and Immigration Appeals Act 1993. The most important part is contained in Article 33 of the Convention, which prohibits the return of a person to a country in which they have a 'well founded fear of persecution for reasons of race, religion, nationality, political opinion or membership of a particular social group'.

In practice the problem for applicants is that the onus lies with them to prove, not simply what happened in the past, but that the persecution will occur on return. This has made it difficult for asylum seekers to find 'proof' or documentary evidence of the likelihood of persecution. What constitutes 'well-founded fear', 'persecution', 'race, religion, nationality, political opinion' or 'social group' are all the subject of interpretation and case law. People who are not recognised as refugees under the terms of the Geneva Convention may be allowed to stay in the UK for temporary periods, for example on humanitarian grounds (see **Humanitarian Protection** and **Discretionary Leave**). Asylum statistics for 2004 show that of around 34,000 asylum applications that year only 3 per cent were granted refugee status with 88 per cent refused (Home

Office, 2004). Given that the countries which currently generate most asylum applications (Iraq, Pakistan, Zimbabwe, Somalia to name but a few) remain unstable, gripped with war or civil conflict or are reeling from the impact of natural disaster, it is not difficult to see the limitations of current systems. Refugee status is now a rare outcome for the thousands of asylum applicants and many who are allowed to stay do so with lesser status, temporarily, without full citizenship rights, with an uncertain future and an insecure place in our communities.

[DH]

Unaccompanied Asylum-seeking Children

See also **Age Assessment**.

Thousands of asylum-seeking families in the UK have children. In these circumstances children, like their parents, will be supported via **National Asylum Support Service (NASS)** arrangements. This includes no choice dispersal, 70 per cent subsistence and access to a school place. There is also a wider layer of children within families subject to immigration control, that is, non-UK citizen families who may face restrictions on their rights and entitlements. For example, these children may never have met or be likely to meet granny or auntie because **immigration controls** systematically inhibit family reunification. There are therefore many children who experience the impact of immigration controls, both within the community and, indeed, in **detention.**

The **social work** profession's focus on children and immigration has to date largely been around a much smaller, but arguably more vulnerable group, that of unaccompanied asylum-seeking children (UASC). I have chosen to use this terminology because it appears to be the most popular in the social care literature but 'young separated refugee' is perhaps a more accurate descriptor. 'Unaccompanied' can imply a conscious act on behalf of parents to 'send' or 'abandon' their children so it is important to unpack language and speak to the realities, not mythologies, of asylum experiences. Parents may have taken incredible risks to get their children out of a country to escape war, armed conflict and persecution, rape, prostitution or serious poverty. Of the almost 3,000 UASC who sought asylum in the UK in 2004, the main countries of origin were Afghanistan, Iran, Somalia, Vietnam and Iraq (Home Office, 2004); this tells its own story about the reasons for separation and flight. The 'Separated Children in Europe Programme' has prepared a 'Statement of Good Practice' for this group and prefers the word 'separated', defining separated children as:

> Children under eighteen years of age who are outside their country of origin and separated from both parents, or their previous legal/customary primary caregiver ... Separated children may be seeking asylum because of fear of persecution or the lack of protection due to human rights violations, armed conflict or disturbances in their own country. They may be victims of trafficking for sexual or other exploitation, or they may have traveled to Europe to escape conditions of serious deprivation. (SCEP, 2000)

The statement includes principles commensurate with general childcare principles. For example, the best interests of the child should be the primary consideration; they should be treated as children first and foremost; their views should be sought in decisions which affect them; they should be able to maintain their language, religion and culture and have access to interpreters.

In considering the UK situation it is fair to say that there is concern about whether these best practice principles are being adhered to (Ayotte and Williamson, 2001; Stanley, 2001). A key concern is the UK governments continued reservation on the UN Convention on the Rights of the Child to asylum-seeking and non-citizen children. Additionally, these studies show that asylum-seeking and refugee children do not receive the level of care and protection they need, despite the fact that unaccompanied children have the same legal entitlements as citizen children, for example, rights enshrined in the Children Act and Human Rights Act. What studies do show is chaotic and unsupportive arrivals, differential experiences of support depending on where they present, use of inappropriate accommodation, variable access to education, despite the fact that this group have a high commitment to education and seek it out proactively, and considerable anxiety about what will happen when they turn eighteen years of age.

So, what are the support arrangements for this group of young people? Unaccompanied asylum-seeking children are the responsibility of the local authority social services department where they first present. The Children Act 1989 places a duty on these departments to assess children in need. Historically, Section 17 of the Act involves meeting those needs 'by providing a range and level of services appropriate to those children's needs' and Section 20 means the child is assessed as needing to be *accommodated*. In practice this has meant very different packages of care, for example, foster care or residential placement under Section 20 and unsupported bed and breakfast type accommodation under Section 17. If accommodated, 'looked-after' children become entitled to key workers, care plans and leaving care services, services which will not follow Section 17 assessments. Following research and publications in 2001-2003 (Stanley, 2001; Refugee Council, 2003) highlighting these inconsistencies, the Department of Health clarified policy on this matter and issued a circular (Department of Health, 2003) clearly stating:

> Where a child has no parent or guardian in this country, perhaps because he [sic] has arrived alone seeking asylum, the presumption should be that he would fall within the scope of section 20 and become *looked after*.

Recent research by the Refugee Council (2005d) indicates that there has been some improvement in the situation, with local authorities largely responding to the circular, at least partially. However, disparity continues to exist between services being provided and some authorities are still supporting children under Section 17. The research also refers to the 'Hillingdon Judgement', which brought clarity to the position regarding leaving care services. This secures the right to leaving care services for this group, considerably increasing local authority responsibility. Unfortunately this appears to be the most inconsistent area, with many young people simply not accessing this level of help. This is a major area of concern given what we already know about the levels of anxiety about transition at age eighteen that have been articulated by this group.

A significant issue in all of this is **age assessment** and the centrality of defining the point at which an asylum-seeking child turns eighteen because of the differential services for children and adults. A new National Register of Unaccompanied Asylum-seeking Children, which will allow electronic access and will include photographs, is being presented as a way of improving processes for children and more efficiently keeping and sharing accurate information among professionals. The concern is that the register may be used as a way of identifying those eligible for removal, once again begging big questions about the social work profession's involvement in what are essentially immigration control systems, not child welfare systems. There is also a drift at the moment to the use of specialist social workers at the main ports of entry and screening units, which also seems to indicate that the profession is now firmly entrenched in the machinery of immigration control. Such rationalisation and specialisation may well represent better value for money, for example in streamlining services and reducing age disputes. However, another consequence may well be to reduce the rights and choices of those arriving without the protection of carers.

[DH]

Further reading
Rutter (2003)
Wade *et al.* (2005)

Visas

One accurate, if cynical, way of defining the term visas would be to say that visas are what most asylum seekers have not got when they arrive in the UK, nor can they obtain in their countries of origin for the specific purpose of departing their country to seek international protection elsewhere (see **Trafficking and Smuggling of People** and **Voluntary Return**). Nor can you get a visa to escape the cycle of poverty, corruption, war and oppression into which your country has spiralled; nor to find better healthcare in the West, using treatments that are only available to the super-rich in your country; nor to avail yourselves of a rational, protective response to domestic violence which cannot be expected from your country's authorities.

The most common categories under which visas to enter the UK are granted are for visitors, for work, education and training, or as a spouse/fiancé of a person already settled in the UK.

Visa, a Latin word meaning 'things that are seen' – and not just the photograph on your passport, which can be readily seen and matched with an actual physiognomy. The UK needs to 'see', to be reassured of a valid reason to visit the UK in one of the categories just mentioned, and which the endlessly revised **Immigration Rules** precisely define. One could name just about any country in Africa, Asia, the Caribbean or South America and find that its nationals were subject to 'visa regimes', thus becoming 'visa nationals', to use the shorthand term to denote persons requiring 'entry clearance', that is, visas to travel to the UK.

Many of these countries – Afghanistan, Algeria, Democratic Republic of the Congo, Ghana, India, Jamaica, Nigeria, Pakistan, Sierra Leone, Uganda and Zimbabwe – have one thing in common: all have been and continue to be the country of origin of people who have claimed asylum in the UK. Writing in 1998, John Morrison, in a report for the **Refugee Council** on the trafficking of refugees stated:

> ... the British government has explicitly linked a visa requirement to any country in the world which starts generating a significant number of asylum seekers who arrive in the UK ... in the case of Sri Lanka, visa restrictions were imposed two years after civil war began in 1983. In 1987-8 ... the then British Home Secretary Douglas Hurd MP commented that the immediate spur to this proposal has been the arrival of over 800 people claiming asylum in the three months up to the end of February. (Morrison, 1998, p. 25)

The imposition of visa controls thus appears historically as a reactive solution to the unwelcome arrival of large numbers of poor and disenfranchised people from what were often former British colonies, now Commonwealth member states. (It is also useful to be reminded that people were claiming asylum as long ago as 1988 and that the phenomenon is not of more recent origin, although the respective discourses of left and right on the subject were less in evidence at that time. It is doubtless reassuring to note that the government was, even then, on the case and vigilantly protecting the UK against uninvited guests.)

You do *not* need a visa to visit the UK if you are from South Africa or the European Union, for example. You *do* need one if you are from the Philippines, but with the well-established employment of Filipino men and women in the UK's health service and domestic service industries and with the importance to the Filipino economy of foreign remittances, it is relatively easy for work visas to be obtained. (Go, 2005, pp. 243-5)

I mention this to illustrate that visa regimes are essentially used to control the entry of potentially dangerous persons to the UK and, indeed, whichever country chooses to impose visa controls on foreign nationals. For example, if I, as a British citizen, wish to enter the USA as a tourist, I do, strictly speaking, need a visa to do so, but as I am a national of a country which is perceived as not posing a threat to US homeland security and providing I am careful to answer 'no' to the question as to whether I am entering the USA in order to engage in acts of terrorism, then I should be allowed to enter the USA on the 'visa waiver' scheme. I have been 'seen' to pose no threat to the country I am seeking to enter.

Similarly, Filipinos, for example, are seen, historically, to pose no threat to the UK's economy and are in fact welcomed into the UK for the positive contribution they make. I may be mistaken, but I do not think that many, if any, asylum seekers are of Filipino origin.

Therefore, visa regimes are historically selective on the basis of the economic and political conditions which prevail globally and locally at any one time. The unregulated nature of asylum seeking, which may cause applications from a particular country to escalate unexpectedly, is thus unwelcome by governments which impose **immigration controls**. There is also no escaping the fact that, as far as the UK is concerned, the greatest danger is considered to come from the indigenous populations of the world's poorest nations.

The solutions to the situation whereby current visa nationals could be allowed to travel legally to seek asylum, employment or healthcare without prior 'entry clearance' are not easily reached.

Could all immigration controls be abolished, with complete freedom of movement for all persons? This is not quite as utopian or dystopian as it sounds (Hayter, 2000; Humphries, 2002), but is, I suggest, highly unlikely in the current climate of fears about global terrorism. If controls were to be abolished, then current prevailing patterns of migration, from the poorest to the richest countries, would simply continue and feed Western capitalism's insatiable demand for cheap labour so that the relatively wealthy can continue with their labour-lite lifestyles. The 'sending' countries would see a depletion of their own labour force as the most skilled continued to seek employment in the West. Global imbalances of wealth and development would increase:

> Without accompanying measures to deal directly with poverty and political oppression, open borders would not be certain to benefit those who are today's refugees. Better opportunities for economic migrants with education and skills in First World labour markets might crowd out

the poorest and most oppressed, who could therefore have the least chance of improving their position through exit. This is why redistribution of resources and democratisation processes would be integral to achieving justice with freedom of movement. (Jordan and Düvell, 2002, p. 253)

I suggest that it is not the abolition of immigration controls that is required, but a more finely tuned system that actively strives to establish a new order of relationships between producing and receiving nations.

The 'Development Visa' (DV) proposed by Michael Jandl of the International Centre for Migration Policy Development in Vienna is one such alternative to existing visa regimes whose function is solely to exclude on the basis of arbitrary criteria of fear and risk and whose very existence is the root of the extensive and lucrative trade in the smuggling of people, who, by desire or necessity, wish to bypass these regimes:

In economic terms, migration control strategies … can be targeted at the supply side, at the demand side, or at the intermediary structures. Thus, supply side measures would consist in any policies that reduce the migration potential in countries of origin, for example in the promotion of political stability and human rights, and, in the long run, in fostering economic growth and income opportunities through development policies. Demand side measures would consist in policies that curb the demand for irregular migrant workers in destination countries … Finally, migration control policies may target the intermediary structures of illegal migration, for example by instituting stricter border control measures, higher document security standards or higher fines for human smugglers.

Unfortunately, migration policies today are too often narrowly understood as comprising only this last category of interventions. (Jandl, 2005, p. 7)

Jandl's proposal for the development visa (DV) is that existing visa regimes imposed on the countries with high records of 'irregular' migration (including, therefore, asylum seekers) be replaced with the selling of legal entry permits to any eligible would-be migrant at roughly the prevailing price of current smuggling fees. The legal entry permits thus obtained would be known as DVs (Jandl, 2005, p. 7). The fee demanded for the DVs would be divided into three parts:

> One third will go to targeted development programmes in the sending country, supervised by an appropriately selected development agency. One third will be reimbursed by the DV office [the locally established agency for the issuing of the *visas*] to the DV holder in person upon the return of the migrant within the specified time limit of the DV. Should the DV holders not return in time (either because they seized the opportunity to gain another legal residence in their host country … they will lose this part of the DV fee. Finally, one third will go to the DV Social Security Deposit … designed to cover basic health and welfare expenditures on behalf of the migrant, should the need for such expenditures arise. (Jandl, 2005, p. 9)

The advantage of this proposal is that it understands international migration as a result of global economic differentials, rather than an opportunistic whim. It also attempts to create a new order of interdependence between sending and receiving countries that aims to make global migration substantially benefit the development of the former. It makes no mention of asylum seekers, but the same channels of clandestine migration are used both by those seeking international protection and those migrating for other reasons and who are currently forced to use asylum procedures in order to gain regularisation of their status, which may then open avenues to employment.

Its disadvantages are that it would require a level of international co-operation, which hardly exists at the current time. It also seems heavily bureaucratic and intrusive with a high level of documentation and border controls which may be difficult to implement unless its benefits are immediately tangible.

One might argue that the time for such co-operation has come, concerted action which moves away from self-interest and the emphasis on preventing unwelcome migration to 'Fortress Europe', still in evidence at the conference on European migration held at Rabat, Morocco, in July 2006. (Le Monde, 11 July 2006)

....

It's a fact, emigrating to Europe is the dream of many Africans. But the barriers between our hell and your paradise are as high as the sky. (Bassong, 2006, p. 9)

These are the opening lines of a novel entitled *How to migrate to France in twenty lessons* by Luc Bassong, a French novelist of African heritage. Isaac, the main protagonist, is desperate to obtain a visa which will enable him to settle in France, and the narrative leads up to the climactic moment of his interview at his country's French Embassy. The official in charge of assessing Isaac's suitability speaks first:

Monsieur, France needs dynamic immigrants.
That's me – I'm breathing fire!

We need punctual workers – no excuses about oversleeping.
I never sleep!

We need men and women who can be discreet about certain things.
I tell lies all the time!

We need people with good critical faculties.
I criticise everything!

We expect them to say no sometimes.
I never say yes!

But who are ambitious all the same.
I want to run the planet!

We need ... how old are you in fact?
It depends.

We need young people.
I'm 20.

But not too young.
I'm 30.

Mature, even.
I'm 40.

Thank you, monsieur, you seem just the type of immigrant that we don't need at the moment. I won't show you out. I think you know the way.
Stuff the lot of you!

As per usual. Thank you for your visit.
(Bassong, 2006, pp. 127-8; translation PF)

In fact, as Gondola illustrates in his study of the Congolese *sapeurs* and *mikilistes* (*sapeur* = young Congolese male fashion victim and *mikiliste* = the same person when he becomes a savvy man-about-town in the European city where he has obtained or hopes to obtain his *papiers*), the dream of Europe is implanted through contact with those who have made it there:

> The geographical migration that transports the *mikiliste* from the undeveloped third world to the Cities of Light in the North constitutes only (one) stage in this migratory process. The *mikiliste* is an individual who first experiences Europe, *his* Europe, in Africa. His knowledge of the northern world is updated by the accounts (always wildly embellished) of young people who return home on vacation – that is, when they have not been deported there – to show off their clothes … Young potential *mikilistes* spend most of the daytime hours with groups of *mastas* (friends) where the conversations, recycled a thousand times over, revolve, of course, around girls, and sometimes music, but especially Europe … It is there that they learn to cheat and get around the Parisian metro, which nightclubs are trendy, and which brand names are fashionable. They learn of the opportunities for lawful integration as well as various illegal schemes to circumvent administrative measures intended to block their entrance into this paradise. (Gondola, 1999, p. 28, emphasis in original)

If the migrant succeeds in getting to France, for example without a visa, his application for regularisation may be refused (which is the fate of Bassong's fictional Isaac) and he will be forced to join the growing army of *sans-papiers*:

> Lacking a residency permit, often without permanent shelter and unemployed, the *mikiliste* finds himself torn between a precarious stay and a return home which he associates with dishonour and failure. (Gondola, 1999, p. 29)

The whole visa game is one whose rules are slanted towards the most desirable in social and economic terms. Isaac, in Bassong's fictionalised account, simply improvised as best he could in the circumstances. The young Congolese studied by Gondola are attracted by the idyllic conditions which they imagine are awaiting them in Europe. When they are spat out by a system that does not want them, when the inevitable expulsion from paradise occurs, the need to improvise becomes associated with the very fact of survival.

[PF]

Voluntary Return

See also **Trafficking and Smuggling of People**.

Something has happened. You're scared and need to get out of this place. You are not usually the sort of person who does things on impulse. You would like to carefully plan your escape by obtaining a copy of the UN Convention on the Status of Refugees of 1951, and check that being given international protection is only possible to certain categories of people. Having assured yourself that you fitted into one of these criteria, you would have then preferred to conduct extensive research as to which country offered the best chance of protection and which one offered the best package of support for people claiming asylum, and you would have chosen Belgium as you know several people who have already gone there.

You would then have gone to the Belgian Embassy in your country's capital city and enquired about visas for people suffering persecution. You would have been told that there are none, but that you could apply for a visa if you have a job offer in Belgium or have a college course lined up, for example.

You know all this already. You know how obsessed the Europeans are with having the right papers, so you ask around. Someone knows someone who regularly arranges travel to countries which might interest you. Western Europe is probably the best bet – it isn't too expensive, the equivalent of £800 should do it, flight and travel documents included. You'll need a passport-size photo and a deposit up front; the rest will be collected at the airport.

Of course you haven't got that much, but don't worry, 'Uncle' will lend some of it, plus interest and you can pay him back when you start your job in France, Belgium, England or wherever you end up. As for the rest, you'll have to sell most of your possessions and property, if you have any. And there is a slight problem: where you end up depends on which countries 'Uncle' has visas for this week. The Belgian stamp has worn out and he'll have to get another one made, but the UK one is just fine. One more thing, 'Uncle''s friend will have to fly with you. Once you're at the airport and through Immigration (this usually makes people quite nervous, but don't worry, the printer does a really good job) you just give the passport back so we can use it again.

Good luck with the asylum application. Don't forget to let us know when you get a job.

So you claim asylum, have your interview at the Immigration and Nationality Directorate screening unit, are refused, appeal and are refused again. This is not what is supposed to happen. One day you get a letter from the Home Office, informing you that, since your asylum application has failed, you must leave the UK without delay, and as you haven't got any money to do this, there is an organisation, the International Organization for Migration, which will help you with your travel arrangements. Thank you for your interest in the UK, sorry things haven't worked out and goodbye.

This is all very well, you think, but what exactly is waiting for me when I get home?

I had to sell my home to pay to get here; I have nothing left back home. I'm still wanted by the police for that incident with the leaflets; I've no job and my country's economy is in a state of collapse anyway. We all know what happens to people who are returned to my country with one of those special passports they give you: you are kept at the airport for hours, maybe days – they beat you and call you a traitor and try to extort a bribe before they release you, if you're lucky not to end up in the central jail. Then there's 'Uncle': he's not going to be pleased that I can't repay his loan, and he's bound to come looking for me and try to shut me up so that I can't reveal any details about his little travel business.

How can I go back? How can I?

....

Lawyers' waiting rooms, Immigration Service reporting centres and detention centres all carry advertisements for the services of the International Organization for Migration (IOM), whose motto is

'Managing Migration for the Benefit of All'. It was founded in Brussels in 1951 as the Intergovernmental Committee for European Migration. In some respects it became an operational arm of the United Nations High Commissioner for Refugees (UNHCR), assisting in the resettlement of those displaced by war in Europe, and it has developed a global role in this task up to the present day.

In the UK it is responsible for running the Voluntary Assisted Return and Reintegration Programme (VARRP), which, since 1999, has offered assistance to asylum seekers who want to return permanently to their country of origin.

The VARRP is open to asylum seekers of any nationality, whose asylum claim is under one of the following criteria:

- Waiting for a Home Office decision
- Refused by the Home Office
- Appealing against the asylum decision
- Withdrawn asylum application. (IOM website: www.iom.int)

The programme thus seeks to create order out of the perceived chaos of unmanaged or 'irregular' migration, which is the normal state of affairs for those who seek asylum in the West, and as the story that began this entry seeks to show.

The VARRP criteria imply a degree of freedom to choose one's future, which is comparatively rare among asylum seekers: being open not only to those who have been refused but also to those who are still awaiting the outcomes of their applications suggests that a significant number of people may have second thoughts about what they are doing, may decide that it is not worth the bother of being dragged through long bureaucratic processes and simply give up. If they choose to do this, then the VARRP is there to help, just in case. There are surely serious moral implications in offering assisted return in these circumstances especially for those whose appeals may have their initial refusal decisions overruled. It seems to be the assumption that as 'most asylum claims fail anyway, why bother waiting, it's better to get out while you can'.

Rational management of people – seen as raw numbers – seems, therefore, to take precedence over the inherently ethical basis of seeking, and giving, international protection to those in need of it.

In 2002, the Home Office published an evaluation of VARRP. Among its key findings were that:

> VARRP [at this time without the 'reintegration' element] provided significant cost-savings for IND in comparison with removing unsuccessful asylum seekers following the completion of the asylum process.

It also reported that:

> Asylum seekers were provided with a dignified, timely departure by VARRP and achieved return to countries via routes that IND was not accessing. A high level of user-satisfaction was reported.

It is reasonable that asylum seekers should be given a choice of whether or not to return to their country of origin, especially if their claims fail. Their exclusion from the **National Asylum Support Service (NASS)** system in the event of a negative decision leaves them destitute and without accommodation. The support package offered by the VARRP normally consists of the provision of travel documents, costs of travel and a sum of money to be provided in kind towards the cost of training or the start-up cost of a small business. VARRP applicants are normally offered emergency or **Section 4 support** while their applications are being considered. In 2005, Iraq was one of the countries in which the IOM was playing a major role by assisting Iraqi Kurdish people to return home by safe routes. However, there remain many countries where this is difficult, if not impossible, due to the fragile nature of national and local economies caused by political instability.

It is apparent from the 2002 report quoted above that one of the effects of VARRP is to reduce the cost to the Home Office that would otherwise be incurred in detaining and removing failed asylum seekers.

The same assumption could be made about the decision in December 2005 to offer an additional £2,000 to asylum seekers who volunteered for VARRP.

It remains to be seen how many would respond positively to this apparently tempting offer. It also remains a fact that the act of seeking asylum in the UK cannot be seen as having entirely rational foundations, and whose outcomes can be processed in managerialist terms by the Home Office and the IOM. Even the promise of 'planned reintegration' cannot assuage the real fears of individuals who will not contemplate return in any circumstances due to their subjective certainty that there is nothing safe for them back 'home', in whatever terms they wish to construe the reality of which only they have knowledge.

[PF]

Further information

www.iom.int

www.iomlondon.org

The 2002 Home Office evaluation of voluntary return is at:

www.homeoffice.gov.uk/rds/pdfs2/r175.pdf

Welfare

As with access to paid **employment**, the granting of refugee status, **discretionary leave** and **humanitarian protection** opens the door to the mainstream UK benefits system from which asylum seekers and others subject to immigration control have been excluded by virtue of Section 115 of the **Immigration and Asylum Act 1999**. Indeed, it is possible for refugees and their dependants to claim Child Benefit, Child Tax Credit/Working Tax Credit, Income Support and Housing Benefit or Council Tax Benefit backdated to the date that asylum was first claimed. However, in the course of 2006-07 it is possible that the government may enact legislation for the removal of this backdating concession (CPAG, 2006, p. 1421).

Refugees and others granted various types of leave to remain in the UK are also automatically considered to pass the 'habitual residence' and 'right to reside' tests which are further layers of control deemed to protect the allocation of benefits only to those who have a 'genuine' right to be in the UK (CPAG, 2006, pp. 1439-41). These welfare controls are a further sign of the all-pervasive importance of sovereignty, nationhood and citizenship on which the state leans in order to distinguish between the deserving and undeserving, all depending, ultimately, on being in possession of the right piece of paper at the right time.

But: go to a party held by a refugee mother to celebrate her being reunited with a separated child; go to a church service attended by people of many nations and languages; go to a social event organised by those who defend the rights of asylum seekers; go to a wedding reception laden with gifts for the bride and groom that have somehow been provided in spite of the most abject poverty – there you will find music, gaiety, dancing, rejoicing, smiles, and you will be unable to distinguish between those who have the 'correct' documents and those who haven't. You will find a spirit of solidarity that transcends barriers and borders. You will find joy in adversity, and hope where it has no right to be, according to the gloomy tenets of divisive legislation and rules.

This is not 'welfare': it is 'well-being' or 'faring well', which demonstrates resilience and determination. We who work with asylum seekers and refugees need to be at these moments of celebration if we are invited. We need to know that there is a life after rejection, humiliation and destitution. We need to be at these joyful moments just as we need to offer what is sometimes our only contribution to the well-being of an increasingly marginalised section of society – and that is our presence.

[PF]

References

ADSS (Association of Directors of Social Services) (2006) *Age Assessment*. Accessed online at: www.adss.org.uk/publications/guidance/ageassessment.pdf

Arango, J. and Jachimowicz, M. (2005) *Regularising Immigrants in Spain: A New Approach*. Migration Information Source. Accessed online at: www.migrationinformation.org/Feature/display.cfm?id=331

Asylum Aid (1999) *Still No Reason at All: Home Office Decisions on Asylum Claims*. London: Asylum Aid.

Ayotte, W. and Williamson, L. (2001) *Separated Children in the UK*. London: Save the Children and Refugee Council.

Bassong, L. (2006) *Comment Immigrer en France en 20 Leçons*. Paris: Max Milo.

BASW (British Association of Social Workers) (2003) *Code of Ethics for Social Work*, p. 5, Principle 3.2.2.(a) Accessed online at: www.basw.co.uk/articles

BASW (British Association of Social Workers) (2004) *Notice to Members on Asylum and Immigration (Treatment of Claimants) Bill*. Accessed online at: www.basw.co.uk/articles

Bateman, N. (2000) Advocacy Skills for Health and Social Care Professionals. London: Jessica Kingsley.

Berger, P.L. and Luckmann, T. (1971) *The Social Construction of Reality*. Harmondsworth: Penguin. (First published 1966).

BID (Bail for Immigration Detainees) (2006) *Facts and Figures about Detention in the UK*. Accessed online at: www.biduk.org./immigration/facts

BID and Asylum Aid (2005) *Justice Denied: Asylum and Immigration Legal Aid, A System in Crisis*. Accessed online at: www.asylumaid.org.uk/Publications/Justicedenied.pdf

Bilger, V., Hofmann, M. and Jandl, M. (forthcoming) 'Human smuggling as a transnational service industry: evidence from Austria'. *International Migration*, Special issue on Human Smuggling.

Blackwell, R. (2005) *Counselling and Psychotherapy with Refugees*. London: Jessica Kingsley.

BMA (British Medical Association) (2002) *Asylum Seekers: Meeting Their Healthcare Needs*. London: BMA.

Boseley, S. (2006) NHS turns away failed asylum seekers with cancer. *The Guardian,* 29 June 2006.

Bracken, P. and Petty, C. (eds) (1998) *Rethinking the Trauma of War*. London: Free Association Books.

Brandon, D. (1995) *Advocacy Power to People with Disabilities*. Birmingham, UK: Venture Press.

Bruegel, I. and Natamba, E. (2002) *Maintaining Contact: What Happens when Detained Asylum Seekers Get Bail*? London: South Bank University. Accessed online at: www.biduk.org/library/publications

Burnett, A. and Peel, M. (2001a) 'What brings asylum seekers to the United Kingdom?'. *British Medical Journal,* 322, pp. 485-8.

Burnett, A. and Peel, M. (2001b) 'Health needs of asylum seekers and refugees'. *British Medical Journal,* 322, pp. 544-7.

Cemlyn, S. and Briskman, L. (2003) 'Asylum, children's rights and social work'. *Child and Family Social Work,* 8, pp. 163-78.

Cohen, S. (2001) *Immigration Controls, the Family and the Welfare State*. London: Jessica Kingsley.

Cohen, S. (2003a) *No One is Illegal*. Stoke-on-Trent, UK: Trentham Books.

Cohen, S. (2003b) 'Dining with the Devil'. In Cohen, S., *No One Is Illegal*. Stoke-on-Trent, UK: Trentham Books.

Cohen, S. (2006) *Deportation is Freedom: the Orwellian World of Immigration Controls*. London: Jessica Kingsley.

Cohen, S., Humphries, B. and Mynott, E. (2002) *From Immigration Controls to Welfare Controls*. London: Routledge.

Collins, S. (2000) 'Counselling'. In Davies, M. (ed) *The Blackwell Encyclopaedia of Social Work*. Oxford: Blackwell.

CPAG (Child Poverty Action Group) (2006) *Welfare Benefits and Tax Credits Handbook 2006/7*. London: CPAG.

CPPIH (Commission for Patient and Public Involvement in Health) (2006) *Unheard Voices: Listening to the Views of Asylum Seekers and Refugees*. Birmingham, UK: CPPIH.

Cuffe, J. (2005) 'Failed asylum seekers in the Congo'. *Areté*,19, pp. 96-103.

Cunningham, S. and Tomlinson, J. (2005) 'Starve them out': does every child really matter? A commentary on Section 9 of the Asylum and Immigration (Treatment of Claimants, etc) Act, 2004'. *Critical Social Policy*, 25, 2, pp. 253-75.

Darnbrough, A. (ed) (2004) *How to Access Disability Services: A Guide for Organisations in Contact with Refugees and Asylum Seekers in London*. London: National Information Forum.

Department of Health (2003) *Guidance on Accommodating Children in Need and their Families*. Local Authority Circular (2003/13). Accessed online at: www.dh.gov.uk/PublicationsAndStatistics/LettersAndCirculars/Local AuthorityCirculars/AllLocalAuthorityCirculars/LocalAuthorityCirculars Article/fs/en?CONTENT_ID=4003946&chk=kx09kw

Fekete, L. (2005) *The Deportation Machine: Europe, Asylum and Human Rights*. London: Institute of Race Relations.

Fell, P. (2004) 'And now it has started to rain: support and advocacy with adult asylum seekers in the voluntary sector'. In Hayes, D. and Humphries, B. (eds) *Social Work, Immigration and Asylum: Debates, Dilemmas and Ethical Issues for Social Work and Social Care Practice*. London: Jessica Kingsley.

Free, E. (2005) *Young Refugees: A Guide to the Rights and Entitlements of Separated Refugee Children*. London: Save the Children.

Freire (1996) *Pedagogy of the Oppressed*. London: Penguin. (First published 1970).

Gibbons, A. (1999) *A Fight To Belong*. London: Save the Children.

Gibney, M.J. and Hansen, R. (2003) *Deportation and the Liberal State: The Forcible Return of Asylum Seekers and Unlawful Migrants in Canada, Germany and the United Kingdom*. Geneva: UNHCR.

Gibney, M.J. and Hansen, R. (2005) 'Deportation'. In Gibney, M.J. and

Hansen, R. (eds) *Immigration and Asylum From 1900 to the Present*. Santa Barbara CA: Clio.

Go, S.P. (2005) 'Filipino Diaspora'. In Gibney, M.J. and Hansen, R. (eds) *Immigration and Asylum From 1900 to the Present*, Santa Barbara, CA: Clio.

Gondola, C.D. (1999) 'Dream and Drama: The Search for Elegance among Congolese Youth'. *African Studies Review*, 42, 1, pp. 23-48.

Good, A. (2007) *Anthropology and Expertise in the Asylum Courts*. Abingdon: Routledge-Cavendish.

Hayes, D. (2004) 'History and context: the impact of immigration control on welfare delivery'. In Hayes, D. and Humphries, B. (eds) *Social Work, Immigration and Asylum: Debates, Dilemmas and Ethical Issues for Social Work and Social Care Practice*. London: Jessica Kingsley.

Hayes, D. and Humphries, B. (2004) *Social Work, Immigration and Asylum: Debates, Dilemmas and Ethical Issues for Social Work and Social Care Practice*. London: Jessica Kingsley.

Hayter, T. (2000) *Open Borders: The Case Against Immigration Controls*. London: Pluto Press.

Home Office (2004) *Statistics on the Control of Immigration*. Accessed online at: www.homeoffice.gov.uk/rds

Home Office (2005a) *Asylum Statistics*. Accessed online at: www.homeoffice.gov.uk/rds

Home Office (2005b) *Integration Matters: A National Strategy for Refugee Integration*. London: Home Office.

Home Office (2005c) *Controlling our borders: Making migration work for Britain. Five Year Strategy for Asylum and Immigration*. London: Home Office.

Home Office (2006a) *Fair, Effective, Transparent and Trusted: Rebuilding Confidence in our Immigration System*. London: Home Office.

Home Office (2006b) *Report on the Gateway Protection Programme*. Accessed online at: www.ind.homeoffice.gov.uk/6353/6356/10611/resettlementpamphlet.pdf

Home Office (2006c) *Asylum Statistics First Quarter 2006 United Kingdom*. Accessed online at: www.homeoffice.gov.uk/rds/pdfs06/asylumq106.pdf

Home Office/ADSS (Association of Directors of Social Services) (2003) *Guidelines on the Completion of IND Age Assessment*. London, Home Office.

Humphries, B. (2002) 'Fair immigration controls – or none at all?'. In Cohen, S., Humphries, B. and Mynott, E. (eds) *From Immigration Controls to Welfare Controls*. London: Routledge.

Humphries, B. (2004) 'The Construction and Reconstruction of Social Work'. In Hayes, D. and Humphries, B. *Social Work, Immigration and Asylum: Debates, Dilemmas and Ethical Issues for Social Work and Social Care Practice*. London: Jessica Kingsley.

ICAR (Information Centre about Asylum and Refugees in the UK) (2006) *New Asylum Model*. Accessed online at www.icar.org.uk/?lid=6002.

Integration with Diversity in Modern Britain (2002) White Paper, p. 108, Cm 5387 HMSO.

IPPR (Institute for Public Policy Research) (2006) *Irregular Migration in the UK*. London: IPPR. Accessed online at: www.ippr.org/uk/ecomm/files/irregular_migration.pdf

Jandl, M. (2005) *The Development-Visa Scheme: A Proposal for a Market-based Migration Control Policy*. Geneva: Global Commission on International Migration.

JCWI (Joint Council for the Welfare of Immigrants) (2006) *Immigration, Nationality and Refugee Law Handbook*. London: JCWI.

Jones, C. and Novak, T. (1999) *Poverty, Welfare and the Disciplinary State*. London: Routledge.

Jordan, B. and Düvell, F. (2002) *Irregular Migration: The Dilemmas of Transnational Mobility*. Cheltenham, UK: Edward Elgar.

Kenny, C. (2004) 'We thought we were safe, but we're not' *Community Care* 2/9/2004, pp. 32-3 accessed online www.communitycare.co.uk/articles

MacDonald, I.A. and Webber, F. (eds) (2005) *Immigration Law and Practice in the United Kingdom*. London: Butterworths.

Medical Foundation for the Care of Victims of Torture (2006) *Extending our Reach: Annual Review 2005-6*. London: Medical Foundation.

Moorehead, C. (2005) *Human Cargo: A Journey among Refugees*. London: Chatto and Windus.

Morrison, J. (1998) The Cost of Survival: The Trafficking of Refugees to the UK. London: Refugee Council.

NCADC (National Coalition for Anti-Deportation Campaigns) (2003) *Annual Report 2002/3*. Accessed online at: www.ncadc.org.uk/annualreport002/3

Prison Reform Trust (2004) *Forgotten Prisoners; The Plight of Foreign National Prisoners in England and Wales*. Accessed online at: www.prisonreformtrust.org.uk/foreignnationals

Rawlings, R. (2005) 'Review, revenge and retreat'. *Modern Law Review*, 68, 3, pp. 378-410.

Refugee Action (2006) *The Destitution Trap: Research into destitution among failed asylum seekers in the UK*. London: Refugee Action.

Refugee Council (2003) *Support Arrangements for 16 and 17 Year Old Unaccompanied Asylum Seeking Children*. Refugee Council Briefing Paper. London: Refugee Council.

Refugee Council (2005a) *Response to NASS Policy on Dispersing Asylum Seekers with Healthcare Needs*. Accessed online at: www.refugeecouncil.org.uk/publications

Refugee Council (2005b) *Asylum Seekers with Special Needs*. Accessed online at: www.refugeecouncil.org.uk/publications/researchreports

Refugee Council (2005c) *Tell It Like It Is: The Truth About Asylum*. Accessed online at: www.refugeecouncil.org.uk/news/myths

Refugee Council (2005d) *Ringing the Changes: The Impact of Guidance on the Use of Sections 17 and 20 of the Children Act to Support Unaccompanied Asylum Seeking Children*. Accessed online at: www.refugeecouncil.org.uk/publications

Refugee Council (2006a) *First Do No Harm: Denying Healthcare to People whose Asylum Claims have Failed*. London: Refugee Council. Accessed online at: www.refugeecouncil.org.uk/downloads/rc_reports/Health_access_re

port_jun06.pdf

Refugee Council (2006b) *Information Service Subscribers Update July 2006.* London: Refugee Council.

Roberts, K. and Harris, J. (2002) *Disabled People in Refugee and Asylum Seeking Communities.* Bristol/York: The Policy Press/Joseph Rowntree Foundation.

Robinson, V. and Segrott, J. (2002) *Understanding the Decision Making of Asylum Seekers.* London: Home Office.

Robinson, V., Andersson, R. and Musters, S. (2003) *Spreading the Burden: A Review of Policies to Disperse Asylum Seekers and Refugees.* Bristol: The Policy Press.

Royal College of Psychiatrists (2003) *Psychiatrists Call Attention to the Desperation of Asylum Seekers, but Warn Against Over-medicalisation of their Distress.* London: Royal College of Psychiatrists. Accessed online at: www.rcpsych.ac.uk/press/preleases/pr/pr_462.htm

Rutter, J. (2003) Supporting refugee children in 21st Century Britain: A Compendium of Essential Information. Stoke-on-Trent, UK: Trentham Books.

SCEP (Separated Children in Europe Programme) (2000) *Statement of Good Practice.* Copenhagen: SCEP.

Schuster, L. (2003) *The Use and Abuse of Political Asylum in Britain and Germany.* London: Frank Cass.

Seddon, D. (2006) *Immigration, Nationality and Refugee Law Handbook.* London: JCWI.

South London Citizens (2006) *A Humane Service for Global Citizens.* Available online at: www.londoncitizens.org.uk/files/Lunar%20House%20Final_Small.pdf

Stanley, K. (2001) *Cold Comfort: Young, Separated Refugees in England.* London: Save the Children.

Summerfield, D. (2001) 'The invention of post-traumatic stress disorder and the social usefulness of a psychiatric category'. *British Medical Journal*, 32 (2) pp. 95-8.

Taylor, A. (2006) 'Your money or your life'. *Community Care,* 27 July-2 August.

UNHCR (United Nations High Commissioner for Refugees) (1992) *Handbook on Procedures and Criteria for Determining Refugee Status*. Geneva: UNHCR. Accessed online at: www.unhcr.org/publ/PUBL/3d58e1364.pdf

UNHCR (United Nations High Commissioner for Refugees) (2006) 2005 Global Trends. Geneva: UNHCR. Accessed online at: www.unhcr.org/cgi-bin/texis/vtx/events/opendoc.pdf?tbl=STATISTICS@id=4486ceb12

Van Kessel, G. (2001) 'Global migration and asylum.' *Forced Migration Review*, 10, pp. 10-13.

Wade, J., Mitchell, F. and Baylis, G. (2005) *Unaccompanied Asylum Seeking Children: The Response of Social Work Services*. London: British Association for Adoption and Fostering.

Williams, P.D. (2004) 'Why failed asylum seekers must not be denied access to the NHS'. *British Medical Journal*, 329, p. 298.

Willman, S., Knafler, S. and Price, C. (2004) *Support for Asylum Seekers: A Guide to Legal and Welfare Rights*. London: Legal Action Group.